STRANGE RIDE

A RUCKSACK UNIVERSE NOVEL

ANTHONY ST. CLAIR

RUCKSACK PRESS

CONTENTS

"For all my wanderings, no journey compares to the road toward what we hope for, yet no destination is harder to reach than hope."

—Guru Deep, *Travels Through the Third Eye*

PART I

THE GOLDEN CITY OF DEDALO

1

THE WORLD BEYOND THE WALL IS NOTHING TO SEE AT ALL

Beyond the prison bar-gray skyscrapers of the ringwalled city of Dedalo, beyond the endless blue sky unmarred by clouds, beyond the brown empty wasteland plain, the green world was waiting. Soarsha was certain of it, was ready to narrow her bright blue eyes and stand tall and ride forth, a mighty new ten-year-old ready to take the bold leap from boring classroom to daring destiny—and then she sneezed.

Standing before the wall-mounted blackboard at the front of the classroom, Yadda paused and stared at Soarsha. Well, the kid's name wasn't really Yadda, but the dull-eyed, empty-faced eejit did nothing but yadda-yadda on about nothing, so Yadda was the name Soarsha liked to use. Though really, for that matter, any of the thirty kids in class could be named Yadda. And pretty much anyone in the city. Though right now it would have been nice not to feel like the entire city was staring at her.

The whole class was definitely staring at Soarsha. Even Mr. Adbad was. Usually he was nice, but now tension fluttered, barely restrained, throughout his short wiry frame. His thin limbs tightened behind his tweed suit, and his outstretched legs loosened as he tried to appear relaxed while he leaned against his desk, taking care not to disturb the full, dusty box of tissues sitting at the edge of one corner. Behind his gold-rimmed glasses, the skin around his brown eyes wrinkled and creased to match his brow. Overhead lights glinted off what seemed like a sudden sheen of sweat on the teacher's pale bald head.

Soarsha drilled her gaze into the curved wooden back of Yadda's empty desk in front of her. Her tan, freckled cheeks burned. She wanted to pull her purple hat down low. The hat already covered her head so much no one could see so much as one hair on her head—though right now Soarsha wished the hat was a helmet that could cover her entire face.

Soarsha tried to find some calm in her deep breathing, the way Garen—her and her dad's happiness coach—had taught her, but all the calm fluttered away like dust on the breeze. The others always stared at Soarsha, especially when she did even the most normal things, like sneeze. Or dream. Or cry. The more normal she acted, the more they hated her. Mr. Adbad would try to say that wasn't true, but he knew as well as Soarsha that this one sneeze might as well have been a violation of some ironclad classroom law, a piercing of some illusion that she wasn't doing her part to maintain. Soarsha knew that punishment and retribution would be waiting outside, in the fenced-in paved recess area at the back of the skyscraper in the southwest quadrant of the circular city, closer to the outside, walled edge than the taller buildings near the center. The school ate up the first three of twenty stories. Sometimes there were rumblings that powerful people wanted nothing more than to tear up the meager playground and kickball area and put in more stacked floors for the resigned and bewildered souls that poured anew into the city each morning.

Soarsha sneezed again. Yadda glared at Soarsha with broken-glass eyes; something unfamiliar glinted too, but Soarsha couldn't figure out what it was. Yadda's eyes probably never knew what it was to cry, or to laugh so hard you cried. Eyes that didn't see how hard it was to never know the warm soft coziness of being snuggled up between two parents instead of just against one. Soarsha glared at the yadda-yadda kid. Whatever their name was. This was exactly why Soarsha couldn't be bothered to learn any of their names.

"Sorry," said Soarsha. "Don't mind me. Besides, we all know what you were going to say anyway."

Mr. Adbad shook his pale bald head. "Soarsha…"

Soarsha sighed. She'd heard the expression her whole life. It was practically the city's motto, shouting in silent big letters from billboards and murals all over the city. Everyone said it, usually when they were shaking their heads and talking about something difficult. As if anything beyond the city were impossible, just as anything hard wasn't worth trying.

What did they know? They knew what the signs told them. They didn't know anything for themselves.

"I know, I know," said Soarsha. "They were just getting to the good part and I had to ruin it. Here, I'll say it for you: The world beyond the wall is nothing to see at all. There, it's like you didn't miss a breath."

Yadda's eyes narrowed and darkened so much, you could have used the kid's glare to lay down another stretch of black street. Not even one of the ring roads throughout the city. You could use it for one of the straight roads dividing the ringwall's circle like a plus sign combined with an X across all eight compass points, spanning from the thick tall beige wall that surrounded the city's perimeter like a manacle, to the sky-poking needle of the Spire at the center of Dedalo. Far outside the school window, the Spire gleamed, golden and pulsing like a heartbeat with a gentle light, and surrounded by its own gateless, doorless, impassable silver-gray wall.

Soarsha shrugged. "I guess it bears repeating," she said. "Maybe for once—"

She sneezed again. The class almost laughed. But yadda-yadda kids didn't laugh. No one in Dedalo ever did. Except her. And sometimes her father, Das. No wonder people thought they were so weird.

The chalk-clouded room always stuffed her up. She'd even sneezed out the memory of what she was going to say. She was certain it was going to be snappy, the sort of wit that Gleaming Head himself would have been proud of, the sort of wit that any hero worthy of being one of the Wandering Heroes, the roving joy warriors known as the Mrazas, would have at the ready, like a hard stick or some reliable knives or a pair of curved swords across your back. It was the sort of snappy comment only to be expected of a new ten-year-old, basking in her birthday power.

Unless, of course, that birthday girl was Soarsha. Maybe quick wit was one more present she wouldn't get. Like a school day without teasing and bullying. Or another day never knowing what happened to her mother in the dim days just before Das brought his daughter, all he had left in the world, behind the walls of the golden city, the only somewhere in a nowhere world, where the buildings reached like flightless angels to try to touch the cloudless blue sky above.

All the while, Yadda glared at Soarsha. Recess was going to suck even more than usual.

With Soarsha quiet, Yadda took the opportunity to drone on some more. It didn't matter that there was nothing but barren wasteland beyond the wall. *Yadda-yadda.* All you ever needed or wanted was in Dedalo. *Yadda-yadda.* Soarsha rolled her eyes, then looked away from Mr. Adbad's face and traced a swoop of fine yellow particles in the air above the desks.

Yellow chalk dust swirled around the classroom in pale imitation of the golden dust ever dancing above the black streets of the city of Dedalo, to the tops of the skyscrapers. Sometimes Soarsha wondered if the dust liked to start dancing at the lower skyscrapers near the ringwall, stair-stepping up the ever taller buildings as the dust loop-de-looped to the center of the city. But not even the dust could reach the top of the Spire. Nothing and no one could. No one ever went in or out. Which made sense. People said the Spire didn't even have a door.

Soarsha glanced out the window, toward the northeast. The Spire rose beyond the tops of all the other skyscrapers, golden and gleaming, as if the endless flurry of dust were what happened when buildings had dandruff. It really did look like the thin, long, needlelike tip of the Spire pricked the sky. Did it poke through? If it did, what was on the other side? Whether day or night, the Spire always seemed lit with a pulsing golden light.

Inside the top of the Spire, a silver-gold light glinted, as if some celestial child had mixed sunlight and moonlight like paints.

The glint was gone just as soon as she had seen it, but Soarsha still smiled. That glint, that little gleam, was a promising thing to see on her birthday. Everyone said that the eye of god lived in the top of the needle of the Spire. If you saw the glint of light, god was looking at you.

A silence seemed to have come over the classroom. Along with a sense of something changed. Something vacant.

Uh-oh.

Soarsha looked away from the window. Sure enough, Yadda had finished yapping and had sat down, filling up the desk in front of Soarsha.

Mr. Adbad had straightened up and was staring at her. "Soarsha?" he said again.

"Aye, Mr. Adbad?" She tried not to smile. Her saying "aye" instead of "yes" always annoyed him, as if it reminded him of something he didn't want to remember. But her dad liked to say how her mother always said "aye," so Soarsha had long ago decided she would too.

Her teacher sighed. "No one is currently at the front of the classroom."

Soarsha's cheeks burned again. Sweat needle-pricked her underarms, threatening to turn her lavender T-shirt a dark purple. She hoped the dark purple corduroy of her overalls would be enough to give her some cover, though right now she was starting to worry she was going to pee all the way down to her purple boots.

"Sharing Day," said Soarsha.

"That's the day," said Mr. Adbad. "And your birthday, of course, right, class?"

No one replied. There wasn't even a nod.

"I thought that, well, you know, it's my birthday." Soarsha tried to smile, but it was hard with her bared clenched teeth. "So Sharing Day skips me today, right?"

Mr. Adbad shook his head. He even rolled his eyes. "You could share what you thought was so fascinating outside the classroom that you no longer needed to listen to your classmate's sharing."

"Oh," said Soarsha. "That..."

She had a feeling that she shouldn't mention seeing the glint of light at the top of the Spire. It was one of those things that people said happened, but if it actually did happen to anyone, no one ever talked about it happening to them. As if you didn't want other people to feel left out. Or didn't want them to get jealous and annoyed. That sort of fury could fall over the city like shadows after sundown, and the nighttime streets of Dedalo had enough problems.

"I..." Soarsha looked around, from classroom to window to the lump in front of her impersonating a person. Then Soarsha smiled. And pulled the smile back down, as if pulling the shades down in her and her father's tenth-floor apartment in the south-west quadrant, even closer to the wall than her school was.

"There was a roar," said Soarsha. She let her voice drop into a tight whisper. "I thought I heard the scathtor."

Mr. Adbad rolled his eyes. He even stood up.

"The scathtor? Come on, Soarsha," said Mr. Adbad. "Every city has its shadows. No city, not even this one, has a shadow monster that a few nights each year roams the night streets and steals people."

Soarsha's eyes narrowed. "The way you say that, Mr. Adbad," she replied, her voice even and careful, "it's as if you're implying there are other cities out there somewhere."

Now it was Mr. Adbad's turn to go red-faced.

"The world beyond the wall is nothing to see at all," he replied. Displeasure simmered in his voice, honing it sharp and flat, like a claw or a sword swinging toward Soarsha's purple-hatted head.

"Please get up and share what you've brought to Sharing Day." Mr. Adbad's eyes narrowed. "Now."

2

———

GREEN PLACES

The key was to stick to the safe plan. That's what Garen, the happiness coach, had discussed with Soarsha and her dad at last week's lunchtime appointment. That's what Soarsha tried to remember as she carefully unfolded her wiry frame from her desk and started the impossible steps on the unmarked yet unwavering path to the front of the classroom.

The floor swung close, and Soarsha doubled over. Her boots squeaked.

Out of the corner of her eye, she was certain she saw Yadda smile—and saw Yadda's leg flash back out of Soarsha's path before Mr. Adbad could notice anything afoot.

Trying not to blush amidst the stares, Soarsha staggered to the front of the classroom. She hated being in front of people who hated her, but she tried to find the big breaths again, the deep breaths. She tried to remember everything Garen had said.

Imagine the yadda-yadda kids were upside down. That would turn their frowns upside down. That's what Garen had said, his calm voice emanating from a face that always looked like red-hot iron about to be hammered into any shape but what it wanted to be.

Share what she was looking forward to tonight. Talk about the action, Garen had said. Everybody likes action. Everybody likes feeling like their hearts are racing, especially in a quiet city like Dedalo.

And talk about the cake. What kid didn't like chocolate?

Inside, Soarsha's soul shrugged. These kids. They probably didn't like anything good. Something tasty might make them smile. Still. Soarsha tried to imagine the kids upside down. Now they were smiling. It was kind of sweet, actually.

"Sharing Day today also happens to be my birthday," said Soarsha, but she knew her voice was small. As small and insignificant as any affection from the kids in the room to a kid like her. Still. From the corner of her eye, Mr. Adbad gave a nod. A small smile. Keep going.

Soarsha nodded back, imperceptible to anyone else but her teacher, and inside she told herself to speak up.

Talk about the things the yadda-yadda kids like, Garen had said. Well, he always told her to stop calling them yadda-yadda kids. If she changed her attitude about them, maybe they would change their attitude about her.

Soarsha's eyes narrowed. But that was the problem.

Why was she always the one who had to change? Why didn't anyone else ever have to?

Soarsha stood straight. Mrazas didn't go through life hunched over. People who walked with their heads down didn't see who was coming up fast to give out a swift kicking. Wandering Heroes stood straight. Saw things as they were and as they could be. And Soarsha might be an unliked kid in a boring city in the middle of nowhere, but dammit, at heart she was a Mraza. They might be made up, but what they talked about was real: courage and being true to yourself and seeing clearly what was and what could be.

And that, as Soarsha started to speak again, was when everything went wrong.

"Tonight my dad and I are going to hang out at home, eat

sushi, then chocolate cake with purple icing, and then we're going to listen to *Wandering Heroes* on the radio," said Soarsha.

"That show's as stupid as you," said Yadda.

Mr. Adbad's eyes narrowed and he sat up. "It's Soarsha's turn to share and your turn to listen."

Soarsha opened her mouth to start speaking more, but then she stopped. Closed her mouth. Stared at Yadda. Stared at all of them.

In front of Soarsha, the bored kids slumped in their desk chairs and glared at her. That wasn't so bad, though. The few who were smiling under bright eyes were the ones who really worried her. Especially once this period was over and it was time for recess.

As faded yellow as the paint on the classroom walls, the chalk dust in the air tickled Soarsha's throat. No one else ever seemed bothered by it. Maybe they were too bored and half-asleep to notice. Or maybe it was just another thing that only Soarsha cared about, like what was in the top of the golden Spire at the center of the city, or what lay beyond the wall that surrounded the city.

Like where her mother had gone that her father couldn't remember, except that sometimes, when he thought that Soarsha was asleep, he still sobbed about it.

Soarsha tried to imagine what Gleaming Head and Jilly the Kid would do right now. She stood up straighter and refused to look away from the kids around her.

"All of you hate me, and that's your deal," said Soarsha. "None of you know me, and I don't know you. But it's my birthday, and it's my sharing time for Sharing Day. So I'm going to share something that scares me. Because that's what heroes do. I don't want to be a hero. I don't think I'm a hero, but you don't have to be a hero to try to live up to the things heroes do."

Some of the kids were sitting up now. Looking at Soarsha in a way that she'd never seen them look at her before. As if she were a person, and not some unidentifiable goo that could walk and talk.

"My dad brought me to Dedalo right after we lost my mom," continued Soarsha. "When he remembers, it's likes it hollows him out. He can't get out of bed for days. Losing my mom hurts my heart too. There's a hole in my heart shaped like what a mom's love must feel like. As far as I know, all of you know what it's like to have both parents. I'm glad you do. I hope none of you ever know the hurt that I know. So today, my birthday, this stupid Sharing Day, I'm going to enjoy every moment I have with my dad. But I'm doing something else too."

Soarsha smiled. She saw Mr. Adbad stand, and she was certain that a dark flash, like some sort of dark beacon, was flashing through the shadows of his brown eyes like a warning light. But she ignored it.

Soarsha thought she'd feel listless, depressed, and more scared. She did feel scared, and she did feel sorrow, but it was as if those feelings were next to her, not at the heart of her, as if she were riding the No. 33 bus home, and depression and fear were separate cars driving along next to her. In the little bus of her heart, Soarsha felt strong. Brave. And it surprised her. She wondered if this was the Wandering Hero part of her. Or maybe something from her dad, the inside strength that he liked to talk about as being so much more important than outside. Or maybe it was something else. Maybe it was something from her mother.

Soarsha smiled bigger, and she stood taller, and she held the gaze of the yadda-yadda kids around her. She might not know her mom, but maybe she knew her strength. Maybe she was as powerful as Sapphire, the Wandering Hero who, with her twin short sticks, was as mighty in battle as Gleaming Head himself.

"On my birthday I wish for one thing," said Soarsha. "To be where I know both my mother and my father, not just one or the other. So the thing I'm going to share... is my dream."

Her voice had soared like her name, though she'd tried not to let her excitement fly too high. That was the key. Whether you were ten like Soarsha or... what was it, a thousand, like her dad, you had to be just excited enough to make people want more, but not so excited that people thought you were crazy.

To her right, Mr. Adbad leaned on his wooden desk and stretched out his legs. His gaze seemed patient, but edging toward "I won't stop you yet, but get on with it." Soarsha sighed. Tried to breathe in, but breathing felt fast and shallow. Dad had said it was all about the breathing. So she slowed hers. Remembered what he had said: When you were nervous, the world felt fast, so you had to slow yourself down.

The hat had never felt so tight. She almost felt tempted to take it off, but she never took off the hat in front of others. Not even in front of her dad. That devotion was usually a comfort, the one mission she could stick to in a city with no adventure. Right now the hat might as well have been a hot air balloon. Maybe it would start to rise, and take her with it. As she drifted out of the school, she'd fly past the couple of stories at the bottom of the skyscraper, then she'd soar past the high stories, full of apartments or offices or whatever else.

"Beyond the wall," began Soarsha, "there is life. Green grass. Horses run free. People live without bounds. Without walls. There is an entire world waiting to be discovered. Green lands roll through hills as far as you can see, as far as you can dream. There is rain in the air, clouds in the air. You can smell salt, and you can just hear the crash of distant waves on a shore that is as close as your hopes."

She paused. The yadda-yadda kids were staring at her. Bored. Down eyes and rolling eyes and eyes full of hostility. No-one-cares eyes.

But Soarsha didn't care either. She breathed in and kept going.

"I dream that I'm standing with my mother," said Soarsha. "We're outside our home. It's not an apartment in some building that gets in the way of the sky. It's a little lone cottage, where green land surrounds us. The sky is just beginning to blue up and golden-shine again after a rain. Mom and I are standing together. I don't wear my hat there, because I don't need it, because I'm with Mom."

Soarsha grinned and chuckled. "Our hair is the same. Our eyes are the same, as blue as the sky after the clouds clear. We hold hands, and we watch the path before us. The path that curves upward over a low hill. My dad is coming home. We've been waiting for him to get home, waiting for so long, it feels like. Just at the top of the hill, where the path goes where I can't see, I can just start to see something. The top of a head. My father. Coming home. He's almost visible, and I'm about to see him, and he's about to be with us—and that's when I wake up. Wake up and wish I could have my dad, my mom, and me, together in that place. That's what I'm sharing today. What you share is what you can make happen. So hate me if you want. Make fun of me if you want. But it's my birthday, and I'm going to keep believing this dream can come true."

Looking around, Soarsha wondered why she might as well as have been talking to empty desks. The strength was fading now, like the image of her mother when the dream faded. The sweating was back, but she was trying to ignore it, and shouldn't it be time for recess by now already?

"Thanks for listening anyway," she said.

Mr. Adbad shook his head, stood up to his full height, and crossed over to Soarsha. Still shaking his head, he gently motioned for her to sit down.

"The world outside the wall is nothing to see at all," he said. His voice was gentle, but it reminded Soarsha of when her dad was cooking, and the lid on the pot trembled from the heat and the pressure trapped inside, trying to escape.

"I didn't say anything about seeing it," said Soarsha. "It was just a dream." She turned away, her face hot, but she could hear

Mr. Adbad sigh, and could practically hear his head shaking. Great. Probably another note going to Garen and her dad.

Soarsha's cheeks burned. Sharing the dream had felt so right. Maybe they would understand. Maybe they would care. But they didn't. No one understood how hard it was to feel like all you wanted to do was run and sing in a place that demanded you keep still and silent.

Ignoring the stabbing stares of her classmates, Soarsha gazed out the window. Far past the soaring slender Spire, she could just see the city stretch and stretch—until it hit the wall, which rose like a frozen tsunami of sand, beige and boring and unbreakable.

Stupid wall. It had defined her whole life. Before passing through the only gate to enter the city, Soarsha had had a mother. Her father had had his wife. But inside the city? There was no mother here. The world beyond Dedalo might be lifeless, but at least it wouldn't be boring. Soarsha glared at the wall and stuck out her tongue.

Her eyes widened, she snapped her tongue back into her mouth quickly. Soarsha's cheeks reddened more. Maybe no one had noticed—

A shrill voice giggled. "Wow, Mr. Adbad!"

Soarsha turned her head. One of the yadda-yadda kids had noticed. They never missed a chance to make her day worse.

The shrill voice continued. "She must not have liked you making her end her sharing early. She stuck out her tongue at you!"

Soarsha shook her head and turned. "I did not stick out my tongue at Mr. Adbad."

Mr. Adbad's voice was as calm as the wall was thick and tall. "At what then?"

Soarsha sighed. Waited for the giggling to turn into painful, loud laughter.

"At the wall."

The thunder of thirty children bounced off the ceiling and walls and floor.

As it subsided, Mr. Adbad said, "Why stick out your tongue at the wall?"

Soarsha sighed. Her eyes felt hot, but she held his gaze. "Because I hate it," she said. "It makes everyone in the city think there's nothing else beyond this lame city. No fields of green. No color. No smell of rain."

Mr. Adbad shook his head. "Soarsha," he said, his calm voice edged with thunder. "Have you experienced these things?"

Soarsha's face reddened again. "No."

She looked toward the window. Easier to look at the faraway thing she hated than at the nearby person wielding inescapable truth. "I've been in Dedalo as long as I can remember."

"Then you have no basis for thinking there's anything beyond the wall worth experiencing," replied Mr. Adbad.

Soarsha said nothing.

"I figured as much," said Mr. Adbad. He looked upon his entire class. "Next for Sharing Day."

Soarsha ignored the next kid sharing, and instead stared hard at the wall, as if trying to punch a hole through it.

3

THE TROUBLE WITH BIRTHDAYS

The trouble with birthdays is they were supposed to be fun.

Cake and ice cream. Friends smiling and everyone happy. Just-right gifts for a new ten-year-old, on the cusp of teendom but still in childhood. Parties and squeals and running around and enough sugar to last a month, but that was no reason not to have another slice of chocolate cake with icing as thick as the sidewalk and as purple as Soarsha's hat.

Soarsha understood that's what birthdays were supposed to be like. In some other world, maybe that's how they were. This world seemed to tie friendship either to being quiet or to saying only what you were supposed to say, thoughts and words as useless but ever present as the golden dust swirling overhead. The yadda-yadda kids ignored the dust the way they ignored everything that wasn't part of the secret code they knew about life and the city and each other, the code that Soarsha either didn't understand due to some personal flaw or that she'd been locked out of.

Still, the yadda-yadda kids could have their fun. The dull dark gray of the playground equipment looked like bones, skeletons rising up from the scraggly patch of scrub that passed for grass but was more yellow than green, and didn't even come up higher than the soles of shoes. Kids hung from monkey bars and swung on swings. They went down slides and climbed through hollow cubes and spheres, little versions of the skyscrapers they would spend their lives moving through. Some of the kids clung in groups like mud clumping on Gleaming Head's boots after a rainstorm over the grass ocean in the world of *Wandering Heroes*. In one group, Yadda was clutching a big red rubber kickball, the textured kind that scratched you up like falling on pavement and skinning a knee.

Soarsha looked down from the yadda-yadda kids and dropped her gaze back into the comic book spread out on her raised knees so the pages rested on her upper legs. She stretched out her back against the chain-link fence at the back of the recess courtyard. Across from her, on the other side of the yadda-yadda kids and the worn equipment, the dark rectangle of the door at the back of the school hung open like a yawn. Even the back of the school was lined with red brick, to make the building feel warmer, homier. Yet as soon as the school ended, three stories up, the bluish-gray steel of the rest of the twenty-story skyscraper soared, a one-legged skinny giant wearing a dark red shoe.

Soarsha had already read this issue of *Wandering Heroes* three times, but she didn't care. It was a trip she was happy to take again and again. Besides, the new one should be waiting for her at home—the perfect gift for her birthday. She'd start reading it as soon as she got home, while she waited for her dad to finish work.

For now, though, Soarsha's eyes widened as she flew alongside the Wandering Heroes. She always imagined herself nearby as they went on their adventures, riding through the tall green grass ocean known as the Cuan Féir. Sometimes she hovered overhead or beside them, a ghostly observer, not changing or disturbing events as they unfolded. Other times, after reading a comic, she would set it aside and, with eyes wide open, dream bright and aloud in her mind. She stopped being an observer and became part of the story. Soarsha the Mraza, one of the last joy warriors, a Wandering Hero. Identical twin sister to Jilly the Kid. Gleaming Head regarded both girls as the daughters he never got to have, and Sapphire and Shirtman were like an aunt and an uncle. Together, they weren't just the warriors of love and joy; they were family. A just-right family, living to help and bring together a hurt, scared world that didn't yet see its potential.

In the comics, Jilly the Kid rode Starcall, a golden horse who had a silver-gray, four-pointed star between its eyes. In Soarsha's daring dreams, she and Jilly always rode side by side. Soarsha's horse was the same size as Jilly's but Soarsha's horse was silver-gray, with a golden four-pointed star between its eyes. The top and side points were short, but the bottom star angled downward like lightning, and that's why Soarsha had named her horse Stormgather.

By night, when the Mrazas weren't in the midst of some terrifying adventure or helping people in need all across the Cuan Féir, Jilly and Soarsha would sit by a fire's embers, sipping tea and telling their own stories of how the Magical Mraza Twins would gather the storms and call down the stars, wiping monsters and fear and evil from all the world, from the barren brown wasteland, to the mountains, to the oceans, and throughout the Cuan Féir.

Sometimes Soarsha wondered what world *Wandering Heroes* was set in. When she and her dad listened to the weekly radio show—not to mention the stupid ads, which always either annoyed or depressed her dad—the Mrazas talked as if there were some sort of brown barren wasteland at the edge of the Cuan Féir. Gleaming Head didn't like to talk about it, though, and whenever it came up he would look away, or change the subject, or get irritated. No one knew why talk of the wasteland bothered him so, but he would only say that this was not the time to talk about it. Soarsha wondered if it ever would be, or if it was just one of those annoying things comic writers did to keep you so fascinated and intrigued that you kept reading the next issue, to see if maybe, just maybe, this time Gleaming Head would reveal what scared him so much about the wasteland beyond the Cuan Féir.

Soarsha turned the page. After surviving a daring adventure, the Mrazas were settling in to what should be a serene night at camp. Relaxing by the fire, they were telling stories when, just as they felt safe—

A big red rubber kickball soared high and to the right of Soarsha's head, missing her by less than a foot. The fence clanged and clattered like amateur thunder, and the thin crisscrossed strands of steel wire wobbled and shuddered as if they were made of gelatin. The high sun traced the ball's dark shadow on the ground as it bounced and rolled back toward the waiting hands of Yadda.

Soarsha sighed. Didn't even let her blue eyes widen. She just looked down at the yellowed, patchy dry grass beneath her. No eye contact. That was key. Eye contact was a sign you were going to stick up for yourself. Inside, though, Soarsha's mind shook its head. She should have seen this coming. Should have sat closer to the wall of the school, so she could rush inside. Now, the playground and all the yadda-yadda kids stood between Soarsha and safety.

She should have known. Yadda was going to want revenge. What better day than Soarsha's birthday to torment the girl no one liked?

Tugging the curved front brim of her purple hat over her forehead, Soarsha felt around the lower perimeter to make sure that not so much as a single hair was showing. The school used to try to make her take the hat off, but after her dad had a word with the principal, no one told her to take it off anymore.

She wondered what Dad had told them. Surely not the truth?

Since she was a little girl, Soarsha had sworn that no one—not even her dad—would see her without her hat on, until the day she found her mother again. She kept her hair cut short so none of it peeked out.

The hat had become her one talisman against the hole in her

and her father's hearts. Dad always said that wherever Mom had gone after Soarsha was born, it was somewhere better, and she was waiting for them there. Soarsha didn't ask why her mother got to be somewhere better while they had to be trapped somewhere terrible. Her dad said her mother lost, and they wouldn't find her again in this world. No matter what Das said, Soarsha was convinced that somewhere out there, beyond the wall, in the strange world outside Dedalo, her mother was out there. Waiting for her family to find each other and be whole again.

Soarsha let Yadda glare. She didn't even close her comic. Let the yadda-yadda kids come. There was no pain they could cause worse than what Soarsha already felt. No pain hurt like a hole in the heart that you knew you could never fill.

Still. Soarsha kept her head low. Better to look down, away from the sky and the sun and the dust. Better to look away from the nearby street, where your imagination would want your feet to follow your gaze. She'd be miles away before she hit the wall.

Besides, if she looked down, the kids might think she was broken enough to be left alone. If she looked up, the kids might remember rocks were easy to throw.

Sometimes Soarsha wished she could act like a hero. Gleaming Head would have looked them in the eye. The flames that burned gently in his dark eyes would have blazed up like the sun emerging from behind an eclipsing moon. Gleaming Head would have grabbed the ball out of midair, wrapped both hands around it, torn the ball in two, then gently dropped the two jagged rubber fragments at Yadda's feet.

That's all it would have taken. Everyone would have gotten the message.

But Soarsha knew she wasn't a hero. Heroes didn't have holes in their heart and fathers who could sob for days and barely get out of bed. Children in a schoolyard didn't terrify heroes.

If there was anything Soarsha wanted for her tenth birthday, it was, for just a moment, to feel as alive and mighty as a hero. To know the power of the joy and love of a Mraza. Or maybe, if she were really lucky, Gleaming Head would ride his golden horse out of the radio, out of the pages of her comic, and onto the city's black streets, arriving in Dedalo to find Soarsha at last, Jilly's lost twin sister, and take this lost girl home.

But there were no heroes. Not in this city. Not in this world. Not in herself.

Soarsha set her forehead on her knees and wrapped her arms around her legs. The kids closed in.

Just another birthday.

4

SOARSHABAITING

The thing about a city like this was that when you are surrounded on all sides by tall buildings, anyone could look down and see what was happening. But no one did. Or if they did, they didn't help. Noticing something wasn't the same thing as doing anything about it.

Under the midday sun, the shadows of the yadda-yadda kids nonetheless looked like dark bars, like a jail cell of skinny skyscrapers. The curved blade of children came closer. The back of the fence bit into Soarsha's back.

In the middle of the kids, Yadda held the kickball, by the hip, like a gunslinger ready for a duel.

Yadda snickered. The flat sharp dislike for Soarsha glimmered like firelight in Yadda's eyes, but again, like in the classroom earlier, Soarsha saw something else, some flicker, a flash there and then gone, as if afraid to be seen.

Yadda leered. "Whatcha gonna get for your birthday, Dorksha? A new hat? A new head to put it on?"

Another child leaned forward. "Do you wear that stupid hat because your hair is so gross, Poorsha? Maybe you need a haircut, Poorsha." The child leaned in. "Or a shave."

Soarsha tightened her arms around her legs and stared through her knees toward the cracked black pavement.

Of course they wouldn't let it go. Her sharing had felt so brave at the time. Now she realized that all she'd done was get noticed. Nothing good came from getting noticed by the yadda-yadda kids. They'd never like her. Never think she was like them. That's what cut deepest. In some part of her soul that she only looked at under the safety of her bed blankets at night, Soarsha knew she was different. She just didn't know how. Or why.

Maybe the yadda-yadda kids knew, and that was why they hated her. Though, Sharing Day or not, she didn't think they'd be open to explaining. They wanted to play their favorite game: Soarshabaiting.

"I'm reading my comic," said Soarsha. "Please leave me alone. All I've done is sit here and mind my own business. Why don't you mind your own?"

Yadda's head shook. Then the child's free hand shot out and yanked away the comic.

"Hey!" Soarsha started to sit up, but the crowd of children all seemed to have eyes that flashed red, red like faraway flames. Soarsha sat back and let the impassable fence bite into her back again.

The crescent of jeering, pointing, chuckling kids stood around her. It would have been nice to be left alone. She understood she was as likely to have friends as it was for the Spire to fall over. She just wished she knew why.

Yadda took a step forward. "Why do you wear that stupid hat? Is your hair as ugly as your face?"

Another child. "Maybe she doesn't have any hair!"

And another. "Let's find out!"

A hand batted toward the hat.

Without thinking, Soarsha grabbed the wrist attached to the hand. She wasn't a Mraza, and Gleaming Head wasn't riding his horse through the school and out the door to save her, but even if she wasn't a Mraza, she could damn well act like one. Soarsha stood quickly, thrusting her body forward while she pushed the wrist away from her. The child attached to the wrist squealed, then tumbled backward and fell over.

The children leered. Some looked back at the fallen child, but no one went to help the kid up. Instead, they moved toward Soarsha.

"No!" Soarsha raised up her arms as the children tried to knock away her hands, but soon there would be too many and someone would grab the hat, and then Soarsha would have broken her mission, failed the mission, and she would never find her mother, never get to grow out her hair, never be with her mother and see their matching, flowing hair ripple in the breeze while they waited for Soarsha's father to come home. Soarsha tried to cover her eyes, cover her face, and above all protect the hat, but there were too many hands now, too many children too close, and they smelled like musty lemons about to go moldy, but dry and tired liked an old shut-in's closed-windows house.

A thin line of pain flashed like lightning down her left cheekbone.

As one, the hands fell away. The children gasped and stepped back. Soarsha looked from kid to kid, wondering what in the world was wrong with them. She touched her fingertips to her cheek, and they came away with little red smears. Some random fingernail must have caught her face. She wanted to scream at them. Fingers near her eyes. Breaking her skin.

But she smiled as she held up her fingers and the children leaned back.

"It's just a little blood," said Soarsha. "What's the matter?"

The children were backing away. A path opened between them. She rubbed the blood off her cheek; already the little line of ouch was oozing less. Barely a graze. She rolled her eyes. The things that freaked people out.

Yadda took a step forward. "She's even weirder than we thought!"

The children shifted toward her again. Soarsha wished she could leap to the top of the Spire, where no one could follow. She rubbed her fingertips on her cheek again, but no one cared. Soarsha wrapped her arms around her head, her hat, her face, as the storm of hands approached.

"Back away from her now!"

The voice rumbled across the school grounds like a tiger's roar.

Soarsha's eyes widened. Maybe she had gotten her wish. Gleaming Head was coming for her, with Jilly the Kid by his side, ready to bring their lost Mraza back into the family of the Wandering Heroes.

Soarsha dared to peek through the space between her elbows.

The yadda-yadda kids went quiet. Tall and slender, with the beginning of a softer belly than he might have preferred, the tweed-suited hero charged with calm fury between the ranks of children. With just enough of a turn of his head to let each child know he had seen them—he had marked them—Mr. Adbad stepped in front of Soarsha.

All she needed was an outstretched hand. A little warmth and kindness. Just someone to lead her away.

"It's her birthday," said Mr. Adbad. "And this is how you treat her?"

Soarsha closed her eyes and clenched them shut. This was not the help she wanted. This is not what Gleaming Head would have done. Gleaming Head would have reached out his hand. Maybe lifted Soarsha onto his shoulders. At the least he would have held her hand, and they would have walked away, side by side.

Several of the kids shrugged. Yadda smirked. "Who cares?"

Mr. Adbad saw the scrunched *Wandering Heroes* comic in Yadda's hand, and he held out his own. Yadda's eyes rolled, and with a huff Yadda handed over the comic.

Looking from side to side, from child to child, Mr. Adbad's eyes seemed mystified. That was the thing about Mr. Adbad. As heroes went, there was no stronger, craftier, more qualified hero… at teaching you how to play chess. Or at handing out a just-challenging-enough quiz, even if the other lame-o students thought all the quizzes were too tough and were done just to make them fail. Mr. Adbad could explain anything out of a book, even out of a comic book, which raised his worth substantially in Soarsha's eyes. Mr. Adbad was great at describing why a squirrel's tail was fluffy—even though, when Soarsha thought about it, she had never seen a squirrel anywhere in Dedalo.

While Mr. Adbad could take in seemingly limitless knowledge about squirrels and numbers and stories and multiplication tables and how to make a volcano out of baking soda and vinegar, there was one slight but really big problem. He seemed to know something about the world that the children didn't.

The trouble was, he knew nothing about the children who comprised so much of his world.

"Poorsha's probably so poor her dad sold her birthday so they could have dinner," said another kid.

Mr. Adbad shook his head. This is where things always went wrong. He tried to be so wise. Stand so tall.

A mob of children could make anyone feel like they could be cut off at the knees. Especially since that's where the kids had their best reach.

Soarsha lowered her head and took in a hitching breath. Her eyes felt hot and puffy. "Please let me leave," she whispered.

Mr. Adbad glanced down at her.

"What's that?" said Mr. Adbad. "You might vomit?"

Soarsha lifted up her head and peered up at him, one eyebrow raised. The other children backed away as if she had already transformed into a puke cannon. Mr. Adbad cocked his head. Behind them, at the bottom of the gray leg of the twenty-story gray-glass skyscraper, the red brick shoe of the school waited.

With a small smile, Mr. Adbad held out his hand.

Soarsha sighed. Put her hand in his, and let him lead her toward the school. He wasn't Gleaming Head. Not by any stretch. But for now, he would do.

Yadda glared at Soarsha, as if Yadda wished to transform into the scathtor and pounce, shadow claws out, on the birthday girl.

Silence followed Soarsha into the school, the horrible silence of children trying to figure out how to fulfill their delayed retribution. Once through the doorway, Soarsha could hear low angry murmurs.

Poorsha the teacher's pet.

They ought to burn her stupid hat.

And her too.

Soarsha's eyes burned, but it wasn't just the flat, powdery chalk dust, in the classroom, tickly and pasty in the throat. Mr. Adbad tossed the comic book on his desk and leaned up against the blackboard. Soarsha wondered if he knew that his entire back was always covered in yellow powder. Behind his back the other kids liked to snicker and call him yellowtail. Soarsha cocked her head. Or maybe Mr. Adbad did know. Only he didn't care. Maybe it was actually a joke on the other kids.

"They're never going to like me," said Soarsha. "No kid here has ever liked me."

"Surely you have friends," said Mr. Adbad.

Soarsha's cheeks flushed. "If I do, could you tell me who they are?"

Mr. Adbad looked away, but not before Soarsha noticed some shadow of disappointment or regret in his gaze.

"I'm sorry, Soarsha," said Mr. Adbad. "Your school life has been far harder than anyone deserves."

"You think?"

Mr. Adbad chuckled. "A good teacher tries not to set students apart too much," he said. "Not play favorites. You are outspoken and difficult, but you are also insightful and brilliant." He sighed.

"And not one of those things, I realize, plays well with kids around here."

Typical, thought Soarsha. Maybe there was a world where smart kids had friends. "If only my social life were as good as my grades."

"Then you wouldn't be you," said Mr. Adbad.

Surprise flashed in Soarsha's widening eyes.

"You're brilliant, Soarsha," said Mr. Adbad. "You're kind too. That's part of what always surprises and impresses me about you. You've known things in your life that the other children can't imagine. If they try to, it terrifies them."

"Why?" said Soarsha. "What makes them so scared of me?"

Mr. Adbad had no reply.

Soarsha's face felt hot. This wasn't how a tenth birthday was supposed to go. Kids were supposed to squeal and eat cake and celebrate with their friends. Not wonder if they'd ever have a friend.

"I'm sorry about the little ruse out there," said Mr. Adbad at last. "It was the easiest way to set things up. I'm letting you leave early, on account of your unfortunate birthday illness that came upon you all of a sudden. I've already phoned your dad's office that you're heading home, and they're letting him know down at the construction site."

Soarsha turned to look at her teacher. Mr. Adbad had been looking out for her, and she hadn't even known it.

Maybe he was more of a hero than she'd given him credit for.

She tried to smile. "I must be really sick."

Mr. Adbad winked. "Nothing some sushi and chocolate birthday cake can't cure."

His eyes flashed, and his face for a moment looked blank. He reached up to his jacket's inside pocket, then he shook his head and lowered his hand.

"Silly old teacher." Mr. Adbad ran his hand over his bald head.

"I get absent-minded. Sometimes I think I must have lost my thoughts along with my hair."

Soarsha shook her head. "Did you forget something?"

Mr. Adbad looked around a moment. Then his eyes widened. The teacher lifted himself away from the chalkboard. He picked up the *Wandering Heroes* comic and set it in Soarsha's hand.

"Wouldn't want you to miss this," said Mr. Adbad. He grinned. "New issue's out today, you know."

Soarsha's eyes widened. "You like *Wandering Heroes?*"

"I know them quite well," he replied. "You and your dad won't be the only ones listening tonight."

Soarsha stared at the comic, then at her teacher. "Mr. Adbad?"

"Yes?"

She shook her head. "Never mind. It's stupid."

"No," said Mr. Adbad. "Everything we wonder, we wonder for a reason."

She sighed. Found her courage again. The way Jilly the Kid would want her to. "Are the Wandering Heroes... real?"

Now Mr. Adbad sighed. He leaned down to Soarsha's height and looked her in the eye.

"I wish they were," he said. "I can tell you something that is real, though."

"What's that?"

"This life can be so hard and confusing," said Mr. Adbad. "Like you can never find your way through a dark maze. Life is a labyrinth that can be confusing and scary. Sometimes you might feel aimless, without a way onward. But there is a path for you. I promise. No matter what happens here at school, there are better things out there for you. You'll have the best life possible in this world." He smiled. "At least, as long as I have anything to say about it."

"Thank you."

"You're welcome," he replied. "And I mean it. Things will get better." He nodded toward the classroom door. "Now, shift it. Get moving before someone figures out I'm helping you fake out of school due to a sudden onset of birthdayitis."

Soarsha nodded and started toward the door. The golden chalk clouds parted as she made her way. She stopped only once, to gather her purple jacket and purple backpack from her cubby along the wall. As Soarsha reached the door, Mr. Adbad called her name. She paused and looked at him.

"Be yourself," said Mr. Adbad. "The more you are you, the more the other kids will come around."

Adults always confused simple solutions with painless ones. "But that's the trouble," she replied. "The more I'm myself, the more the other kids hate me."

Before Mr. Adbad could say anything else, Soarsha left the classroom.

5

RUMORS GROW

The golden dust fell as silently as the endless throngs of people walked. It was as if only the traffic had permission to make noise: the whirs of cars, the honks of taxis, the rumble-snorts of buses. The high sun found its way through the obstacle course of skyscrapers, swinging and leaning and backflipping through until a few rays found their lonely way to the street.

Soarsha stared as high as she could, trying to see the tops of the tallest buildings. Maybe the dust's job was to guide the sunlight from the sky to the streets. The streets were where people needed the light the most, after all. Seemed a shame it was so plentiful in the sky, and in such short supply down here.

The straight lines of the skyscrapers seemed so still and cold compared to the warm air. It was nice to think of Dedalo as being warm, but Soarsha rubbed her arms as the city's endless chill pushed through her jacket. People tried to act like it was warm, dressing in thin clothes and talking about sunshine, as if enough repeated lies would rub against the truth, and the friction would raise the temperature. Soarsha zipped her too-thin jacket up to her chin and tried to imagine how warm the sun must feel on the

Cuan Féir. As far up toward the sky as she could see, the endless golden dust fell, powdery as fluffy snow yet never touching the ground.

Snow. She'd never seen snow. Except in pictures in the textbooks. The air here was always clear. No clouds ever obscured the sun. There was night. Then there was day. It always felt abrupt, like slipping when you thought you were walking just fine. Or like a glass falling off a table. The graceless sun never seemed to arc across the sky. It seemed to dash up fast, as if afraid of slipping back down behind the horizon and embarrassing itself. And it rushed down to the other side of the sky just as quickly, just as suddenly, as if the sun had a bus to catch and was running late.

Soarsha walked faster, both to keep warm and to get to the bus stop in time. Often she walked to and from school. After all, walking was free. But today was her birthday. Surely the city wouldn't collapse because a poor birthday girl decided to treat herself to a bus ride.

The No. 33 would take her home. She'd sit and look out the window—that way, she wouldn't have to see some inevitable depressing scene: a girl who wasn't Soarsha sitting with a mother who wasn't Soarsha's. The details didn't matter. Holding hands and telling jokes. Laughing and giggling. Or flustered and red-faced, clearly annoyed with each other or running late or having a generally crappy day. It didn't matter. More mothers and daughters rode buses than dust fell from the sky. As ever present as mothers and daughters were, Soarsha always had to look away. Seeing them did nothing but remind her of the dull ache in her heart.

It'd be nice to get home early. She could read for a while—with a little luck, maybe the mail would have already arrived and the new issue of the *Wandering Heroes* comic book would be waiting for her, like a birthday present sent by the post office. She'd get her homework done too, though. Once Dad got home from work, her real birthday could begin. The prize after the torment. Just her and Dad and a cake. She thought of the full tight round belly she'd have. And the thrill that would arc through her lightning when her dad turned the dial on the giant brown boxy radio with its top curved like an arch.

That was all a girl needed. The hole in Soarsha's heart panged again. Well, okay, not *all*. But it would do. It would be enough. Especially since there wasn't an alternative anyway.

As Soarsha left the school behind and made her way toward the bus stop, a newspaper box shouted at her:

Rumors Grow as Five Vanish Near Ringwall.

She wondered what Mr. Adbad would have to say about that. Every year there were similar stories, always beginning around Soarsha's birthday and ending two days later, the same day as the anniversary of when her father had lost her mother and brought Soarsha to Dedalo. Was there a shadowy monster in the night? Did it take people for a few days, then vanish until the following year? Usually, the rumors went, the scathtor only took people who wanted to leave Dedalo.

Soarsha looked over her shoulder.

No scathtor behind her. Not this time anyway.

What would it take for the scathtor to decide it needed to take someone? Did they just have to be thinking constantly about leaving the city? Planning an escape? Or did the scathtor only target people who were actually trying to find a way out, from scaling the wall to breaking through the gate during the few seconds it was open each morning, when the day's sole inbound bus entered the city?

Soarsha looked over her shoulder again. And wondered when the time would come that she'd look behind her and see it there —part person, part shadow—the scathtor that took and never gave back. Did it have claws? Did it have monster breath that stank of ripped-raw, rotten flesh? Were its eyes dark like shadows too? Or did they glow like red-hot coals fresh from a furnace? Furry or scaly? Horns? Wings?

Every black street made her wonder which sidewalks, which roads, held some taloned footprint. Maybe there'd be a deep impression, a sign the monster had a massive bulk, like a small skyscraper out for a bloodthirsty stroll.

Soarsha gulped.

She definitely needed to look over her shoulder more often.

A soft breeze wafted through the city, carrying exhaust and a scent like warm dry paper. It made Soarsha long for rice—rice that was slightly piquant from vinegar and savory from salt and with just the slightest tinge of sugary sweetness. Soarsha thought of sushi, but the scathtor was stalking through her mind. Every thought of the scathtor made her wish it was already later in the day, and she was home—home and waiting for the sound of her father opening the door. Her dad would never let the scathtor get her. He would always protect her. Never let her come to harm. Dad always wanted the best for her. In all this stupid lifeless lame lukewarm city, at least she could count on the warmth and strength of her father's love.

With its clear, closed-in back and sides, the bus stop wasn't a fortress, but at least it made Soarsha feel like she was safe inside one. Besides, there was plenty of light left in the day, and so far everyone thought the scathtor only came out at night. Still. The No. 33 was taking forever. She could wait, though. The scathtor only came out at night. Soarsha shook her head. How did people know that? If people were vanishing during the day, it wasn't as if they could tell others about the change of plan.

Soarsha glanced over her shoulder. Stared right and left.

There was no monster.

The monster was behind her.

There was no monster.

The monster was behind her.

There was no monster.

A rumble filled the air. The low roar brought with it a gross wind, earthy and stinky, with a rancid edge. Soarsha's eyes widened. She'd been looking over her right shoulder, but the sound had snuck up from her left, where she wasn't looking. She whipped her head around, ready for the pounce, hoping it would be quick, sorry to miss her dad and her birthday and anything else that was to come, but maybe she'd finally see her mom again—

6

SILENT FANGS IN THE ROARING SHADOWS

The No. 33 bus, all light gray and dull red, like a scabbed knee, rumbled to a stop and opened its doors to the birthday girl.

Soarsha leaped inside, hoping her face wasn't red and tear-soaked.

Carl, the bus driver, grinned and called out, "Soarsha!" His dark-gray shirt rippled as he waved her inside. Carl's dark skin was a deep rich brown, nearly black, the sort of color the city's nights wished they could be. His short curly hair reminded Soarsha of what her textbooks said snow looked like. And his eyes were always as kind as her father's.

Despite herself, Soarsha smiled as the doors hissed closed. She was safe. The good ole 33. Good ole Carl. He waved her forward. Soarsha pulled the fare out of her pocket, but Carl reached out a steady hand and covered the fare box.

"You and your dad have been riding my bus since you came to this city ten years ago," he said. "You think I don't know what day it is?" He nudged his head toward the seats. "This one's on me."

"Thank you," said Soarsha.

With a grumble and a shudder, the ancient bus pulled back

into traffic. The driver barely even looked around at the onrushing cars, trucks, taxis, and scooters. Didn't need to. A bus made its own way, he always liked to tell Soarsha, and other people's jobs were to get out of it.

As the No. 33 rumbled along one of the golden city's coal-black diagonal spoke streets, Soarsha stared out the front windscreen toward the wall.

It was one thing to want to leave. But to actually leave? The world beyond the city was a wasteland. No one lived there. There was nothing there. No life. No other cities. Just a road. That was all. A lonely road in a barren plain. No matter what she otherwise dreamed. Wasn't that the point? Wasn't that what Mr. Adbad and her dad and Garen the happiness coach all wanted her to settle for, for her own good, for her own—happiness? No. Coming to terms with that wouldn't bring happiness. Resignation maybe. Begrudging complacency. But not happiness. Happiness lived in a green land where a woman waited for her family to return.

Soarsha wondered if there were any truth to the rumors about the monster in the shadows amidst the dark places of the city's winding streets. It reminded Soarsha of an ancient legend Mr. Adbad had told the class about. It took place somewhere that didn't exist anymore. Crease. No. That wasn't quite right. Soarsha's brow scrunched.

Crete.

That was it. And in the legend there was a big maze. No. Not a maze. It had been called a labyrinth. Massive and winding, in the middle a monster called the minotaur waited to devour all who wandered the impossible path.

Maybe the minotaur and the scathtor were cousins.

Soarsha tilted her head. If they were cousins, what were the family reunions like?

The No. 33 growled to a grinding stop at a red light. Dedalo's coal-black streets had a way of always glistening, as if the dry, cloudless world had just rained. Her schoolbooks talked about weather and seasons, but those phenomena seemed as mythical as the minotaur and its labyrinth. Only cool sunshine and deep darkness covered the golden city. No clouds. No rain. No seasons.

People made their way along the sidewalks. The bus rumbled off again, passing by block after block of coal-black streets and high massive gray buildings. As the bus passed through another intersection, something tugged at the edge of Soarsha's sight. She whipped her head around to look. Instead of the usual glistening shadow-black of the other streets, this cross street was a light, silvery gray.

She had never seen—or at least never noticed—a silver-gray street in Dedalo before.

Soarsha turned to look out the window on the opposite side of the bus.

The light gray street continued. Then, at a bend, there was black again.

Weird.

Why was one street silver-gray, when all the others were black? Were there other silver-gray streets?

She looked away. What did it matter whether some streets were black and maybe—maybe—some were a different color? It wasn't as if some magical silvery street was going to show her the way out of Dedalo. No one left Dedalo. Not of their own volition. As far as she knew, anyway.

Her eyes narrowed. Maybe there was another reason for newspapers talking about people vanishing. Maybe it had nothing to do with a minotaur or a scathtor or anything else. Maybe, just maybe, you never saw those people again because they got out after all.

Soarsha grinned. Saw her bright-smiled, bright-eyed reflection in the window.

A little bit of hope made a big birthday present. It didn't fill the hole in her heart. But it made Soarsha think that maybe, just maybe, someday she could.

Staring out the window, Soarsha let the dust dance away her thoughts of the scathtor, of the hole in her heart, and of whether or not people ever left Dedalo. Sometimes the golden dust brushed against the windows of the bus. Sometimes it pressed up against the tenth-floor apartment where Soarsha and her dad lived in. Whenever it did, Soarsha wondered if the dust were peering through the window, trying to figure out what was going on.

Soarsha pressed her palm to the window.

"I know how you feel," she said to the dust.

The blocks jittered past as the rumbling bus shook and shimmied, always teetering on the edge of rasping to a halt yet never going still. Not once did she see another silver-gray street. Or maybe she hadn't really seen a different-looking street after all. Maybe it was just some strange confluence of dust and light. Or a birthday girl's wish for adventure. But there were no adventures in the golden city. If anything ever surprised Soarsha about Dedalo, it was how quiet the place always felt. Deep inside, Soarsha had this feeling cities weren't meant to be so quiet.

Soarsha turned and looked toward the center of the city, outside the window on the opposite side of the bus. Somewhere near the big central needly Spire was a skyscraper where, at street level, a bus station waited to devour in its shadows the local buses, then vomit them back out onto the streets. And every day, once a day, the city gate opened, and one bus—only ever one bus—shuddered out of the wasteland, into Dedalo, down the black street from the northern end of the city to the bus station.

New people came every day. Yet the city was always quiet. And no one ever left.

Soarsha shook her head. Home was a place you could always call weird.

She pulled the stop-request cord and waited for the bus to slide with a gasping grace to the curb. Instead of getting out through the rear doors, she walked up to the front door, so she could thank Carl again for the ride.

He shook his head. "You deserve all the good this world has to give, Soarsha."

She tried to smile, but her eyes felt hot all of a sudden. "Thank... Thank you, Carl."

"I mean it," he replied. Then he lowered his voice, and looked up and down the bus, as if to make sure no one was too close.

"And there's one other thing," he said. He leaned in closer to her.

Soarsha leaned in too. "What?"

"That silver-gray street you saw isn't the only one."

Soarsha stood up straight, lightning and icicles running up and down her skin and through her veins.

She started to open her mouth, trying to find her voice again, but Carl just jerked his head toward the door.

"Don't go looking yet," he said. "Ride again tomorrow, and I'll tell you more."

The doors whispered shut behind her as she stood on the solid sidewalk, her feet and stomach grateful to no longer be sitting in the rattling trap of the bus. No one else was out. Whenever she left school at her normal time, the streets always felt so full. So many soundless people, quiet except for the screams in their eyes, wandering lost and confused yet, Soarsha assumed, with some sense of where they needed to go.

No streets near her building were silver-gray. But as a bus driver, Carl would know the city better than anyone. What would she learn when she rode the bus to school in the morning?

Her eyes widened. Maybe he knew the way out of Dedalo. The way to get the gate to open so you could leave. Or maybe he knew another way out. Maybe some secret passage in the bus station?

The bus turned a corner. Before it disappeared, Soarsha waved, and she hoped Carl saw it.

The high square façade of the forty-story building's gray stone bumped out from the main body of the building. Inside the square, a tall narrow arch yawned high, four times as tall as Soarsha. Glass double doors filled the arch, gangly, narrow, and strange, like transparent rabbit teeth. Soarsha always felt like she was walking into a giant mouth.

Just as she neared the door, Soarsha stopped, turned around, and stared down the diagonal spoke street toward the wall. What would it be like to step outside the city, to see and feel and hear and taste and smell the world beyond the wall?

Would it be terrifying?

Would it be amazing?

Would it be a little bit of both?

Soarsha couldn't help but suspect that it would be a little bit of both. Her dad liked to tell her that sometimes life was terrifying. Sometimes life was amazing. The best parts of life were usually a little bit of both.

Across the street, in the shadow of another skyscraper, something moved. Some shape. Shadowy and indistinct. The overall shape seemed like a person, except the head. The head had a strangeness to it. A gauzy darkness flowed there, a non-person strangeness that was all terrifying without any amazing, like shadows trying to be a human head.

A whispered rumble shattered the silent cool air, like a tiger purring and growling as it neared. Soarsha trembled, the way she shook when she stood near the edge of the street and a fast bus passed by, nearly close enough to knock her off her feet. Her body felt like it was covered in a thousand wet ants determined to crawl up her nose.

She turned and opened the door to the building, all too glad to rush into the open mouth as long as it kept her away from what she was certain were silent fangs hiding just behind the roaring shadows.

7

AND NOW... WANDERING HEROES!

A hundred warriors must have changed their minds and fled —the lucky ones. Holding the locked little wooden chest tight, Jilly the Kid sighed and looked over what was left of the battlefield. If only they all had chosen to flee.

A dozen of the few remaining soldiers formed up into a group and approached Shirtman. He stood with his feet as rooted as a tree, twin curved knives raised near his face and stretching down the underside of his forearms. He shifted back his shoulders. His white shirt, with no buttons on the front, just a fabric panel, shifted and whirred. Jilly wished she were close enough to read it. The strange designs didn't often make sense to her, but then again, she wasn't the target.

The shirt froze in its message of the moment. Soarsha thought she caught a glimpse of artfully rendered flames, and perhaps a sword making its way to a not-usually targeted part of a soldier.

Ten of the troops turned red, then pale, then turned and ran from the field. The final two soon lay before Shirtman. They wouldn't be going anywhere ever again.

Nearby, Sapphire's blue eyes flashed like stars. The mere heat and intensity of her light melted swords and turned armor so hot that many soldiers lay around her in a sort of pale puddle. Twenty soldiers stood in a half-circle around her. They looked into her eyes—and her eyes looked into them.

Twenty soldiers fled. Off, Jilly had no doubt, to live rather different lives.

And then there was Gleaming Head.

The leader of the Mrazas had made clear that this battle was no place for a child, not even a ten-year-old. Her job was to protect the chest, and to ride like hell if anyone came near her. Still, from Jilly the Kid's place at the edge of the battlefield she could see Gleaming Head, in the center, at the heart, of the fray. He was always truest where the fighting was thickest, Sapphire liked to say. Though, as Shirtman added, it wasn't because Gleaming Head liked to fight. He just figured that if fighting had to be done, he wanted to end it as quickly and decisively as possible.

Fifty soldiers closed in on the ancient hero. His twin curved swords flashed like silvery tornadoes.

Make that forty.

Half of them must have finally seen the ever-burning fire in Gleaming Head's brown and black eyes. They too made the smart choice and ran away, toward what Jilly hoped were long and peaceful lives.

After continuing to make bad choices, the remaining vanquished soldiers were left to return their bodies to the earth. As the Mrazas cleaned their weapons, they sang soft songs that the souls of the departed would return—and next time live better decisions. Nearby, in a small village where the protected had trembled in fear and hope, calls of gratitude now rode on the wind like guardians, like messengers, flying across the Cuan Féir to proclaim to all corners of the living world that once again the Wandering Heroes were victorious.

The sun set, burning blazing orange through a pale blue sky

with a few long thin purple clouds. They left the battle joyous for life yet sorrowful for life's conflicts, richer in love, hope, and wariness. They emerged not just as saviors of another day, but as kinder people, more determined than ever to find the key that could unlock the true hope of the world. On the path of the living star, the Wandering Heroes rode off into the glorious sunset, over the Cuan Féir, toward what they hoped would be a night of rest and a new day of fewer troubles.

Granted, the Mrazas hadn't expected so much trouble over the little locked wooden chest that Jilly held close. But if you learned anything as a Mraza, it was that trouble usually saves itself for the moments you least expect it. Then you figured out whether or not you really were someone who could leap into the fray with a smile—and a smiling heart.

Riding to the right of Gleaming Head, Jilly the Kid kept one hand firmly on Starcall's reins. The other hand she traced over the little wooden chest, boxy on the bottom but with a curved top. Black iron bands covered the top and sides. Covering half the front of the chest, a thick black steel padlock had blunted swords, axes, lock picks, maces, and prayers—though Jilly's curiosity remained keen as ever.

Jilly rode with her heart, feeling Starcall's stride as the Mrazas made their way to camp. Yet part of her heart remained focused on the chest. It wasn't just that hundreds of people had died wanting to take it. It wasn't just that Gleaming Head had trusted her, Jilly the Kid, a mere ten-year-old and the youngest Mraza ever, with the honor and duty of carrying the chest. No, something else pulled her attention to the chest, as if her soul were a magnet. Somewhere, somewhere, the key was waiting. They didn't have it yet, but Jilly the Kid could feel the day was near. Once they had the key, she could finally see what was inside the chest. Supposedly no one knew—though she suspected Gleaming Head did, but wasn't willing to say, All Jilly understood was that battle after battle had made it clear that plenty of people were willing to die to take the chest for themselves, contents unknown but certainly not undesired.

"Go with love," said Shirtman.

"Go with joy," said Sapphire.

"And go ever onward," said Jilly the Kid.

Gleaming Head reared his horse and shouted, "Go, Mrazas!"

SOARSHA TURNED THE LAST PAGE OF THE BRIGHTLY COLORED comic book, to the full-page panel that every issue of *Wandering Heroes* closed with.

Through the tall green grasses, Gleaming Head rode hard on his brown and black horse, the color of his eyes, and Sapphire and Shirtman were to his left. Jilly the Kid rode on his right. Her long red hair streamed backward in the breeze, like rain stretching horizontal in a high wind. Jilly leaned low over Starcall, a determined, golden glint like a spark in her bright blue eyes. Soarsha was certain she could see a similar glow in the dark shadowy gloom of the locked chest's keyhole.

Below them, bold gold letters outlined in orange said, "see you next time, heroes…"

8

HAPPY 10 RAINBOW

With a sigh, Soarsha closed the comic and set it on her pillow. She loved that finale. She just wished that the new issue had been waiting in the mailbox like a birthday present. Oh well. Sometimes all a birthday girl could eat was disappointment. Maybe the comic would arrive tomorrow.

But what adventure! What revelations! What a wide world they could wander in! A world without walls. A world without limits except their own—and even then, if the Mrazas knew anything, it was how to break past their own limitations and keep going and learning and doing—

Maybe they were on their way to rescue her. Soarsha loved to imagine it. It was still her favorite make-believe. Well, other than having a mother again.

Sitting up in bed and surrounded by the lavender walls of her room, Soarsha stared out the window of the tenth-floor apartment. She tried to see past the faraway ringwall. Maybe, just maybe, she could glimpse dust clouds kicked up by four galloping horses. No luck. Turning toward the little gauzy sachet that hung above her bed, Soarsha squeezed it. The scent of lavender filled her room and her soul, pulling the edges of her mouth into a smile. Her dad loved to tell her how lavender had been her mother's favorite scent. She grew it around their cottage, and she always smelled of it.

Up here, ten floors from the streets where the shadows were deepening and darkening, the fears of the scathtor faded like shadows in tomorrow's sunlight. Soarsha let her imagination roam with the Mrazas, across the Cuan Féir, as the Wandering Heroes made their way to the gate of Dedalo. Soarsha wanted to feel the ringwall shake and tremble. She wanted to hear it crack in two and watch a massive section of the wall crumble like a hand smooshing cake into crumbs.

The Mrazas would ride through the city and cut down the scathtor. They would find Soarsha and her dad, and give them their very own horses. Soarsha raised an eyebrow. She'd have to ask her father what he would name his horse. Together they would ride out of the city and into a world beyond Soarsha's imagination.

From outside her bedroom, a creaking sound snuck through the empty apartment.

The front door.

Soarsha sat up. Eyes wide. Wondering—

"Where's my birthday girl?"

For the first time all day, Soarsha's face brightened, and she ran out of her room, past the silent black phone on the wall, to the large, light-blue-walled room that encompassed the apartment's entryway, living room, and dining area.

"Dad!"

Soarsha leaped and wrapped her arms around her father's broad hard shoulders and his soft, black, tight T-shirt. His otherworldly scent filled her world: strange spices, hot greasy dust, high piercing sun, a hint of cold beer, and garlic hitting hot oil in a pan.

Das rested his head against her hat, and she could tell he was trying to breathe in the scent of Soarsha's hair. He said that the scent of Soarsha's hair, with its hints of old hills and salty sea, reminded him of her mother. Setting down his daughter, Das closed the door, then hung his dusty work jacket, the same faded blue denim as his jeans, on a hook on the back of the door. He set his black lunchbox and small black backpack on the floor next to the door. With a sigh he turned around, leaving the workday things behind him, then he smiled at his daughter and said, "How's my Rainbow?"

Her heart beat like giggles. "Better now."

"That kind of day," said Das. "I've had those too." He patted her shoulder with his right hand. "Even birthdays." For a moment he winced, hard enough to make his brown ponytail bounce, as if some painful memory had lanced his heart, and his eyes clouded in pain.

Soarsha knew the look, and she reached out for his left hand. The comfort of his right hand on her shoulder faded as he grabbed his chest, fingers paling over his heart. Then Das breathed in deeply and moved his hand higher, digging into the neck of his shirt until he found the pendant on its brown leather cord. His hand wrapped around the little disc of silver-gray clay, a swirl of curving lines and jagged-round edges. He never said much about it, only that he'd had it since they first arrived in Dedalo, like a welcome gift from the city. But she noticed that whenever her dad needed to clutch the pendant, the dimness in his eyes brightened.

Soarsha thought about telling her father what had happened during recess, and about Mr. Adbad, but she decided it could wait. This time of year, when her dad's pain came fast and never knew when to leave, she didn't want her dad to slip down the long dark chute of misery that was so hard for him to climb back out from. Whenever that happened, she set the card on his bedside table: a Soarsha rainbow, she called it—with an extra arch of purple above the red, because the only problem with rainbows was they needed more purple. On the card she'd written, in big purple letters, "Rainbow Needs You." Her dad said that remembering this always helped him find his way back—and it was why he liked to call her Rainbow.

Horrible children did horrible things, and it had been a horrible birthday so far. But the birthnight could be perfect. Maybe at their appointment tomorrow with Garen she could talk about what had happened. But not tonight. Tonight was finally shaping up into what a birthday could be.

Her dad touched her face, and she saw what looked like understanding gleaming softly in his jade-green eyes. "I'm okay, Soarsha. Really." He kissed his daughter's forehead. "And what happened at school… It's not okay what happened."

"You mean the kids?" said Soarsha. "Or do you mean me at sharing time?"

Das tried to keep his body relaxed, but Soarsha could see the conflict in his gaze, the struggle of encouraging his daughter to be completely herself yet also wanting to shield her from a world that didn't understand her. "A bit of both," he said at last. "Mr. Adbad told me all about what happened at school. I don't think it helps when you talk about the dreams."

"They don't feel like dreams, though, Dad." Soarsha took a step back. "They feel like things that… that haven't happened yet but are going to happen. They feel real, like you know one step will lead to another, and my steps lead me to what's happening in that dream."

"I understand," said Das. "Dreams can motivate us. But Rainbow, these dreams aren't leading you anywhere."

"The yadda-yadda kids."

Das chuckled. "They have names, you know." He shook his head, the way he often did when he was trying to restrain a laugh. "It might help if you learned them."

Soarsha held his gaze. Why learn the names of people who don't like you? "It might help if any of them were worth knowing."

"Well, once you decide someone is worth it, I know you'll

never let go of their name." Das leaned in close and grinned. "Thank goodness you came down with that horrible case of birthdayitis."

Soarsha's lips scrunched. "You're not mad?"

Das shook his head. "I know school is hard. You learn your subjects and push your mind, and that's what I care about most. I want you to have the best life here that you can. I know you try to fit in with the other kids but you just don't feel like you belong." His bright eyes filled with concern, bewilderment, and a peppering of frustration. "I've never understood why the kids are so mean to you."

"Do you think that if we moved somewhere else—maybe, you know, another city—the kids there would be nicer?"

A spear of sorrow pierced Das's eyes. "If there were somewhere else."

Soarsha shrugged. "I know," said Soarsha, her voice lowering and her hope collapsing. "I know. The world outside the wall is nothing to see at all."

Das patted her shoulder. "It's rough being here," he said. "It's not easy for me either." He leaned down and put both hands on her shoulders. "But we've got each other," he said. Then he winked. "You know what else we got?"

Soarsha shook her head.

Das reached back, picked up something, and held it between them; he must have set it on the floor just before Soarsha had hugged him.

"We've got cake!"

Soarsha's eyes widened. The cake was covered in light-purple frosting, and dark purple-red jam spelled out, "HAPPY 10 RAINBOW!"

"Dad, it's beautiful!"

Das grinned. "As beautiful as you, Rainbow." He nodded toward the kitchen. "Did you check the fridge?"

Soarsha shook her head, then ran into the kitchen, every surface the yellow of faded gold, to yank open the fridge door.

"I'm sorry I didn't make it myself this year," said Das. "This new skyscraper Nabraig has me working on is a massive project, and these foundation stages always take up more time than I'd like."

"It's okay, Dad," said Soarsha. She reached in and pulled out the large black tray, as long as the fridge shelf was deep and half as wide. The little shapes beamed with color: the gleaming white of the rice, the purple-reds and pinks of tuna and salmon, the bright yellows and oranges of pickled vegetables, and the deep green of lovingly wrapped strips of nori sea greens. Even fresh out of the fridge, the scents of soft-sharp vinegar, earthy rice, and the sea-salt kiss of fish floated up to her. Setting the tray on the counter, Soarsha took a step back, afraid she was going to start drooling all over the dark field of sushi.

"I mean, don't get me wrong," said Soarsha. "There's nothing better than your sushi, but if I have to choose, this is still way better than no sushi at all."

Das kissed the top of her head through the hat. "That's the spirit, Rainbow."

9

TWO PIECES OF MOM

I n the front room, as the sun set over the golden city, daughter and father sat on the faded brown coach, with cake, sushi, and a pot of green tea on the coffee table in front of them, and the radio silent against the opposite gray wall. As they ate they talked about their day. Her father told her about how the new building was rising higher into the sky.

"Steel beams are sticking out of the ground like dinosaur bones," said Das.

Soarsha raised an eyebrow. "What's a dinosaur?"

Das leaned back. "You haven't learned about those in school?"

"Nope."

"Dinosaurs were animals, some smaller than you, some as big as your school," said Das. "Millions and millions of years ago they roamed the world."

"What happened to them?"

"No one knows for sure." Das flung up his hands. "Most people think an asteroid slammed into the world, and the explosion made the world change so that nearly everything, not just the dinosaurs, couldn't live anymore."

"That must have been a huge explosion to make it so nothing could survive," said Soarsha.

A familiar faraway look came into her father's eyes, like when you spotted someone on the far side of a crowd. You were certain you knew them yet couldn't quite recognize them. Sometimes her father looked like he wasn't just trying to travel back through the unreliable time machine of memory. He looked like he was trying to traverse void-ridden dark canyons of time and space, to reach worlds beyond, to head toward some long-ago memory that day by day was becoming as faint as far stars.

Soarsha looked toward the window, though the world beyond the glass was now dark. "How long ago was that explosion again?"

"Oh, something like nearly two hundred millions years ago."

"Oh."

"Why?"

Soarsha chewed another piece of sushi before responding. "If the world was so terrible and nothing was alive, I guess I was wondering if maybe that's why there's nothing beyond the city."

Das looked toward the window too. "I don't know if anyone knows," he said. "New people come in, just like you and I did ten years ago. We build upward and upward so everyone can fit within these walls, but no one talks about the world outside."

"I wish you'd tell me about it," said Soarsha.

"I wish I could," said Das. "You're old enough now to know, but the memories aren't there anymore. The thing about passing through those gates, Rainbow, is it's like the world you knew fell away. The city is so big and tall, and there is so much here, that whatever life and world you knew before... it might as well be a dream. Coming to the city is like waking up, and you know what waking up does to dreams."

They ate in silence for a while. With less than half the cake remaining, Soarsha set her plate on the table and snuggled up to her father. "Tell me again," she said.

Das chuckled. "Even though I can't remember it all?"

"Especially because you can't remember it all," said Soarsha. "That way we both remember all you can."

"The world was different then," said Das with a smile. "Where we were before the city."

"What was the place called?"

Her dad shook his head. A shadow dulled his bright green eyes. "I'm sorry, Rainbow," he said. "It's just not there anymore." He glanced toward the window and the unseen wall beyond.

Das rubbed his daughter's head through her hat. "Sometimes I think it's not just getting out of the city that's hard. It's like anything that was with me before the city somehow got left beyond the gates, as if my memories didn't have the right visa."

Soarsha turned and looked up at her father. "What's a visa?"

Das shimmied a little, as if the answer should have been as obvious as air being the answer to the question of what they were breathing. "A visa is a country's way of saying you have permission to visit," said Das. "It's usually a stamp or sticker that goes in your passport."

"Um, Dad?" Soarsha shook her head. "What's a passport?" Something else didn't make sense either, but she figured she should try to unravel the mystery one confusion at a time.

"A passport is a document you carry when you travel," said Das. "It's a little booklet. Mine had a dark-blue cover with gold lettering and designs on the front. Inside, your passport says who you are and what country you're from. There are also blank pages inside, for stamps for when you arrive in and depart from a country, and of course for the visas."

Ah. That was the problem. That was the confusion.

Soarsha touched her father's hand. "Dad?"

"Yes?"

"What's a country?"

Das stared at her. "A country." For a moment his gaze went far away, as if he were trying to find the answer by peeking at something in his across-the-universe past. "A country is a way people say what land and culture is theirs. The world had nearly two hundred countries."

"Oh, so they were all cities too," said Soarsha.

"Well, cities usually exist inside a country," said her dad, "though sometimes you have a city that is its own country. What was it? Hong Kong. That was one. Hong Kong was a city that was its own country. But usually countries have rural areas, and small towns, and villages, and cities of different sizes, and each city has its own distinct look, based on the culture and resources of the people living there."

"Two hundred countries," said Soarsha. "I can't even imagine one country."

Das squeezed her close. "I suppose you can't."

"Are countries and cities one of those things that went away when, you know, when all the things happened and we lost Mom?"

"I can't remember the name of the country anymore, where your mother and I lived," said Das. "When I think back now, the world before the city, the world before you, is a red-and-black flash."

"And that pain in your chest?"

Das shook his head. "I wish you didn't notice."

Soarsha snuggled up to him. "It's my job to notice, Dad. You're all I've got."

"You're still a kid," said Das. "Amazing and precocious though you are. It's my job to take care of you, not the other way around." He sighed. "But you're right. Sometimes my chest hurts, and my mind feels hot, as if my memories are burning up, like wood crackling in a fireplace."

"I'm sorry," said Soarsha. "I didn't mean to make you feel—"

"Don't you worry about that." Das kissed her head. "Being alive is all about feeling many things at the same time and trying to make sense of it all. I learned to live with that a long time ago. Sometimes I feel like there's so little I can give the one person in this world who matters to me."

Then he smiled. "At least I can give you what little I have left of your mother."

He turned to the little table by the couch and picked up a small package wrapped in purple construction paper and topped with a bow made with strips of the same paper. "So, Rainbow, that's exactly what I'm going to do."

He handed her the present. "I always wanted to give you this when you turned ten, when you were on the cusp of your journey growing into the marvelous woman I know you're going to be."

The paper crinkled as Soarsha pulled it off, revealing a little hinged box as bright blue as Soarsha's eyes. A scent like sunlight on lavender filled the air.

Soarsha glanced up at him. "This is really for me?"

"Happy birthday, my daughter."

With a grin as big as the sky, Soarsha opened the box. Inside, on a brown leather cord like her dad's, a crescent-shaped, polished, cloudy purple stone lay on a bed of soft white cotton. The lavender scent filled and embraced Soarsha, a blanket of calm and contentment, the way she imagined her mother's embrace would feel.

"It's beautiful, Dad." Soarsha lifted out the cord, letting the full necklace unfurl, the cloudy purple stone glinting in the light. "But what is it?"

Her father smiled and touched her face, his rough yet gentle hand warm with kindness. "It was your mother's." He looked away slightly, lowered his gaze, but Soarsha could tell he was trying to hide the pain in his face. "I just held onto it for a while. It's time it went to her daughter."

Soarsha handed the necklace to her father, and he fastened it around her neck. Father and daughter nuzzled their foreheads together, smiling. For a moment both of them held the pendant together, the little purple, lavender-scented crescent the only thing they had of the lost woman they both loved.

Soarsha's eyes were wet, but she could tell her father was

managing to keep his dry. Holding the pendant in her fingertips and rubbing the smooth surface of the purple stone, Soarsha let the lavender scent fill her as she nestled in closer and rested her head on her father's chest. Sometimes Das would tell her about how, when they first came to Dedalo, he would pat her back and sing to her when they felt sad about losing her mother. And on her birthday, he would always tell her about her mother.

"Your mom and I hadn't been certain about children," said Das. "Our lives had... complications. We both engaged in the world in some very different ways. I, especially, hadn't been sure about changing my traveling ways."

Soarsha didn't understand this talk of traveling, but she just wanted to listen to him, so she didn't ask. But how could there be a world where people travel all over the place? Sometimes, when he could find the memories, her father would tell fantastical stories of places as real as they were faraway. He could never remember the names of the countries, though. Not anymore. But he could remember the feel of the places.

One country he especially loved to tell her about. The memories seemed the most recent, the closest to his heart. It had been a hot place, with the smells of spices everywhere, and the sound of an ageless world both falling apart and building up, all at the same time.

Dinai, he sometimes called that country, pronouncing it "die-nigh." He said that never felt quite right, but it was the best he could do, as if he had puzzle pieces he couldn't fit together the right way.

Dinai.

It sounded like an amazing place, and Soarsha wondered what Dinai was like. What anywhere was like, if it wasn't here. Or if there was anywhere else. Maybe there wasn't anymore.

Soarsha sighed. Not that she would ever know.

"In the end," her father continued, "your mom and I realized we wanted a child. I was excited to share the world with her, but we both felt like there was something missing from the family we made." He squeezed Soarsha closer to him. "We realized that what was missing, was you."

He stroked her cheek. "I was excited to share the world with someone new, someone the world would want to make itself worthy of. Your mom gloried in how it felt to have you growing inside her." Das smiled. "She would touch her belly as if she were holding the very world in her hands."

Das kissed Soarsha on top of her hat, but she could still feel the pressure of his lips on top of her head. "As far as I'm concerned, Rainbow, she was. And now I am."

He paused there. Soarsha let the story sink in, like the warmth that starts to glow inside you when you've dived under cold blankets, but now they've warmed up and the golden safe tingling feeling starts coming back, blood to bone and skin to soul.

She looked up at her dad. "Why did you name me Soarsha?"

Das smiled, and excitement, respect, and pride rose in his voice like the sun arcing up high in a new day's sky. "It was a name very special to your mother," he said. Then his eyes narrowed, and his voice plummeted like the city's dust falling through still air. "I can't remember why, though. I think she named you after someone who meant a lot to her. Someone she looked up to."

Soarsha sat up and kissed his cheek. "It's okay, Dad." She smiled. "Hey, I have two pieces of Mom then."

Das shook his head. "What do you mean?"

Holding up the pendant, Soarsha said, "I have this, plus what Mom named me. That's a piece of her she gave me the day I was born."

Das breathed in a ragged breath. "Sometimes you're so wise it's scary," he said. "I don't know how I managed to deserve such a marvelous daughter, but whatever I did, I hope I keep doing it." He shook his head. "I'm sorry I can't remember more about her."

"It's okay, Dad."

"It's not okay at all," Das replied, "but it's nice of you to say so." Blue pain dulled his green eyes. "Still. It is what it is. We are where we are, and we will make the best of life that we can. Right, Rainbow?"

Soarsha took his hand and squeezed it. They both sat up tall.

"And you know what we better make?" Das grinned, though the smile didn't make it past his mouth. His green eyes seemed duller.

She smiled back. "What?"

"We better make cocoa and turn on the radio," said Das. "*Wandering Heroes* will be on soon."

10

AND NOW, BACK TO WANDERING HEROES

Tall grasses swayed in the wind like green waves that had danced and flowed however they damn well chose. The last clangs and cries had faded, like the calls of flying birds as they vanished beyond the horizon. Between the green hills under the afternoon golden sun, fallen bodies covered the valley floor like the end of a gruesome harvest.

Another day, another battle.

Jilly the Kid knew that she should be tearing up. Such a waste of life and all that dahl. But there were no tears in her dry eyes, and she wondered why that was. It wasn't that the Mrazas—the Wandering Heroes, the Joy Warriors—celebrated death or lived only for battle. Quite the contrary. Gleaming Head always maintained that he'd love nothing more than to just kick back in an evening, after a long day's ride across the ocean of grass, and drink a quiet beer. It was the rest of the world that kept putting itself before him for a kicking.

Sometimes they could skip the battle part. Sometimes. When people's hearts shone through, and the blinding hatred in their eyes cleared like breaking clouds.

Sometimes people made the right choice.

The bodies seemed to sink into the bent and broken grass. Sometimes they didn't.

Jilly the Kid wondered how much of the Cuan Féir had been fertilized by days like this.

Turning away from the carnage, Jilly could see a look similar to her own on Gleaming Head's face. His eyes were dry too, but she figured he must have emptied his soul of tears long before she was a dream, much less a baby. Even now, as he cleaned his twin curved swords, she could see the resignation in his brown and black eyes. Not regret. Not sorrow. But the calm resignation of someone who had done what he'd needed to do—and wished dearly that he'd been able to find another way. Yet always his eyes gleamed with wariness, kindness, and hope, like the eyes of a father.

Again Gleaming Head had refused to let Jilly anywhere near the battle. She was to protect the chest. She stared at it. What was so important that thousands would risk their lives for what was inside?

Gleaming Head would say only that she was more precious than the world understood. Yet he did not despise them or feel rage toward them. He had ridden out to the field, trying to persuade the army to leave. They didn't even have to drop their weapons. They just had to change their minds and go home.

A few did. Not enough. But a few was better than none.

Then the others had charged the ancient hero.

It still made Jilly shake her head. By now, you would think everyone knew better.

Gleaming Head's namesake brown bald head had shone like a beacon in the golden sun. With one bound he had leaped off his horse, drawing his swords as he landed on both feet.

The soldiers had come. None who had tried to kill Gleaming Head survived.

And none had gotten near Jilly. Really, that seemed to be even more important to Gleaming Head than anything else. He'd been increasingly protective of her lately, though he wouldn't say why. Not that she understood. She was just another poor child, around nine or ten years old—no one really knew—who wore sackcloth dresses and tried to keep the worst of the mud and muck off her feet. No one wanted her. No one liked her.

Until the Mrazas had found her. Not just found her but made her one of their own.

A salty, iron-edged scent wafted across the field. Jilly didn't like that. She hoped they could leave soon, but she knew they wouldn't. Gleaming Head would insist that all the fallen be treated with dignity and honor, regardless of why they died. He said it was the least the dead could hope for, and the least the dead could do.

Not that that made any sense. But Gleaming Head was the sort of adult who usually didn't sound like he made any sense and instead was too busy being more profound than the noon sun was bright.

Swords clean, Gleaming Head sheathed the twin blades and nodded toward the wooden chest—still padlocked, chained, and closed—that Jilly the Kid cradled in her arms.

"Word travels faster than hope," he said. "It's as if the whole damn world wants what's inside that chest."

"Is there anywhere we can go that we'll be safe?" Jilly replied.

Gleaming Head's eyes flared, like grease thrown on a campfire. He opened his mouth, then stopped himself. The ancient hero turned away, toward the south, and did not answer.

Far from the battlefield, outside the village they had defended as much as they had protected the chest and their own skins, the Mrazas graciously received the thanks of those they had defended from the bandits. Much of the thanks came in the form of food, hardy and long storing. Much of the food came in the form of the cheese common to the area, dried on sunny rocks for days. While the cheese looked like albino slugs, it was often harder to chew than rock—though more flavorful. Usually. Then again, empty saddlebags made anything satisfying if it led to a full belly.

Gleaming Head liked to make Jilly the Kid laugh when he would tell her that once, in a far-off land with no villages, his horse had thrown a shoe. With no nails to be found, he carved pieces of cheese into slivers and nailed them into the hooves. To this day he had never had to re-shoe his horse.

Jilly never knew which of Gleaming Head's stories were real and which he was making up. Or maybe, she was starting to realize, there wasn't much difference.

The grasslands of the Cuan Féir swept along the plains for the spans of countries, of continents, of what felt like half the world. It was said that somewhere far away, beyond horizon after horizon, the waves of grass did indeed break. They crested and fell, shorter and smaller, until they faded to tan nubs at the toes of the great wasteland beyond the grass ocean.

Gleaming Head never went near the wasteland. Only one adventure would have him cross it, he once told Jilly the Kid, and that day had not yet come. When it did come, Jilly feared he would shed more tears than the rainclouds that swept over the Cuan Féir like an ocean in the sky.

Reaching up to his chest, Gleaming Head touched his fingertips to the long, brown leather cord that he wore in multiple loops around his neck. There was nothing on it; he just liked the cord, he said. It was a reminder, he had once told her, that there was a hole in his heart, an empty place that he hoped he could fill someday. Soarsha had said she figured heroes didn't have holes in their hearts. Gleaming Head had smiled, and said that every hero had a hole in their heart: Loss and pain told you what was wrong in the world—and showed you the way to mend it.

Jilly the Kid looked at Gleaming Head. "For all the adventures you've faced over your long years," she said, "why do you fear the wasteland?"

Gleaming Head touched his not-daughter's shoulder, looked

her in the eye, and replied, "The day I leave the Cuan Féir, I will never set foot in the grasses again, or soothe my soul with the soft sound of the breeze through the green and gentle blades. I wield the swords because sometimes swords are needed." He swept his strong hand over the tops of the grass. "But these are the only blades I care for."

Other than the wasteland, there was one day he absolutely would not talk about. The day that reminded him more than ever that the key to looking forward, never back, was that it was a kindness to those who would otherwise know nothing but more suffering.

It was the day that turned the spark in his gaze to a raging fire amidst a stormy night.

The day Gleaming Head had ridden so hard and so fast, he had nearly lost not only his happiness but also his horse.

It was the day he had doubted everything about himself. The day he had drawn his swords not out of joy and protection but out of rage. The day he had wondered if the world was far worse than he had feared. The one time he had wanted not to save the world but to burn it down, because surely no world deserved to live in the midst of the horrors that people did.

It was the day he had found Jilly the Kid.

Gifts and gratitude received, the Mrazas bowed and took their leave from the village. There had been a time when they gratefully received any village's hospitality, but a recent adventure had gone rather badly, full of betrayal. Now Gleaming Head preferred to camp in the wild, away from settlements, away from people whose hearts could turn with any wind or thought.

Before Jilly knew it, the Wandering Heroes were riding again. The chest still rode with Jilly, and Jilly's horse stayed next to Gleaming Head's. The ancient hero kept glancing at her. At the chest in front of her. Each time, she saw something in his eyes that she hadn't seen once during the battle.

Fear arced like lightning through the ancient hero, through

the man who said she was the daughter he had never had. She saw the fear of a man who did not like what he was riding toward, but nonetheless accepted his path.

As they rode, Jilly noticed something else in Gleaming Head's eyes: a little silver-gray flicker, like a little spark of hope. Though Jilly couldn't understand how he could be so fearful and despairing, yet also ride high on some little hope that, if it were a breeze, couldn't sway a blade of grass.

Time after time, Jilly tried to ask him what was in the chest. Time after time, he would not answer, except to say that she would find out when he did.

That night, by the fire, Gleaming Head said little. He sat half in light and half in shadow, nodding at the conversation, but offering nothing of himself.

After dinner, Shirtman and Sapphire took hands and wandered off into the night. One time Jilly the Kid had been about to ask if she could go with them. But that was the thing about adults. Even the nicest ones had a way of making the air around them really still and hard and cold when they didn't want you around, as if by will they could summon an invisible wall between you. Jilly didn't entirely understand what they were doing that made their walks so secretive, but whenever Shirtman mentioned how he loved looking up at the sky, she couldn't help but think he was admiring something other than the stars.

Tonight, though, Jilly was glad Sapphire and Shirtman had left. She carried the small wooden chest over to where Gleaming Head sat in silence, watching the fire and occasionally stoking it, and she sat down next to him.

He didn't even look at her.

Jilly smiled a little. Set the chest on her lap. "I could pick this lock in ten blinks. Three if I hit the spot lucky the first time."

Gleaming Head turned so quickly she only realized he had moved when she felt the simmering heat of his gaze on her.

"Don't go near that lock." No mirth. No smile. His eyes were cold fire, and his mouth was as flat and sharp as his swords.

"Wouldn't dream of it." Jilly refused to look away. "But you've hardly said a word since we left the battlefield. I know there's something about me and this weird chest that you don't want to tell me."

Gleaming Head sighed. "It's not that I don't want to tell you."

Jilly the Kid rolled her eyes. "It's just that you won't. It's not the first time."

"That's not it at all, actually." He poked and dug at the fire with a stick, as if hoping answers were hidden under the coals. "Ever since we got that locked chest I've been trying to figure out how this little chest connects to you, and you to it. The connection is there. I just don't know how or why... or what is going to happen when we get there."

"When we get where?" Jilly sat back. The cool edge in the night was like the back of a chair against her spine. "You always act like we just wander and see what happens."

Gleaming Head chuckled. "We do that too, but often we have some direction." He picked up the small chest. It was so slight. Hardly of substance at all, really. Yet when he removed it from Jilly's body, she felt both like a heavy weight had been taken off her—and that part of her was moving away from her, and she wanted it back as much as she wanted a fresh inhale to follow her exhale.

The black iron padlock glinted in the firelight. "I know what's inside, but I don't know what's inside," said Gleaming Head. "I know the overall, but not the specific."

"I don't see what that has to do with me."

"I don't know what it has to do with you either," said Gleaming Head. "Only that it does have to do with you. It's always been with you. You're connected."

Jilly the Kid shook her head. "I thought we'd found it a while back."

"Nope." Gleaming Head sighed. "I'd been keeping it hidden, keeping it safe, until the time was right and you seemed mature enough for the responsibility."

Jilly's brow scrunched. "But you found me when I was a baby."

"You weren't a baby," said Gleaming Head. "I don't know how, but I don't think you were ever a baby. You were a kid, Jilly. It was years ago, yet you were the same then as you are now. You've never been Jilly the baby or Jilly the toddler. You've always been Jilly the Kid."

"That's impossible," said Jilly. "People... start as babies. We... age."

The lines around Gleaming Head's eyes deepened as his gaze twinkled. "I haven't aged in centuries. For all I know you sprang into this world as a ten-year-old child. And you've stayed that way. But the only thing with you was that chest. Now... Now I know where it needs to go."

Jilly the Kid took his hand. "Across the wasteland."

Gleaming Head squeezed her hand, but she could still see the fear in his eyes. "I don't know what's going to happen. There is no path. I'm hopeful."

"But you're also terrified."

He said nothing. The ancient hero's face looked so tight, as if some powerful grief and despair were exploding and crashing inside him, but he would not let them out. Jilly squeezed his hands, those hands had seen rough work, hard living, fierce battle. Yet still, the hands were gentle.

"We'll find out together," she said.

"I'll do all I can to keep you safe," said Gleaming Head, his voice soft but tight. "Thing is, I just don't know that I can anymore."

Jilly's eyes tightened. Nothing terrified a child like the fear of an adult they thought was fearless. "Whatever happens, maybe it's because it won't be your job any longer to protect me. Maybe it's time that I go on to whatever you've been keeping me safe for."

"That's just it," said Gleaming Head. "You've become like a daughter to me. I don't want to let you go."

Jilly the Kid rested her head on his shoulder. "But that's exactly when it's time for you to have to let me go."

They held hands and looked at the sky. She could feel and hear his steady, slow heart, which must have beat more times than the stars had twinkled. She wondered how much longer Gleaming Head and Jilly the Kid had to travel together.

The generous night gave the Mrazas deep, untroubled, uninterrupted sleep. Once they were riding again, south against the eastern rising sun, Jilly looked back. Their camp seemed so empty —and in her heart she felt she might never know another peaceful sleep.

The Mrazas rode across the grassy plain, toward the place, said Gleaming Head, where at last the chest would be safe.

"AND THAT," SAID THE RADIO ANNOUNCER'S VOICE THROUGH the big brown boxy radio with its arched top, "is the end of tonight's episode. What's in that chest? How is Jilly connected to it? And where, oh where, are the Mrazas going this time? Find out this and more! Join us for our next adventure next week with... *Wandering Heroes!*"

Soarsha and her father clapped, then her dad turned off the radio. Soarsha got into her pajamas, and did her bedtime routine, and her father gave her a big hug.

"Are you and Iandel still going for a drink?" said Soarsha.

Das held her gaze, but she could also see a nervousness in his eyes. "Is that okay with you if I meet up with her?"

Soarsha tried to keep her voice steady. "People say the scathtor is out there."

"I have no interest in leaving this city," replied Das. "Home is where you are."

Images of the scathtor, of a padlocked wooden chest, of the yadda-yadda kids, all rushed liked an army through Soarsha's sleepy mind.

"Okay," said Soarsha. "Go."

Tucked into bed, Soarsha listened for the soft click of the apartment door when her father left. She was so tired, sliding fast down sleep's slide, but somehow, she thought in the dark, the apartment had never before felt so empty.

11

WHAT THE BUS DRIVER SAID

A perfect birthday night erased whatever had been bad about the day. It left you a joy that couldn't be ascribed to sugar, but to something else, something you may not be able to name or comprehend, but you knew it was there, as solid as the world.

The trouble with a perfect birthday, though, was the next day. When you woke up and had to get through that first terrifying moment when you doubted the birthday had happened, or had been nothing but a vivid dream. Yet Soarsha had slept as peacefully as the Mrazas. She woke refreshed, ready for whatever the day would bring.

She just hadn't expected it to start at the bus stop.

With backpacks slung over their shoulders, Soarsha and her father sometimes rode the bus together in the morning, her in her purple shirt and overalls, and him in his black shirt and blue jeans, though Das got off a few stops before Soarsha so he could walk the rest of the way to the construction site.

"I like the fresh air," he would say.

And Soarsha would giggle. "You work outside, Dad. How much more fresh air do you need?"

Her dad would shrug and take on the half-stern, half-cartoonish rigidity that he put on when he wanted to sound especially fatherly. "Well, you should always get some fresh air," he would pontificate. "You never know when you'll get another chance."

As much as Soarsha loved riding the bus with her dad, today she looked forward to when he would say goodbye. Once he got off the bus, Soarsha planned to move up toward Carl and find out what the bus driver knew about Dedalo's silver-gray streets.

Even the golden dust and the skyscrapers seemed to shiver in the low gray morning sun, while Das told Soarsha about his drink with Iandel.

Soarsha grinned. "Did you kiss her?"

"Kiss who?" Das stumbled. "Kiss Iandel? Um, no."

"People do that, you know," said Soarsha. "I mean, you didn't kiss Iandel… but you have done it before." Heat flushed over her face. "I mean kissing—but, well, you've done, well, you know, *more* before—obviously, since, well, I'm here. Ahem." Her voice faded and her face felt flushed; her words had felt so much brassier and tougher and more grownup in her mind. Apparently being ten was not the same thing as feeling grown up.

"Okay," said Das, "clearly we need to talk about a few things." He grinned. "As for Iandel, no, we didn't kiss. It's not that kind of friendship. She's great, and I think we find… comfort in each other's company. But kissing her… I don't know, Soarsha. It'd be like kissing my sister."

Clearly grownups had very complicated feelings. Soarsha didn't know what to say. She knew as much about kissing as she did about having a sibling.

"Don't you ever… you know," said Soarsha.

"Oh," said Das, with a slow long nod. "Do I think about being with someone else?"

"Well, yeah," said Soarsha. "I mean… in *Wandering Heroes,*

Shirtman and Sapphire love each other. You loved Mom so much... but doesn't it... don't you feel... lonely?"

Das smiled. "My wise Rainbow. I miss your mother. I miss what we had." He leaned in a little and chuckled. "Right down to the kissing. Maybe someday I'll want to find something like that again, another love, or at least someone to be with who's more than a friend."

Soarsha shook her head, and her eyebrows scrunched under the brim of her purple hat. "Why don't you?"

Das cocked a shoulder. "Because I don't want to. The only girl I care about is next to me. Being your dad, honoring the love your mom and I had, being there for you as you become the marvelous woman I know you'll be... that's what matters to me right now." He smiled, and tapped his forehead against hers. "Now, the moment you grow up and move out, who knows. But for now... nah. I miss your mom too much, and I want to be there for every moment my daughter is growing up."

Soarsha reached over and took his hand, and gave it a squeeze. Das squeezed hers back.

"I love you, Dad," said Soarsha.

Their gazes touched. "I love you, Rainbow," said Das.

The No. 33 lumbered up to the curb, gasping and sputtering, as if it had barely escaped attack. The shuddering bus always looked rough, but right now Soarsha wondered if it were about to fall over from exhaustion.

The doors squealed open. Soarsha took a step, ready to say hello to Carl—and she stopped.

"Morning sweetie," said the driver—but it wasn't Carl.

Soarsha had never seen this woman before.

"Where's Carl?" said Soarsha.

The woman looked away from Soarsha, only for a moment but enough for Soarsha to see the dark look that passed between the woman and Das. One of those coded looks adults gave each other, as if they could temporarily send messages through their gazes. Soarsha glanced back at her father, and he tried to put away the fear flashing across his face.

"Carl... didn't make it in today," said the woman. She jerked her head toward the seats. "Morning rush, you know."

Das paid their fares and they sat down a few rows from the front. Das stared out the window, as if searching the shadows.

"Why isn't Carl here?" said Soarsha. "What are you not telling me?"

Das sighed. He reached down into his backpack and took out the morning paper. "I didn't want to say anything," he replied. "I don't like these sorts of rumors flying around the city without proof."

Soarsha stared down at the loud tall black ink:

SCATHOR SPOTTED MOMENTS BEFORE BUS DRIVER VANISHES

Tears trembled in Soarsha's eyes.

"Dad, did the scathtor take Carl?"

"Carl's cared about you as long as we've been here." His voice shook. "This whole scathtor thing... sometimes I think it's a bunch of hooey dreamed up to sell more papers. Whatever happened, I bet everything will be fine tomorrow."

Soarsha looked away from her father, back to the newspaper on her lap.

Or nothing was fine. Maybe the scathtor had leaped from the shadows to take someone she knew and cared about.

Her eyes narrowed. But why Carl?

She thought back to the shadow she had seen yesterday, and to Carl's words—the last thing she'd ever hear him say.

Carl noticed she had seen a silver-gray street, and he planned to tell her more about it.

Eyes widening, her fingers went to the purple crescent pendant. It was no wonder, she thought, that her dad held his tightly when he felt upset.

What if the attack wasn't random? What if... What if the scathtor had taken Carl because the scathtor knew Carl was going to tell her about the streets? She'd always wondered why the scathtor's attacks and sightings only happened around her birthday and the anniversary of when she and her dad came to Dedalo. Soarsha looked back up to her dad. She needed to tell him about Carl and what Carl was going to tell her. Das was staring out the window again. She reached for his shoulder, about to tug on his jacket, but she stopped.

If the scathtor took Carl because he was going to tell Soarsha about the silver-gray streets, then if Das knew what Soarsha knew, the scathtor might take her dad too.

Soarsha lowered her hand.

No. She couldn't tell her dad. Or Garen. Or Mr. Adbad.

She'd have to learn about the silver-gray streets herself.

And find Carl.

The No. 33 neared her father's stop. He hugged her, but his face was still tight. Ten years old or not, amazing birthday or not, the tenth anniversary of their arrival in Dedalo was tomorrow.

"Dad? You okay?"

"I'm fine," said Das. "Really. A good morning's work and I'll be totally myself for when we meet at Garen's during lunch."

"My birthday was yesterday," replied Soarsha. "Do we really have to go see him?"

"Once a week," said her dad. "You're not having an easy time of it."

"Neither are you."

"He helps," said Das. "He just helps."

Soarsha sighed. She knew her dad was right. But she didn't like Garen. He was like a pretty pot on a blazing stove, shiny and red. You wanted to reach out and touch it, but the closer you got the hotter it was.

"Will we ever get happy enough not to need a happiness coach?"

Das set a gentle hand on his daughter's cheek, then her shoulder. "You're a kid." Das tried to smile, but no grin could dissolve the pain in his eyes. "There's so much you don't know. So much I keep from you."

"Like how the scathtor took Carl," said Soarsha. "Maybe that's the problem."

He shook his head. "That's the job. I'm not trying to hide you away. Things happened when you were so young, Rainbow. It's a parent's job to get their children ready for the hard stuff. That includes shielding you so all the hard stuff can't smash into you at once."

Soarsha's eyes narrowed. "I can handle more than you know."

"There is so much more to handle than you know," replied Das. "Think of it this way: If you don't need Garen, I do. So how about you keep your old man company?"

Soarsha sighed. "Fine."

Das leaned forward and touched his forehead against hers. "What do you get when the sun meets the rain?"

Soarsha looked away. Her cheeks felt a little flushed.

"A rainbow," said Soarsha.

"That's what your mom always liked to tell me." The bus rumbled to a shuddering stop as Das kissed her forehead. "See you at lunchtime." He stepped off the bus with a wave, which Soarsha returned.

Soarsha stared at the empty space where her father had been. She still felt the odd urgent press of his strong hug, a coat she never wanted to take off. The constant sun shone through the dusty sky. Where had her parents been that had rain—and where they could see what a real rainbow looked like?

"The rainbow is what you get when the sun meets the rain," repeated Soarsha. She shook her head. Her dad must have been the rain to her mother's sun.

Before she knew it, the bus dropped her off. Soarsha rushed

inside the school, torn between wanting the morning to fly by so she could see her dad and get away from today's yadda-yadda torments, and wanting time to crawl, seconds like eons, anything to delay sitting down again with Garen the happiness coach.

12

THE HAPPINESS COACH

The bright lime greens of Garen's walls reflected in the smoky glass windows, but Soarsha did her best to ignore Garen's garish office. Fifty floors up from the black streets of Dedalo, golden dust drifted against the blue of the sky, glinting in noon light.

Located in the center of the northeast quadrant, halfway between the ringwall and the central Spire, the building was sited on one of the strange city blocks that bowed gradually so that the skyscraper façades curved with the contours of the streets. Garen's large window wall looked out toward the southwest, though Soarsha never bothered to try to find her school. While the innermost buildings were the city's tallest, Garen's office was situated so that Soarsha could see down one of the diagonal streets that ran to the Spire and from the Spire all the way to the ringwall.

Soarsha stared out the window, the only time she got to be so high up. The city was beautiful; Soarsha had to give Dedalo credit for that. It wasn't ugly and horrible. Blocky or slender, shorter near the ringwall or taller near the center, every building had an angular grace and a subtle gleam. Above all, though, Soarsha loved to look out beyond the wall. You actually could see over it from up here. The brown wasteland of the cracked plain staggered out to the edge of sight, on a dusty, hazy horizon that for all Soarsha knew was dust kicking up as the world crumbled over an unseen edge.

And still, Soarsha thought, she longed more than anything to see the world beyond the wall for herself.

She traced the lines of the city from the ringwall, through the streets—but saw none that were silver-gray—and finally arrived at the base of the Spire. All streets near the heart and center of the city emptied into the central ring road. It curved around the short sibling of the ringwall, which surrounded the Spire, as if cordoning it off from the rest of the city.

Soarsha and her dad had sometimes walked around the inner wall, touching the smooth, crackless, seamless stone. Yet everyone in the city knew that while the inner wall may be shorter than the outer wall, it was just as tough and impenetrable. Unlike the outer wall, the inner wall had no gate. No one ever came in or out of the Spire, or if they did, they did so by some means no one else could see.

Yet the Spire, the same silvery gray as the inner wall, rose higher than anything else in Dedalo. Sometimes the Spire seemed so tall the sun itself could perch on the top and balance there, like a porcelain ballerina on a brass needle spinning in a music box. Soarsha stared at the beautiful building—and at the very top, in the chamber where people said god lived, a bright light winked at her.

Her mouth fell open. Before she could think much about the light winking a second time, a door clicked closed. Garen and her dad must have finished their grownup talk in the outer office and had come into Garen's main room.

Soarsha turned. Whenever Garen was around, the world felt ten degrees hotter. His red button-down shirts, orange pants, and short blond hair must feel like they were constantly being steamed, and his pale skin looked like a boiled dumpling.

"Happy birthday!" The gleam of Garen's smile never reached his dark green eyes. He leaped up as if he'd stepped on something sharp, and clapped his hands and smacked his heels together as he came down. "Ten years old! Wonders of the city!"

Garen lunged forward sideways, right hand outstretched, like a fencer. Soarsha couldn't help but giggle. The happiness coach could be very annoying, but he was also undeniably handsome.

She held up her hand, and Garen took it, and gently kissed the air just above her skin.

"Soarsha," he said, "you marvelous girl. Before you know it, your father won't let me give you that little kiss anymore."

Soarsha rolled her eyes. He was cute, but he wasn't *that* cute.

Garen winked at her and stepped back. He swooped his arms to his left, steering father and daughter toward the angular, dark-gray squashy chairs that had been arranged so they faced each other, with Garen's chair facing both from one end. In between all the chairs, a long low orange table gleamed in the lights. Everything in Garen's office gleamed, like a toothy white smile angled too perfectly to the noon sun. In the middle of the table, a dusty box of tissues sat like a stone, the limp white thin paper the only thing in the office that didn't look new and shiny.

"It really is amazing," said Garen. "You've come so far."

Soarsha sat down. Saw nothing but the green wall. A large, framed, black-rimmed, painting looked like someone had run an unbroken swooping line of silvery-gray paint all over a dark canvas.

"It'd be nice if other people could come a ways too," said Soarsha.

Garen blanked the expression from his face. Soarsha always thought it strange that being a happiness coach often meant looking so neutral.

"Mr. Adbad and your dad told me all about yesterday," said Garen.

"Other people are the only thing that upset me," replied Soarsha. "They just... They just seem so limited. Even worse, they want to be."

Garen leaned back in his chair but kept his gaze fixed on Soarsha. "How was school this morning?"

Soarsha thought again of all the things she'd been expecting. Another kickball to the head. Stuck-out tongues and jeers and rude rhymes about her name. Poorsha. Boarsha. Dorksha. Double-palm slaps to her ears. Trip-ups in the hallways. Grabs at her hat. Soarsha just wanted to mind her own business and learn. Hell was other people at school.

"Surprising," said Soarsha. "I figured everyone would be messing with me... but no one did. It's like I wasn't there. Which wasn't great either, but it was better than being bullied."

Even Yadda had left Soarsha alone. What few times they saw each other, again Soarsha saw a strange glint in Yadda's eyes, flitting and gleaming behind the fury of Yadda's dislike for Soarsha. One time there was a softness in Yadda's eyes, even, but the moment Soarsha had caught Yadda's gaze, the other child had dashed off, as if suddenly needing the toilet.

"Maybe that's progress." Garen tilted his head to one side. "If you could do anything, Soarsha, what would it be?"

That was easy. "I'd leave the city and see the world."

Garen's mouth fell open, and his face contorted into a grimace. As if by reflex, his right hand shot up toward his chest, not over the heart, but to the center. His fingers seemed to clutch around something under his shirt, though when he did his dim eyes brightened. Even with his mouth open, he shifted his jaw side to side, as if grinding his teeth.

"Soarsha..."

Her eyes narrowed. "You think I don't know everyone says it's impossible?" She shook her head and stood up. "I know it's not possible. But you didn't ask what was possible. You asked what I would do if I could do anything."

"But... Soarsha," said Das, "why see the world?"

Soarsha turned and looked at him. "You always tell me how you and Mom were these world travelers," she said. "Have you forgotten?"

Das shook his head and looked away.

"I want to travel because maybe then we could find Mom," she said.

Das turned to hold his daughter's gaze again. "Your mother isn't missing."

"She's out there somewhere," said Soarsha. "Can't you feel it, Dad?" She ran her fingers down her arm, as if for a moment she had felt a gentle hand there. "I can. Sometimes I'd almost swear I can see her face in some of the specks of dust."

Garen looked from father to daughter, daughter to father.

"Das," he said.

But Das kept staring at his daughter. She suspected he was also seeing a day ten years ago tomorrow, the day that he didn't realize would be the last time he'd be with the woman he loved.

"Das." Garen's sharp voice cut.

Das's head snapped toward Garen. "What?"

"Maybe there's something to what Soarsha is saying."

Das shook his head. "You know as well as I do..."

"I'm not saying that you try to leave the city." Garen chuckled. "No sense bringing the ole scathtor onto your trail, right?"

No one else laughed, and Garen's chuckle trickled away. "Anyway," he continued, with barely a pause. "I'm saying... explore the city more. How often have you ever taken Soarsha around the different quadrants? Or the inner wall? It's lovely. The material is amazing, and being near the Spire lifts both the gaze and the heart. And the ringwall at the city's edge? It's a wonder of engineering and architecture."

"I don't see the point," said Das.

"The point," said Garen, "is that life is about knowing what your limits are, but that's not all life is about. Sure, you need to know your limits. What's more important for Soarsha—and for her happiness—is that she gains a better understanding and appreciation of all the good things in the place she does have. Is the city finite? Sure. So is life. So is the world. Finite is not the same thing as trapped. This city is finite, but it can feel boundless, limitless, full of possibilities without end. Soarsha is seeking answers, Das. You only find answers by getting to the heart of the matter. If the two of you undertake some exploring together, she'll find what she needs."

Garen looked at Soarsha. "What do you think?"

"I... I think that could be... really cool." She smiled.

Das sighed. "I know when I'm outnumbered," he said. "Soarsha, I'll start taking you on little tours to different parts of the city."

"Every day?" said Soarsha.

Garen chuckled. Soarsha glared at him. Unscathed, Garen said, "Let's start with once a week. Get a feel for it."

Soarsha smiled. "Could we start today?"

Das stood up. "Iandel and I were supposed to have drinks again this evening, after work," he said. "You know how it is. When we get close to the day."

Garen tilted his head to one side. "She's an embalmer, Das. It's not as if shuffling her client appointments will make them mad," he said. "Maybe you can meet up later this evening instead."

Das sighed and turned to look at his daughter. "I'll take you today. After work. I'll rearrange things with Iandel. I've got an afternoon meeting with Nabraig, but after that I'll knock off. We'll pack a picnic dinner, I'll pick a bus route, and we'll go. Spend the evening seeing a part of the city you haven't been to before."

Soarsha arched an eyebrow. "Which part?"

"Ah-ah." Das waggled his index finger back and forth. A light had come on in his eyes, as if the wanderer part of her father's past was coming back to life. "It's a surprise. Father's prerogative."

"Are you excited?" said Garen.

Soarsha grinned. "I am."

Das gave her a large broad smile in return. When they hugged, she could feel his love from his face and his embrace.

"I'm excited too," said her dad, "This might be the just thing we both need."

For a moment, a troubled look crossed her dad's face. Garen noticed right away.

"What's wrong, Das?"

Das chuckled. "You know, Garen, I can honestly say nothing much. I just realized I left the light on in the kitchen this morning." He shook his head. "If that's my biggest worry, I'm a pretty lucky guy."

The three of them laughed. Golden afternoon sunlight streamed through the window. And a brighter light, silvery and gray, gleamed in her father's eyes, the light of new paths and possibilities.

13
____

NO MORE MEAN

When the final bell rang, Soarsha didn't even stop to tell Mr. Adbad goodbye. Anytime she'd looked at her pendant, his face stormed with the same fear and irritation he showed whenever she said "aye." Soarsha all but flew out of the building and down the stairs, sitting at the bottom to wait for her dad. The afternoon sun gleamed with the bright pure light of promises about to be fulfilled. In the heights of the city, the golden dust danced with glee for the father-and-daughter adventures that were about to begin.

The bell's clamorous tone still rang in her ears. Students filed past, a thick stream branching off as children went their separate ways for the day. Yet there was no sign of Das.

Soon the kids were gone, and Soarsha was alone. The absence of people had a surprising warmth to it, a comfort, like a blanket made of sky. She stared at the streets, waiting for Das to come into sight, yet all the while feeling like she'd made a mistake.

Her back prickled. Soarsha turned around—and saw Yadda standing there, just inside the shadow of the doorway, staring at Soarsha.

Soarsha's eyes narrowed as she stood. Her heartbeat pounded.

Something that felt like steel flooded through her body, hard and strong and ready for anything.

"What?" said Soarsha. "Come to throw something else at me?"

Yadda's gaze dropped to the floor. Voice low, almost a mumble, Yadda said, "I'm sorry."

Soarsha leaned back, but being turned around, the strange position made her stumble off the step. She smacked against the bottom stair, and was starting to tumble—but suddenly hands were under her arms, steadying her and helping her get to her feet.

Now Yadda was standing right in front of her. Eyes wide. And so brown. With a bit of amber. Soarsha had never noticed that before. They were really pretty eyes. Soarsha's heart was beating faster than what she would expect from a stumble. Maybe that was the thing. For the first time, there was no dull fire of dislike in Yadda's eyes. There was only the something else, the flickering flitting thing that fled as soon as it realized Soarsha had noticed it.

"Finley," said Yadda.

"Whatley?" said Soarsha, her head shaking and eyes blinking.

A nervous smile. A near-giggle. "I know you have a hard time with names. My name is Finley. And I'm sorry I'm so mean to you. You're... so much smarter than everyone else. And you're so alive." Finley's voice dropped to a whisper, but the gaze stayed steady. "And you're really pretty."

Gaze softening, Finley leaned forward, full lips closed but sticking out. The world around Soarsha had turned into honey, thick and made of golden shimmers. The air rippled like little waves. Soarsha's skin went prickly all over. Finley's lips were so close, the beautiful amber eyes closing, and Soarsha felt her own lips rising, her own eyes closing—

Soarsha leaned away, and with wide eyes took a step backward.

Finley's eyes and mouth popped open. With a gasp, Finley stepped back too. "I'm sorry," said Finley. "I didn't... I shouldn't..."

Soarsha shook her head, but her hot belly and trembly every-thing felt like it wasn't moving the way it should.

"It was really nice of you to say sorry," said Soarsha. "But I don't know you. I only know that you're mean to me. An 'I'm sorry' and a little bit of nice doesn't sweep away all the mean and earn you a kiss."

Finley walked back up the steps, hands out, toward the door-way. "You're right," said Finley. "I... I like you, Soarsha. I have ever since I first saw you. No one else did, though. I was afraid of them. I was afraid of you." Finley sighed. "And I was afraid of myself."

"That's why you've been mean to me all this time," said Soarsha.

"Yes," said Finley. "But I won't be mean to you anymore."

Soarsha took a step toward the other child. They were both ten. And Soarsha had heard the little whispers and giggles. Kisses on the playground. The way your skin buzzed and sparkled when your fingers brushed a hand that you wanted to feel squeezed tight within your own.

"We could... get to know each other," said Soarsha. "Maybe... see if we can be friends? Then, you know, we could see."

Finley's eyes brightened. "Are you saying you like me too?"

Soarsha shrugged. "I... I don't know." She smiled. "But I could."

Finley nodded. "Okay. No more mean." Voice thick and crack-ing. "I really am sorry."

Soarsha sniffled. "No more mean."

Finley nodded. "Only nice. Because that's how friends treat each other."

Soarsha could see it. A friend. Maybe something else. But a friend. That would be really cool.

"I'm waiting for my dad," said Soarsha, scuffing her foot on the step and looking down. "But... maybe, you know, if you don't have anything else to do, maybe you could, you know, wait with me."

Finley smiled. "I'd like that."

Soarsha smiled back, and Finley took a step from out of the doorway.

From inside the school, a roar shook the brick and the steps and the two children.

Soarsha and Finley looked around. Now the air had turned to hot broken glass, but Soarsha still felt slow and sludgy, heavy and light, at the same time.

"Finley?" said Soarsha. "Come here."

Finley was almost at the stairs. From out of the shadows, a flash of darker shadow swept forward. The rumble-roar filled the air again. Something swept around, like a dark tornado wrapped in a cloak, and topped with swirling shadows trying to form a shape like a human head. Tapering, curved shadows swept forward like blades, and a blur of shadows surrounded Finley.

"Soarsha!" yelled Finley.

Then both shadow and child were gone.

Soarsha took a step forward. "Finley?"

Silence.

Soarsha's eyes trembled. There was no sign Finley had ever been there at all.

Before she even realized it, Soarsha was running. Away from the school. Past the bus stop. Toward home. She had to get away. Had to run. Because Soarsha felt in her heart what she had seen with her eyes. Finley had wanted to be her friend—and now she was gone.

Just like Carl had wanted to help her then had vanished.

No, not vanished. Been taken.

Soarsha ran through the city like lightning through the skies of her dreams. She realized why now she had felt like she was making a mistake. Tears streamed down her face. Now and again the trudging people would stop and stare at the crying running child, faces agape at the sight of tears, but no one spoke to her, or tried to help.

Soarsha swore at herself. If she hadn't made the mistake, Finley wouldn't have tried to kiss her. And Finley would still be there. Maybe not Soarsha's friend, but at least... around. Alive.

Soarsha's eyes burned—and she realized her other mistake, while she was waiting for her dad. She'd gotten it wrong. Her father hadn't said he'd meet her at school.

He said he'd meet her at home.

Soarsha ran faster. Toward home. Toward her father. And away from the school, grateful for every step she put between herself and that horrible shadow in the doorway. She knew what had taken Finley. And Carl. Knew what she had seen.

The scathtor.

Lingering sun still hung in the sky as countless people moved through the city in strange silence, as if the soundtrack of the world was playing in a different theater from where the film was showing.

The door clonked against the wall as Soarsha bounded into the apartment, her body heaving from the running. In the kitchen, light gleamed, and Soarsha smiled through what was left of her tears. She shut the door and dropped her backpack nearby, but kept her shoes on.

"Dad! I need your help!" Her words tripped over each other. She had no idea how she was going to explain what had happened. Finley. The almost kiss. The scathtor. The gone child.

She hoped he would believe her. She hoped she could say something coherent.

But she didn't expect silence and light to be the only things coming out of the kitchen.

She called out toward the kitchen again. "I'm sorry if I made you worry," said Soarsha. "I hope I didn't make you mad..."

Looming silence, deep as shadows, like light made of lies.

Soarsha's almost smile faded. The tears threatened her eyes again.

Soarsha took a cautious step toward the kitchen doorway. "Dad?"

But something wasn't right. No matter how upset he might be, he would answer her, at the least to say he was too upset to talk right now. She felt like she knew the answer to a question on a test, then later realized she had forgotten to fill it in.

The doorway loomed, and the light seemed bright, but the light, there was something wrong with the light—

Soarsha stepped inside the kitchen and immediately saw what was wrong.

The kitchen was empty.

Her chin trembled. That was the problem. And she remembered. At Garen's office, near the end of their session. Her dad had said he'd accidentally left the kitchen light on. Light was the only thing happening in the kitchen. No yummy smells—nor the occasional spicy words that Das immediately reminded her she was not to repeat. Yet.

Maybe he'd gotten worried and gone looking for her. That must be it. Otherwise he'd be here, he'd be waiting. But the kitchen wouldn't be clean. There would be food out. And either dishes ready to be washed or dishes already washed.

Turning, Soarsha walked back to the front door—and found the other problem.

Her father's jacket wasn't hanging in its usual place. His black lunchbox and small backpack weren't on the floor by the door.

Soarsha shook her head.

Her dad hadn't come home and then left. He had never come home at all.

Her eyes widened. What if the scathtor hadn't taken only Finley?

Soarsha tore open the front door. Sprinting down the hallway, she stopped at the elevator and stabbed at the buttons. Beating on the doors didn't make the slow cars come any faster. Soarsha kneed the doors as if they were a bully, then with a glare turned and slammed the stairway door open.

In the lobby, Soarsha glanced at every corner. The lobby was big enough for people to stop and chat while they checked their mailboxes, but wasn't so big that a tall, muscled man like her father wouldn't be noticed. Busting through the front doors of the apartment building, Soarsha dashed out to the street. The city's gray silent throngs were going here and there, from school and work to home and bar and wherever else it was that adults went when their days were done.

"Dad!" Soarsha's eyes widened as she yelled. She turned her head from side to side, trying to catch the slightest glimpse of the only person she had left in the world.

No one spoke to her or asked if she was okay. No one even looked at her. To the northeast, the endless needle tip of the Spire stared down, all-seeing yet non-caring, without so much as a wink of light from the top.

The rumbling engines of passing cars and taxis were the loudest sounds in the otherwise silent city. The No. 33 bus rumbled by, driven by the woman from this morning.

Soarsha leaned forward, her neck tight and her head stretched upward. She yelled again. "Dad?"

Rain wet and needle sharp, she felt a prickly heat poke at her eyes.

The city continued on its lonely way.

No one turned for Soarsha. No one ran to her. No dad-strong arms picked her up and held her close to the heartbeat she'd known since she first arrived in the world.

A teardrop fell from Soarsha's cheek and plopped on the sidewalk. A moment later some passerby's foot stepped on the teardrop and ground it into the cement as they passed, without so much as a glance at the scared and lonely child.

"Dad..." Soarsha whispered, a hope and a prayer as brief and fading as a teardrop on pavement.

He wasn't there. Wasn't approaching through the crowd, delayed but hurrying, relieved to see her and glad she was okay and sorry he'd made her worry.

With her eyes dry yet burning, and without another glance at the street, Soarsha turned and went back into the apartment building. The wildfire panic blazing through her burned out, and the world's sounds had faded to a soft buzz. Numb and moving slow, she vaguely remembered going to their mailbox and getting the mail, the normal sort of thing she would do on a normal day. She pulled out the thin stack of envelopes—all of them were small. No *Wandering Heroes* comic. Not that it mattered, really. What did finding a comic matter when she couldn't even find her dad? With staggering, stuttering, quivering steps, Soarsha made her way to the elevator and laid her head on the doors. Through the brushed metal she could feel the slow hum of the descending cars.

This time it was good to wait. Every moment was a chance she might hear her dad say her name. Feel his strong gentle hand on her trembling shoulder. See the love and concern in the grass-green ocean of her father's worried yet relieved eyes.

The doors opened. Soarsha got into the elevator alone.

Back in the too-quiet apartment, Soarsha snapped the lock closed on the front door, then she turned and put her back up against the wood. The mail tumbled to the floor with a soft sound like water splashing. Tears trembled in her eyes, then tumbled out. Chin quivering, Soarsha's knees gave way. The child alone in her home sank down to the floor and cried, and cried, and cried, and knew for the first time no one would hold her in their strong safe arms.

14

AND NOW, THE CONCLUSION OF THIS EPISODE OF WANDERING HEROES

When Jilly the Kid wasn't looking directly at it, the locked wooden chest glowed with a gentle golden light. It pulsed at the edge of her sight, like breath or the heartbeat of someone you loved. Whenever she looked down, though, the light went out.

The Mrazas had been riding for days, at a brutal pace that Gleaming Head would not let up on. Jilly the Kid knew they were riding south, but only because the sun told them so. The Mrazas barely stopped for food or relief, much less rest. The horses were keeping their heads as high as they could manage, but everyone, including the horses, looked ready to fall over. Starcall's coat shimmered with sweat. Sometimes Jilly could feel the horse shudder, and almost stumble.

Yet Gleaming Head pushed them all the harder.

Other than the steady, if tired, beat of the hooves pounding the earth, the Mrazas were silent. Gleaming Head told no stories. Sapphire and Shirtman didn't get caught up in any of the usual funny conversations they liked to have. Jilly asked no questions— and she realized, on the fourth day, that maybe the reason Gleaming Head was making them ride so fast and so hard was not only to prevent her from asking questions, but to prevent him from having to answer them.

Now as they soared across the Cuan Féir, a dull fury began to glow in Jilly's heart. They always talked about where they were going. Family meant talking things through. Family meant relying on each other—and relaying to each other what they all needed to know. Yet the steely set in Gleaming Head's eyes told Jilly that right now the ancient hero no longer saw his family. He saw only the road ahead, and perhaps some destination that only he could see.

Jilly the Kid noticed something else too.

The grasses of the Cuan Féir were getting shorter. Less dense. Patches of earth were visible now, dark brown and rich. Pace by pace, the earth seemed to be getting lighter, drier, with occasional cracks. Now Jilly the Kid understood why Gleaming Head said nothing. He didn't have to speak. The earth itself was telling them everything they needed to know about where they were going.

The bottom edge of the big orange sun was about to meet the edge of the land to the west. Jilly was certain her eyelids were about to have a similar meeting. She lashed the little chest all the tighter, and she wrapped the reins around her wrists, then grabbed them again, terrified she was going to slip into sleep and fall off Starcall.

Once again Jilly's eyelids drooped, and once again she forced them open. But her arms were limp and her legs were limp, and it was too much, too many long days of endless riding. The wet mud of her body wanted to slump against the back of Starcall's neck. The gravity of sleep pulled Jilly's eyelids down, and pulled her body toward the horse's neck, and started to pull her downward, toward the waiting ground where the grass was sparse, short, and brown, no longer a green ocean but like the scrubby foam of waves where living sea gave way to parched sand.

"Mrazas!" Gleaming Head's voice cut through the air like

thunder, like a tiger's roar—like the shock of hearing his voice for the first time in days.

The ancient hero's right hand swung up in a fist, halting when it was level with his head.

Starcall scrabbled to a stop, and so did Shirtman's and Sapphire's horses behind them. Jilly's eyes widened. The sleep leaped away from her like a mischievous animal caught out.

"We're here," said Gleaming Head, and he hopped down from his horse.

Sapphire and Shirtman dismounted. Jilly did too, but carefully, awake yet still so tired she didn't trust her body to come down via anything so much as resembling grace or skill.

There they stood, horses and riders. The Mrazas. The Wandering Heroes. The joy warriors of love, with bright eyes and open hearts, despite all else. There they stood, at the end of the Cuan Féir.

Mere steps away from their tired feet, what remained of the brown nubs of grass surrendered to a jagged edge where the brown scrub met the brown wasteland that mastered the world as far as the eye could see.

"The wasteland," said Gleaming Head. "The Barrenburn."

Sapphire stood to the left of Gleaming Head. "There's nothing there," she said.

But Gleaming Head shook his head. "Our road is there," he replied, "and our road is all we need." He tried to push his words through the famous thunder-boom low roar of his voice, but Jilly could still hear the tight fear behind the show of confidence.

Jilly stood to the right of Gleaming Head, and Shirtman came up next to Sapphire.

"This is the place," said Jilly. She took Gleaming Head's hand and would not let him pull away. "The place you fear to go." Her voice tightened. "The place you know you will not come back from."

The tears Gleaming Head could not cry softened his voice,

but he tried to mask his fear with gruff kindness. "It's also what I told you," he said. "The one place we can go where you might be safe. Until the time is right."

"There's nothing out there," said Shirtman. "What are we supposed to do? Hide her in the cracks of the earth?"

"We don't have to," said Gleaming Head. "We'll rest here tonight. In the morning, we head that way." He pointed, and the Mrazas all looked with him to the south.

It was faint, shimmering in the distance like a mirage. But they all saw it, at the edge of the horizon, the only thing on the wide, flat, dusty, empty plain of cracked earth that didn't look devoid of even the memory of life.

Rising from the Barrenburn was what looked like a city, surrounded by a curving wall. High buildings swooped up to a tall central golden needle that shimmered in the evening light.

Something, though, at the near edge of Jilly's sight made her look down.

The chest was glowing—even as she stared at it. The light pulsed, first near her, then fading as the glow intensified toward the far side of the chest, then repeating—and always the light was its most intense where the chest was pointed toward the city. The metal and wood and whatever lay hidden inside weren't just something to carry, but a guide, a compass, to lead them where they needed to go. Standing at the edge of grassland and wasteland, the Mrazas gazed out toward the golden city in the far distance.

And somewhere, some place nearby yet where neither Jilly nor any of the Mrazas could see, something else glowed. Bold gold letters, outlined in orange, that said, "SEE YOU NEXT TIME, HEROES..."

PART II

THE 33 GOES ALL THE WAY

15

———

THE HEART OF THE CITY HAD NO HEART

All night long, the scathtor chased the little girl through the city of no escape.

In the darkness of the black-walled labyrinth with streets of silver-gray, the scathtor's rotting flesh stench snapped like whips, stinging Soarsha's nose, body, and soul. The monster was always in shadow, so she could only catch glimpses, never the whole. A thick arm, ropy with twisted shadows. A muscle-gnarled leg. A bare torso, dark with fur or skin or scales, she could never tell. Not once could she see beyond the swirling shadows of the head to glimpse the scathtor's face.

The streets shuddered with the low rumble-roar of a hungry monster ready to pounce.

The monster's shoulders were so broad, sometimes Soarsha could squeeze through passageways where the scathtor got stuck. Whenever this happened, Soarsha squealed with glee, the cry of a child victorious. The stink would fade and she would run on, down the silver-gray path of the city's labyrinth, trying to find the way out.

Yet always, always, she would pass an intersection, round a corner, and the stench would claw at her, try to grab and never let her go. Then the scathtor would step out of some bend she hadn't seen, as if it had appeared out of thin air. With a bellow and a snort it would chase her again. Whatever progress she thought she had made, Soarsha would have to turn around, double back, try another corridor, always, always, with both the stench and the claws ever closer to grabbing hold.

She stopped to a wall, a shining, silver-gray ring. From the center the Spire gleamed golden and rose to the sky. She found no gate, and no matter how hard she beat on the wall, no help came.

The heart of the city had no heart.

A hot breathy bellow snagged her by the ears. She turned around, her back against the wall. The scathtor's claws rose, then fell. The monster came clear, no longer obscured by light or darkness. Its body looked like a grownup's, but the head was all swirling shadows. Yet as the scathtor got closer, the shadows seemed to part, and the scathtor's face began to become visible, dark eyes solid and sorrowful behind swirling shadow. It roared, and claws ripped toward her—

Soarsha sat up on the couch, sweating, body heaving. The dream clutched sharp and hard at her like claws. While she slept, the sun had set. Night had risen again after all, rolling its darkness over a world where a little girl had no father. How many hours had slipped by in too-early sleep, down the labyrinth where the scathtor chased her and its tigerish growl followed her everywhere she turned? Soarsha wasn't sure how long she had napped, or when fear had given way to exhaustion. She was certain only that she had wasted time.

She turned toward the front door. Maybe, though, maybe—

No sign of her father's things. No Dad sitting next to her, maybe gently stroking her cheek with his knuckle the way he sometimes did. No delicious smells from the kitchen.

"Dad?"

She felt stupid calling out his name, but if he was there, and he could hear her, he'd respond. The too-small apartment was too silent, though. No father. Just a daughter who'd already lost her mother, and now her father.

Soarsha got up from the couch. She passed by the phone and went into her dad's room. Maybe he'd fallen asleep too. She flipped the light switch.

"Dad?"

A golden glow shone on a tidily made, yet empty, bed.

Soarsha sat on her father's bed and stared out through the dark windows, her knees pulled up to her chest and her arms wrapped around her legs. Lit rectangles of bright windows gleamed in every skyscraper as far as she could see. People would be behind those windows. Families. Single people. Children and their grownups. Doing whatever people did. Soarsha didn't know any of them. Didn't know or understand this city, yet still she looked, trying to see, trying to understand. This was the deep longing of all places and ages: To look upon a world where you did not belong, yet desperately wish you did.

Rising from the bed, Soarsha went over to the floor-to-ceiling window and sat down so her left side was against it. She leaned her cheek against the cool glass. Outside, the golden dust twinkled like dancing stars. Her dad had once told her a story about traveling in a place where at night flying bugs lit up, yellow-green in the gloom. Soarsha didn't believe him. Still didn't. Then again, glowing bugs didn't make any more sense than ever-falling dust. Maybe he hadn't been telling her some strange tall traveler tale after all.

Off in some corner of the city where she couldn't even tell where the sound was coming from, a rumble like a tiger's low growl made the windows shake. Sweat popped out from all over her. Even ten floors up and behind glass, she scooted backward on the bed, as if the scathtor could leap up from the street below and burst through the window.

"Get it together, Soarsha." She shook her head. "This isn't what the Mrazas would do. No matter how scared they felt.

They'd turn that fear into action." Her eyes narrowed. "And that's what you're going to do."

Staring out the window, Soarsha wondered where her dad could be. An accident at work? A late meeting? She shook her head. He would have called. Someone would have, maybe even Nabraig herself. Soarsha had only met her once, years ago. All she remembered about the businesswoman, though, was her intense, confident air, like a golden hug combined with a punch in the shoulder. Nabraig's certainty wrapped up Soarsha like a warm sweater and filled her with what felt like unlimited potential. Maybe that's what it felt like to have the sort of power Nabraig had; she was the only person Soarsha knew of who was regularly on the ninetieth floor of one of the city's tallest skyscrapers. Soarsha wished she had some of that confidence right now.

Or there was Garen. His happiness seemed the sort that he left at the office. The simmering frustration under his skin, though, that he took home. Even if it were a fire in his soul, the happiness coach always glowed from inside. Garen shone like a lighthouse—not that Soarsha had ever seen one, of course, but the one in the photo Mr. Adbad passed around had been quite beautiful. Soarsha wished she could shine like that.

Iandel was the strangest. Pale and quiet, she seemed like she was drained by being out in the world. The embalmer always seemed to prefer bodies to people—maybe because bodies were quieter.

Soarsha sat up. Iandel. Of course.

Das and Iandel were supposed to have drinks tonight. Maybe Das had forgotten about his and Soarsha's adventures and gone out with Iandel as planned. Sure, Soarsha would be mad at him. She smiled. He would feel terrible. And guilty. That would easily be good for a few extra sushi dinners and chocolate cake desserts this week.

From its perch on the wall near Soarsha's bedroom, the silent black phone sprang to life with its clamorous ring.

Soarsha scrambled up and ran to the phone.

"Hello?" A smile already launched over her face. It had to be her dad. Sorry he'd forgotten—

"Soarsha? Oh, thank goodness."

Soarsha's smile fell away. That wasn't her father's voice.

"Iandel?" she said.

"I was wondering if your father was home," said the embalmer. "He and I were supposed to meet up tonight."

Soarsha's body went rigid. "He... He's not with you?"

"No, dear." The embalmer's voice was always chilliest when she was trying to sound warmest. "I assumed something came up, or he forgot."

"He isn't home." Soarsha's voice cracked. "I saw him this afternoon, and he was supposed to cancel with you because our happiness coach assigned us this great adventure, but he's not here..."

Soarsha's voice was flooding away fast now, as the tears streamed down her face. She didn't want to cry. Not over the phone with her father's weird friend who only liked being around bodies. Iandel was freaky. Soarsha had never liked being around her. She wasn't mean... She was just... distant. As if she had found herself somewhere she hadn't intended to be, and had yet to make peace with it.

"You poor child," said Iandel.

Soarsha wiped away snot and tears and tried to sound like a brave ten-year-old, instead of the terrified kid who was trying not to drop the phone.

"I'm... okay."

"Nonsense. You don't know where your dad is." The calm steadiness in Iandel's voice surprised Soarsha. The embalmer was silent so long, Soarsha thought she had hung up, but then Iandel spoke again. "Soarsha, stay where you are, okay?"

Soarsha shook her head. "Why? I need to find my dad, Iandel." Her eyes widened. "Wait! Iandel! The scathtor! It's real... It might try to get you!"

She waited for Iandel to reply, but there was nothing—nothing except a strange annoying beeping sound, that Soarsha realized had been there ever since Iandel had told her to stay put. Soarsha looked at the phone. "Iandel?"

Nothing. The connection was gone, the line silent.

16

IN THE DOORWAY

The trouble with waiting for someone was knowing there was a chance they wouldn't arrive. And the trouble with knowing someone might not arrive was the guilt that ate at you because you were convinced you had failed to give them the vital information they needed to protect themselves against the horrible monster that right this moment might be devouring them whole.

After Soarsha hung up the droning phone, she went back to the window and sat down again. Outside the window, just inside the thrum of the traffic, like a ragged sickly dark gray thread woven amidst silver, the howls of the scathtor chomped through the gloomy night all the way to Soarsha's ears and soul.

What was the scathtor? Where did it live? Where was it now? Why did it come out? Who was it searching for—or who had it already found?

The glass was cool against Soarsha's forehead. She felt a little hungry, but not enough to bother with eating. She wanted to run out onto the sidewalk again, and dash from one end of the city to another, seeking out her father. But that was the sort of thing a scared little child would do. Not someone who was ten. Not someone who could see being an adult, being a woman, before her. A woman didn't run around in a panic. A woman felt the pain and the fear, and turned it into strength, understanding, strategy, and action. A woman got ready for whatever was to come, then made it sorry it had come for her.

Soarsha's eyes narrowed. She didn't understand how she knew any of this. But she knew.

In her reflection, a sheen had come back to her eyes. Not fear and panic, though. Connection? Strength? Confidence? A warm trickle went through her like a breeze, like a warm mug of cocoa in her hands, like, she suspected, what it would feel like if her mother's hand were squeezing her hand right now.

Her hand wrapped around the pendant, and a hint of lavender filled the room.

Bright and powerful, the eyes staring back at Soarsha looked older, with more sorrow, yet more joy too. This, she was certain, was what her mother's eyes looked like. Ready and strong. Scared, but powerful enough to transform fear into love and power. Soarsha smiled bigger. No wonder her father loved her mother so much.

And her mother, Soarsha realized, would not be sitting on the floor with her head against the window. So Soarsha stood. Her mother would be thinking, taking into account everything she knew, trusting her mind, her feelings, and her instincts.

Soarsha closed her eyes, and she thought. Iandel was on her way, but that wouldn't be enough. Her father didn't spend time with many people.

Garen. They had just seen Garen. He would help.

Nabraig. She'd want to know where Das was, nearly as much as Soarsha. Soarsha knew good and well that Nabraig's company owned the properties, but without Das any project would halt like a sprinter tripping before the finish line.

Who else?

Mr. Adbad. If anyone would be worried, it would be her

teacher. He knew how much her dad meant to her. He would know that Das needed to be found, for Soarsha's sake. He would help.

Once Iandel arrived, Soarsha would explain the plan. They'd gather the right people, scathtor be damned. No monster was going to take her father. Or if it had, no monster was going to keep him. Soarsha would fight like all the Mrazas if that's what it took to get her father back.

Going to the phone, Soarsha called and left messages for Garen and Mr. Adbad. She was about to call Nabraig, but her belly was squealing and chattering like an engine trying to turn over without fuel. Grabbing a snack from the kitchen, she ate quickly. It was no picnic, but an adventure was definitely on its way. After she ate, Soarsha opened her purple backpack, took out her schoolbooks and supplies, and set them on the purple bookshelf near her bed. She loaded up the backpack with snacks, fruit, and a couple of water bottles from the fridge. She left the old *Wandering Heroes* comic in the pack but wished she had the new one to take with her, so once she found her dad, he could read it to her. Oh well. One more thing she didn't have right now.

Her eyes narrowed. But she would have her dad back, dammit. She would.

She had just zipped the bag when there was a knock on the door.

Iandel. Thank goodness. And about bloody time. The night wasn't getting any younger. Soarsha slung her backpack over her shoulder and ran to the door. She yanked it open—then stood back, eyes wide.

The brown-skinned, bald woman before her stood tall, broad and solid, wearing a tulip-yellow silk blouse under an open navy blue jacket and pants, as if a harvest moon had hidden behind the curtains of the night sky. Over her left shoulder, a brown leather strap crossed her torso to a matching messenger bag, thick and bulging with, Soarsha presumed, lots and lots of boring grownup documents. It would figure. All that paper, and not one comic. Adults just never knew their priorities.

The woman shifted. Her amber eyes and the tawny, light-brown skin of her bare head caught the golden gleams of the apartment's lights.

Soarsha's face scrunched up in confusion, and she took a step back.

"Who the hell are you?" said the girl to the stranger in the doorway.

The woman cocked an eyebrow. "Does your dad know you talk like that?"

"You're not Iandel," replied Soarsha.

"Of course I'm not Iandel," said the woman. "Whoever the hell that is. How do you not know who I am? I've been your father's boss for as long as you've been in this city."

An annoyed line tightened Soarsha's lips. "You're Nabraig?"

The woman raised an eyebrow and studied Soarsha as if the doorknob had started talking. "I also was figuring I wouldn't need to sleep out here," replied Nabraig, her voice a dry sharp crack, like thunder in Soarsha's dreams. "Will you be asking me in or should I find a sleeping bag?"

"Um... come in." Soarsha stepped out of the way, and closed the door after Nabraig came inside.

"I'm looking for your father," said the businesswoman.

"That makes two of us," replied Soarsha.

Nabraig tilted her head to one side. "What are you talking about? I called earlier, by the way, but no one answered."

Soarsha wondered if that had been when she was running out to the street searching, or maybe when she had fallen asleep.

"I don't know where Dad is," said Soarsha. "I... I've been trying to find him. He was supposed to be here when I came home from school."

Nabraig's eyes softened. "Your adventure. He told me after lunch. He said he had to go up the structure one more time to check a few things, then we were supposed to meet before he headed home to wait for you. Trouble is, I never saw him again. Neither did anyone else on site."

A hot flood ran up Soarsha's face. Her eyes felt hot, but this brusque stranger was the last person she wanted to cry in front of.

A hardness glinted in her eyes, but Nabraig's face softened. The businesswoman now seemed strangely familiar, as if Soarsha had known her for years. She knew what her dad thought about Nabraig, though. No matter the situation, he liked to say, Nabraig was tough, but she was fair, with a kindness that came out at the most surprising and unexpected times.

"Oh child," said Nabraig. "You must be terrified."

Even though it felt like worms crawling on her skin, Soarsha let the fear come through on her face and in her eyes. Might as well. It was true: She was terrified.

"That also makes two of us," said Nabraig. "I know your father has his problems."

"He's never let me down," said Soarsha. "Don't you dare start thinking you can sack him—"

Nabraig shook her head. "He's never let me down either. The last thing I'd want to do is sack him. I'm worried precisely because he's so reliable. But..." She looked away from Soarsha, as if pondering, then her fierce gaze returned. "You and I both know this time of year is hard on him."

Soarsha said nothing, wondering how much Nabraig understood.

"It's a weird time of year," Nabraig added. "This time of year, about ten years ago, I lost everything too. One moment it was like so much potential was before me. The next, it was all gone." Her hand went up to her neckline, and she seemed to squeeze something right behind her blouse. Soarsha hadn't noticed before, but Nabraig, like her dad, wore a brown leather cord around her neck.

"Next thing I remember," said Nabraig, "I was on the bus to

Dedalo." She chuckled, the warm of the old memory brightening her eyes the way a cup of cocoa could brighten Soarsha's. "The same bus you and your father were on. That's where he and I met. We've done a lot of good work since then." The gleam in her eyes faded. "The details of my old life have long since faded, but the heart never fully forgets the feelings. Sometimes there's still a pain in me, like a hole in my heart. Some hurts never go away, I guess. But we do what we can with them."

"I feel that way too sometimes," said Soarsha. "About my mom. I never knew her."

"But you know you should have known her," said Nabraig, her voice soft. "That's why it hurts."

Nabraig was brusque, her words covered in sharp jagged edges, like a cheese grater. But Soarsha could see what her father meant. There was kindness there too, rounding off the sharp parts so she was less likely to cut someone. Soarsha smiled at the businesswoman. For the first time since Nabraig had knocked on the door, Soarsha liked her.

Another knock pounded on the door, and Soarsha dashed to open it.

Soarsha knew Iandel wasn't tall and slender. Yet somehow when Soarsha saw Iandel, the embalmer always seemed gaunt. It must have been some sort of visual trick, as if someone's profession were a filter through which you saw them.

The embalmer was short and muscular—probably from lifting all that dead weight every day. Iandel's devil-red suit flowed from her short boots to her flowing pants, from the swell of her hips past the thin lapel, up to the top of the matching silk blouse. A brown leather cord wrapped around Iandel's throat. Thick, wavy blonde hair cascaded loosely down Iandel's back to her shoulder blades, and her blue eyes glinted in the lights of the apartment. What few times Soarsha had met Iandel, she was weird but nice—

"Well," said Iandel, voice flat, "hurry up."

"Sorry?" said Soarsha.

Through windows and walls, the rumble-roar of the scathtor rose, as the shadow monster roamed the labyrinth of the city, looking for souls who wanted to leave.

"Dad," said Soarsha.

Iandel stepped back from the doorway and raised an arm toward the elevator. "Now come on," she said. "I know where he is."

17

WELCOME BACK TO WANDERING HEROES

Clouds never touched the blue sky above the Barrenburn. No rain, mist, or morning dew softened the hard dry air. The cracked brown ground was hard as stone and made the horses wince, as if the furious earth were pounding back at the hooves.

Every moment they rode, Jilly the Kid missed the soft whisper of the Cuan Féir's swaying grasses. She missed cool mornings when taking a breath was like sipping water. The little locked wooden chest in front of Jilly the Kid pulsed toward the city. In addition to the tall, slender, golden needle thing in the center of the city, gray buildings radiated out, taller near the center and shorter near the massive encircling ringwall. Jilly had never seen anything like it, not even in her dreams.

Sometimes she looked behind her, wondering what marauding army or fierce solo warrior had been brave or foolish enough to follow them.

"Our only danger lies before us," said Gleaming Head, without so much as a glance behind him. Every time he looked toward the city, Jilly could see it in his eyes: fear. Resignation. And a glint of hope, though Jilly was certain it was getting dimmer, like the last coals of a campfire going dark.

Jilly stared at the city ahead. If many people lived there, shouldn't it be louder?

Near the end of the Mrazas's second day crossing the Barrenburn, the wall of the silent city loomed like a mountain. As the Wandering Heroes got closer, Jilly saw now what seemed like a golden veil over the city, as if endless small things were floating in the air.

Such a strange, strange place they rode toward.

Midway between afternoon and evening, the sun dropped from sunflower gold to campfire orange as the Mrazas neared the wall. At a signal from Gleaming Head, the horses stopped about a hundred meters away. Jilly was grateful the sun wasn't casting the wall's shadow over them. The high wall looked as thick as the earth beneath her feet, and felt as tall as the mountains that ringed the Cuan Féir. If the wall's shadow had fallen on them, Jilly was certain she would have turned Starcall around and headed back toward the Cuan Féir, armies and marauders be damned.

Without the beating of the hooves, though, the Barrenburn's hush returned. So thick was the silence, Jilly couldn't hear so much as the breathing of her friends, or even her own heartbeat. She touched her fingertips to her wrist, and sighed—at least she still had a heartbeat. The silent sunlight had even stopped warming her skin. Everything near the city was cool and quiet, on the brisk brink of chill and far beyond the edge of eerie.

Yet they were here. Jilly reached down and touched her fingers along the pulsing wooden chest. They had reached the one place where Gleaming Head thought they could be safe. Though even in the strange city, it may be difficult to pass unnoticed when they had a chest that pulsed with light as if it had its own heartbeat.

The Mrazas dismounted and stood in the not-cool, not-warm sun. It was good to be on her own legs again, and Jilly patted Starcall's neck gently. She leaned toward the horse's ear and whispered, "Thank you, my friend."

As she leaned away, Jilly realized something she hadn't noticed before. The Mrazas had all ridden abreast each other. Now, though, Gleaming Head, Sapphire, and Shirtman had formed a line in front of Jilly the Kid. Like a guard.

Or a shield.

"What are you doing?" said Jilly.

"This city is not easy to enter," said Gleaming Head. His voice cracked with a pounding of fear and uncertainty.

"Maybe we should find somewhere else," said Jilly.

"There is nowhere else," replied Gleaming Head. "There is only this place." With a sigh, the ancient hero turned and approached Jilly, flanked by Sapphire and Shirtman.

Shirtman laid his hand on Jilly's left shoulder, followed by Sapphire's hand on Jilly's right. Looking into their eyes, Shirtman's vivid green and Sapphire's bright blue, Jilly the Kid felt like she was looking into the eyes of the parents she did not know.

"You are truly one of us," said Shirtman. "I want you to know that riding with you has been a joy." Jilly glanced down at his ever-shifting shirt. The designs swirled. Then stopped.

"Today Is The First Day Of The Best Of Your Life," said the shirt, in bright orange letters on top of a blue background, as if the sun were writing on the sky. Then the design swirled again. When it stopped, the letters were a light silvery-gray over deep green, like mist on a field.

"Over The Hills Or Over The Sea, I'll See You Soon. Namaste La Vista, Baby."

Jilly the Kid chuckled. "That's just weird."

Sapphire could read it too, and she smiled. "He's always saying weird things like that. Kind of endearing." She winked. "Usually."

Sapphire leaned in closer to Jilly, and her beautiful eyes crackled like lightning.

"You're an amazing kid, Jilly," said Sapphire. "But you're just getting started. No matter what happens, trust yourself. Know that those you love most, even if they seem lost, you'll find them again. Just trust the way before you, and lead onward with an open mind and an open heart."

Sapphire and Shirtman hugged Jilly. Tears filled Jilly's eyes, and the others sniffled. Then the two Mrazas stepped back, and Gleaming Head came up to her. The ancient hero sank down to one knee, so the hero and the child looked at each other with level gazes.

"I want you to know, Jilly," said Gleaming Head, "that I love you. I've loved you like a daughter ever since I first found you. I knew then that you were special. Special in ways you don't even know yet. Coming here breaks my heart, but this is the path I must follow, in order for you to take the path you deserve."

Jilly stared beyond her friends, her family, to the wall. There didn't even seem to be a way in.

"What's in there for me?" she said.

"I don't know the shape of it," said Gleaming Head. "Only that my heart tells me it is where you must go. Just remember: Some paths you only know when you travel them not with your feet, but with your soul."

"That doesn't make any sense," said Jilly the Kid. Sometimes it'd be nice if grownups could just talk plainly.

"I know it doesn't sound like it makes sense," said Gleaming Head. "But in time you'll know, you'll feel, that it makes sense. Then you'll understand that wisdom as your own."

The ancient hero kissed her forehead. "Whatever happens," said Gleaming Head, "you stay here. When the time comes, you go into the city. No matter what."

"I thought we were going together," said Jilly the Kid. "I can fight."

"Your fight, your path, your quest, your adventure." The ancient hero's voice trembled as Gleaming Head touched her cheek. "Whatever you call it, it's on the other side of that wall.

Our fight, though, is right here. When it's done, we will go together. I just don't know entirely how we will accompany you."

Before Jilly could ask what he meant, from behind the massive wall, yet as if it were right across from them, a howl, a roar, a rumbling cry, rose up from the city.

Gleaming Head sighed. He stood and looked away.

"What's happening?" said Jilly.

"What must," said Gleaming Head simply. "Now stay behind us, with the horses. Do not try to help. Wait until the time is right."

"But when—"

"You'll know," said Gleaming Head. "Remember: You will always know, and you will always have what you need."

Standing in a line with Gleaming Head in the center, the three Mrazas, the last of the Wandering Heroes, drew their weapons, left Jilly and the horses, and went toward the wall.

"The dim day of my darkest dreams is here," said Gleaming Head, "but I know that even in the depths of this deepest shadow, brightness shines beyond." He tightened his grip on the twin swords. Shirtman and Sapphire nodded.

"Your dream," said Sapphire, "has been our dream too."

Shirtman shifted his feet a little. "Now we live it, face it, as we were always meant to. Together."

Jilly stood by Starcall, as Gleaming Head had instructed. But she had also unlashed the little wooden chest and held it close to her body. The light was pulsing faster.

From the top of the ringwall, a black line began to form, straight and vertical, sweeping downward until it reached ground. Then, with a clank and a shudder, two massive doors, invisible until now, hinged backward, in toward the city.

The gate opened slightly, just enough to let a figure pass, alone, with no one or nothing else behind it. At least, it seemed like a figure. She couldn't make out anything but what looked like a shadow.

Something at the edge of Jilly's vision pulled her gaze downward. Jilly's eyes widened. The little chest's light had gone out.

"Go with love!" shouted Shirtman.

"Go with joy!" shouted Sapphire.

Jilly's breath hitched, but she found her voice, as clear as she could manage. "Go ever onward!"

Gleaming Head twirled his swords. "Go, Mrazas!"

The dark figure of swirling shadow emerged, with thudding steps like boulders crashing. A shadowy, indistinct head lifted toward the sky. The same howling cry roared and sobbed out of the shadowy monster, shaking city, wall, sky—and Jilly's heart. The gate closed. With more thudding steps, the shadow monster approached the Wandering Heroes, and the last stand of the Mrazas began.

18

OUTBOUND BUSES

The nighttime streets were even emptier than Soarsha had expected. A few people wandered the streets outside the apartment building. Each soul had the look of someone glancing every way with each step in the hope of making it inside to somewhere safe before the scathtor took them. The clear starless sky pulsated, as if smacking the golden dust toward the streets. The black streets themselves looked like rivers, frozen in a snapshot, as if the city wasn't really alive, as if nothing was really alive, and the truth was that everyone in the city might as well be a statue that now and again got to experience the joy and pleasure of a moment of movement.

The dark shadows between buildings pulsed like the sky, as if creatures in the shadows wanted to leap out, devour the golden dust with black tongues, and with spiked fists shatter the golden rectangles of windows into darkness. As the building's doors closed behind them and the exposed, night-chilled air pressed in around her, Soarsha realized for the first time how much the apartment felt like a fortress. The safe walls. The sturdy window. The height. Down here at street level, the world felt naked.

Soarsha was certain she had heard another rumble-roar. She

couldn't tell where it came from, but it didn't seem close. Trouble was, since she didn't know where her father was, Soarsha couldn't decide if the scathtor being far away was a good thing or a bad thing.

The eerie quiet, occasionally pierced by the scathtor's rumble-roar, had Nabraig and Iandel looking everywhere except at each other. Both the businesswoman and the embalmer reached up and rubbed at their chests, right above their hearts, as if in pain. Then each reached higher, and seemed to clutch on to something behind their shirts, just as Soarsha had seen Garen do earlier.

Soarsha looked from one woman to the other. "Are you two okay?"

Nabraig turned and looked at her with an armored soul. "You ask too many questions, kid."

"You're supposed to be such a great businesswoman," said Soarsha. "Don't you ask a lot of questions too?"

Nabraig opened her mouth. Then closed it. The corners of her lips turned downward, and Soarsha feared she had annoyed the businesswoman.

Then Nabraig nodded. And chuckled. Then smiled. "I do indeed," she replied. "Questions lead to answers, like steps along a path."

Iandel snorted. "Questions are an excuse to yap," said the embalmer. "This way."

A shadow passed over Nabraig's gaze, but she said nothing. Whatever objections she had, she tucked them away and started following Iandel.

Before them the many streets of the city stretched. Soarsha saw they were on one of the straight diagonal spokes that took them toward the center of Dedalo.

"Speaking of questions," said Nabraig to Iandel, "where are we going?"

Stopping at an intersection, Iandel peered down the dark streets.

"Wait," said Nabraig. "I thought you knew where Soarsha's father is."

"I think I do," replied Iandel as they continued. "I just don't want to encounter that... that thing."

Nabraig snorted and scoffed. "The scathtor? That's fake news. Something to scare people. Cities always have weird ways of keeping people in line."

"I don't think so," said Iandel. She glanced upward, far above Nabraig's head, toward buildings the height of the sky-snagging one where Nabraig worked. "Some of us work a little closer to the ground and see things you might not."

"I see plenty," said Nabraig.

Iandel turned to her, blue eyes fierce and sharp. "You know what I see sometimes?"

Nabraig rolled her eyes and hardened her voice. "Too many dead people?"

"If only," said Iandel. "Each year, this time of year, sometimes I hear that rumbling sound around the funeral home. When I go to see what's happening, I discover bodies gone. I see a mystery. People gone. Taken by the scathtor."

Nabraig's face flushed and seemed pale. "I'm sorry," she said. "I didn't..."

Shaking her head, Iandel looked away from Nabraig and pointed toward the city center. "I think Das went to the bus station."

The moment Iandel finished speaking, though, Soarsha felt certain that the embalmer had more to say, only she was trying to communicate the rest to Nabraig without speaking. Soarsha fought the urge to roll her own eyes. Grownups always thought they were being so sneaky with how they looked at each other. As if a ten-year-old couldn't read their weird secret gaze language.

The two women and the girl crossed the ring road and heading down the sidewalk of the diagonal street.

"You might as well tell me," said Soarsha.

"Tell you what, sweetheart?" said Iandel. As if.

Now Soarsha did roll her eyes. "The thing that you want to tell Nabraig as soon as you manage to have me out of earshot for two seconds. Whatever it is that you think I'm too young to hear." She stopped and put her hands on her hips. "I'm going to tell you this right now: If it involves my dad, I don't care that I'm ten. I don't care that I'm a kid or that you think I'm too young for whatever it is you know or think you know. He's my dad, not yours. Whatever you have to clue each other in about, you'll tell me. If he were your dad, or your husband, or your son or whoever, you'd have the right to know. He's my dad. You will tell me."

Iandel sighed. Looked away. "Look, kid..."

Soarsha's eyes narrowed. "My name is Soarsha."

"Soarsha..." Iandel looked at her but seemed to struggle to hold her gaze.

"If it's about my father, I deserve to know."

"He said something to me last night," said Iandel. "I didn't think much about it at the time. After you called me, I started to wonder."

Nabraig leaned in. "What did he say to you?"

Iandel took a deep breath. "He said that he wondered what time the outbound buses leave."

Soarsha looked from one woman to another. "There aren't any outbound buses. Everyone knows that. One bus enters the city. Other buses travel around the city. No buses ever leave."

"Still," said Iandel. "Whatever he meant by it, I think he's at the bus station."

Soarsha looked from one woman to the other. "Are you trying not to say that you think he's leaving the city without me?"

Iandel opened her mouth. Closed it. Looked away.

"Of course you are," said Soarsha. "You didn't want to tell me because I'm a fragile child who can't hear brutal truths. Well, here's the difference between a kid and an adult: Adults always think people are going to do the most terrible, most stupid things they possibly could. Kids know that sometimes adults are stupid and mean, but stupidity and meanness aren't inevitable. Just because it's possible to do a bad thing doesn't mean it's what a person is going to do."

The embalmer turned and looked back at Soarsha. The businesswoman smiled.

"You know, Soarsha," said Nabraig, "your dad occasionally does some pretty bone-headed things. But I'd put down good money that having you was the smartest thing he ever did."

Iandel sighed. "We're going to find your father, Soarsha."

"Not just him," replied Soarsha. She quickly told them about Carl and Finley.

"I bet," said Soarsha, "that whatever happens to the bodies the scathtor takes from Iandel, the same thing happened to Carl and Finley. We're going to find the people the scathtor has taken. We're going to get them back."

The women stopped. "That's a big order," said Nabraig.

Soarsha looked from one woman to the other. She might be shorter than them, but she felt taller. "I'll do it myself if I have to." Soarsha tried to sound braver than she felt. "But I'd prefer not to have to do this alone."

Far away in the dark distance, the scathtor roared.

Soarsha's mouth settled in a thin, flat half-smile. "After all, I'm just a kid."

Iandel and Nabraig looked at each other. They seemed to be having another of those wordless grownup eye conversations. Whatever they discussed with gazes and expressions, though, at least they kept going along with Soarsha. Before the women looked away from her, though, Soarsha was certain she saw a look on their faces like what she sometimes saw on her father's, like when he was feeling proud and said he wished her mother could see her right now.

The three of them made their way down the silent street. Each block was emptier than the last. Soon nothing was around except for two women, one girl, endless dust, and the shuddering lights of the skyscrapers above.

Until, at last, the brick walls of the bus station, just a few blocks from the walled center of the city, came into view. It was, of course, just the bus station, but everyone called it the old bus station. As if implying there was a new one. Or to remind themselves that at one time it had been new, if only in their minds and hearts, when each person arrived in the city and saw the bus station for the first time. Like the school, the bus station took up the ground-floor level of a skyscraper, this one over eighty stories since it was so close to the center of Dedalo.

The bus station walls were brick. At one time, some shiny long-ago new time, perhaps the brick had been red, like bright blood from a scraped knee. Nowadays the bricks were the dull brownish maroon of a scab. Above the bus station, soaring as high as Soarsha could manage to see, gleaming blue-gray steel and matching glass held a dull dark sheen, like a straight razor shaving the cheek of the endless sky.

No buses were rumbling about right now. Soarsha wondered how many were still out in the city, lumbering around like old lost beasts, wandering until they found their way back to their brick pens deep inside the station.

"I haven't been to the bus station in years," said Iandel.

Nabraig shook her head. "Me neither."

"Don't you take the bus?" said Soarsha.

"Not from here," replied Nabraig.

"Come to think of it," said Iandel, "I don't think I've been here since I first came to the city and the bus dropped me here."

"Wait a sec." Nabraig stopped. "When did you come here?"

Soarsha and Iandel stopped too.

"Ten years ago," said Soarsha. "Me and Dad, after we lost my mom. I thought you knew that."

"No. Not you, small fry." Nabraig tilted her chin toward Iandel. "I meant you."

A funny scrunched look passed over the embalmer's face. "Ten years ago too. Why?"

Nabraig's eyes softened. "We were on the same bus. I didn't recognize you at first—you know how the memories fade."

Iandel's voice lowered. "Do you remember where we came from?"

Nabraig shook her head. "I barely remember the bus ride. But I remember you now. You were the most brilliant soul on that rackety old rig. I remember feeling like I just might make my way in this place, if people like you were around."

"That's one of the nicest things anyone has ever said to me," replied Iandel.

"Maybe that's one of the downsides of being around dead people so much," said Nabraig.

"Wow," said Iandel. "You really know how to follow up a compliment so it's like it never happened."

Nabraig opened her mouth. Closed it. "Sorry," she said at last. "I just... I want to thank you. I mean, sure, you were just riding the bus, same as I was. But it gave me hope, and hope always seems in short supply here."

"Kind of like a warm day?" said Iandel.

Nabraig chuckled. "Exactly like that."

"Arriving here is the only time I've been to the bus station," said Soarsha. "Dad's never brought me here since, and I've never ridden a bus back to the station. It's kind of weird, you know? This is where I first came to the city, but I've never been back."

"Life's like that, kid," said Nabraig. "You think of something, some place, that was so integral to you, but you hardly ever get back to it. There's always so much else to be getting to, to be getting on with, that it becomes harder and harder to think of where you came from."

The three of them reached the entrance of the bus station.

Then a shadow leaped down in front of them.

19

GOLDEN LIGHTS IN THE DARK CITY

The last thing Soarsha remembered was the scathtor screaming—and Nabraig screaming right back at it.

The world had turned both vivid and intense, while at the same time dark.

A pain in her back.

The scathtor?

No.

Iandel had shoved her. That was right. Shoved her and told her to run. Run and not look back, or stop, or interfere, or anything else.

Soarsha looked down and nearly stumbled. She was still running. Stopping, Soarsha looked around. She didn't even know where she was. The bus station wasn't in sight. Neither were Nabraig or Iandel. Or the scathtor. She hoped the others were okay. Her throat felt tight. If they weren't, though, if the scathtor had taken them too, then that would be Soarsha's fault. Like Carl. Like Finley.

Like her dad too?

Still. The city was so still. She reached into her shirt and held the pendant, hoping the scent of lavender would calm her. As she took a deep breath, she looked down. The streets of the city were a deep black, the black of night skies and windowless rooms in the dark. But her mind flashed back to yesterday's bus ride, when for a moment she had seen a street that was light gray. Almost silvery.

Now, standing near the edge of the street, Soarsha saw another gray street. Light gray. Almost silvery.

She looked in each direction as far as she could. The street curved, and at some point seemed to curve again. Tucking the pendant back into her shirt, Soarsha followed the silver-gray road, hoping that it might lead her back to the bus station, to her dad, to a new tomorrow in a place with no walls. It would have been nice. To maybe not be lost, but to trust that the city itself was guiding her to somewhere new. It would have been nice. The sort of thing you could have relied on to happen in a story.

But Soarsha knew good and well she wasn't in a story. She was in a strange place, for sure. The city that might as well have no world around it. Yet in Soarsha's dreams she never saw the city. She never walked the hard streets. Instead, she roamed and wandered soft curving turf of bright green, across wide lands where the world was green all the way to the horizon. Where the world kept going. Across the lands and plains, through hills and bright rivers. Through towns and cities. All full of life and people and stories and so, so much more life. More life in one little patch of ground than Soarsha had ever felt all of Dedalo.

The city seemed to have leaned back from her, as if it could hear her thoughts and wanted to put some space between itself and the crazy girl who dreamed of a world of green. Soarsha looked around again, following the silver-gray street. Then she remembered to look up. If she could find the Spire, she could find her way.

Staring and staring, Soarsha looked, and turned, and—

Found it. From behind a cluster of high buildings, the Spire rose. The bus station should be near the Spire. Soarsha might have to wander around some to find it, but as long as she was moving toward the Spire she should be going the right way. Soarsha stared at the street and the Spire and the buildings for a moment longer, getting her bearings and her breath.

From behind her, a long high scratching came, like glass needles dripping onto her eardrum. Like a dull axe on a grinder wheel. Like a claw scraping along cement.

Soarsha whipped around.

From a long dark alley, the sound came. Higher and louder—as whatever was making the sound got closer.

Soarsha's eyes widened. She turned back toward the street and ran.

It didn't matter that she was a little girl. It didn't matter that she was a small soul in the midst of a giant city. It didn't matter that the scathtor was powerful and gruesome and could probably pounce on her at any moment.

Soarsha ran. Because she was going to get to the bus station. She was going to find her friends. She was going to find her dad.

Her eyes narrowed, with sharp glints shining like the streams of sunlight she often saw in her dreams.

Together, friends and father and strange crazy girl, they were going to get the hell out of this damn city.

Soarsha grinned. She was certain her dad would agree she was using the words correctly.

The silver-gray street turned, and Soarsha turned with it. She seemed to be moving in a loop, so that now she was looking toward the Spire. Did the loop now straighten out and run back toward the center of the city? Or was it folding in on itself?

Soarsha kept running, anything to keep the silver-gray thread of hope next to her—and the rumble-roar of the scathtor far behind. The silver-gray street straightened out, then swung around another corner, past a building, out of Soarsha's sight. She ran faster, angling her body and feeling the dust swoosh around her, like starlight for a moment gently pressing on her skin. Soarsha rounded the corner—but the silver-gray street was gone.

Only one of Dedalo's usual black streets ran beside her now, nearly as empty of traffic as the sidewalk was empty of people. Soarsha stopped running. Bracing her hands on her knees, she wheezed, panted, trying to get her breath back.

The street was gone. The thread had broken. Tears pressed at Soarsha's eyes, but she refused to let them fall. Gleaming Head and Jilly the Kid might be dispirited or afraid right now, but they wouldn't cry right now, no matter how they wanted to break those dams of sorrow. They'd turn misery into momentum, depression into direction.

Besides, they were Wandering Heroes, not heroes who carefully consulted a map and never got lost. You wandered because you knew that the way before you was the only way.

Soarsha stared at the street and the buildings around her. She didn't know this part of the city, and from where she was standing, she couldn't figure out where the wall or the Spire were situated. The street seemed to be mostly residential skyscrapers, narrow, and Soarsha passed an alley between two buildings. All up and down the length of the buildings, golden lights glowed. People living their lives. Doing whatever they did in the evenings, or longing for whatever they wished they were doing. Golden rectangles, like strange eyes that didn't see but that could let you see in. Soarsha wondered if anyone inside the building had any idea that on the sidewalk below a lost girl was trying to find her missing father. And how many people, if they did see, would care.

Reaching the end of the block, Soarsha turned, looking up—and finally saw the Spire. Nearby, a massive skyscraper rose, easily a hundred stories tall. But even from a few blocks away, Soarsha could see that the bottom three stories were lined with brick, and a wide, dark rectangular opening loomed like a hungry mouth.

The bus station.

Though she feared what she would find there—or worse, who

she wouldn't find—Soarsha made her way. And thought. Why was the scathtor after her? Why was it attacking people who helped her?

Carl. Finley. Iandel. Nabraig.

Her eyes narrowed, and the tears dried up. And what did it not want her to find?

Garen. Mr. Adbad.

Her dad.

Inside Soarsha, a fire sparked that Gleaming Head would have recognized like his own reflection. A fire like Jilly the Kid when she realized that she was a kid, sure, but only in name. She was more than that. She was a Wandering Hero. A joy warrior of love and the world, despite all else.

Soarsha would be that too. And herself. Whatever that meant.

"I'm going to find what you want to keep from me," Soarsha said to the city, wondering where the scathtor was and if it was about to pounce out at her again. "I'm going to find those you stole. I'm going to find the answers you don't want me to have."

The bus station was nearer now, and its wide black mouth of a bay might as well have stretched as wide as the bottom of the skyscraper.

A roar resounded through the night, no longer bouncing off the buildings but slamming into them, and sending shudders and dust flying through the air.

A lowdown part of Soarsha's brain screamed at her to stop. To turn around and run away from the noise. To find her way back home and never leave her apartment. She'd find her dad in the morning, when there was light. But now she had to be home. Had to be safe.

But another part of Soarsha's brain was saying something else, and was speaking in the calm slow voice her father spoke with. The voice Soarsha dreamed her mother's sounded like. It said one simple thing.

"Keep going."

So Soarsha did. She walked quickly, marshaling her strength and ignoring how weary she felt, ignoring her scared she was. Instead she squished all those feelings into a big bowl in her heart and mind, mixed them and cooked them up into something that would drive her onward.

She was nearly to the bus station. Barely a block to go.

In front of her, near the end of a dark alley, the scathtor stepped out onto the sidewalk, between Soarsha and the entrance to the bus station, and began moving toward her. The concealing shadows around it no longer flung about like some sort of ragged cloak in a hurricane. Now the scathtor seemed to have some sort of calm about it, the eye of a storm of hunger and taking. The tiger stalking before it pounced.

"I'm Soarsha of the world beyond Dedalo," said Soarsha, stopping about fifty meters away from the scathtor. She moved her shoulders, loosening up her body, as she stood with her hands open, yet feeling as if fire and lightning were crackling in the palms by her sides.

Silence floated across the city. Even the dust seemed to have become still. A page of newspaper fluttered overhead, passing them like a shooting star. Golden lights glowed in nearly every window of every skyscraper.

"I'm... I'm a Mraza, a Wandering Hero, a joy warrior of love," the girl continued, sliding one foot behind her slightly, the way Gleaming Head always did in the comic. "You've taken people I care about—and you're going to give them back. Now."

A chittering, stuttering sound tripped its way across the space between them. The scathtor seemed to tremble, as if in some sort of fit. For a moment it even bent over.

And Soarsha understood. The scathtor was laughing at her.

Then it straightened, and still said nothing, but started to move toward her.

Soarsha stood still. There was no Gleaming Head to save her.

No Shirtman and Sapphire to stand by her side. No Jilly the Kid to strategize with. There was only her.

All she knew was how much she wanted to run.

The scathtor came closer, slowly yet ceaselessly. Soarsha didn't move, but she had no idea what to do. She wondered what the scathtor's bladelike shadows would feel like. Being caught in a warm whirlwind? A tornado of knives? Would it hurt? Would there be anything afterward? A single tear hung in the corner of her eye, but even that was too afraid to fall.

The scathtor stopped moving, and shifted itself, like a dark tiger ready to pounce.

A voice, deep and resounding off the buildings, bounced all over the street.

"Soarsha!"

The scathtor looked up, away from her—and Soarsha realized she had one chance to put some distance between her and the shadow monster. Turning toward the sound of her name, she started running. From around the corner near the bus station, a figure emerged—and began sprinting toward her. Even in the dim lights, Soarsha could see the person's face was red, as if some deep rage were simmering and near to boiling within.

"Get away from her!" shouted the running man. "Get away from her now, damn you!"

The scathtor turned. The running man wasn't alone anymore either. Two other figures were with him, as if Gleaming Head, Shirtman, and Sapphire were coming to her rescue. Could it be? As Soarsha got closer to the trio, her mouth fell open, and her eyes widened.

Nabraig. Iandel. They had gotten away too.

And Garen. He'd found her.

A relieved smile crept up her face, just a little, as if it didn't want the scathtor to see. No, these three were not the Mrazas. But they would do. They would certainly do.

Staring at the four of them, the scathtor shifted a little, side to side, as if unsure. With a howl, it ran off, crossing the street toward one of the apartment buildings covered in windows of bright and golden lights.

The three adults surrounded Soarsha and hugged her.

"You're okay!" said Iandel.

"So are you!" said Soarsha.

"The scathtor got confused," said Nabraig. "It took off, but we couldn't find you."

"Thank goodness we found you," said Garen.

Soarsha soaked in their warmth, their presence, their thereness. She wasn't alone after all. They'd found each other. They'd found her. They'd even scared away the scathtor.

And if they had found her...

Soarsha smiled.

Together, they'd find her dad.

From across the street, a crash banged through the air. The four people turned. The scathtor had ripped open the door of a ninety-story apartment skyscraper. Moments later, light after light on the building's first floor went out. Then the second floor. Third floor.

And upward.

Moments later, the completely dark skyscraper emanated an eerie silence, an emptiness, as if every apartment, shop, and space was vacant.

But that wasn't the only thing happening. Even the grownups noticed. Nabraig and Iandel looked up in the air, and held out their hands.

"The dust," said Nabraig.

Soarsha held out her hand, like a child wishing that dwindling snowflakes could gather into a big school-canceling storm. "There's less of it."

"Just a change of breeze," said Iandel with a shrug. "Surely."

Moments later, the next skyscraper went dark, then another. Every time a building went dark, less and less dust was in the air.

Soon every building they could see was dark and empty—and so was the air around them. Soul after soul fell to the whirling embrace of the ragged darkness, as the scathtor moved throughout the city.

Soarsha realized she was clutching her pendant, and the adults were clutching at their chests too. Cocking her head, Iandel let go first and took a deep breath. "Let's get inside the station while that thing's distracted," she said softly.

Like a shield, the three adults walked abreast in front of Soarsha. Together they passed beyond the shadows of the bus station's wide-open bay. Behind them the clear air ached with the absence of the golden dust, and the last lights in Dedalo winked out.

20

AND NOW, BACK TO WANDERING HEROES

Weakening cries of battle bounced off the ringwall again—just as Shirtman and Sapphire bounced off the ground... again. The two Mrazas helped each other up. They did their best to look strong, to face down the shadow monster between them and the closed gate, but even from beyond the battle, Jilly could see the trembling fear and weariness compound as the battle continued endlessly.

Gleaming Head's swords flashed in the weak sun, yet the monster's swirling shadows were like smoke before the blades. The ancient hero's sword work had no effect other than to leave Gleaming Head breathing hard. Jilly hated to see it—hated to know what it meant—but this time when the shadow monster knocked Gleaming Head backward, the ancient hero kept his feet, but staggered and slumped. His swords drooped as if even the tireless hero had grown weary of wielding them.

Still, though, Jilly the Kid stayed with the horses.

She hated it. Hated every inactive moment. Hated being a spectator to the gruesome event of the deaths of her friends. Her family. The only people she knew in this world were going to die in front of her.

Her eyes burned.

And then what?

What would the shadow monster do to her, once it had destroyed the three most powerful heroes in the entire world?

Gleaming Head lunged forward—and some sword thrust must have found something more than smoky shadow. The monster shrieked as its swirling cloak of shadows grew as rigid as blades and icicles. Behind Jilly, the horses reared, neighed, and ran away. Even Starcall, her companion for as long as she had wandered with the Mrazas, had in the end been overcome by fear and left her in the dry cracked dirt, alone.

Well, not completely.

Jilly the Kid held the locked wooden chest closer to her heart. The chest remained dark and still, an insignificant box, just as Jilly knew she wasn't any more significant than any other person—yet here she was, being defended as if she were a queen, a goddess, a mother.

Just like queens, goddesses, and mothers, Jilly realized that soon she would be on her own, with no one to help or guide her anymore. Tears gleamed in the girl's eyes, but her heart, she could feel, was changing and growing, hardening and strengthening, becoming both tougher and suppler. In the chest of a girl, a woman's heart began to beat.

Jilly's eyes narrowed. She wanted to run to them, wielding the chest like a war hammer and bringing it down on the shadow monster with all the might and strength of every day she'd known and would know in the days to come.

But Jilly did not move.

No matter how many times her friends fell, got back up, fell again, staggered, and swayed, they kept fighting. For her.

So she did what they had asked.

She waited.

Her eyes burned with wet fire. Every tight muscle in her body yearned to throw herself between the shadow monster and her friends.

"Wait until the time is right," Gleaming Head had told her. "Remember, you will always know, and you will always have what you need."

Gleaming Head had been flung sideways, rolling across the ground as the shadow monster leaped after him. Whatever blow the shadow monster had struck him with, the ancient hero had screamed—and he had yet to rise up again. With every move now, though, little bits of shadow dripped behind the monster, as if that last sword thrust of Gleaming Head's truly had found something solid. Something that hurt. Something that bled.

Jilly waited for Gleaming Head to get up. He was like the earth, the mountains, the rising and falling of the sun. A constant of the world. But if he were gone...

The monster came closer, ready to rend the fallen body of the ancient hero. Jilly wanted to turn away her burning eyes, but the harder part of her, the steel within her, demanded that she watch. She would see. She would remember. She would know. Always—or however much longer she had left.

The monster was nearly to Gleaming Head. Then Sapphire was there, standing between the furious monster and the fallen hero. Sapphire's blazing blue eyes lanced the monster like spears, yet still it came—albeit more slowly than before. Jilly had lost track of how many times the mere sight of Sapphire's eyes had turned the wills—and boots—of army after army. How many soldiers, how many mercenaries, how many people forced by someone else to fight, had had a change of heart, a vision of new life ahead, simply because they had seen in Sapphire's eyes the chance to wake up tomorrow instead of die today?

Raising her battle sticks high, Sapphire stood her ground as the monster came toward her. So intense was her gaze, the swirling ragged edges of the monster, the walls of the city, all shone with bright blue.

"It doesn't have to be this way." Sapphire stared it in the eyes. Or what passed for its eyes. "It can all be different."

The monster swung what seemed like a curved blade made from shadows. The blade sliced through Sapphire's battle sticks, and was almost to her head—

Sapphire was rolling along the ground, but she came up to her knees, gasping and staggering. Then screaming.

Shirtman was taller than he should have been.

No.

Jilly looked closer. Her mouth fell open, and her chin began to quiver. A dry, coppery scent streaked through the air.

Shirtman had taken the shadowy blade in the heart, and the monster's swing had raised Shirtman off the ground. Jilly caught a glimpse of his shirt.

"today is the first day of the best of your life."

Jilly wondered if that's what the monster had seen—or if, even in death, Shirtman's shirt had changed the moment she saw it. Was the message for her? The monster? Both of them?

Shirtman slid off the shadow blade and slumped to the ground.

Sapphire's scream knocked Jilly back a step. Even the shadow monster staggered. Sapphire's eyes blazed, a thousand lightning storms striking out from one woman. Without even standing, Sapphire leaped off the ground, into the swirling shadows. The cloud of shadow turned blue, shining like every night star being pressed into one small space.

A white and blue flash soared over the Barrenburn, smacking into the ringwall and knocking Jilly off her feet. She rolled, her vision fuzzy and blurry, but she cleared her eyes as best she could as she got back up.

By Shirtman's side, Sapphire lay still. Her hand had fallen on his hand. Sapphire's lightning-blue eyes dimmed, as she stared up toward a sky she could no longer see.

Jilly trembled, and she shook her head. "No!" she shouted.

The shadow monster turned. Staring across the cracked earth, it seemed for the first time to notice the lone girl.

And it ran toward her.

She had no weapons. Little in the way of fighting skills. No powers. Yet Jilly did not run. It wasn't time yet. She was still waiting, and she would have what she needed. Sweeping her foot back behind her, Jilly stood sideways to the shadow monster. She tucked the little wooden chest under her right arm, so her body was between the chest and the monster. In her own chest, her woman's heart surged, beating with fury and grief, with the disbelief that two of her friends had died, for her. But her eyes narrowed, a woman's gaze shining from a girl's eyes, and she saw what was, and she saw what could be, and she saw the love, the joy, despite all else, that her friends, that she, would be willing not only to die for, but to live for.

The girl had watched the battle. Now the Mraza, the woman, stood before the onrushing monster. Sure, it was terrible. Sure, it had killed two of her friends. But she could see something amidst the shadows. Doubt. Yearning. And a blue sheen, as if a light were beating against the shadows, dissolving them slowly into something else, something different, something new.

The monster's hot breath smelled like stale socks.

Kind of pathetic, really. Jilly grimaced.

The shadow monster's arms swirled wide, stretched out as if about to embrace her. Jilly smiled, and held out her hand, fingers up, palm out.

The monster shuddered. It skittered, trying to stop. It wouldn't work completely. Certainly wasn't ideal. But it would do.

The monster's arms closed in on her, shadow pincers that would never let go.

Two silver lines streaked up from the monster's feet to the top of the round swirling shadows that passed for its head.

The monster shrieked, and its rumble-roar made the very sky tremble. Behind it, Gleaming Head swirled his swords and readied another blow.

But Jilly saw it. Just before Gleaming Head did.

The sharp shadow, already moving, a dark pointed blur in the clear air, even faster than the ancient hero's swords, whistled sharp as it swung toward Gleaming Head's heart—and ran the ancient hero through.

Leaping forward, Jilly turned her body as she moved and swung the little wooden chest forward, through the swirling shadows of the monster's torso. In the smoky dark she couldn't see her hand and arm anymore, but she kept pressing forward, pushing—until the little wooden chest was right where she figured the monster's heart, its soul, or whatever it had like those things, must be.

The monster staggered. Stumbled. And fell onto Gleaming Head. The two of them tumbled to the ground, a blur of gleaming swords and swirling shadows, then were still and did not rise or move.

Something else tumbled too. At first Jilly could only hear it, the skittering tumbling solid sound, a strange drumbeat thumping over the hard cracked ground. Then she saw it, as the little wooden chest bounce-rolled out of the monster's shadows. She heard something else, some little snapping chittering sound, something she had never heard from inside the chest until now. The chest tumbled, edge over edge and end over end until, with a thump on one edge and a slight lift up from the other edge, the little chest settled onto the ground, its padlocked front facing Jilly.

From inside the chest, the little smaller sharper noises faded, like glass shards tumbling and then falling still. Silence flooded back across the Barrenburn. Then, from the chest, there came a smaller sound, a soft click that might as well have been a thunder-clap or an earthquake.

The padlock opened and fell to the ground, and the top of the chest opened.

21

STAGGERING IN THE DARK

In the dim, silent bus station, shadows queued up for buses that would never move again. Flickering ceiling lights shrugged brownish cones of light down to the black asphalt of the floor, as if a half-asleep janitor were sweeping the light down from dying glass bulbs. Between each bus's parking bay, bricks in the cylindrical support columns looked smooshed, as if they had tired of carrying the weight of the building above. The buses themselves were quiet and still, engines off, lights dark, like fading, failing beasts gradually giving way from flesh to skeleton to fossil. The bus station was a weary cave, not a hustle and bustle hub for people on their way to and fro, but a final destination where the life-tired went to give up.

After all, there were no more people, except for a few lost souls trying to find one more. Soarsha shook her head, but the understanding didn't go away. They were the last people in Dedalo.

Never had she hoped the voice was so wrong though. Because if it were right, that meant Mr. Adbad and her dad were gone too. Her eyes and face felt tight and hot again. She hoped and hoped that she was wrong. That the scathtor hadn't gotten them. But if the scathtor had taken all the uncountable souls in the golden city, there was no reason he hadn't taken Mr. Adbad and her dad too.

The depressing view of the dim bus station flickered. The world rushed by her, lines and blurs—then stopped.

Garen was holding her by the shoulders. He kneeled down so their gazes were level.

"We're going to find them," said the happiness coach.

Soarsha's voice trembled, but she was past caring about concealing it. "What if they're nowhere to be found?" Sadness tore through her like the scathtor through a building. "What if no one in the city is alive but us?"

"I don't know," said Garen.

"Isn't this the part where you tell me everything is going to be okay? That it's all just fine?"

Garen sighed, and his breath seemed to hitch. "This is the part where an adult knows the last thing he can get away with is lying to a child."

Iandel and Nabraig leaned down too, so all three of the adults were at Soarsha's height.

"What's happening is horrible," said Nabraig, "and we have no idea what's going on either." Her knuckles paled as she clenched the strap of her messenger bag. Fear crackled in her strong voice. The words sounded like they were about to shatter—but were holding steady. For now.

"There's a chance, though," said Iandel. "A chance your dad is okay."

Soarsha shook her head. "Why would he be, when all the others have been taken?"

The three adults looked at each other, and all their gazes held nothing but confusion. "We don't know," said Nabraig.

"Just as we don't know why the scathtor hasn't taken us," said Garen.

"Saving us for last," said Iandel. "Maybe we're dessert."

Nabraig's eyes narrowed as she glared at the embalmer. "Way to cheer things up."

Iandel tilted her head and shrugged, as if she'd just realized where she was and what was happening. "I thought we were being honest."

"We can stay truthful without being brutal," Nabraig replied.

"I never knew my mom," said Soarsha. "Now my dad's gone too." Her voice shattered, and the tears came, hot and thick and endless. The dream flooded back to her—her father and mother, a girl with both parents, together the way they always should have been. Green hills rolling under gray and misty skies. Like a photo held to a flame, the edges of the dream began to curl, burn, and fade to ash.

The three adults surrounded her, and held her close, and Soarsha's sobs resounded off the walls of the silent, empty bus station.

From the shadows behind a wide brick-walled, pale gray upward staircase near the middle of the bus station, a thud smacked the ground.

The flat sound might as well have yanked a cord coming out of the heads of the three adults. Garen, Nabraig, and Iandel stood up and started staring, while at the same time standing in a line in front of Soarsha. The sound had also knocked the tears from Soarsha's eyes, and she took a deep breath.

Well, Soarsha figured, they were right about one thing.

The scathtor wasn't finished with them.

A cone of light shone down to the right of the staircase. Behind it, in the deep shadows under the staircase, scrabbling sounds skittered out, as if a swarm of roaches had fallen out of the steps. Or maybe it was the sound ragged shadows made when they rubbed against themselves.

Without turning around, Nabraig said, "We're going to do all we can, Soarsha."

Soarsha said nothing. She had a feeling that mere minutes ago, many people in Dedalo had just said the same thing. No point reminding the grownups how that had turned out.

Iandel looked from Nabraig to Garen. "You sure we shouldn't just run?"

Garen looked toward the dark, empty, lifeless city. "Where?"

Iandel said nothing, though a glint in her eyes indicated she had some thoughts on a dark place where Garen could shove his head. The three adults stared at the shadows.

Behind the stairs, the sounds seemed like dragging and banging, as if someone were having a seizure while lying on top of metal garbage cans. The sounds began to fade. A strange half-moan, half-sob came out of the darkness, as deep as the shadows and as wrenching as the hole in Soarsha's heart. A half-sliding, half-scraping sound screeched out from behind the stairs, like swords being scraped along the street.

Then a slapping plod. Like something falling. Or taking a step. Followed by another.

From the shadows something dark emerged. Hunched over and staggering, it lurched from side to side, as if drunk, or disoriented, or both. Soarsha tried to swallow, but her throat had frozen. All the moisture in her body might as well have dried up into a desert.

Step by step the shadow straightened up—and then stepped into the dim light from the ceiling bulb by the stairs.

Fearful brown eyes looked from Iandel to Garen to Nabraig, then reached past them to see Soarsha behind the three adults. The brownish light glinted off a hairless head and made the tweed suit browner and rougher and dingier—though Soarsha was pretty certain that wasn't just the light.

Eyes and face trembled. A thin voice pattered like tears on the pavement.

"Is... Is it gone?"

Soarsha stepped past the three adults.

"Mr. Adbad?"

Sadness dimmed her teacher's eyes. "I don't think we'll be having class tomorrow," he replied.

Soarsha ran forward, and she flung her arms around her teacher. "I was so afraid it had gotten you!"

She could feel Mr. Adbad nodding. Hugging her back, he ran a hand over her hatted head. Gradually Soarsha let go, and stepped back a little to look at her teacher. Brown smudges of dirt streaked up and down his face like stripes. His suit was rumpled, scuffed, dirt-smeared, and wrinkled, and one elbow was ripped.

"What happened to you?" said Soarsha.

"I got here a little while ago," replied Mr. Adbad. "Then I saw the scathtor outside on the streets, and I saw the lights start going out all over the city... I figured that whatever was happening, the scathtor must be doing something terrible. So I hid behind there. I hoped that maybe if it came in here it wouldn't find me. I must have slipped though, hit my head... everything is a bit fuzzy. I must have given you all such a fright... I... I'm sorry." He looked again at the three adults.

"Garen," said Mr. Adbad, "it's good to see you, though shame about the circumstances."

Garen gave a stiff nod in return.

Mr. Adbad looked at the two women and shook his head. "Sorry," he said. "Really, I must have hit my head rather hard."

"Iandel," said the embalmer. "I'm a friend of Das's."

"Nabraig," said the businesswoman. "Das works for me."

"Of course," said Mr. Adbad. "Soarsha said she had called the people her father knows."

Soarsha smiled and wanted to hug him again. He had said, "knows," not "knew." Implying that he believed her father was still around.

"I haven't found your father," said Mr. Adbad. "But before the scathtor, I thought I heard something moving around down here."

Soarsha's eyes widened. "My dad?"

Mr. Adbad reached out and touched her shoulder. "I hope so."

The five of them started searching around the buses and the bays, around the staircase and the various doors around the bus station. Returning to the middle of the black pavement, surrounded by the still and quiet buses, the five people stood in a circle, and stared at each other, and didn't know what to say.

Behind Soarsha, toward the entrance where they had come in, a shuffling sound scraped its way across the black asphalt.

The five of them turned. Resigned. Hope dashed. A father not found.

In the shadows near the entrance, the figure shuffling toward them straightened up—and began running toward them. Not one person moved. Not even Soarsha. Her mouth opened, and her breath came in staggers.

Soarsha smiled. Even the dingy light of the ceiling bulbs couldn't dim the bright green eyes staring at them. They hadn't found her father.

He had found them.

22

SMALL PIECES OF A GREATER WHOLE

Her father's jeans were torn. Along the side of his left thigh, blue denim flapped like a flag in a breeze. His black shirt was dusty and scuffed. Little holes and rips ran along the fabric at his shoulders. Veins crackled like red lightning across the whites of Das's eyes. His green irises gleamed not like grass in bright sunshine, not like carved jade, but like some sort of otherworldly potion—or poison. The skin of his face was drawn and tight, as were his hands, up near his chest, palms out, fingers curved like sickles, as if he feared he was under attack.

But he was Das. Her dad. He was here. She could still smell his scent: spices, hot dust, high sun, a whiff of beer, and the first hint of garlic hitting hot oil in a pan.

Soarsha ran toward him, but he took a step back, and she stopped. Staring into his eyes, she noticed for the first time how it was as if a film covered his sight, some blinding glaze of fear.

"Dad?" said Soarsha. "It's me. It's Rainbow."

The glaze of fear shimmered, like paper about to catch fire. Then it faded.

"Soarsha." Das took a step forward. "My... Rainbow. Of course.

I'm sorry." He shook his head, and came to his daughter, and wrapped his arms around her.

"Are you okay?" said Soarsha. "Did... Did the scathtor chase you?"

Das squeezed her tighter. "Um... the scathtor... Yes, Rainbow, the scathtor came after me." He took a breath, and she could feel the ragged air go through him. "I don't know how I got away... Goodness, I must look terrifying to you. I'm okay, though. Really I am."

Soarsha pulled away and looked at him. Already his eyes seemed to be clearing, the film fading. The brightness of her father's green eyes started to look less mad-science-experiment and more the excited green of someone who loved life and the world and his little girl and all the joys little and big. All those love didn't negate the losses and the pains, but it did balance them out and help him find something worth smiling about and living for.

"Why weren't you at the apartment?" said Soarsha.

Her dad hugged her again. A dry sob shuddered through him.

"The scathtor," said Das. "I couldn't..."

He paused, took another ragged breath, then continued, his words slow, as if they were catching on hooks on the way out of his mouth. "I couldn't go back to the apartment. I was worried it might follow me and come after you. I wanted to lose it, then make my way back. Next thing I knew, I was near here. Then I saw all the lights go out, and I heard voices and sounds and didn't think they were the noises a shadow monster would make, so I came to see if there was anyone else left in the city. Thank goodness you found me."

Iandel stepped forward. "Last night, though, you were talking to me about coming here."

Das stepped back. "Outbound bus schedule. I know. That's what a couple of beers can do to you. I did look—but on the way back to the site this afternoon, after my and Soarsha's appointment with Garen." He shook his head, red-hot coals of frustration glowing in his eyes. "There are no outbound schedules. No buses. No routes. Nothing leaves the city. It's like we've always thought. There is only the one daily arrival, then all other buses are local only."

Soarsha looked at the five adults. "Doesn't that seem weird to you?"

"Being an adult," said Mr. Adbad, "means getting used to living with things that are weird and inexplicable."

"I agree with you, Soarsha," said Das. "I do think it's weird. But it's how things are. Sometimes there's nothing you can do about that. You just have to live with what's what." He put his hands on Soarsha's shoulders—though when he moved his arms, he winced. "It's the sort of thing you just have to learn to live with, kid. I didn't make the rules, daughter. I just have to live by them too, and I'm sure that in time you'll learn to be okay with them. Dedalo is all there is."

Taking a step back, Soarsha looked up at her father. His eyes were clear, yet something flickered back and forth in his gaze, as if she were peering into a part of his mind and heart where a battle waged.

"Dad?" She shook her head. "You're not making any sense."

Das shook his head too. "Of course I'm not making sense. Because if there's any adventure you deserve, my dear daughter Rainbow, it's the adventure of getting the hell out of here."

Before anyone could say anything, Das started walking past them, deeper into the station, toward the bus bays. With each step he staggered, a little left then a little right, in the strange box step debate of his mind.

A hot fire of fear blazed up inside Soarsha's heart. She'd found her father. Mostly. But the strange staggering man didn't seem like her dad.

Das trembled—then fell to the ground.

"Dad!" Soarsha ran to him and kneeled down. The others

followed. Standing in a circle, Iandel and Garen and Nabraig, then a sort of empty space, but they surrounded Das and Soarsha. Mr. Adbad stood by Soarsha.

"Everything is as it seems," said Das. He stared at his daughter, stared at the others, but Soarsha wasn't sure if he was really seeing any of them. "That's what's so terrible," her father continued. "Because nothing is as it should be, yet everything is as it seems. Then, when you see things as they really are, how it didn't make sense finally makes so much sense."

Soarsha reached under his head to try to cradle his head in her lap. She set her hand under the back of his neck—then Das winced, and yelped, and skittered to his feet. His right hand smacked the back of his neck as if he were swatting a mosquito. Soarsha's eyes narrowed. What the hell was a mosquito? Mr. Adbad had talked about them in class once, and her dad had talked about how they were brutal in Dinai, biting you and drinking your blood. That was during his travels, though. There were no mosquitoes in Dedalo.

"Don't touch the purple!" Das yelled. His eyes bulged, and little earthquakes trembled across his face, then his entire body.

"What is going on, Dad?" said Soarsha.

Mr. Adbad took a step toward Das. "Das, please," he said. "I don't know what happened, but I do know you're scaring your daughter. Please."

"Soarsha..." Das's gazed fixed on Soarsha, and she realized that he could truly see her again. "Daughter... Rainbow..." He shook his head. "I'm sorry, I'm so sorry..." He fell to his knees.

"Das," said Garen, "are you hurt?"

Das shuddered. "I... I fell earlier. Slipped. Must have whacked myself worse than I figured..." His eyes cleared, and Soarsha could see her father's kind gaze again—well, tinged with embarrassment, but overall, his gaze. "Sorry, it's like it comes and goes," said Das, "but I think it's getting better."

"Damn, Das," said Iandel. The embalmer had moved so she

was standing behind her friend, and she was staring at the back of his neck. "That's one hell of a bruise back here."

Soarsha came over next to Iandel, and she gasped. A long, thick, blackish purple line stretched across the back of her father's neck where it met his shoulders. The line disappeared under the collar of his shirt, but Soarsha was certain that the line ran from shoulder to shoulder.

Stepping back around to the front of her dad, Soarsha kneeled down and touched his cheek. "Are you sure you're getting better?"

He laid his hand over hers. "The moment I saw you, Rainbow, I started feeling better. I'm so sorry I scared you."

Soarsha leaned closer. "You're telling me the truth, right?"

"Always, Rainbow," said Das. He swallowed. "Always."

His right hand came around from the back of his neck and pulled the pendant out of his shirt. He rubbed the silver-gray clay, the way he always did when he was upset.

"Wait a minute," said Nabraig. She took a step closer. "All these years, and I never realized you had one too."

Das glanced at his boss. "One what?"

Nabraig reached into the neck of her own shirt—and pulled out a pendant. Silver-gray, with strange curving lines etched on it.

"That's strange," said Garen, though a jagged edge of irritation roughed up his voice. He, too, pulled out a piece of pendant from around his neck.

"I don't believe it," said Iandel. And the embalmer also pulled out a pendant she wore around her neck.

Soarsha turned, person to person, gazing at each piece. "They all have the same design," she said. "But each piece has a smooth, rounded edge—curved, as if it's a part of a circle."

Coming back to her dad, she smiled at him. He smiled back, nervous, but steadier now, more... him. He held out the pendant toward her. The brown leather cord drooped slightly in the air.

With gentle fingers Soarsha held the pendant in her own hand. So many times he'd shown her the pendant. Said it was a gift from Soarsha's mother, but as far as he could remember it had always been like that. A small piece of a greater whole. The same thing everyone was. We are always incomplete, he liked to tell her, but at least we knew the rest of us was out there somewhere.

On her dad's pendant, the smooth rounded edge was at the bottom right. The right and top edges were jagged, yet rounded off—as if the pendant had been snapped off something bigger.

Soarsha's eyes widened, and she looked from person to person. Small pieces of greater whole.

Glancing from piece to piece, Soarsha held out her hand. "Would you all let me hold them?"

Her father's piece of pendant slipped backward, and bounced back against Das's chest. As one person, the four adults took a step back. She might as well have been waving a lit torch in their faces. Mr. Adbad, though, just looked back and forth from the others, a confused expression on his face.

"You mean... take it off?" said Nabraig. A yellowy paleness had come over her brown skin. The top of her head seemed to have turned slightly green. "I've... I've never taken it off."

The others all nodded. Except for Mr. Adbad.

Noticing they were now looking at him, Mr. Adbad reached his fingertips inside the collar of his shirt and pulled it forward. "Sorry," he said. "No fashion accessories here."

"Please," said Soarsha. "I can see that it must feel strange to be asked... but... please. It might help us."

"Help us do what?" said Garen. The red of his face reminded Soarsha of hot cinnamon candies. "These are part of us, don't you get it?"

"They're... pendants," said Soarsha. "But... you aren't seeing it, are you? You're so busy seeing your own, it's like you haven't even really looked at what the others have. Please." Her gaze softened. "Whatever is going on, I... I believe this is going to help us understand. Find a way forward. Please trust me, Garen, as I've trusted you."

Garen seemed to tremble slightly.

A finger tapped Soarsha on the shoulder.

She turned—and her dad was holding out his pendant to her. His neck seemed strangely bare without it. The brightness of his green eyes had dimmed too, full of doubts and questions—but the light there was a light of trust, and Soarsha smiled at her father as she gently took the pendant into her hand.

"If her own dad can trust her," said Nabraig, her voice trembling and soft, but getting steadier, "then maybe we should too." The businesswoman pulled her pendant over her head and handed it to Soarsha.

"Don't let me be the holdout," said Garen, but as he set his pendant with the others, a red flash blazed momentarily in his eyes.

"I don't see what you're going to make of it," said Iandel.

The others glared at her, and she rolled her eyes.

"Fine, I'll go along." Her pendant made a slight clink as she set it with the other pieces in Soarsha's hand. She started to pull back her hand, but some resistance slowed her, and she seemed to change her mind, started to reach for it again. A hard-eyed glare from Das seemed to shake her. The embalmer stopped.

"Sorry," she said. "I just... as long as I've been here, I've worn it."

The others nodded. Soarsha stared at them, then looked at the pieces in her hand. Each was just a piece of jewelry on some brown leather cord. A bit of personal decoration and solace. No one even seemed to know why they had it, just that ever since coming to Dedalo they had been wearing a pendant. Yet...

Kneeling down, Soarsha set the pieces on the floor of the bus station and stared, searching for something in common. Then she saw it.

Reached out to Iandel's piece, Soarsha ran her finger along the curved edge.

"Iandel's pendant is curved at the bottom and right," said

Soarsha, then she started tracing the others. "Garen's is curved at the bottom and left, and Nabraig's, the top and left. Dad, yours is curved on the top and right."

Das stared at the pieces, trying to understand how this little puzzle could go together—and what it could mean if it did. "What do you make of it?"

"This." Soarsha rearranged the pieces on the ground: Iandel's at the top left, Garen's at the top right, Nabraig's at the bottom right, and her dad's at the bottom left. Each piece had its own combination of curving silver-gray lines, etched into the surface, yet the lines on each piece seemed like they could connect. A space like a plus sign ran between the four pieces, but the outer curves more or less lined up, like four points on a compass, like four pieces of pie—

Soarsha leaned forward.

Like four quadrants of a circular city.

"Do you see?" said Soarsha. "It's like they all fit together. It's like they're connected."

Nabraig looked from one adult to the other. Well, except for Mr. Adbad. He didn't have a pendant, so there wasn't much point thinking about him when it came to this.

"If they're connected," said the businesswoman, "maybe we are too."

"Aren't you, though?" said Soarsha. "Dad's boss. Dad's therapist. Dad's friend." She pointed to the pieces on the ground. "And all of you have this. That can't be a coincidence."

"I don't see how this helps us against the scathtor," said Iandel.

"Or helps us make sense of what's happening here tonight," Garen added. Frustration seethed out of him like steam from a covered pot just coming to a boil. "This is useless!"

"It's mysterious and doesn't make sense yet," said Soarsha. "That's not the same thing as useless." She pointed at the pieces. "Doesn't it seem strange to you that the pieces even correspond with where you live in the city? Iandel's in the northwest, Garen's in the northeast, Nabraig's in the southeast, and Dad and I are in the southwest. Your pieces match that."

"It's not definitive, though," said Mr. Adbad. "I don't know if you remember, but I was on the bus with you too. I caught it late, after you were already on. We all came together to Dedalo." He pulled down the collar of his shirt. "But as you see, there's nothing here."

"For all we know," said Iandel, with an eye-roll and a puffed-out sigh, "they were just part of a collection and we happened to get them as, I don't know, welcome-home prizes from the city when we arrived. We came to Dedalo on the same day, but so did plenty of other people. It's not like there's anyone else here being stripped of their property."

The others were staring at Iandel. Garen nodded with justified sympathy, but Das and Nabraig looked irked.

"Fine," said Iandel. Dismissiveness sharpened the word like a thrown dart. "It might be more convincing if the pieces all actually fit together."

A lightning storm of annoyance flashed through Soarsha. Why did Iandel doubt everything? Wasn't it clear enough? She shook her head. Damn adults (and she was certain she was using the word correctly). They never wanted to believe anything. Adults were always so busy thinking they knew, that they forgot to trust.

"You all came to the city the same day," said Soarsha. "Yet none of you remembers life before the city."

"Don't read too much into that," said Garen. "No one in Dedalo remembers—he glanced at the dark buildings outside —*remembered* much of life before coming here."

"But what do you remember?" said Soarsha. "Even the smallest, most insignificant detail might make the biggest difference."

"This is ridiculous," said Iandel. "Maybe it's time we all went home."

Das took a step forward. "Home to what?" He raised his arm

toward the bus station's wide bay exit. "There's no one out there —you're not exactly going to have any work to do tomorrow. The scathtor has taken everyone!"

"A river," said Nabraig. "I remember a river. Riding on it. Gentle rocking. Like a baby in a cradle must feel."

The others turned and looked at her. "Look," she said, "I don't know if the kid is right or not. But I'm willing to hear her out. Maybe we learn something that helps us. What do we have to lose?"

The others stared at each other. At the ground. Silence fell over the bus station like the deepening shadows, as if the lights above them were getting dimmer.

"Fine." Garen scratched at his heart. "I remember a big pain here. Hot as fire. Big as the world."

"Terrified," said Iandel. "Whatever I was doing, whatever I was, I felt terrified." She shook her head. "But then I felt certain, completely certain, the sort of certainty you think only the sky and the sun must feel." Regret flashed in her eyes. "I don't remember anything else."

Das nodded. "It's like we each have different pieces of the same puzzle," he said. Then he looked at Nabraig. "You remember a river?" He took in a deep breath. "I remember a boat. Then nothing. Maybe a light, maybe a city—not this one, somewhere else—but I definitely remember a boat."

They all looked at each other, though Mr. Adbad just stood next to Soarsha, glancing from person to person.

"I think you're all a bit cracked," said Mr. Adbad. He shrugged. Chuckled. "But under the circumstances, who wouldn't be?"

Das sighed. "Sometimes I feel like our old lives, our old memories, were something we had to throw out of the bus on the way here. Sometimes I wonder if the memories are still out there, beyond the wall, wandering the wasteland like tumbleweeds across a desert."

"Garen told me that to find answers I had to get to the heart of the matter of things," said Soarsha. "At the heart of this matter, you are all connected. I'm certain."

The excitement grew in her now, certainty rising like an elevator going up to the top of the Spire.

Mr. Adbad nodded toward the pendants. "Try fitting them together, Soarsha."

Soarsha looked at him, relieved to hear her teacher's approval, his encouragement. With her fingertips, she nudged the pieces until they touched.

The others leaned in, all watching, all wondering—if they were all connected, if their pendants were small parts of a larger whole, what would that mean for them?

Then Soarsha sat back. The others leaned away from each other, looked away, looked anywhere but at each other.

Tears burned at Soarsha's eyes.

On the ground, the four pieces of pendant did not fit together at all. No greater whole. No connection. No grand design or higher purpose. No heart of the matter. Just a bunch of people spared for the moment from being destroyed.

"Hell with it," said Das. He grabbed his pendant, and as he did Soarsha could see the wildness coming over his eyes again. He put his pendant back on and smiled at his daughter.

"I love you, Rainbow," he said. "We've got this."

Then Das ran toward a nearby bus. He yanked open the door —Soarsha was certain she heard something snap, like the metal of an overwhelmed lock. Before she could blink, her father was sitting behind the steering wheel. Pulling down a visor, he caught a set of keys that fell out. Soon the bus station came alive with the rumble-roar of the stuttering bus, brought back to life in the dark.

23

AND NOW, THE CONCLUSION OF WANDERING HEROES

The little darkness between the barely open lid and rim of the chest might as well have been the abyss between stars. Silence reclaimed the Barrenburn. A smoky orange glow spread across the dimming late-afternoon sky, the first long breath of the coming evening. Jilly's legs trembled as she took the few slow steps toward the chest.

Nearby, the shadow monster and the ancient hero lay intertwined. Gleaming Head did not rise—and now, up close and after the battle, Jilly could see why. The round, black, bloodless hole in the hero's chest must have pierced his endless heart.

Tears fell from Jilly's eyes. Well, not endless anymore.

He'd been right, Jilly realized. The moment he had set foot on the Barrenburn, Gleaming Head had known that he would never return to the Cuan Féir. He would never hear the swish of the grasses again, or feel the rising sun on his face. Not far away, Sapphire and Shirtman lay, holding hands even at the last. Jilly's tears smacked the hard dry ground—probably, she realized, the first rain this wasteland had known for eons.

The Mrazas had died for her. For her, for this weird chest, for her to have a chance at something else. Some better life. Whatever that was.

All alone now, Jilly stared at her fallen friends, and at the monster that had killed them, and at the barren cracked earth, and at the uncaring walls of the circular golden city—and, at last, at the slightly open chest.

The cool wood tilted back without a sound. Inside, on black velvet, five silver-gray pieces of something bigger lay jumbled. Jilly shook her head. Whatever it was must have broken in the falling and tumbling—not that she had known what was in there. If a broken trinket and a wooden chest were what it took to finally stop the strange monster, well, she could live with that.

She glanced at her fallen friends, and her eyes grew hot.

If only she wasn't the only one.

Sitting before the open chest, Jilly reached inside. The warm pieces were made of some sort of clay. The craft was simple, more everyday than elegant, more homey than honored. The broken edges were slightly jagged, but mostly rough and rounded. Four of the pieces comprised the main part of the circular disc, which bumped up in the middle, as if recombined the pieces would point toward the four compass points.

Jilly took out the four pieces and set them on the hard brown ground. The work was simple yet lovely, as rough as people were yet as beautiful as all people could be. The pieces were similar in shape and size. They didn't entirely line up, but she had expected that.

After all, there was one more piece.

Reaching back into the little chest, Jilly took out the fifth piece. It looked like the key to all the others. The one that could transform the little pieces into something bigger. The one that could make them whole. The silver-gray circle was smooth all around, except for where the other pieces had broken off. Top and bottom, left and right, four jagged, rounded-top points rose up. Once Jilly had figured out how to lay the pieces, the fifth piece fitted the rest together perfectly.

And yet.

The center of the fifth piece was a perfect circle, smooth-edged and empty. Along the recombined whole, a polished, shimmering, carved line of silver-gray curved and whirled all around the design, like a strange, convoluted path. There seemed to be a pattern to it, though Jilly couldn't make out what the pattern was, or where it began, or where it was going. Broken, complicated, and hard to follow, it was also beautiful.

Jilly ran her finger over the object, feeling the slight indentation of the curving line, the rough-smooth feel of the clay like fine bark, or rough skin. Her eyes teared up again. The surface of the object felt like Gleaming Head's hands.

Near one edge of the object, something caught her eye. She started to look at it, to move her finger toward it—

Then a cough made her turn away from the object, to the two intertwined bodies lying nearby.

The shadow monster was stirring.

Ragged limbs shook, and flung back and forth.

"No," said Jilly. She tried to scramble to her hands and knees so she could stand, but the monster was moving faster than she was—

The shadow monster rose. Its torso turned, and the monster seemed to stare at her. Then it kept turning, and fell to the ground with a flat smack, and lay still.

"Oof," said Gleaming Head. He coughed, and his body shook.

Jilly slid over to her friend. The ancient hero was trying to move, but he could barely stir.

"Jilly," he said.

"I'm here." She sat next to Gleaming Head, and gently lifted his head so she could lay it on her legs. "I've got you." She touched his face. "It's going to be okay."

He smiled, but he also coughed. "It is going to be okay," said

Gleaming Head, "but not in the way you think. I don't even know how this is all going to go. But I do believe, in all my heart and with all my long years and with every breath of air and speck of sand and blade of grass in this world, I believe it is going to be okay for you."

"You'll be all right," said Jilly. Her eyes burned yet her cold skin puckered. "You're practically as old as the world. What's a little poke, huh?" She stared at his chest, but looked away, back to his eyes, just as quickly.

"We are not family who lie to each other," said Gleaming Head. "And I'm not going to lie to you, Jilly. This is the day of my dread. I knew it was coming. The moment we came to the edge of the Barrenburn, I knew where this path would lead."

Jilly shook her head. "But I didn't want the three of you to die!"

Kindness shone in Gleaming Head's eyes. "For what it's worth, we didn't want to either," he replied. "But for you, for what's ahead for you, we were willing. That's the difference between some horrible fate and a choice that is hard but still right. There is no power and love but what you grow in yourself. We love you, Jilly, and we see that the love and power growing within you are vast. We know there is more for you than what this world could possibly contain. That's why we came here. With grim smiles, aye, but smiles nonetheless. Because we knew that if you could get into the city, you'd have the chance you deserve."

"I don't know how to get inside the city, though," she said. "The gates haven't reopened."

A flicker of trouble passed over the ancient hero's face. "They will," he said. "I'm certain of it. Just be ready for when they do."

Gleaming Head nodded over toward the little wooden chest. "So it opened after all."

"And helped bring down this monster," said Jilly.

"You found the pendant inside?" said Gleaming Head.

Jilly looked from the pieces on the ground, back to Gleaming Head. "You knew?"

"I saw it," replied Gleaming Head. "When I found you. You were wearing it, actually." His fingers tugged on the many loops of brown leather cord around his neck. "I put the pendant in its chest, and thought it would be best if you and the pendant were separated, and that I keep an eye on both of you. I figured that if you weren't together, maybe people would stop noticing you, stop trying to take you. Then I thought the day might come that I could safely return the pendant to you." He chuckled, but it was cold, dry, and bitter as a breeze on the Barrenburn. "Oh well. Even ancient heroes can't be wise about everything."

"What is it?" said Jilly.

"A key," said Gleaming Head. "That's why so many people want it, are willing to kill and die for it. It's a key out of this world."

Jilly shook her head. "To where?"

Gleaming Head's eyes gleamed, as if he himself were at the threshold of the answer. "To wherever is next."

He took the cord off his neck and handed it to her. "Put it back on," he said. "It's time."

"I can't," said Jilly. "It... It broke when I used the chest against the monster. The pendant's in five pieces."

Another flicker of trouble passed over Gleaming Head's face, but he forced a smile. "Things happen," he said. "Not really for a reason, but we make reasons out of what happens. I'm going to trust that this is for the best. It might help you pass unnoticed in the city, until you find where you must go. Keep the pieces safe. When the time comes, the pendant will likely fix itself. Then it will be time."

"Time for what?"

He shrugged. And coughed. "Bugger if I know," he replied. "The thing people never understand about heroes is that our idea of a plan is to make it up as we go, look decently impressive in the process, and seem like we knew all along how things were going to work out. I don't know where the key leads, Jilly." He rolled his eyes back, toward the walled city. "But I'm guessing that wherever the lock is, you'll find it there."

His body arched. Pain slashed across his face. A coughing fit wracked over him like blows from an unstoppable army.

"Please don't," said Jilly. She hated how small her voice sounded, but she couldn't find a way to make it bigger again. "Please don't die."

"Hey, we all have to sooner or later," said Gleaming Head. "Even me. For this to be my time, well, I can't imagine a better way than if my passing helps you in your life. It's been my job—and my joy—to keep you safe, to help you grow. I got you to where you needed to be, Jilly. It's just that I can go no farther."

"You've been like a father to me," she said. "Now I'll have nothing and no one."

Gleaming Head reached up and covered her hand with his. "You are the child I never had, but at least we got to have each other for a while," he said. "No matter who we lose, we still have them. There are others in this world who will help you, even better than I could. Wherever you go, I will be with you, even when you can't remember I'm there. No place in any world could take my love away from you." He squeezed her hand. "Now, Jilly, last of the Mrazas, you go. You follow your path. Find your way and unlock the world that lies before you. Go with love. Go with joy." He smiled at her. One last time. "And go ever onward."

Jilly kissed his forehead. Her words were raspy, barely a whisper, but she found her voice anyway.

"Go, Mrazas," said Jilly.

The ancient hero's eyes closed. For a moment, a soft warm breeze shuddered across the Barrenburn, then the air was still.

Jilly's tears washed over her lost friend, her lost father, and finally, gently, she closed his eyes and laid his head back down on the hard earth. Then she tied the cord around her neck, and tucked the pieces of pendant into her pocket. The chest she laid in Gleaming Head's hands, his swords crossed upon his chest, where he lay next to the shadow monster. Then the last Mraza stood before the walled city and stared at the gate.

"All right," said Jilly. "Let's go where I need to go."

She knocked on the gate. No answer. She pounded on it. Kicked it. Even spat on it. But the gate did not open. The wall of the city remained closed, featureless, and the city as beyond her reach as the sun.

Throughout the long cold night, Jilly did not even try to sleep. She sat over the body of each of her friends, and sang the long slow songs you unlocked only for those you love most. The rivers of her tears carried each soul in a boat of her love, down the lonely way to where, she hoped, they would find peace, and green fields where the swaying grasses were the only blades they ever needed.

Eventually, after what may have been a few moments of sleep, Jilly sat up. She stared at the gate, but not even her glare could force it open.

With a sigh, Jilly looked around the wall and the plain of the Barrenburn, but she saw nothing. The horses had never returned, but she hoped they had found safety.

Then, off in the distance, at the edge of the blade-flat horizon, a spinning globe of dust puffed up.

The cloud got closer, moving slowly yet steadily. Finally, as it neared, a rumbling roar filled the air. Jilly recoiled, and she stepped back, fearing that whatever strange monster was coming for her, it would not see her and would squash her into a jelly-slick footprint on the ground.

A screeching shattered the air and her eardrums and drove fear through her like cold lightning.

Right in front of her, the monster halted. Gradually the dust faded, settling back onto the ground until, at last, Jilly could see what strange monster had crossed the Barrenburn to come, as she had, to stillness outside the gate of Dedalo.

Her eyes widened—though they also still stung with some of the dust lingering in the air.

She had never seen a monster like this.

It was rectangular, with rounded edges at the front and back, yet its rusted, silvery chrome gleamed dimly in the early sun. Clear glass windows stretched like a stripe from the front edge of the monster to the back.

She looked down. No feet would have stomped her into the earth. Instead, four ragged but intact tires stood still on the packed dirt, the only part of the monster touching the ground.

With the hiss of a sick person inhaling, something at the front side of the bus moved. Jilly walked over to it—and saw that an opening, a doorway, had appeared.

A man sat behind a large circle, empty except for some black spokes, and his hands rested on the circle's round black rim. His skin was dark, even darker than Gleaming Head's, but it also shone in the morning sun. His hair was short, curly, and white, and his eyes were as kind as the ancient hero's as he turned and looked at her.

"Need a ride, child?" he said.

Jilly didn't know what to say. She pointed toward the city.

"My next stop, in fact," said the man, "though I'll be darned if I know what my next route is." His smile was a surprise, like thick clouds clearing and revealing a bright noon sun. "Oh well, that's life. You never really know where you're going until you get there." He turned slightly toward her. On his dark gray shirt, a white tag above his heart spelled out one word: "carl."

His shirt rippled as he waved her inside. "Now come on in, child," he said. "Normally there's a fare to ride."

Soarsha reached into her pocket and pulled out the five pieces of pendant. "Will this do?"

Carl shook his head, and he laid one hand over a box, his

fingers blocking some sort of slot. "Your job—your fare—is to take good care of that. Given the circumstances, I'd say it's more important to get you where you're going, don't you think?"

"Thank you," said Jilly as she stepped onto the bus.

"Anytime," said Carl. "Anytime."

The doors wheezed closed behind her. Jilly walked down the center aisle of the bus, staring at the seats. There were two women, one on each side of the bus. There were also two men. No one sat together. But one man looked at her. His green eyes were bright but sorrowful, and they shone like the grasses of the Cuan Féir. He smiled at her. Soarsha smiled back, and sat in the seat in front of him.

"Good morning," said the man.

"Good morning," said Soarsha.

With another rumble-roar, the chrome rectangular beast began moving again, a strange ride toward a strange place—but Soarsha was grateful to at least be in motion.

For a moment she thought she saw a shadow approaching the back window, but it had to be just a trick of the early light. Turning away from the man behind her, Soarsha looked ahead, past Carl, to the beige wall of the city.

From the top to the bottom, a vertical line appeared, then widened—and the gate of the city opened. Jilly held the pieces of the pendant and thought of the bright green eyes of the man behind her. Wary, kind, and hopeful. A father's eyes. Like Gleaming Head's. Before her wide eyes, between the endless rows of skyscrapers and beneath a strange, endlessly falling golden dust, stretched a long, winding, beautiful street of silver-gray.

24

TO THE GATE OF THE GOLDEN CITY

The bus shuddered and sputtered, shaking from side to side like a leashed animal longing to break its chain. A sulfurous, brown-gray stink unfurled, trickling through the air while the back of the bus lowered toward the ground, as if ready to bound out of the station, crash through the city's gate, and rumble along the unfettered world beyond the walls of Dedalo.

From the driver's seat, Das waved for the others to get on, but they stood near the door, jaws open and eyes slack.

"Dad?" said Soarsha. "What are you doing?"

"You're right, Soarsha," he replied. "You need adventure. What's the use of showing someone every corner of their cage?" He shook his head. "Dedalo is a prison, my daughter. That's what it is for all of us, but especially for you. You deserve so much more out of life than what this world can offer you."

Das revved the gas pedal. The bus's rumble blazed up into a roar. "Forget exploring the city." Her dad smiled. "I'm going to bust you out of here."

"But Dad," said Soarsha. "There aren't any outbound buses."

"There are now," replied Das.

Soarsha smiled back at her dad, and she got onto the bus. She sat down on the bench to her dad's right and just a little behind him.

"So," said Soarsha, "we're going to find my dream come true?"

A bright determination glowed in her father's eyes. "We're going to find the world of the rolling green hills, the rain, the warm sun, the salty air. All of it. Soarsha, do you know what a parent wants for their child more than anything else?"

"What?"

He leaned toward her. "I want you to live the fullest life possible." He shook his head. "But I know you simply cannot do that in Dedalo. I don't care that there's a scary shadow monster running around the city and stealing people. I care that you are here, and that this world is yours, and that we are going to do all we can so you can have the full life you deserve. It doesn't matter that the pieces of the pendant didn't fit together. Life doesn't happen because there's some grand design to it all. There is no greater design or purpose or plan. Random people make their own purpose. Random people move the world, and that is exactly what we are going to do."

Das leaned out toward the door, and he looked from Iandel to Garen to Nabraig to Mr. Adbad. "So," he called to the others, "who else is with us?"

The four adults stared one to the other. Three of them shrugged, and lined up to board the bus.

"This is bloody madness," said Iandel, standing outside, hands on her hips and shaking her head.

"Sure it is," said Nabraig. "But what do we have to lose?"

"Our lives," said Iandel.

"You'd be surprised," said Das. "The scathtor has taken everyone in the city but us. I don't doubt it, and I feel it from my soul to my skin. There's nothing here for us anymore, Iandel." He stared at her, kindness and pleading in his green eyes. "Please come with us."

The others got on the bus and sat down in the seats around Soarsha. Iandel shook her head. "You know how to drive a bus?"

With a chuckle, Das patted the wide black steering wheel. "Ask me again after I've done it."

Iandel sighed—but she got on the bus, and sat down in the seat right behind Das. "You'd better earn this, buddy."

"I won't let you down." Das pushed a chrome lever. With a squeak and a swish, the door closed. "I can feel it."

Mr. Adbad leaned forward. "What makes you think you can just... drive out of the city?"

"Carl," said Das. "He drove the bus Soarsha and I took a lot—and he disappeared today, taken by the scathtor. He told me once that there was something about the bus that made the gate open. That's fine, obviously, for when a bus comes in. But for leaving? That's why no buses go near the gate. If they did, the gate would open."

"And, this Carl," said Mr. Adbad, "he's a reliable source?"

"Like I said, he disappeared this morning," said Das. "Maybe he'd said too much."

Staring at her father, Soarsha wondered what else Carl had said.

Garen leaned forward. "It might be helpful if you gave us more to go on."

"I wish I could," said Das, "but I don't think you'd believe me. Look, Garen, all of you, please. This isn't for me. This is for my daughter. You all know good and well I wouldn't put her in danger. She's all I have in the world."

He pulled the chrome lever again, and the door whistled open. "If you think I don't have Soarsha's best interests at heart here, then by all means, get the feck off my bus."

Soarsha's eyes widened. She hadn't heard that word before, but she was never going to forget it.

No one moved. Das closed the door. "That's what I feckin thought."

The rumbling bus shimmied from side to side, trying to dance to the beat of its engine. Inch by inch, the beast of a rig backed out of its den.

Das flicked on the headlights. An amber-gold gleam shone before them, but quickly got lost in the darkness of Dedalo.

Soarsha's skin prickled. "I wish the lights shone farther."

"It's okay, daughter," said Das. "We can see only a little bit at a time, but we can make the whole trip that way."

Garen and Nabraig looked out the windows.

"No sign of the scathtor," said Iandel.

"Doesn't that seem strange?" said Mr. Adbad. "This monster, at least as far as we can tell, wipes out every soul in the city... except for us? Now here we are, not exactly moving in something small and quiet, aiming to escape the city, and the monster is nowhere to be found?"

"Who knows," said Das. "Maybe it's afraid of buses. Keep watching for it, though."

"What are you going to do if we see it?" said Iandel. "Run over it?"

"If you come up with a better idea," replied Das, "be quick about telling me."

The snorting bus sauntered down the city streets. Das drove fast, and the city began to blur by. After a few turns, Das had them on the northbound road leading to the northern edge of the city—leading to the sole gate and the freedom beyond.

Soarsha settled back in her seat. Unzipping her purple backpack, she pulled out her old issue of *Wandering Heroes*.

Nabraig glanced down at the cover and smiled at Soarsha. "Your dad told me you were a fan."

Soarsha's cheeks burned. "Sometimes I pretend Jilly and I are sisters."

Nabraig glanced at Soarsha's hat, wondering about the hair concealed inside. "I wouldn't doubt it," she replied. "Even the way she's drawn, you two could just about be twins." She looked closer at Soarsha's comic.

"Wait, why aren't you reading the new issue?"

"It hasn't arrived yet."

Nabraig smiled. She pulled around the leather shoulder bag she'd been wearing. Unbuckling its flap and reaching inside, she flipped past white papers and yellow papers and black folders and brown folders—then pulled out something bright and colorful.

"Mine came today," said Nabraig. "The finale." She held out the comic to Soarsha. "Why don't you keep it safe for me? Once we've got a dull moment, we'll read it together."

Soarsha blushed and smiled as she slid the comic into her backpack. Her father's voice rumbled through the bus.

"Get ready, everyone!"

Soarsha picked up the comic and slid it back into her backpack, trying not to fold it or wrinkle the cover. Setting the zipped pack on her lap, Soarsha looked up and gasped. They had almost reached the ringwall. This close, the wall might as well have been bigger than the Spire. Jilly's legs tensed, trying to root her feet into the floor of the bus while at the same time her bladder threatened to empty itself.

The road was so short now. And shorter by the moment, as the gate was closer, and closer—and showed no sign of opening.

"Dad..." said Soarsha.

Das didn't so much as turn around. "It's gonna work, Rainbow."

Soarsha grabbed her backpack with one hand, pressing fabric between her fingers and her palm. Her other hand wrapped around her pendant. So much had changed in the day since her dad had given it to her—and so much more was about to.

"Das..." said Mr. Adbad.

"Stop!" yelled Iandel.

"It's not working!" shouted Garen.

The wall said nothing its unbroken mass didn't already say clearly enough.

Das pressed the pedal to the floor. He screamed—a war cry, freedom's demand, a wish for every tomorrow to come with the sight of a world that faded from sight by distance, instead of being cut off by a wall that sprang up to stop how far you could see, how far you could imagine, how far you could live.

Crushing the tweed of his jacket, Mr. Adbad clutched his heart. Everyone else had a hand near their throats, clutching their pendants. Even Das did so as he drove. The four adults screamed their loud prayers of stopping. At the same time they held their talismans of hope that this would work. Maybe Carl was right, and the bus was the key to opening the world beyond Dedalo.

They screamed. They hoped.

But not Soarsha. In silence, she trusted her dad the way the Mrazas trusted each other. And she waited to see the world beyond the wall.

The engine's roar became a steady whir. The bumpy ride smoothed out so much the bus could have taken flight.

Das turned, just for a moment, and glanced at Soarsha. She smiled, and he smiled back. Then he turned, and leaned forward, and pushed the bus forward with gas pedal and will and hope and the certainty that the point of having a dream was to make it come true.

Inches separated bus from wall. Then nothing did.

The screams fell away for a moment, overtaken by the roar and screech of metal. Yet even the screams of six people rose higher than the shrieks of ripping steel and shattering glass. Soarsha held on to her backpack and her pendant. The roof and sides and floor of the bus ripped away, like a horrible flower opening, petal by metal petal. Iandel, Garen, Nabraig, and Mr. Adbad leaped up, surrounding Soarsha like a shield, but there was nothing that could guard against the unbreakable wall that refused to open.

Something ripped the backpack out of Soarsha's hands. She closed her eyes. She didn't want to see what was about to happen. Maybe she wasn't enough of a Mraza after all. But that didn't matter anymore. All she saw, in the green bright place beyond the somber crashing reality outside her eyes and mind, was a land of rolling hills. Soarsha wished, with tears she would never cry, that she could have met her mother. Or at least found out what had happened to her.

But she'd never get to tell her mother hello, or hug her, or hold her hand, or stand on that path and watch for her father coming home. There would be no sound of rain on the roof, or a breeze over the green fields. There would be no sound at all, only screams and ripping and shrieking—then, at least, at last, the relieved exhale, the last breath. The total silence.

PART III

ON STREETS OF SILVER-GRAY

25

FLOWER IN THE WRECKAGE

The unbroken, unmarred wall seemed to grow even taller, as if Dedalo's ringwall were competing with the Spire. Yet now something was reaching beyond the wall—and could stretch even higher than the Spire.

Under the conical amber-gold light of streetlamps, smoke wafted up from the wreckage of the shattered bus, gray as death and blacker than the streets, blacker than the deep night covering and suffusing the city. Thick and rolling as muscles, the smoke rose toward the sky, passing the height of the wall, of skyscraper after skyscraper, until the smoke rose even higher than the tip of the Spire. Perhaps the smoke sought answers. Perhaps it wanted to see for itself what the world looked like from the sky. Or perhaps it just wanted the breeze to tear it apart, end it all, so it wouldn't have to hurt or wonder anymore.

Maybe the smoke just couldn't bear the sight of what was on the street below.

Ripped and jagged chrome lay sooty and scratched on the dark street. The backs and bottoms of red seats lay torn and scattered like the abandoned remains of a predator's kill. Fragments of glass practiced their impersonation of the stars, but their dusty, sooty twinkles weren't going to be competition for the heavens anytime soon. Twisted metal and sagging bars lay scattered.

Amidst the wreckage at the edge of the silent empty city, a strange flower had bloomed.

Four adults lay in a circle, on their sides. Their arms splayed outward like petals, and their backs faced the inside of the circle. No one was bloody or torn. Just still, the feels-wrong calm of the dead. Near their feet lay a fifth adult. A man. He was bald, and his char-marred tweed suit was ripped and scuffed, like armor that had kindly taken all the damage for him. The man lay curled, like a parent comforting a child who'd woken up from a bad dream.

In the center of the bloom, the child lay.

From a scratch on her temple, blood had trickled, yet the thin red stream was already browning, stopping, and hardening. Her purple clothes were dusty, and the knees of her overalls had ripped. Something had torn her purple backpack. Bright papers rustled in a fresh breeze, then fluttered, then floated away like departing souls.

The girl's purple hat lay just off her head. The hat she'd worn as her own armor for as long as she could remember. It was more than a hat. It was Soarsha's armor of hope, her shield against the quiet city's constant abrasion of her soul's brightness.

She would only stop wearing the hat when she found her mother.

All around the top of the girl's head, a small puddle of red—coppery and with hints of gold—shimmered in the starlight. The breeze rustled the child's hair, little red curls reaching toward a new day.

And Soarsha opened her eyes.

The first thing she noticed was the absence of the hat covering her hair, red as fresh strawberries and sushi tuna, red as a Soarsha rainbow under its new and improved second arch of purple. Soarsha felt around, grabbed her hat, and felt all over her head. She winced when she touched her scratch. Otherwise she found no wounds. Not only did her head feel unharmed, but her mind felt… surprisingly clear. Smoothing down the red hair as best she could, Soarsha put her hat back on like a knight putting on her helmet.

Then she sat up and saw what the world, her world, looked like now.

Still trapped in Dedalo. But around her, the bodies of the people she knew, the only people who'd been left—

"Dad?" she said.

Das didn't move. His back was to her, and his shirt had stretched downward, so she could see the purple line across the back of his neck.

"Dad?" she said again. The word floated away with the smoke, and faded too.

Looking from person to person, Soarsha was afraid to move, afraid to touch them, not because she might hurt them, but because there might be no response at all.

A small gasp. Soarsha's eyes widened; the little sound might as well have been a whoop of joy.

Staring from person to person, Soarsha slowly stood up. From her head to her toes she felt a bit sore, but that was all. Nothing was broken. Other than the scratch on her temple, she was fine.

"Soarsha?"

Her dad sat up. He could move fine too. Soarsha blinked, and her brow furrowed. He seemed to be covered in scratches, little furrows, but there was no blood on him, as if the rush of the crash had whooshed it all away.

The others began to stir too. Iandel and Garen, Nabraig and Mr. Adbad. One by one they sat up, all scratched up and sore, but no one bleeding, no one broken, but everyone surprised.

Soarsha took a gentle step, and stared at the wall, and the wreckage, and the people around her.

Nabraig stood up. "How?" She stared at her hands, at the empty scratches like paper cuts that hadn't gone deep enough to bleed. She stepped to the wall, and touched the unmarred surface where everyone had hoped the gate would open.

"We should be dead," said Nabraig. "The bus hit this wall at full force. None of us should have survived."

Das shook his head. "We made it, and that's all that matters," he said. He stepped over toward his daughter. "Isn't that right, Soarsha?"

But Soarsha took a step back and shook her head.

"Rainbow?"

Soarsha didn't know why, but standing next to her dad right now felt too much like standing next to a fallen electrical wire.

"It's a shock," said Das. "But it's going to be okay." He reached for her, to touch her cheek or her shoulder, she didn't know, but she shook her head again and took a step back.

"Nabraig's right," said Soarsha. "We should be dead."

"You're hurt," said Garen, pointing to Soarsha's temple.

"It feels fine," said Soarsha. "A little tender, but considering what could have happened, tender is fine."

Garen shook his head. "I think... I think I remember all of us wrapping ourselves around you, Soarsha," said the happiness coach. "That must be why you're hardly injured. It's okay."

Mr. Adbad said nothing. He staggered around the wreckage some, fingertips on his temples.

Soarsha took a step toward her teacher. "Are you okay, Mr. Adbad?"

"Just... my head hurts a little," he replied. "That's all. My mind just feels all shadowy and foggy." He took in a deep breath, and let it out slowly. Gradually he lowered his fingertips. His eyes seemed clear, but there was a cloudiness there, a dimness, that Soarsha had never seen in his gaze before.

"But given we just survived a bus crash," continued Mr. Adbad, "well, like you said, Soarsha, considering what could have happened..."

"We're okay," said Garen. "Really we are." But even his red face had a paleness to it.

Nabraig stood with her hand on the wall, as if trying to converse with it through her fingertips. Soarsha wondered what the businesswoman was saying—and how much of it was language Das would not want his daughter hearing.

"Iandel?" said Das. He stepped across the wreckage, to where the embalmer stood. Iandel hadn't spoken once, or made a noise, or even moved. She only stared at the wall. Or maybe she was staring at Soarsha. Her gaze seemed so far away, she might as well have been staring from the top of the Spire to the edge of the world.

Thinking about the golden needle in the center of Dedalo, Soarsha turned and stared up toward the top of the Spire. She realized that, since coming to the bus station, she hadn't even glanced at the Spire. She'd assumed it had gone dark, like the rest of the city. It hadn't, but it didn't pulse anymore either. Now the Spire shone bright as the sun—it was even hard to see the sky. The steady golden light gleamed from the Spire, as if the scathtor had shut every shining soul and every golden speck of dust inside the massive building.

The one thing on the Spire that did not shine, though, was the chamber at the top. No glint. Apparently the god there wasn't watching anymore. Attention turned elsewhere. Bored.

Soarsha shook her head. The city was empty. What else could there possibly be to pay attention to?

"Think about what we've got, Iandel," said Das. He was standing next to his friend now, and Soarsha noticed that she felt relieved her father was no longer trying to stand near her.

Iandel stared at Das, but she said nothing. Her mouth hung open slightly. Her mouth and throat sometimes twitched, words like fish in a stream, except they must be getting caught on hooks.

"We didn't get through the wall," Das continued. "But we got here. No monster got us. We survived, Iandel. We survived."

Iandel raised her hands over her face and let out a giant sob. Turning away from Das, Iandel realized she was now looking at Soarsha. Iandel turned away again. Away from all of them. The embalmer kept her face covered while she sobbed so hard and so loud it was as if she thought her cries could hammer a hole in the wall.

The others looked back and forth from one another. Soarsha tried to watch the adults, tried to read their minds through the weird ways grownups looked at each other as if their gazes were enough to communicate. Garen seemed to be trying to get across that it was understandable—after what they'd just been through, what they'd just survived, who could blame someone for a cry? Under Nabraig's furrowed brow, her eyes had narrowed, and Soarsha kept noticing a twitch in the businesswoman's hand, as if Nabraig were pondering when the time would be right to let loose a mind-clearing slap.

Her father wasn't looking at Iandel. He was looking at Soarsha, his I'm-sorry eyes dim and pleading. But Soarsha turned away. It was still hard to be near him or even look at him. Soarsha wanted to cry too, but she held it in. Jilly wouldn't cry. Gleaming Head wouldn't cry. Not right now, anyway. And if Soarsha was going to live like a Mraza, she wouldn't cry either. Besides, if she cried, her dad would try to comfort for, and that was the last thing she wanted right now.

The thought of the Mrazas reminded her of the lost comic. She'd seen the ripped pages scatter from her torn backpack. Now she'd never know what happened to the Wandering Heroes. She'd never know what happened when the Mrazas crossed the Barrenburn, or if the golden city they'd seen in the distance really was a comic book version of Dedalo. Or was Dedalo itself a story version of something else? Wondering about such strange improbable things was far easier than trying to think about her father, and the crash, and the should-be-dead people surrounding her who were all she had left in the world.

Mr. Adbad, though, walked by Soarsha, and her gaze followed her teacher. He stood next to Iandel, and put his left arm around her trembling shoulders.

"Go on," said Mr. Adbad. "Get it all out."

Iandel dropped her hands. Her eyes were red, but dry. No tear tracks carved through the dust on her face.

"But that's the problem, dammit," said the embalmer, stepping away from Mr. Adbad. "There's nothing to get out. Nothing... There was nothing to fear at all... Never was..."

Garen shook his head. "What are you talking about, Iandel? Are you sure you're okay?"

Iandel's head snapped toward Garen. "Of course I'm okay, you idiot," she said.

Das took a cautious step toward his friend. "But you're not making any sense. Maybe you hit your head and aren't feeling quite right."

"No," said Iandel. "I know exactly what I am. And what you are. What we all are."

Nabraig held up her hands. "As far as we can tell, we're the last people in the city."

Iandel shook her head. "We're not the last people," she replied. "I don't know if we're even really people."

"Of course we're people," said Das.

"Then why aren't you bleeding?" said Iandel. "Look at yourselves. Look at each other. All those scratches, but not a drop of blood. All this pain, all this terror, all this trauma we just went through—and no tears."

Garen pointed at her face, and the irritation glared off his own. "This is getting ridiculous. You've been crying."

"Crying?" Iandel laughed. "I've been sobbing, sure, but not crying. You have to have tears to cry. Just like you have to have blood to bleed." She shook her head. "That's what you don't understand yet. You don't have those things. Just like I don't. We're the same, and you know it. We've all been in Dedalo for ten years. So tell me, over ten years, how often have you ever bled? How often have you cried?"

"Well," said Nabraig, "I mean, I'm on site all the time. You sometimes slip, catch yourself on something rough or sharp."

"Go through lots of bandages?" said Iandel. "Have a tough time scrubbing blood out of your clothes?"

Nabraig opened her mouth, but closed it again and looked away. "No," she said. "Now that you say it like that. Never."

Iandel turned to Garen. "So many people you see, trying to find their happiness," she said. "You must go through box after box of tissues every week."

Grinning, Garen leaned forward, snapped his fingers, and pointed at her, "Ah, that's got it," said Garen. "I go through..." He paused. Looked away. Then looked back at Iandel, shaking his head. "I... don't go through any. I think I've had the same box of tissues on my table for as long as I've had the office."

The image flashed back into Soarsha's mind. It was hard to believe that mere hours ago she'd been sitting in Garen's office with her dad, staring at the dusty tissue box on Garen's gleaming orange table. It was maybe, what, half a day ago that they'd been trying to figure out how to deal with bullies and find a way to be happy in the city. Or that she and her dad had planned to go on an adventure—though this was not what she'd had in mind.

Garen took a few steps back, shaking his head. "That doesn't make sense," he said.

Mr. Adbad stood next to Iandel. "It does make sense," he said, his voice soft.

"What do you mean?" said Soarsha.

For a moment the teacher said nothing. Only stared at Iandel, with another of those stupid adult eyeball-to-eyeball conversations.

"You know?" said Iandel.

"I've known for a long time," replied Mr. Adbad. "I'm a teacher who's never had to deal with so much as a bloodied-up skinned knee. And I've also noticed that the box of tissues on my desk has never been used, or emptied, or replaced."

Nabraig and Garen stared at them. "What have you known?"

"Yeah," said Soarsha. "Stop talking with your eyes. Tell us."

Iandel sighed. For a moment the tremor of a sob shuddered over her face, but her eyes looked bright, as if she were relieved not to be carrying a lone heavy burden anymore.

"People in Dedalo don't cry, or bleed, or do so many things," said Iandel, "because everyone here is dead."

26

THE DAILY BUS ALWAYS COMES AT DAWN

The silence of an empty city was cacophony compared to the stunned silence after impossible news explodes.

The six people looked at Iandel. At each other. At the wreckage, not even smoking anymore now.

"Dead?" said Garen. "That's ridiculous. We're here. Why would you say something so stupid, Iandel?"

Nabraig rolled her eyes. "Don't be daft, Garen. Can't you tell she's right?"

Das shook his head. "So many years when I've fallen into the dark," he said, "yet not once have I cried."

"No, no," said Garen. His voice was louder now. "If we were dead, well, we wouldn't be walking around, would we? We'd be, you know, still. That's what you do, Iandel. You know damn well we're alive. You deal with the dead every day. Are you telling me you don't know the difference?"

Iandel looked up at the happiness coach. "Every city has its secrets, and those who know do not tell," she said. "I've known for years, but wouldn't let myself admit it. Then, one night, a body was on my table."

"And you drain them," said Garen, "and, well, you know, you do embalmy stuff." He waved his hand.

"Yes," said Nabraig. "Thank you for summing up her years of training and experience with a hand-wave and a word that doesn't actually exist."

Garen shook his head. "She must not be a very good embalmer, Nabraig, is all I'm saying, if she doesn't know the difference between alive and dead. You'd think it'd be pretty obvious!"

"It is," said Iandel. "You just don't want to see it."

The embalmer held up a finger. "Like I was saying. One night a body was on my table. And you're right. We're trained to drain fluids." For a moment she trembled, as if the fresh horror of the memory's revelation had returned. "But in Dedalo, every body is empty, as dry as tissue on the inside. Not a drop of anything. This night, standing over the body, I was shuffling some papers and got a paper cut. A deep one. The sort that goes from stinging to howling in about two seconds, and stays that way for five minutes that feel like an eternity. It hurt. It damn well hurt. But it didn't bleed. That's when I understood. I was dead too. I just hadn't stopped moving yet."

She turned away. Garen moved toward her, but Mr. Adbad stepped in between them and raised a hand.

"What?" said Garen. "Some kid hit you in the nose with an apple, and you didn't get a nosebleed?"

Mr. Adbad chuckled, his laugh as dry as the dusty air. "I've always known," he said. "That's how the world is. That's how I am. That's how we are." He shrugged, a mix of resolve and resignation simmering in his gaze. "I figured the best thing I could do was get on with helping my students."

"You want us to just consider this true," said Garen.

"I never wanted it to be true," said Iandel. "Das can tell you. The way I've talked about the bodies on my table, it's as if they were friends. They might as well be. People always talk about how death makes you consider how similar we all are. Well, we don't get more similar than that. We're dead, Garen. Where we are, some afterlife, some purgatory, I don't know. But I know we're not alive."

Soarsha looked from one adult to the other. "Then what about me?" she said.

Garen shook his head, and his voice swung sharp. "What about you?"

Soarsha gasped. He had always been so kind, but this jagged edge of his gaze, fiery and furious, cut into her.

The happiness coach started to say more, but he stopped. Instead, Garen whipped around and walked off. His heavy steps jackhammered off the street until Soarsha could barely see his back. Das started to go after him, but Nabraig gently squeezed his hand.

"Let him be," she said.

"You're talking this so easily," said Das.

Nabraig ran a hand over her bald head. "I love what I do, Das," the businesswoman replied. "Negotiation is all about reading people, reading place, reading circumstance. You don't do what I do without learning to deal with things as they are. What Iandel says... It's bewildering. It's crazy. It's just that it's also right. It's completely mad yet completely makes sense. I can't fight the truth any more than I can fight knowing that I'm not growing a sensational silky head of hair anytime soon."

"We don't bleed," said Das. "We don't cry. We just keep going, until the time comes that we don't anymore."

Iandel looked at her finger, as if wishing it could bleed again. "When that happens, then the people come to me... and I, well, I don't even know. I guess somehow I see them on their way. Though I can't imagine where the dead go when they die. I don't even understand where we are now. I remember snippets of things from... the world before. Or I guess I should say, the life before. Heavens. Hells. Places in between."

The embalmer shook her head, as if trying to shake trapped memories loose. "I don't know what Dedalo is. We're not tormented, but there's certainly no everlasting peace and joy. If anything, I think Dedalo is some sort of waiting place. A place where the dead linger... until..." She shivered with confusion. "I don't know. Just like I don't know where we go from here. Or if we do."

Soarsha stared at them. Adults. Always so wrapped up in the big stuff, they never noticed what was right in front of them.

"I cry," said Soarsha. "I bleed. In a city where the dead do neither, what does that make me?"

Not even her dad knew what to say. The adults stood around Soarsha, Soarsha with the tear tracks on her cheeks and a thin streak of crusty brown blood on the side of her face.

Mr. Adbad came over, and took her hands. "We know the truth, Soarsha, and so do you." He tried to keep his voice gentle and calm, yet buried inside the words was an edge he didn't want her to feel.

"It's why I've tried to keep you safe from the other kids," continued Mr. Adbad. "They don't like you because they sense you're different. Unfortunately, some people don't like different, and the dead are still people. Deep down, I think, the children know it most of all. That difference is what they hate. Not what's in you, but what isn't in them: Life."

Das gave a thin smile. "You dream, and care, and live big no matter how small the world around you," said her dad. "You don't respect limits, not the walls, not what others say, nothing. In a world that is dead and of the dead, you dream of a world that lives and is of the living."

"You're not dead," said her teacher. "You're alive. More alive than everything here, than this city, than this entire world. In a city of the dead, Soarsha, you are alive. And you're the only one."

"You've known this too?" said Das. "I thought I was the only one."

"Dad?" said Soarsha. "You knew?"

"About you being alive?" Das smiled, and a light came back to his eyes. "Even in a world of the living, Soarsha, you'd be more alive than anyone else. Your boundless heart. Your horizonless mind." He turned and raised his arm toward the wall. "That's why I wanted to get you out of here. Maybe, I figured, just maybe there'd be somewhere out beyond this place that was as alive as what you deserved."

Soarsha took a step back, letting Mr. Adbad's hands drop. "Then you... when you crashed... if I'm alive, Dad, I can die too."

The light faded from her father's eyes. "I'm sorry, Rainbow. I'm so sorry..."

She shook her head. "What if I'd died, Dad? What if I'd died?" The tears came again, hot and fresh and flooding. Sure, he hadn't meant to. But that didn't matter. He had.

"I guess..." Das raised a finger to his collar. "I guess I figured that there was already enough death here, and you didn't have to worry about it."

"But you didn't know."

Das sighed, and he turned his head, hoping that maybe if he looked in the right direction he could find the right words. "I thought that since dying hadn't killed me, then there was nothing to worry about."

Before anyone could say anything, Das reached up and pulled down the collar at the back of his shirt. The long purple line had faded slightly, but just looking at the bruise made everyone wince.

"After we left Garen's this afternoon, and before my meeting with Nabraig," said Das, "I was back on site to finish up a few things. I'd gone up high, to look out over the site. Think through some next steps. I was up high enough to see beyond the wall, out to where the sun was getting low in the sky to the west. It was beautiful, Soarsha, so beautiful. Yet all I could think about was the hole in my heart."

Das shook his head. "Tomorrow is the day, Soarsha," said Das.

"The tenth anniversary of when we came here. Of when I lost your mother."

Mr. Adbad shuddered, as if he'd just remembered he'd left the oven on. His eyes narrowed, as he stared at Das with what looked to Soarsha like concern. Her father's eyes looked so dim now, so dark, as if the light she usually saw in her father had faded to wisps of smoke and failing embers.

"I haven't wanted to mention it around you, but that hole in my heart is a chasm, my Rainbow," said Das. "It's eating me up. I love you. I want joy for you, despite all else. But no matter what I do, this hole in my heart is getting bigger. It's eating me from the inside, Soarsha. Sometimes I'm afraid that by the time it's done a dark hole of nothing and misery is all that will be left of me."

Das looked up, toward somewhere across the city where, under the dark sky and above the empty streets, the steel skeleton of his and Nabraig's latest project rose.

"When I was up high today, for a moment all that darkness came and took everything from me," said Das. "All my hope. All my love. What was left of my memories, and what remains of my dreams for my daughter."

Das shook his head. Soarsha could see in his eyes that at that moment, he wished more than anything that he could cry. "I felt like all the energy was going out of me. And I... I fell, Soarsha."

Tears trembled in Soarsha's eyes, and her voice shook. "You... went off the building?"

Das laid his hand over his heart. "I didn't mean to. I didn't want to. But all the... well, not life, but... vitality left me. It was like I didn't have bones anymore. Next thing I knew, I was falling. Ten stories, down to the ground below." He glanced at the empty city behind them. "Thing is, nobody saw. No one knew it had happened. During the fall I managed to turn and look up at the sky. All I thought about was you, and your mom, and how I wanted nothing more than to see the two of you again."

"But you're here," said Soarsha.

"Everything went dark for a while," said Das with a nod. "I hit pretty hard—and that line across my neck and shoulders is where I hit. It should have killed me, but it didn't." He raised his palms. "That's when I knew. I knew I was dead, because I didn't die. And didn't bleed. And didn't cry. Like Nabraig said, it was the only thing that made sense." He chuckled. "Good thing though, I suppose. You could say being dead saved my life."

He tried to smile.

Soarsha ran over to him and put her arms around her dad. "I'm glad you're okay," she said.

He ran his hand over the top of her hand. "I don't know if I would say that I'm okay," he replied. "It hurt like hell. Still stings. And as you saw, I was pretty woozy for a while. And, it turns out, I'm dead. So I won't say that I'm okay." Das kneeled down and looked his daughter in the eye. "But I'll tell you what I believe, Rainbow."

"What?"

He smiled, and held her gaze, and a little gleam came back into his green eyes. "I'm not okay, but I believe we will be. We didn't get out of Dedalo, but we will."

Soarsha looked away from him, toward the wall. "It didn't work, Dad."

Das punched his right fist into his left palm. "Then we'll try plan B."

Nabraig came over to them. "I agree," she said. "We wait until the morning bus arrives."

"Exactly."

Mr. Adbad said nothing. He seemed to be lost in his thoughts, and only stood still and looked toward the center of the city, where the golden Spire rose to the sky.

"When the bus comes," said Das, "the gates open. During that moment we'll get out."

Garen came back into the light of the streetlamps, his eyes set with determination, but his voice was soft. "It's worth a try."

Garen looked at Soarsha. "I'm sorry," he said. "I was mean to you." He shook his head. "Even the dead can feel jealous."

"It's... It's okay," said Soarsha.

"Not really," said Garen, "but it's nice of you to say so. It makes sense, though. Ten years in Dedalo, and it's my job to help others find their happiness, but all I think of is how miserable I am. I've always been yearning for what I lost, only I didn't know what it was. Now I do. I lost my life and my memories of that life. They're gone."

"Not all," said Mr. Adbad. "Not yet."

"Do you have things you don't remember?" said Iandel. "Holes in your mind?"

"And in my heart," said Mr. Adbad. "Things I remember knowing, but it's hard to remember the things themselves, like knowing I used to be able to speak a language, but I can't speak the language itself anymore."

"Exactly," said Nabraig.

Behind them, a glint.

Soarsha turned—and smiled.

"The sun's coming up." Her fingers sought out the comfort of her purple crescent pendant and the lavender scent that whispered from it like light from the sun.

"The daily bus comes at dawn," repeated Das. "The daily bus comes at dawn..."

The six of them stood in a line, just off the road, near the gate, so they could dash through right away.

The sun rose over the wall.

Dawn turned into sunrise, which turned into morning, the morning of the tenth anniversary of when Das lost Soarsha's mother, and all six of them rode on the bus to the golden city.

Yet the gate stay closed, and the world beyond the wall stayed silent, and on that day, no bus came to the city of Dedalo.

27

FLUTTERING IN THE BREEZE

No bus.

No gate.

The sun rose higher over the empty city.

No way out.

Soarsha sat down. She dropped her pendant and let it fall back behind her shirt. "The world beyond the wall," she said, "is nothing to see at all." Maybe it was true after all. Like everyone said, even if they didn't know themselves.

Tears wanted to come again, but she was tired of letting them out. Crying had had its moment. Sure, the living could cry, but that didn't mean they had to all the time.

What would the Mrazas do? Gleaming Head might be able to figure out a way to bound over the wall. Perhaps Shirtman's shirt could... confuse the wall? Sapphire's gaze would... Soarsha thought and thought. Sapphire would stare at the wall until it decided it'd be better off turning itself to dirt and going to fill a garden somewhere.

What, though, would Jilly do?

Soarsha wished she'd had a chance to read the finale issue of *Wandering Heroes*. See what happened when the Mrazas crossed the Barrenburn and reached what must be Dedalo. Yet for all her wondering and pondering, Soarsha could not think of what Jilly would do.

"I'm sorry," said her father.

Soarsha stiffened, but she also didn't pull away when he sat down next to her and put his arm around her shoulders. "Not just for this," he added. "For... everything. A parent wants the best life for their children. You've never been happy here, and I want you to find where you can be happy."

"Maybe the other kids had it right, Dad." Soarsha's face felt hot, and suddenly she wanted nothing more than to sleep. "All my dreams... all my wishes to be somewhere else... where have they gotten us?"

Das set his fingers under her chin, and gently lifted her face up to meet his gaze. "Your dreams are something to live for," he replied. "The question is, how are we going to make them come true?"

"Look, I know you're trying to make me feel better," she said, "but there's no way through the wall. We can't wait here forever, Dad, and no gate is opening." Soarsha's eyes burned. Deep inside her mind she told the tears, with Dad-unapproved words, exactly where they could go.

"Maybe my dreams are just a wish that can't come true." She shook her head. "Maybe... Maybe it's time to let my dreams go."

Around them, the sun rose higher, its meager warmth slightly better than the night's chill. No one else spoke. All the others sat or stood here and there amidst the wreckage, mining their memories for something they could recall from their old lives, or trying to think of what to do next, or maybe, heck, for all she knew, wondering when maybe the scathtor would come for them and all this could be over. Did the scathtor take the living too? Or would there come a time when Soarsha would be the only soul in the golden city?

She stared out toward Dedalo, though it wasn't much better to see the abandoned buildings and the empty streets. It was one thing to feel lonely. It was another thing to wind up completely alone. If they couldn't get out of Dedalo... Soarsha shuddered. The scathtor would return. Then Soarsha would be alone... or else she would find out if the living could die in the land of the dead.

Her dad shifted toward her and squeezed Soarsha close. A breeze blew past, full of gray, choking dust. Under Das, something shifted.

A fluttering sound filled the air.

Soarsha looked up.

"What is that?" she asked. The exhaustion fell away.

"I don't know," her dad replied.

Their heads turned this way and that. The others noticed the sound too, and began looking around.

Soarsha looked down. "Dad?" she said.

Das looked down too, then all but leaped sideways.

Under him, paper flapped. No bland and boring black and white newspaper page either. But a page of bright colors.

A page from the finale issue of *Wandering Heroes*.

Soarsha snatched up the page before the breeze could steal their last hope.

The gleaming yet wrinkled paper was battered and creased. Little black charred chomps around the edges looked like the bus wreckage had been nibbling at the page.

Yet there she was.

Jilly. The massive panel of the splash page made her look so small compared to the ringwall. To the child's right, across brown cracked ground, the beige wall of Dedalo rose so that even at the top of the panel the wall kept going, out of sight yet never out of mind, rising through the clear, hazy, empty blue sky. The horses were gone, as if they had run away, and Soarsha knew that something terrible must have happened for the horses to leave the Mrazas.

Soarsha's eyes tightened. Jilly's back was to the reader, but her loose red hair was unmistakable. Her body seemed tense, with feelings that wanted to explode out of her, but she was reining them in, trapping them inside, trying to transform them into something else. Mrazas didn't just feel things, they transformed them. Fear into love. Fury into action. To be a Mraza wasn't just to change the world, it was to change oneself.

To the right of Jilly, two panels, one above the other, were overlaid over the main art. In the top one, Sapphire and Shirtman lay still, their hands touching. And in the other, Gleaming Head lay with some sort of strange shadowy monster, and it was hard to tell where the hero ended and the shadow began.

They were all dead.

All except for Jilly.

Soarsha felt her body tighten too, and again she thought of how much she and Jilly resembled each other.

"So that's what happened," said Nabraig.

Mr. Adbad came over, and Soarsha pointed at the page. "They died," she said, tapping the shadow monster as if she wished she were punching it. "Fighting that..." She looked up at the others. "It looks like the scathtor."

Mr. Adbad stared at the monster, inked as it was in blacks, as if evaluating how accurately the scathtor had been translated from afterlife to comic. "I hope we never have to take that close a look, Soarsha."

"But it does," she said. "I saw it. If the wall there is like the wall here, and if that's the scathtor... I think the comic isn't just a comic. It's almost like this is... this is something that happened."

Iandel pointed at Jilly. "I wonder what she's looking at."

Soarsha peered closer. "Oh," she said. "She's leaning over something, like a little wooden chest that's come open."

The breeze picked up—and knocked the paper from Soarsha's hands.

"No!" she yelled, trying to spring up to grab it, but the breeze had knocked the paper upward, out of the child's reach.

Mr. Adbad lunged forward, trying to grab it, but the breeze danced around him. Soarsha was certain she heard it laugh.

"No!" shouted Garen. "This damn city's taken enough from us!" He leaped, swiping his hand toward paper. The breeze took it out of his reach too—but his other hand came up from behind, and he snatched the paper out of the air.

As he did so, something moved.

A page unfolded.

And Soarsha smiled. It hadn't just been a page. It had been an entire spread from the comic.

Everyone circled around her now. Soarsha smoothed out the spread on the ground, and they peered at the new panels.

No.

One panel.

On the new page, one large panel looked over Soarsha's shoulder, and showed what was inside the little wooden chest.

"Everyone," said Soarsha, "hand me your pendants. Now."

The others looked around.

Das glared back. "You heard my daughter."

One by one, Soarsha set each piece on top of one of the pieces in the comic. Four pieces of ink and color and space—and four pieces of clay. That matched the art exactly.

And in the middle, though, was something else.

A fifth piece. Circular. With points like the points of a compass rose. In the center of the fifth piece, the wreck had torn a small hole in the paper, but it was only a small part of the bigger whole, and the overall picture was clear.

"We're missing a piece." Soarsha's voice rose like the morning sun. "That's why they didn't fit together before. It wasn't because they don't match, or because they're not part of something bigger, something whole." She looked at the adults. "It's because we don't have all the pieces."

"There's something else," said her father. "Look at the lines."

Finger trembling, Soarsha touched the top of the pendant,

where the missing fifth piece had a point like the north point of a compass rose. A twining line curved all around the page, but now, with the fifth piece, it was clear. The line wasn't some strange meandering, not some incomprehensible pattern.

Mr. Adbad leaned in closer. "It's a labyrinth," he said.

"Oh great," said Nabraig. "A maze isn't much of a map."

Mr. Adbad shook his head. "A maze and a labyrinth aren't the same thing," he replied. "A maze has many paths, dead-ends, tricks and twists. Soarsha?" He nodded toward her.

"Aye?"

"Could you please trace the line?"

"Okay." As she touched the page, a hum filled her, like a stream, like a little bolt of lightning, like the relief and excitement of seeing the face of someone you loved but hadn't seen in far too long.

"A labyrinth," said Mr. Adbad as Soarsha traced the line over drawing and clay, "looks complicated, and it has many curves and turns, but it's ultimately only one path. One beginning. One destination. And one way to get there."

Soarsha traced, following the curved line near the center, then swooshing around and back toward the outer edge. Gradually her finger came ever closer and ever closer to the center. Then the path would swing her away—yet again she would find herself closer, and closer, until she traced along the art of the fifth piece in the comic—and reached the hole in the center.

"One destination," said Mr. Adbad. "The center of that piece is the center of the labyrinth."

"That's a great little relaxation exercise," said Nabraig. "How exactly is it supposed to help us?"

Relaxing? Soarsha wanted to laugh. Her heart was pounding. The answer seemed to be right in front of her, as if it were just past the horizon, like when she dreamed she was standing with her mother, and her father was about to come into view.

From the center, she moved her fingertip and set it back at

the beginning of the labyrinth. At the top point of what looked like north on a compass rose. She knew now what Jilly would do.

Jilly would think.

"I am a Mraza," Soarsha whispered so that only her heart could hear. "So I will act like a Mraza. Move forward with love and joy, despite everything else. Go, Mrazas."

She smiled. Maybe they didn't need the gate after all.

"North," said Soarsha. She gently slid the pieces of pendant off the page to the ground, then she stood. Turning, she held the page in front of her. Her gaze followed the north point—until she stood at north.

The northern edge of Dedalo. At the gate.

"Dad," she said, "could you put your back to mine?"

With a nod, he did, and Soarsha handed him his pendant. His warmth was a comfort. They held each other up, and Soarsha used it to help her voice stay steady.

"Point directly south," she said. "What do you see?"

She couldn't see his face, but she was certain he smiled. "The center of the city," he replied. "The obvious center of the labyrinth."

The others put on their pendants too, then all six people stood together, staring south, toward the center of Dedalo.

Where the Spire rose to the sky.

"The fifth piece of the pendant must be in there," said Soarsha. "At the top, I reckon. We find that... I think we'll find answers."

And maybe more, she thought but didn't say. Like what happened to the others. Like Carl. Like Finley. Like my mother.

"Soarsha?" said Nabraig. "What's on the other side of the pages?"

Soarsha looked at her. "Huh?"

Iandel nodded at the page. "It's printed on both sides."

"Oh, right." Soarsha turned the page over. On one side,

Gleaming Head was showing Jilly the leather cord around his neck. On the other page, Gleaming Head was speaking.

"The pendant, complete and whole," said Soarsha, "it's a key."

Garen pointed at the page. "So we complete the key."

Nabraig touched his shoulder. "Then we find the lock."

Iandel touched Nabraig's shoulder. "We open it."

Das held his daughter's hand. "Then we see where it leads."

"There's just one problem," said Mr. Adbad.

Hands fell away from shoulders and Das dropped his daughter's hand.

"What's that?" said Soarsha.

"We don't know where to find the labyrinth," said Mr. Adbad. "This is a city. It's full of streets."

But Soarsha shook her head.

"We know," she said. "The answer is right here." She pointed at the page, and she pointed to where the pendants hung on the necks of the four adults.

"The pendants are silver-gray," she said. "And there are silver-gray streets in Dedalo. I've seen them. Glimpses, then they're gone. But they're there. They must be part of the labyrinth."

"But there's not one here," said Mr. Adbad.

Soarsha started to speak, but stopped. He was right. The street they stood on was black. Black as the scathtor. Black as the night they had barely survived.

What would Jilly do? Soarsha thought.

Then she smiled.

Jilly would get the right perspective.

Soarsha looked at Mr. Adbad. "A labyrinth has only one starting point, right?"

"Yes," replied her teacher. "And one center."

"The heart of the matter," said Garen.

Soarsha walked through the wreckage, until she reached the wall. She pushed at it. Just in case. It didn't open, but hey, it was worth checking one more time.

Then she turned around, and shuffled backward until the wall was against her back, the unyielding stone cool through her shirt and jacket and overalls.

And she smiled.

"Some paths you only know when you travel them not with your feet, but with your soul," said Soarsha. "Come stand next to me."

Excitement flowed from her like dust on the wind. The page rustled in a gentle breeze, but Soarsha held the paper firmly in her right hand, and kept it by her side. Her left hand she raised and pointed down the street. Her father stood to her right, along with Nabraig, and Mr. Adbad stood to her left, along with Garen and Iandel.

"Oh my goodness," said Iandel. "I don't believe it."

"A path of questions," said Soarsha.

"And maybe, at the end," said her father, "answers. A key in a lock."

Beyond the wreckage of the bus, from the wall as far as they could see into the city, the black street had turned to silver-gray.

28

A PATH OF DAY AND NIGHT

From the wreckage behind them to the Spire far, far away in the center of the city, the air above the street shimmered. Iridescent streaks of light flowed down, like looking at a stream of water slicked on top with a rainbow of oil. Then the air seemed to harden, as if the light had become a curved ceiling with straight sides, a tunnel of light and air.

Alone in the sky, the tip of the Spire glowed golden in the morning light. Then, inside the windowed chamber at the top of the Spire, a white light flashed—and then shone on them, steady, not pulsing or going out. Just shining, like a star that had moved from the sky to the city.

Soarsha tried to take in the sight, hold it in her mind and her soul. She wished she could fold up the image before her and tuck it into the pocket of her overalls, next to the folded-up page of the comic. Soarsha was certain, certain of her heart, as certain as Gleaming Head would have been. Their destination was the Spire. What they sought, they would find there. Yet as Soarsha gazed at the top of the Spire, the light seemed to fade.

Her mind screamed no, but the voice at the top of her mind

soon spoke more softly, yet the rest of her mind could not refuse to listen.

The light in the Spire wasn't fading. The entire city was.

The tunnel of light surrounding the six wanderers hardened—and grew opaque. The city winked out of sight. Still there, presumably, beyond the wall and ceiling of the tunnel, but not for them to see again, Soarsha figured, until they emerged from the labyrinth and found themselves, she hoped, inside the Spire. After all, the wall surrounding the Spire had no gate, no opening at all—so if they didn't come out inside the building, she had no idea how they were supposed to get inside.

"Well," said Garen, "I wonder what happens if we try to take a wrong turn."

"You can't get lost in a labyrinth," replied Mr. Adbad. "That's the difference."

Iandel touched the hardened, yet still slightly shimmering, wall. Her fingers pressed against it—then seemed to start passing through it. She pulled back her hand. "It stings," she said, wincing. "Could we even leave this path if we wanted to?"

Nabraig reached down and picked up a chunk of metal that must have come off the wrecked bus. She chucked it at the wall. When the metal made contact, it paused, stopping its path in midair and pressing against the wall—then it soared through. Moments later, a sharp ringing sound resounded, followed by a hard thwack.

"It must have hit something outside and bounced back," said Das.

Soarsha reached toward the wall then pulled her hand back. "But it didn't come through again."

Mr. Adbad touched the wall. "So we have to assume," he said, "that if you go through, you can't come back."

The six of them looked at each other.

Das fixed his gaze on his daughter. "Are you sure about this, Rainbow?"

The final piece of the pendant. A way out of Dedalo. Her mother. The answers to everything they sought. What else might wait in the center of the labyrinth?

Soarsha smiled—she knew there was only one way to find out. She smiled at her father. "I've never been more certain."

The six began walking. By agreement, Das and Soarsha were at the front, then Garen and Nabraig, and Iandel and Mr. Adbad brought up the rear. While opaque, the straight walls and curved ceiling of the tunnels still shone with a swirling iridescence. The tunnel felt closed in, sure, but at least it made a pretty path. Bright as morning, the way gleamed straight and clear.

"It's like we're heading straight toward the Spire," said Soarsha. "Maybe this will be easier than we thought!"

No sooner had she said it than the labyrinth curved. They walked for ages, it felt like, especially with nothing to go by inside the tunnel. Soarsha said nothing, though she was certain that her cheeks must be red enough to glow.

"It's getting darker in here," said Das.

Soarsha blinked, and realized her dad was right. The bright walls had dimmed, like a sudden nightfall. Moments later, she could hardly see in front of her face, but she knew that in the city beyond the tunnel, it was still morning.

"What if we go off the path?" said Soarsha.

"Put your hands out," said Das. "You can feel for the wall."

From the back, Iandel's voice marched to the front. "Everyone stop."

Soarsha did, and turned around, not that it made any difference in what she could or couldn't see.

"What's wrong?" said Soarsha.

Mr. Adbad's voice stepped lightly up in response. "Iandel, I told you I'm fine."

"You looked clammy as hell to me," said Iandel. "If we weren't dead I'd expect you to be mopping the sweat off your head."

"I... Tight places and I don't get along well," replied Mr.

Adbad. "This tunnel... It creeps me out. But I'm okay. For Soarsha. I'm okay."

Soarsha felt her father touch her hand, but she pulled away. A cold uncertainty deepened the darkness between them, then she heard her dad say, "Do you want to come up here, Mr. Adbad?"

"The longer we talk about this," the teacher replied, "the longer it takes to get where we're going. Or for us to suddenly wind up with something behind us that makes this darkness seem like daylight."

They started moving again.

Now that her eyes had adjusted, the dim tunnel wasn't so bad. Soarsha could see farther than she thought. Without the distractions of the light, in fact, she was noticing details she hadn't picked up on before. The darkness sharpened her sight, focused her vision—and, she hoped, her thinking. In her mind, the labyrinth image on the pendant made sense.

She wished she could fly. Thick sunlight would warm her skin. Above all, though, she could look down. She bet she'd see it then. The ringwalled golden city of Dedalo, with its black streets, both concentric rings and straight lines on the compass points, from the center of Dedalo to the wall that separated the now-empty city from the wasteland beyond. And she'd see the labyrinth, imprinted on the city like the pattern on the pendant.

Soarsha wondered how long they'd been walking. Occasionally she thought she could hear Mr. Adbad mutter something—airing his fears, perhaps, or cursing where he was. She was also just as certain that, now and again, she could hear Iandel whispering for him to shut the feck up, only the word didn't sound like feck.

She felt her dad move closer to her again.

"Soarsha?"

Her eyes narrowed. Her dad's voice might as well have been rubble on the path. "What?"

"You seem... distant."

"It's the darkness," she replied. "Makes me seem farther away than I am. I'm right here." Her hands stayed by her side though, and she kept walking. At the same time, her face felt hot again.

What had he been thinking?

The squeals and shrieks came back—not just of the metal ripping, but also of the fear tearing out of Soarsha, out of all of them.

All because of him.

"You said you wouldn't let harm come to me," said Soarsha. Before her father could say anything or reach for her, she walked faster, getting out in front.

So alone. Even with the others around her. So alone now. The only person alive amongst the dead. Yet they felt like family.

All she wanted was a normal life with a normal family. All she wanted was to know her mother—or at least learn what happened to her. Was that too much for a daughter to ask?

No. But trusting her father's word wasn't supposed to be too much to ask either.

She walked faster.

"Please slow down, Soarsha." The pleading in Das's voice was trying to slow her down. He'd wanted to go fast. Why shouldn't she?

"I'm sorry, Soarsha."

His voice came through the shadows. She'd seen so many shadows. Lying there. What happened to the living if they died in the city of the dead? What could have happened, if more had come out from her head than a trickle of blood? Part of her wanted to turn and go to her dad. Take his hand again. Smile at the I'm-sorry honesty that she knew was coming from the deepest part of his big deep heart. And part of her wanted to kick him in the head. Even if he couldn't bleed, he could hurt.

Soarsha stopped. The voices warred in her now, one forgiving and loving, one furious and a hotter red than her hair. Finally, she opened her mouth—but she didn't get to say anything. Or see anything either. The tunnel went black, full of fear and gasps. Full of shadows—and behind them, a low, rumbling roar.

29

THE ONE THING LEFT

Screams happened, along with scratching sounds. Soarsha had hardly turned, had hardly seen the others turn, when Iandel screamed, "No!" and "Mr. Adbad!"

Then dark silence covered everything but Soarsha's pounding heart.

The light returned—but as an insult. The day-bright glow was back, as if the tunnel were its own high noon. All the better to see clearly, but at a time when Soarsha had never wanted to see less. If the tunnel had stayed dark, she could have convinced herself it was only a trick of the shadows. She realized she was clutching her pendant, but for once no scent of lavender filled the air. The fear, the loss, the flat, hot scent of the terror or understanding overpowered everything, even the scent that reminded Soarsha of her mother.

In the clear pure light, though, tricks could not survive. Only plain truth, and the truth pounded at Soarsha, talked calmly at her soul, but never had she so badly wanted silence. No. Not silence. Their voices. And their presences. Here. Not the emptiness where only the memory of Iandel and Mr. Adbad remained.

The space behind the remaining four people was not untouched, though.

Slowly, Nabraig stepped away from Garen, and with careful step approached the rent pavement, and she sank down to her knees. Garen kneeled next to her and ran the tips of his fingers along the parallel ridges separated by narrow gulfs.

Nabraig's voice trembled. "It... It slashed through the pavement like a knife cutting into a block of cheese." For once, the businesswoman wasn't even trying to gird up her words with confidence and mild bravado.

"The scathtor," said the happiness coach, though his flat voice was as empty as the air around him. "It found us. It followed us."

Soarsha stayed back, but Das kneeled down with the other adults.

"What did it do to them?" said Das.

"I guess... it took them," said Nabraig. "Like the others." She took a step back. "Maybe it finally realized it still had some work to do."

"Killed them... Collected them," said Garen. "We have no idea what it's done. But if it emptied out the entire city, why not take us too? Why only two?"

Das shook his head and stood, at the same time clutching his piece of pendant through his shirt. "I don't know. Maybe what it did earlier... weakened it. Like working out too much. Maybe it's... sore?"

Soarsha stared at him as he clutched the pendant. How his eyes always got a little brighter when he did.

Or maybe there was something harder about them that was harder for the scathtor to deal with, she thought. Something about the pendant. Something about each other. Soarsha shook her head a little. Something she couldn't see in the bright light, but so close—

Out of the corner of her eye, though, something snagged her

gaze and she turned. The adults were so busy muttering their theories about the scathtor, the souls, Iandel, and Mr. Adbad, that they didn't see Soarsha kneel down to the edge of the street where the wall began to rise.

She'd almost missed it. No wonder too. On a street of silver-gray, it'd be easy to miss seeing something the same color. And Soarsha hadn't seen it. No. The slender, brown sinuous line had caught her eye, because it stuck out, was out of place, and Soarsha knew exactly what it looked like and felt like to stick out and be out of place.

The hard pavement both smooth like paper and rough like sand, and Soarsha's knees throbbed slightly as she leaned forward. Her fingertip traced the jagged end of the narrow, brown curvy line, then followed it to the middle. She rested her finger on Iandel's silver-gray piece of pendant.

Looking at where the adults were obsessing over the slashes in the pavement, Soarsha rolled her eyes, but she also made herself think. Perhaps the pendant had come off while Iandel struggled with the scathtor. Maybe the scathtor had ripped it off, like perhaps the pendant pieces had some sort of protective power, but only if they were being worn?

Soarsha shook her head. That could be the case. Her eyes narrowed. But it didn't *feel* like the truth. She thought back to the Wandering Heroes, and she pulled the piece of folded-up comic out of her overalls pocket.

No. What felt true was that the scathtor hadn't touched the piece of the pendant. Maybe it was afraid to. Soarsha pulled the piece of pendant off the pavement. So light in her hand. So different from the heaviness in her heart.

Iandel had yanked off the pendant. Broken the cord. And flung it here, hoping they would find it, a clue in the labyrinth.

Soarsha's eyes widened. She turned her head toward where, beyond the opaque tunnel, the gently pulsing golden Spire rose above the city. Iandel had given up her piece of the pendant, in the hope that Soarsha would fit the pieces back together.

They had to get to the Spire. Had to find the fifth and final piece.

As tall as she could manage, Soarsha stood. Put her shoulders back. And looked at the adults.

"Get up," she said.

"But Soarsha," said Das, "we have to make sense of this."

She held up the comic book page and Iandel's piece of the pendant. "This is all the sense we need. We know our path. Iandel ripped this off her and threw it to safety before the scathtor took her."

Garen glared at her. "There's no way you can know that."

Soarsha shook her head. "Whatever you think I know or don't know, know that we have to keep going. We have to get to the Spire. The sooner the better. Before the scathtor returns and picks us off one by one."

Garen took a step toward her. "Look, kid, I know this is hard."

She walked right up to him, almost close enough to touch, and she stood on tiptoes and stared him in the eye.

"And that's why you're going to listen to me." She leaned in closer. "The one who's alive." Soarsha tried to make her voice sound like Gleaming Head's. "Iandel's not here anymore. Mr. Adbad's not here anymore. There's nothing we can do—except one thing. We're moving on."

Das and Nabraig got up and stood next to Garen, and Das nodded his head toward his daughter. "You think that's best?"

Tucking the folded-up page and the piece of pendant into her pocket, Soarsha breathed in deeply. This had to be right. "We won't find answers here," she replied. "But in the Spire, we will. I'm certain."

"Okay," said Das. The pleading was back in his eyes. Maybe some of this agreement was to try to get her to forgive him. But it didn't matter. As long as they followed.

"You lead, kid," said Nabraig—and for a moment Soarsha thought she saw a hint of a smile.

They set off again, faster now, but they walked abreast, with Nabraig to Das's left, then Soarsha, then Garen to Soarsha's right. The turns were coming faster now, and the tunnel stayed bright.

"I think we're close," said Soarsha.

"How can you be certain?" said Garen.

"I'm not." Doubt tugged at her, but she kicked it away. "I'm not certain of much of anything. Just... when I think of how the labyrinth design looked on the page, the way the turns and runs and curves are near the center, I keep thinking that this must be what walking that design must feel like."

"I hope you're right," said Garen.

Soarsha looked at him, and she didn't try to keep the fear out of her eyes. "So do I."

Behind them, close as nightmares, a rumbling roar filled the tunnel.

Garen's head turned. He leaped backward, so that Das and Soarsha were behind him. Nabraig joined him. They both stood like warriors, hands up, legs bent slightly. They looked at each other—and smiled.

Then the tunnel went dark again. Soarsha couldn't see anything. Part of her wished she couldn't hear, but the highest part of her mind was grateful for hearing. If she couldn't see her friends fighting, or see them being taken or killed or whatever the scathtor was doing, at least she could hear it. Know their courage. And know, from that last look in their eyes, their love, their affection, and how they had, without a thought, stood between Soarsha, her dad, and the onrushing danger.

A slender cone of swirling shadows—like an arm, perhaps?—swept out toward Soarsha. She heard Garen's voice shout out, and the shadows were gone. For a moment she had seen Garen, his face so red it could have been a torch. Nabraig was calling out, and there were thumps that shook the tunnel.

A red glow came.

Soarsha realized she had closed her eyes. Opening them, she saw that light had returned to the tunnel. She tried to breathe in deeply, though her jaw, her chin, were already quivering, waiting for the assault of the absence where Nabraig and Garen had stood their ground.

Nabraig and Garen nodded toward each other—then raised their hands in a high five.

"Well," said the businesswoman, "if I'd seen your face, that alone would have made me run."

The happiness coach chuckled. "I guess even shadow monsters have a nose you can sock 'em in. Remind me never to make you mad."

Soarsha looked from one to the other. "You... You scared off the scathtor?"

"Looks like it," said Nabraig.

A whisper of a roar fell through the air.

And Soarsha looked up.

Just as the scathtor let go of the ceiling and fell toward them.

The limbs, the torso, indeed looked like person, or at least a person's shape. Soarsha thought she could see legs and arms, and hands with splayed fingers. All that was solid, dark, and human shaped.

But the head.

Shadows swirled like a slow, small tornado, except for a swirling circle, like an O, that was like a mouth. The scathtor's roar got louder and louder as it fell.

Then the shadow monster was on them. Soarsha rushed through the air. Surely she must have been flung, and the wall was coming up behind her. Her eyes widened. She'd be thrown out— unable to get back in—

Hard pavement scratched at her through her clothes as she skidded to a stop. The wall was just behind her. At least she was still inside the labyrinth.

Then her head smacked the pavement. The world shook, and turned darker than the scathtor. By the time the brightness returned to Soarsha's sight and the world was standing still again, she sat up.

And found herself alone.

30

THE IMPOSSIBLE IMPASSABLE WALL

Shaking, Soarsha pushed herself up and slowly, achingly rose to standing once more. Her face trembled. At least the scathtor was gone, but the others, her dad...

Ridges rose up from all over the street. All around Soarsha, the pavement was slashed again. Inside, she could feel the Spire. So close. But it might as well be in another world.

She'd never make it. The next time the scathtor came, there'd be nothing she could do against it.

"Soarsha!"

Her head whipped left.

Das stood. Staggering, he half-limped, half-walked to her. Soarsha ran to him. He was okay. He was here.

"The scathtor threw me," said her father.

And he'd landed near her. Something in Soarsha loosened, relaxed—she hadn't seen him because she hadn't looked in that direction.

They threw their arms around each other, and Soarsha rested her head against her father's chest.

She felt the voices in her again. One furious. One forgiving.

"I could have gotten you so hurt," said her father. "You must be so mad at me."

Soarsha squeezed him tighter. "I am mad at you," she said. "But I can still forgive you."

Das kissed the top of her head through her hat. "How about I not drive any more buses into walls?"

With a laugh, Soarsha looked up at him. "That's a good start."

"Wherever we go from here," said Das, "if there's sushi and chocolate cake to be found, you can have as much as you want."

"For a month," said Soarsha.

"For a week," said Das.

Soarsha's eyes narrowed. "Two weeks."

Das chuckled. "Deal."

They let each other go, but stood next to each other and stared across and up and down the empty street.

"Do you think the scathtor has taken the others to the Spire too?"

"I do."

Das breathed in deeply, and let out a long, slow sigh. "Then we'd better get there as quick as we can. The day is slipping away."

The day. Soarsha's eyes widened. The day.

"Dad?"

Das gave her shoulder a squeeze. "Yes," he said. "The tenth anniversary of when we lost your mom. And when we came to the city."

"I'm sorry we're here," said Soarsha.

"Wherever you are," said Das, "is where I need to be." He touched his hand to her cheek. "That's what your mom would think too."

"I feel like... there's something important about today," said Soarsha. "Ten years. I don't know what it is, though. But it's there. Like something I don't remember, you know?"

"I feel that too," said Das.

"It's like something that happened when I was a baby," said Soarsha. "It's there. It's part of me. But I don't remember it."

Das's face was all scrunched up.

"Dad?"

"You were never a baby," said Das, his voice so small.

"What?"

"You were never a baby," he said again. "But you were always my daughter."

"I don't understand," said Soarsha.

"I don't either," replied Das. "But I think we will."

They started to walk. Ready to get away from the slashed-up street. Then Soarsha stopped.

"Wait." She dashed off.

"What is it, Rainbow?"

Soarsha stared into ridge after ridge, shadow after shadow, searching but finding nothing. Maybe they hadn't had a chance to. Maybe it hadn't occurred to them. Maybe the scathtor didn't mind the pendants at all—

On the other side of the street, a light glinted.

Soarsha ran to it. And found two pieces of the pendant.

"I think you're right," said Das as he stood next to his daughter while she tucked Garen's and Nabraig's pendant into her pocket. "I think they all realized they had to leave their pieces for you." He put both hands on her shoulders and looked her in the eye.

"If the scathtor takes me," said Das, "I'll do the same."

Soarsha shook her head, and her body felt both hot and cold. "Dad, it won't..."

Das shook his head. "You know it will."

Reaching behind his neck, Das unfastened his pendant and handed it to his daughter. "In fact," he said, "I'm giving it to you now. So you have it. No matter what."

"Dad..."

He touched her cheek again. "It's what Gleaming Head would

have done for Jilly. And it's what I'm doing for you."

She stared at the pendant. Stared at her father. Her eyes were hot, but she also felt calm, and strong, and knew that while what he was doing was hard, it was also right. Just like a Mraza. Just like her. Just like him.

With a nod, Soarsha put the fourth piece of the pendant into his pocket.

They started walking fast, leaving the slashed streets behind, and then they ran. Around the curves they went—until, almost without realizing it, they came around a corner, and the world opened up again.

The tunnel of the labyrinth was gone. Behind them, the walls and ceiling stood for a moment—then collapsed. The two of them turned around, just in time to see the last shimmers fade. The silver-gray street darkened, and turned once more to black.

Das and Soarsha stared at each other.

"Only way is onward," said Das. "Dead or alive, that never changes."

They turned back around. Across the circular street from where they had emerged, the golden Spire rose to the sky and continued its gentle pulse of bright and dark, like a heartbeat of light. So close up now, the Spire was thicker than Soarsha had realized. The height made it look skinnier to her, but the Spire was nearly as wide as the city block where it sat.

Except, of course, for the wall.

The silver-gray wall surrounding the Spire stood, tall and smooth... and blank. While they had emerged from the labyrinth, though, no gate opened before them. No section of wall slid back or dissolved or did anything whatsoever to reveal a secret entrance.

The Spire rose. Yet the silver-gray wall remained gateless, doorless, with no way in.

"I don't understand." Making sure the four pieces of pendant were safe, Soarsha pulled the comic book page out of her pocket, unfolded it, and stared at the center of the labyrinth. "We must be at the center. We made it, Dad. This is where we're supposed to be."

"Just because you do the right thing," her dad replied, "doesn't mean you get some reward. Or if you do, the getting it still doesn't have to be easy. Come on."

"What's the point?"

Das looked at her. "The point is that we got here. And we're going to find a way in. No matter what. It's here. We just have to find it, Rainbow."

She followed her father. He walked right next to the wall, keeping it to his right. She stayed to his left as they walked around it.

And around. And around. Soarsha lost track of how many times they circled the wall.

But there was no way in. No keyhole or barely perceptible switch or lever or pressure plate or anything. No gap or crack or big bright sign that said, "Push."

Just a barrier, keeping them away from the one place they wanted to go.

"I'm sorry," said Das. They stopped walking, and he looked at her, his eyes dim.

"First I hurt you," he said. "Then I failed you. You've always deserved so much more than this, my daughter. My Soarsha. My Rainbow."

"Just one time, Dad," said Soarsha. "Please. For me." She leaned in. It was a cheap shot, but it was still right. "For Mom."

Das stiffened, then his chest heaved and he started off again. They went around one more time. One more search. He pushed at the wall, punched it, pulled at the pavement, leaped at it. Yet with every fall and tumble and wringing of his red-knuckled hands, the wall mocked them with its silent stasis. It remained unclimbable. Unbreakable. With no way through to the Spire beyond.

Once more they rounded the turn that brought them back where they began. It looked the same as ever, except for the swirling shadows of the scathtor waiting for them.

Soarsha screamed and staggered backward. As she stumbled her hand opened. The page of the comic book tumbled away on the empty air and was gone.

The scathtor flung its arms wide and lunged toward her.

The shadows had a heat to them. And a smell. Like hard concrete baked under endlessly hot sun. Like the hot coppery iron scent of blood. Like a wish for life and to be alive, once spring-green and vibrant, now rotting in disappointment, like walking through a forest on the spring edge of summer and smelling the decay and renewal as every step pressed on the endlessly cycling earth beneath.

Soarsha's eyes widened. How did she know things like forests? How did memories remember things she had never lived?

The swirling tornado of the scathtor's head came to a stop. Shadows in the front pulled back, like a mouth stretching into a tall wide O shape, like staring into the top of a whirlpool or a black hole. Yet slightly higher up from the mouth, behind the thinner shadows there, was something else. Brown, not black. Almost familiar.

She closed her eyes. Wondering what would be next. If anything.

A roar filled the air, like a tiger or a dragon or, Soarsha realized, something even fiercer.

A father protecting his child.

Her eyes opened. Das was in front of her, moving faster than she had ever thought her father capable. His hands and feet were a blur as he lashed out at every scrap of shadow that came near Soarsha.

The scathtor roared.

"Not my daughter!" shouted Das. "No more!"

The sorrow was gone—turned into rage. And something else.

Forgiveness flooded her heart. Along with a warm river of love for her dad, and her mom, and for being alive. Her dad knocked the scathtor backward, then turned slightly toward his daughter.

She expected to see rage like Garen's, or determination like Nabraig's, or to hear shock and surprise, like Iandel's and Mr. Adbad's.

But in her father, there were none of those things.

His face was calm. With a small smile. His green shone like the grass in her dreams.

"Joy and love," said her dad, his voice caring and even and true as the fabric the universe. "Joy and love," he said again. "No matter what else. Onward."

Soarsha smiled. Then the scathtor knocked her father backward, and Soarsha went backward too—until she felt the smooth, featureless silver-gray wall against her back.

And she realized something.

Her dad knocked the scathtor away, and the two of them fell to the ground, rolling and tumbling.

Soarsha turned so she could see both the fight and the wall.

The wall.

She raised her hand.

All the times they had walked around the wall, her dad had touched it. But not once had she.

Fingers splayed, Soarsha laid her hand on the silver-gray wall.

With a scream, the scathtor threw Das off it, leaped up, and moved quickly toward Soarsha.

Das knocked into the scathtor from its side, and they tumbled away from Soarsha again. She pressed against the wall—and felt nothing.

Turning, Soarsha now saw a wide gap in the wall. And beyond it, across a simple flat space of silver-gray stone, the Spire rose. Not only that, but a door faced her—closed, but clearly a door.

Soarsha turned. "Dad! Come on!"

Looking up, Das saw the opening too, and he started to move

toward her. But the scathtor saw his hesitation—and it reached up under Das's chin, grabbed him around the throat, and with one hand lifted Soarsha's father off the street.

"Dad!"

She started to run toward him. The hell with the Spire. The hell with the wall. Something was trying to hurt her dad.

Turning as best he could in the scathtor's grip, Das shook his head. "No! You keep going!"

"You've got to come with me!"

Das kicked the scathtor, and the monster released him. Das landed, and staggered slightly, but righted himself.

"You go through," he said. "I won't walk through with you, but I'll still be with you. Just like Mom."

Her face was hot again. "No," she said, but her voice was smaller than the pieces of pendant in her pocket. The hole in her heart throbbed—and grew bigger.

"Yes," said Das. "You must. Remember, Soarsha: You will always know, and you will always have what you need." Then he turned. The scathtor had swung a sharpened shadow toward his heart. But Das did the same. His hand no longer seemed like a hand; it was as if he had somehow swung a sword. No. Not swung a sword. Become a sword. Her father wasn't a sword, of course. But he moved like a sword moved.

Das and the scathtor fell—and were still. But Soarsha could see her father, clutching the scathtor, trying to keep it still long enough for her to get away.

"Go," said her father. "Onward, and seemingly alone, yet always with those who love you."

The scathtor seemed to reach into Das's heart—but her dad also seemed to reach into the scathtor's. Around them, above them, the windows of the empty skyscrapers shattered.

Tears running down her face, Soarsha stepped through the gate. The wall closed behind her, and she could see her father no more.

PART IV

THE CENTER IS NOT THE HEART

31

LAST SOUL IN THE GOLDEN CITY

The silence of the empty city pressed down on Soarsha's shoulders. No sound came from her father or the scathtor, but Soarsha doubted that the scathtor was dead. She smiled for a moment, though: Her father had really given it a kicking.

My dad can beat up your shadow monster, she thought.

She laughed, her voice the only sound in the city of the dead, tinkling like rain along what was left of the windows in the surrounding skyscrapers. The laugh faded. Uncertainty trembled through her now. Fear for her dad. Fear for the others. Above those whispering voices of doubt, smaller voices got bigger, louder, clearer, and stronger.

The answers are inside the Spire.

The only way is onward.

Soarsha reached into her overall pocket. She breathed in, closed her eyes, and pulled out everything she felt there.

Then, finally, she let herself open her eyes and exhale.

In her palm, all four pieces of the pendant were there—and unbroken. Or, rather, not broken any more than they already were. With a sigh, she returned the pieces of pendant to her pocket, then reached up to her neck and pulled out the little purple crescent stone that her father had given her for her birth-day. No scent came now, as if the lavender infused in the stone had exhausted itself.

Her birthday. Barely two days ago. When there were people in the city. Or souls. Whatever was here. But there had been a father and a girl, and sushi and chocolate cake, and snuggles and stories and laughter and the warmth of the heart. All the things that made life—or whatever this was here—worthwhile.

Now, nothing. Leaning back, Soarsha stared up the impossible height of the Spire and rubbed the little stone between her finger and thumb, and relished the slight pressure of the brown cord around the back of her neck. Trying to follow the full length from bottom to top of the tapering needle of the city's tallest structure was like trying to look at every star in the sky. The scale was so immense, her gaze kept slipping, or leaping upward, or flitting off to the side to see the darkening sky again. If she'd been trying to climb up the Spire from the outside, she would have fallen off a thousand times.

Well, not a thousand times, she thought. Just once is all it would have taken.

It also didn't help that the Spire glowed with golden light as rich as melted butter. Soarsha closed her eyes, tilted her head back as far as she could, then opened her eyes again. The needle met the sky. Even here, at the bottom of the Spire, as she looked up, a white glint at the top of the Spire looked back, as if staring through the floor of whatever was at the top of the Spire.

Whatever that god was doing, Soarsha thought, I wonder if they're enjoying the show.

After all, with no one else left in Dedalo, Soarsha's little soul was the only show in town. While the light inside the top of the Spire glowed brightly, the daylight on the Spire was fainter and dimmer now. Afternoon was giving way to evening, and Soarsha realized she needed to get moving. Whatever was significant about today, this tenth anniversary, she needed to have it figured out by midnight. If she didn't, something unique, something singular, was going to be lost, never to be found again.

Dad's depending on you, said the small strong voice inside.

So is Mom.

Crossing the gray stone between the wall and the Spire, Soarsha stood in front of the door. Maybe it was like the wall: If she touched it, the door would open. Soarsha raised her hand again, splayed her fingers, and rested her hand on the door.

Nothing happened. The door had no idea the only living person in Dedalo was there.

"Hello?" It felt so silly to call out when she knew in her heart there was no one inside, but she might as well try.

She looked at and felt and listened to and even licked the doorway. While there was clearly a door, there was no apparent way to open it.

Or maybe it was the wrong door. That was always the trouble, her dad had liked to say. Things that seemed obvious and apparent were, in fact, obvious and apparent, but rarely useful or correct. Soarsha shuddered, and her eyes felt hot. It was one thing to know her dad was dead. It was another to think of him not in the now, but in the past.

Walking around the Spire, though, did not reveal another way in. The golden material of the Spire stretched to the sky and dug into the ground, and the only thing different about the structure was the one door that had been facing her when she came through the wall.

Returning to the door, Soarsha put her back to it and pushed.

"Come on!" she yelled. "Come on!"

The door did not yield.

Her legs shook. It'd been a day. A day of walking and fearing. A day of running and crashing a bus into the wall. A day when she now found herself completely alone, in a massive city that might as well have been a cemetery of souls. The concrete of exhaustion poured through her body, until she was too heavy for her legs to bother holding her up anymore. She sank down, back against the door, until she was sitting on the gray stone. She might as well be the last speck of dust in the city. The world. No mother. No father. No friends. No one who even knew her name. Completely and utterly alone. Iandel had said that what the monster took did not come back. After taking Finley and Carl, and then every soul in the city, and then Iandel, Mr. Adbad, Garen, Nabraig, and her father, Soarsha didn't expect the scathtor to suddenly start giving back what it took.

Of course, she reckoned, she could probably open up the gap in the wall again. The scathtor was there, waiting, furious to have been wounded, impatient to take the last soul in Dedalo. Soarsha wondered what it would feel like when the shadow claws sank not into a dead soul but into living flesh.

But Soarsha didn't get up to go to the gate. Too tired. Too exhausted. Too empty.

A tear fell down her cheek. Well, not totally empty yet. Still a few tears left. So Soarsha laid the back of her head against the wall, and cried. Eventually, as the tears finished, she noticed how warm the stone felt. Warm like the air near a candle flame. She had never sat next to a fireplace, she knew she hadn't, but she also knew that this was exactly what it felt like, to sit cold bones by the living flickering fire, and as if by some sort of magical transfer, feel the warmth and light and life transfuse into the your own body and soul.

Rolling back her stinging eyes, Soarsha looked up toward the top of the door. Then her brow scrunched, and she sat up. The concrete of weariness crumbled out of her as she scrambled to her tired feet.

At the right edge of the doorway, she noticed something she hadn't seen before.

A little depression. Almost like a hole, curved and slender.

The only change in the entire texture of the entire doorway and the entire Spire.

A hole.

Keys fit into holes.

"What key, though, do I have?" said Soarsha. No piece of the pendant would fit the small hole, which seemed barely bigger than the tip of her thumb.

Her touch didn't do anything to the Spire. She had no proper key. Nothing else around the Spire looked any different from anything else. The pieces of the pendant were too big to be useful here.

Fear wrung more tears toward her eyes, but she pushed them back. She'd had her time to cry. Now was her time to keep going. Onward. The way a Mraza would. The way her mom and dad would want her to.

She leaned in closer and stared, and traced her fingertip around the gentle curve. Her eyes widened.

"It has to be," she said. "Or else I truly have nowhere to go."

The hole wasn't just a slender curve.

It was a crescent.

Soarsha smiled. Leaning back and standing straight, she reached up to her neck again and pulled out the little purple stone her dad had given her. A last hint of lavender whispered in the air, then faded. Soarsha lifted the pendant off her neck, just as her father had done with his own pendant moments ago.

Soarsha pressed the little crescent stone against the depression.

It clicked against the surface. But did not go in.

Hot frustration pressed at Soarsha now, and the low voice, the low growl in her mind started chittering at her. But she breathed, and the better voice high up in her mind told her that there was only one way. Only one fit. Precise.

Soarsha slightly turned the little stone. Stared closely at its edges and the edges of the keyhole.

Then pressed again.

The little crescent slid into the keyhole, this time with a click like the first turn of a switch, the first turn of a gear, the first excited step to watch the sun rise on a new day.

Removing the stone and putting the pendant back around her neck, Soarsha stepped back. She stared up at the top of the Spire. A white glint of light seemed to wink back at her.

Silvery light spilled out of the door as it opened. Soarsha smiled, and stepped into the glowing silence of the Spire. The door closed behind her. She stood in a softly lit, narrow silver-gray room—which began to softly shake. Soarsha shot out her hands and braced against the walls. Then the floor, and the little elevator car surrounding her, began to rise.

Soarsha relaxed and returned her hands to her sides. The door had closed without leaving so much as a slight gap or crack, as if the material were all one substance, one surface, that had now become solid and one again. No pad of buttons was anywhere to be seen, nor were there any gaps or hatches or any differences whatsoever in the surface. No controls. Only up or down. The street or the sky.

The elevator rose quickly; the new anchor of her stomach wanted to fall through the floor, but after a few minutes she got used to the feeling. It was strange, but not painful. She felt a little woozy, but not in danger of hosing down the elevator floor with what little was in her empty stomach.

She thought of when there had been people in the city, people she could walk by, or pause near, and listen to what they were seeing. Knowing the height of buildings at a glance had been a minor hobby of many people in the city. Twenty-seven stories. Ninety-five. Forty-two. Yet no matter how many buildings a person had effortlessly and immediately cited the height of, whenever their gazes landed on the Spire, they said nothing. If they guessed at all, it was a number they shared only with themselves, like a secret lottery ticket that, if they guessed right, would let them out of the city.

As the elevator rose, Soarsha wondered how many people had

been making up numbers when they looked at the building. They weren't specifying. They were guessing. Numbers in the dust. A way to pass the endless time.

What else were people just guessing at?

Everyone knew that there was no way out of the golden city of Dedalo. Just as everyone knew that even if you did get beyond the northern gate, the world beyond the wall was nothing to see at all. Everyone knew that the silver-gray wall surrounding the Spire had no gate. And everyone knew that the Spire had no door.

Now, as the elevator rose, Soarsha stood in the center of the narrow car and began to realize something.

What everyone knew was not a damn thing.

Everyone also knew that the scathtor was taking people. Her father knew that her mother was lost.

What else was she about to learn?

Soarsha didn't try to count or guess or estimate the endless stories the elevator climbed. For a little while she wished the walls would transform into windows, but at the same time she liked being in the simple, apparent, tight space of the elevator. Closed in. No one around. No hidden places where the shadows could grow claws. Soarsha hadn't felt this safe since the last time her dad had hugged her.

The elevator's speed changed. A subtle whisper of slow. She might have missed it, if not for the lightening of the anchor in her belly. With a little gasp, a machine's sigh of relief, the elevator puffed to a stop. Soarsha didn't even stumble. She instead took a deep breath, and stared at the door, and waited to see what would happen next.

And she waited. She cocked her head.

The door didn't open.

A slow-burning panic began to rise in Soarsha, little flames growing hungrier for flammable calm. She turned around and around again. Perhaps she was facing the wrong wall. She touched the walls, pushed at them, looked for little depressions where the stone might fit.

Nothing.

No way out.

With a hard low thunk, the floor of the elevator shifted. Perhaps the bottom was about to fall out—and the entire ride had been a ruse. To rise to the sky, only to fall to the unforgiving ground below.

But the floor didn't fall. Instead, the walls of the elevator looked shorter.

Soarsha looked down, and understood.

There was no door to open. Nor was the floor falling. It was rising.

The ceiling, however, hadn't changed. No magical hatch opened. No gaps appeared in the solid material to assure her that she was simply rising to the top, as opposed to being squashed into jelly between the floor and the ceiling of the elevator car.

Soarsha crouched down. She balled her hands into fists. Forget panic. Those little fires got burned up in bigger ones. Fury. Justice. Purpose.

She wasn't going to die pressed into a thin disc, like a cookie sandwich with an unspeakable filling. She roared. She'd punch her way through the damn ceiling. Her fists pattered on the unmoving ceiling like dust against the skyscrapers—and had about as much effect.

"No," said Soarsha. "No…"

She wanted to close her eyes, but she forced them open. If the last soul in the golden city was about to die, she at least would see it happen for herself—and know that it was real.

32

BEACON IN THE DARK

Gaze fixed and unwavering, Soarsha stared at the center of the ceiling. Then it stared back.

A little circle appeared in the center of the material, dark like the pupils of her own eyes. Then, as the circle in the ceiling got bigger, curved gaps began to appear, radiating from the hole in the center to the edge where the ceiling met the wall. The lines turned the ceiling into a circle of curved triangles, like teeth, but the teeth weren't growing. They were shrinking, pulling back from the center as the hole got bigger and the gaps got wider, until the ceiling had completely retracted.

Soarsha stood tall, her feet slightly apart, as the floor of the elevator raised her through the gap where the ceiling had been. Moments later, the floor leveled out with the floor of where she was now, and stopped. The sky, the streets, entire world spread out around her, with no walls, ceiling, or floor to obstruct her view.

The top of the Spire.

Soarsha smiled, and looked down and up and all around at the clear expanse above and beyond and below her.

The world was so much bigger than people imagined.

Here she was at last: on the cusp of all answers. The fifth piece of the pendant. Her mother... or at least what had happened to her. A way to find those the scathtor had taken. At last. She was here. And she was ready.

Soarsha smiled. Yet as the floor plate stopped moving, the slight jerk of the loss of momentum made her stumble forward, off the silver-gray square she'd been standing on—and out over the empty air a world above the hard black streets far below.

Soarsha shrieked. She was falling forward now, no way to go back, no way to catch herself, no way to do anything but watch the streets get closer until they were too close.

She thrust her hands out in front of her—and hit something solid. So did her feet and knees.

Solid, but invisible.

As she shifted her hands backward, a low stuttering squeak replied to her pounding heart like a laugh. Leaning her weight on her right hand, Soarsha raised her left hand and rapped gently on what was beneath her.

A hollow knocking sound filled the top of the Spire.

Soarsha smiled. Knocked again. And stared through what she could feel but could not see.

Glass. The entire top of the Spire was made of glass. Perfectly solid. Perfectly clear. The top of the Spire wasn't made of windows; it was all one window, curved and round, jointless, flawless, and perfect. And, Soarsha hoped, unbreakable.

Getting back to her feet, next to the silver-gray floor that had brought her to the top of the Spire, Soarsha turned slowly and marveled at what she saw. Nothing blocked her view. Above her, the sky was close enough to touch. Below her, she could see straight down the golden length of the Spire. From here, the streets of Dedalo might as well have been black thread.

Her head felt light. She swayed slightly, blinking. Gradually her body and mind adapted to the strange feeling of standing in midair. The world steadied—and, at last, the city made sense.

Turning slowly, she saw the long, straight streets, north, east, south, and west, radiating out from the wall surrounding the Spire to the ringwall at the edge of the city. She saw the concentric circles, mostly perfect, of the ring roads radiating from wall to wall. The streets were black, except for a winding silver-gray path, complicated yet simple. From here the labyrinth looked so beautiful, but the lovely design clashed hard with the slashed pavement, black terror, and loss of friends and father that Soarsha had survived to get here.

Tears stung Soarsha's eyes. Even in the dying gloom of day's fading light, even empty of souls and golden dust, even with all that had happened, the golden city of Dedalo really was beautiful.

If what came after death could be so beautiful, thought Soarsha, how beautiful could life be?

She let herself walk now, though for the first steps she kept her eyes closed. She opened her eyes again only once her mind stopped yelling at her that she should quit trying to walk on air, that sooner or later the illusion would break, break like thin weak glass, and she would fall, and fall, and fall...

But Soarsha smiled. She wouldn't fall. Not here. For all she knew, from here she could fly.

Soarsha's footsteps made no sounds, and there was a slight give in the glass floor, like what walking on clouds and daylight must feel like. Crossing the floor, Soarsha walked as far as she could, hands out in front of her slightly, using the ending daylight to guide her to the southwest. She stopped only when a bonk on her nose told her she had reached a wall. Behind her, the small disc of the elevator platform seemed at least a block away.

Looking down toward the southwest quadrant of the city, she found the building where she and her dad lived. Her eyes tightened. Had lived. No matter what, she knew, there was no going back there. Nor was there a dad to live with. Not anymore.

Following the straight street to the western edge of the city, Soarsha's gaze leaped over the wall, across the barren plain below.

More than ever she saw the resemblance between the wasteland of the world before her eyes, and the Barrenburn, as Gleaming Head had called it, drawn on the pages of *Wandering Heroes*. The plain of the Barrenburn extended to the edge of sight. Yet even as she strained her gaze to see as far as possible, Soarsha was certain that just at the edge of the farthest she could force herself to see, a fuzzy green line began, wavering in her sight like slender blades of tall grass in a gentle breeze.

Green. Soarsha's eyes narrowed. There was something about green, something she had noticed but not marked. Now it pulled her gaze back from the edge of the grassland, following the last dim daylight across the Barrenburn, over the wall, back across the vast expanse of the circular city, to the base of the Spire itself, right back at the center of Dedalo. Down below, just across the street to the south, a square green warehouse squatted, the size of an entire city block. And the only building in the city, as far as Soarsha could see, that wasn't a skyscraper.

Soarsha stared at it. And remembered. Nabraig had talked about it. She hated it, and wanted to tear it down and replace it with another skyscraper, only that apparently the "old codger" who owned it wouldn't negotiate with her. She and Iandel had been talking about it, and so had Nabraig and Das, a potential new project.

The last of the light faded, and night's darkness came quick as a falling blade. Soarsha couldn't see any skylights in the rusted, corrugated metal roof, but there must have been cracks or gaps in it somewhere. From inside the warehouse, as long as the block-sized building yet thin as paper, a golden light began to shine, the same brilliance as the Spire, a beacon in the dark calling to her. She gazed at the light—then the light from the warehouse went out, and the squat green building was dark.

Turning to look across the top of the Spire, Soarsha could more or less approximate where the other walls were. She could also see where the narrow, round shaft of the Spire met the top, marked only by the silver-gray floor panel in the center of the room.

Again Soarsha's stomach felt like a heavy anchor. She dashed across the glass to the floor of the elevator, and searched frantically, yet she found no buttons or switches or hatches or subtle keyholes or pressure plates. Nothing to indicate a way to open the elevator, or lower the floor, or leave the top of the Spire at all. The edges of the silver-gray plate seemed to meld seamlessly into the glass—no gaps, no sign that there was any way back down.

Soarsha took a step back. Just like the elevator door and perhaps even the gap in the gate, this was another one-way trip. For all she knew, maybe the elevator itself had vanished too.

Whether floating on light or floating on darkness, the glass top of the Spire was beautiful. The city below and the world beyond the city were beautiful. But she hadn't realized that it was all a beautiful trap, and it had caught her.

Then Soarsha remembered: the white gleam, which she had seen so many times from the world below. The staring glint in the Spire. The sign that the god was looking at you.

Yet as Soarsha looked around the top of the Spire, and ran to and fro, along the perimeter and end to end, there was nothing here. No light. No being. No presence. No nothing. Just a girl at the top of the world, who for the first time wished she were back on the simple streets, where the Spire had once been something to look up to and hope you'd see a light.

There was no god here. Not any more than there was a way out.

No were there answers. Or a fifth piece of the pendant.

Soarsha's face felt tight.

Nor was her mother there. Or anything that might explain what had happened to her. Only a terrified girl who had lost her dad, and her world, and her hope.

Night lay thick over the city now, and the darkness had cut off any sight of the world. Head down, Soarsha walked back over to the southwest part of the glass. She lay down, and fixed her gaze on the building where she and her dad had lived. Then she closed her eyes and wished that, if she were to open them again, it would be to find answers before her.

The girl lay floating on the dark. Below, a world away, a harsh, low, rumbling roar reached up from the black streets and scraped at the glass below her sleeping face.

33

FIRST STORM OVER DEDALO

Blotting out the night's darkness, the faint light glowed a soft silvery blue, and as if with fingers touched Soarsha's face.

"Soarsha."

The voice was familiar. Not a shout or a whisper in the dark. Just calm and even, with a hint of a laugh. A voice of love and joy. Maybe that was why she bothered opening her eyes, though she'd closed them moments ago. Nothing left to lose. Nowhere to go— and nowhere she could go. Exhaustion, despair, and futility gnawed at her.

"Soarsha."

Getting to her knees and then to her feet, Soarsha ignored the dark sky above and the dark city below. She looked only toward the center of the top of the Spire.

Where the ghost floated.

"I guess it makes sense," said Soarsha. "Other than me, everyone here is dead." She shook her head. "I'm sorry," she continued. "That means you're dead too."

Carl, the disappeared bus driver of the No. 33, floated toward her. He wasn't wearing his uniform anymore. Instead, he wore a white tuxedo with a white tie, silvery and blue in the soft light.

The combination made his dark skin as lustrous as moonlight—and Soarsha smiled to see how the tux matched his hair. It was his eyes, though, that held her. Dark and kind, with a ready honest laugh, just like his voice.

"I am dead too," said Carl, nodding. He floated in front of her. "I have been for longer than I can remember."

"The scathtor took you," said Soarsha.

"It did," said Carl. "And it took me here. And the others. They're here, in the Spire."

"My dad?"

Carl started to respond, but paused. "You'll get to that, okay? There's something I want to go over with you first."

Soarsha cocked her head. She didn't like it, but she wanted to trust him. But they would get to it. "Did the scathtor hurt you?"

"Actually." Carl smiled. "No."

"No?"

"The scathtor's not what you think, Soarsha," said Carl. "All of us, in this city... There are cities like this all over the place."

"Because you're dead."

"Because we're... waiting," said Carl. "After we died, we went to another city. A city of gates. Not like Dedalo, though. The buildings were low, and the streets were narrow, and my oh my, they had the best mango lassis. Every soul had a choice to make. Every soul entered through the Fall Gate to the west. There was a Spring Gate to the east, and through there we would go on to whatever was next for us. There was a Summer Gate, to the south, the one used most rarely."

"Why would it be used so little?" said Soarsha.

"Because not only was it a path back to the land of the living," said Carl, "it was a way back to the life you had before. A way to pick up where you left off."

"What's the gate in the north, then?" said Soarsha. "I take it that's the one you took?" She leaned forward. "The one my dad took?"

"The Winter Gate," said Carl. "It's... many things, but it's mainly what people decide it's going to be. Some hold to a belief that they must be punished, so they go through to whatever hell or torment they believe is theirs to endure."

"Please tell me that's not what you did," said Soarsha. "Or my dad..."

"Not in the slightest," said Carl. "Some of us... we go through the Winter Gate because we know there's something we need to wait for." He kneeled down, so he was level with her gaze. "Just so we're clear, Soarsha, the souls in this city weren't all waiting around for some living girl to show up. Their fates aren't bound to yours, and vice versa. There is, however, a time. A reckoning. A time of decision. For all of us here, our times are all at the same time. Why it's like that, well, as I used to say when I was alive, that's way above my pay grade."

"So you're saying that the scathtor took everyone... all your souls... because... it was time for you to leave?"

"That's right," said Carl. "The bus, the gate—none of these are a way out of the city. The Spire is." He cocked his head. "For me and a few million other souls, anyway."

Soarsha sighed. What he wasn't saying was as clear as the glass under her feet. "But not for me," said Soarsha. "I came all this way." She shook her head, and forced the tears back into the furnace of her heart. "*We* came all this way. But now they're all gone. I'm alone."

"So you take me to my cue," said Carl. "Before I left, I made it clear that I wanted to be the one to explain things to you. The big stuff. And one other thing."

That was nice. But rocks felt like they were tumbling through her soul. "Why not my dad, though?" said Soarsha. "Why not my mom?"

"That's the thing you haven't learned yet," said Carl. "You mom isn't here, Soarsha."

"But my dad has always said he lost her," said Soarsha. "Right before he and I came here."

Carl leaned in closer. "Did he ever say she died?"

Soarsha opened her mouth. Closed it. "No," she replied. "Not once. Not ever."

"He didn't know," said Carl. "He lost your mother not because she died..."

Soarsha's eyes widened. "But because he did." She took a step backward, her head shaking, her breath staggering. "My mother... My mother is alive."

"She's not here." Carl raised his hands a little, just below his shoulders, his palms pointing to the sky. "This is a place of the dead, Soarsha. Not the living."

Carl smiled, and he winked at her, then reached out to where her hands were. He didn't hold her hands, she realized, but she could feel him, a slight pressure, like a kind hand on a cheek hot with tears. Nor was his touch the cold clammy chill of ghost stories. Instead, it was the warmth of a person whose soul had learned to live with their hurts and turn them into love and joy, despite all else.

"Your mother, you amazing child, is alive," said Carl. "Alive. And waiting for her daughter."

Soarsha trembled, and her chin quivered. "But... where?" she said.

"Back where you came from," said Carl. "The world where you were alive. Where your dad was alive. Where your mother still lives—and wants to hold her daughter again."

"Thank you," said Soarsha. "Thank you for everything. Every kindness." A memory flashed like lightning through her mind, as recent as a couple of days ago yet feeling like years past.

"Thank you for letting me on the bus," she said, though the memory faded so quickly she was both glad she said it yet puzzled as to why.

"Be kind where we can," said Carl. "People spend lives and afterlives searching for the meaning to life. You've already got it."

"Kindness," said Soarsha. "Joy. Love. No matter what else."

"And, above all," said Carl, "living your truest self for the best life you can manage."

Floating upward slightly, Carl started moving back toward the center of the top of the Spire.

"There's one other thing you need to know," he said. "About the scathtor. And that pendant in your pocket."

"I could also do with a way out of here," said Soarsha.

Carl smiled. "Don't worry," he said. "It's coming."

"What about the scathtor?"

"Now that I'm about to leave," said Carl, "I remember what happened the day you got on the bus. Not all of it, but most of it. When you were outside the city."

"Like Jilly," said Soarsha. "Am I Jilly?"

"Better to say that Jilly is you," said Carl. "When you got on the bus that day, as we came into the city, something else got on too, only we didn't know until it was too late."

"The scathtor," said Soarsha. "I thought it had died, along with the hero who killed it." The color fell out of Soarsha's face. "If Jilly is me, then you're saying that Gleaming Head... and that shadow monster in the comic... they lived too? And still do?"

"More than that," said Carl. "Both survived, but neither was as they were before. They are soul and shadow, melded, trapped together as the scathtor. On the bus, it tried to fight you—"

"And my dad," said Soarsha. "And Iandel, and Garen, and Mr. Adbad, and Nabraig." Confusion trickled through her. "But it didn't take us."

"You and those pieces of pendant vexed it," said Carl. "You stopped it. That shadow is here to help souls move on—but a living vivid vibrant girl like you stumped it good. The scathtor fled the bus. The others... you... your memories were hazy. Mine are too, but as we neared the bus station, I remember you taking this long cord off your neck, cutting it into shorter pieces, and giving each of the people riding with you a piece of that pendant to wear."

"I did all that?" said Soarsha.

"Your time in the city, and the power of the scathtor, have made it hard to remember, even for me—I had to be on the edge of life to find the memories again," said Carl. "The hero and the shadow are one. Find the scathtor, and you'll find your way—and, I figure, do a lot of good in the process." He nodded toward the sky. A golden glow was edging into the darkness, but not the glow of dawn.

"It's time for me to go," said Carl with a grin. "Onward. What I was waiting for, it's time for me to go to it."

"I'm happy for you," said Soarsha.

Kindness and joy gleamed in Carl's eyes. "I am too," he said. "And I'm happy for you."

"I'm trapped up here," said Soarsha.

"No you're not," Carl replied. "It's just not quite time for your ride."

Floating above the center of the room, halfway between sky above and city below, a blue and silver glow began to surround Carl.

Soarsha's eyes widened. "Carl?"

"Yes?" He leaned slightly forward from the glow, so she could see his face more clearly.

"The day you vanished, when the scathtor took you," said Soarsha, "what were you going to tell me?"

Carl chuckled. "I was going to tell you about the silver-gray streets, and what little I knew of the labyrinth," he replied. "In short, I was going to tell you everything you managed to figure out yourself." He nodded toward her. "Keep that in mind, dear girl. You don't need us to tell you anything. You already know. It's just a matter of when you understand."

"Good luck, Carl."

He leaned back into the light. "You too, Soarsha. You too."

Then the glow faded, and Carl was gone.

Only after the darkness returned to the chamber did Soarsha realize that Carl hadn't told her what she needed to know about her father.

Soarsha smacked her leg. She wanted to kick the glass, stomp at it, but that was the sort of thing a kid did, and she didn't feel like a kid anymore. But for a moment, just a moment, she wanted to rage like one. She shook her head. The one thing she needed to know.

"Where will you go, Dad?" said Soarsha. "What were you waiting for?" She closed her eyes. "And why didn't you take me with you?"

Through her closed eyelids came a blue and silver glow.

"Dad?" Soarsha opened her eyes and stared again at the center of the chamber.

But her father wasn't there.

Soarsha's eyes widened. "Finley?"

"Hi," said Finley. The child floated like Carl did, but didn't wear a tux. Finley was wearing overalls that looked a lot like Soarsha's, but the silvery blue glow made it hard to tell the color. Like Soarsha, too, Finley wore a low-brimmed hat.

"It suits your eyes," said Soarsha.

"I'm here because I asked to be," said Finley. "I didn't get to be your friend. I... I didn't get to make everything up to you. I don't have long, but I wanted to be the one to tell you."

"Look, that's really nice," said Soarsha. "And I don't want to sound like it's not good to see you..."

"Your dad isn't here," said Finley.

"He's gone on already?" Soarsha turned away. The hole in her heart felt as big as her heart now. As big as the darkness beyond the Spire. As big as the universe, and just as empty.

"That's not what I mean," said Finley. "Your dad is waiting for you. Only he's scared, because he doesn't know where you are, or what's happening with you."

"But my dad... he's dead too," said Soarsha. She waved her hand toward the dark sky. "So shouldn't he be... you know... moving onward with the rest of you?"

"I don't remember how I died," said Finley. "I know what's happened to me, and what Carl told you. It's all true. We came to Dedalo to wait. I know what I was waiting for, and that it's time for me to go. I also know that's why your dad isn't here, Soarsha. He's still waiting."

Soarsha shook her head. Anything to keep from crying. "What could he possibly be waiting for?"

"Remember how Carl told you there were gates in the other city?" said Finley.

"Aye."

"We're all leaving to go back to the city of gates," said Finley. "It's time for us to leave the Winter Gate, and take our turn going through the Spring Gate. On to what it's time for us to do."

"But that's not what my dad is waiting for," said Soarsha.

"No," said Finley. "But not just your dad. Iandel, Nabraig, Garen, Mr. Adbad. It's... It's complicated, Soarsha. But there are things for you to learn." Finley leaned closer. "The scathtor isn't done either. You will have to face it again... and you will have to face it alone."

Soarsha looked down through the floor. "I might have plenty of worries up here," said Soarsha, "but apparently a shadow monster isn't one."

"You aren't staying here," said Finley. "You're going back to the city."

Soarsha looked around the empty chamber. "Elevator seems to be out of order. Besides, I thought the fifth piece of the pendant would be here," said Soarsha. "I came to the center of the city. The end of the labyrinth."

"That's why you haven't found the pendant here," said Finley.

"It's not at the center of the city. It's at the heart of the city, and the center is not the heart."

"Wise dead people talk in riddles a lot," said Soarsha.

Finley leaned forward and laughed a small laugh. "I'm still a kid too."

Stepping closer, Soarsha stood near Finley. Then she leaned in and kissed Finley on the cheek, and it felt like touching a puff of warm sunlit air.

"I've got to go now, Soarsha," said Finley. "Thank you for helping us. And know that it's almost your time."

"What do I have to do?" said Soarsha.

Finley smiled. "You'll see. You'll know. And then you'll do."

The silver and blue glow suffused the child. Then Finley, like Carl, like every other soul in the city, was gone.

Soarsha sighed. "I hope you're going where you want to be," she said, thinking of Finley, and Carl, and every other soul.

The Spire shuddered. The golden light grew brighter. Soarsha fell to her hands and knees. She looked through the glass, down toward the streets and the bottom of the Spire—and she gasped.

From the street upward, the Spire started going black. Darkness spread from the bottom of the Spire up the length of the structure, faster than thought, faster than light, faster than the elevator. Not only the Spire, though. Any lights left in Dedalo—streetlights, stoplights, anything that shone—winked out. In moments, from the Spire to the wall, the entire city was dark.

Soarsha turned over so she could look up. Golden dust, shining like sunshine, poured out of the top of the Spire. The dust rose, glowing and scattering across the sky like golden stars. A galaxy of souls hovered in the sky, wanderers in the dark who made their own light everywhere they traveled. As one, every soul, every bit of golden dust, gave a single, silvery flash, as if saying thank you to the girl at the top of the Spire. Then the dust vanished, leaving a dark empty sky over a dark empty city.

Soarsha stared at the sky and city and the unknown places beyond. So many questions were still unanswered, though.

Where were her parents?

Was there a way out of Dedalo?

And, for feck's sake, how was she supposed to do what she was supposed to do if she couldn't even get out of the Spire?

From the edge of her gaze, a glint of silver-white light made her turn.

The soft light glowed throughout the chamber, gauzy like clouds at the edges, but solid as a moonlit wall in the center. The light was so bright Soarsha raised her arm over her eyes, trying to shield her sight.

Was some sort of portal opening?

Was her mother about to step into the chamber, arms open, ready to take her daughter home?

The glow faded—and Soarsha cocked her head.

She had not expected that.

In the center of the chamber, no one floated. No mother appeared with hair as red as her daughter's. No dad or scathtor. No god or other mystical being. No portal or doorway or elevator. Heck, Soarsha would have been happy with a ghostly rocket ship, if only it could take her out of the Spire.

No. Instead of any of those things, what had appeared in the center of the chamber was a sinuous, spindly silver and gold stand. From the top of the stand, two prongs rose in a U shape. Between them, light swirled—and a tall, narrow, oval mirror appeared.

Soarsha walked carefully to the mirror. Around the top of its glassy edge, an inscription appeared:

The Center Is Not The Heart

Along the bottom, another arose:

You Are The Gleam In The Dark

"All this time," said Soarsha to the mirror, "I thought that people knew what they were talking about. That there was a god here. But there's nothing here. It's empty." She shook her head.

She had thought this would make her dispirited, but it didn't. In fact, she realized as she saw her smiling face in the mirror, she was happy. Peaceful.

"No one is here," she said to her reflection. "Except for me. I'm here. Everyone who lives, every soul that persists, we are here. Wherever there's darkness, we can shine. We are the heart. We are the center. Your soul is the only god that matters."

Beneath her feet, far below the dark Spire, a golden glow began to shine. Not from the Spire. Not from the soaring skyscrapers.

From the squat, ugly warehouse.

It too had gone dark, like the rest of the city. But no more. Now, the same light she'd seen before shone out from the warehouse. A beacon. Where she needed to be.

If only she could get there.

The Spire shuddered. From the street upward, tearing, breaking sounds erupted, like thunder from the ground. Below Soarsha's feet, above her head, all around, the glass chamber at the top of the Spire began to crack.

The sides of the chamber fell away, and the cold night air swooped in like ghosts. Below the chamber, a crack exploded, so loud Soarsha covered her ears, but even as the sound faded, the world pulsed with a strange echo.

The top of the Spire began to tip.

From the edge of the floor and ceiling, the glass shattered and fell, a hard sharp rain—the first storm over Dedalo.

There had to be a way down. Had to be. She hadn't come all this way, learned so much, only to be crushed and shattered by falling to the street. She grabbed the mirror with both hands, and pressed her face close.

The center is not the heart.

You are the gleam in the dark.

"In the dark, I shine!" Soarsha screamed. She had no idea what she was saying. Nothing made sense, but at the same time, she knew exactly what did make sense. "I am the heart. Now... take me to the heart!"

The glass floor splintered around Soarsha's feet. The mirror filled with golden light, surrounding Soarsha, as the Spire shattered into pieces and plummeted to the empty streets below.

THE SUMMER GATE

34

LAST OF THE MRAZAS

The following quiet was warm blankets on a cold night. That was the thing about silence that came after a horrible noise, or the stillness that came after the world had shaken. When you could feel the stillness or hear the quiet, you realized you were still alive to know what had been and what now was.

Soarsha opened her eyes, but at first she saw little. The gleam of the golden flash must have overwhelmed her vision. Little by little, the golden glow faded and the deep, dark night over the city reasserted itself. The wreckage of the Spire lay tumbled across the city, like the snapped vertebrae of some ancient gargantuan creature. The silver-gray wall that had surrounded the Spire had also been destroyed, and rubble lay jumbled all over the black streets.

Some bright glint caught her eye, though. Glancing up, Soarsha smiled. High in the sky, right around where the top of where the Spire used to be, a little white light, like a star come to earth, glinted at Soarsha, as if winking. The white light looked exactly like the one she used to see glinting back at her from the top of the Spire, and she wondered what it was. Then the star faded, and was gone.

As it vanished, the rumbling began. Soarsha's eyes widened.

Instead of the scathtor looming in the darkness, though, Soarsha realized the buildings were shuddering. Every skyscraper in Dedalo shook. First one by one, then in unison, every skyscraper collapsed—roars and rumbles and great groanings and screechings—until all around Soarsha, from the center of the city to the ringwall, a wasteland of rubble was all that remained of Dedalo.

That, and the wall. That remained standing, and unbroken.

Looking around her, Soarsha realized that she was now standing just south of the Spire, across the street. She turned, and saw the green squat, square, ugly warehouse, as windowless as deep secrets—and the only structure left in the entire city. The golden light was no longer shining. Tremors of fear went through Soarsha, but faded just as fast. If the light had been there to beckon her, it had done its job.

And now, she understood, she needed to do hers.

In the center of the corrugated green wall facing her, there was a door. She raced to it, and marveled at how her body felt suffused with energy. She door looked closed, and she feared it might be locked. The door looked to be a massive sheet of steel, mounted top and bottom on rails, so the door could roll across the wall. At the right edge of the door, a curved metal handle stuck out. Soarsha stepped up to it, and planted her feet—but a crackling, scrabbling sound made her leap back.

Leaning down, Soarsha poked a finger at what she'd been standing on—and stood up with a gasp and a cry, wincing and holding her index finger.

Under a short shard of glass, a small bead of blood bloomed like a little rose. Soarsha grimaced, but she pulled the shard out of her finger and threw it as far away as she could. Then she peered down again. Silver-gold light glinted on little shards of glass, but Soarsha didn't see any light around her. Her eyes widened. The light must be inside—the light she'd seen from the top of the Spire.

In the center of the shards, in the gap where the door had tried to close but hadn't been able to, a bent, broken pair of eyeglasses lay.

Glasses, Soarsha realized. Just like Mr. Adbad's.

She stood. The others must be inside. Iandel, Garen, Nabraig, Mr. Adbad. And if they were there... Her dad must be inside too.

But if they were in there, then there was a good chance the scathtor was in there too.

Soarsha's eyes narrowed. She reached into her pocket and checked the four pieces of pendant. She thought of the scathtor's eyes, that one glimpse she'd gotten when the shadows had briefly parted.

Then Soarsha grabbed the door handle, put all her weight against it, and shoved the door open.

Silver-gold light flew out through the doorway, covering Soarsha and filling the air around her.

Before her, parallel walls ran toward the center of the warehouse. But she recognized the turns she saw too.

The building wasn't just a warehouse.

It was another labyrinth.

She took a step back.

One day walking home from school, she had turned a corner only to have the rank fist of rotting meat stink punch her in the face. Down the block, it turned out, the butcher shop's refrigeration had gone out over the weekend. Hundreds of pounds of meat had rotted, and the smell was like a wall.

The stink coming out of the warehouse was even worse.

She pinched her nostrils shut, but there was nothing she could do to stop the burning feeling covering her eyes, as if she'd accidentally squirted her face with lemon juice.

Stumbling backward, Soarsha started to think she had this all wrong. Was this really what she had to do? Was this really the way forward? Nothing had worked out the way she had expected. Finding her father had resulted in a bus crash. Following the labyrinth to the Spire had ended up with the scathtor taking everyone but her. And in the Spire itself, she hadn't found her mother or the fifth piece of the pendant or anything she expected.

Now she was all alone. No one to make choices or protect her. What did she have to show for all she'd done over the past day? A bunch of wrong answers and strange paths behind her, and little else. Her dad was gone. Everyone she knew was gone. She was a lonely little girl in a vast, rubbled city, helpless and weak and incapable.

Then Soarsha grinned. She had indeed taken strange paths. But on each path she had found something that kept her going. Even if what she found or where it led hadn't been what she expected, she still had been able to go on.

Just like now.

Besides, there was nowhere else to go. Just toward whatever was at the end of this labyrinth. She knew the path might not unfold in the way she expected, so she threw away her expectations. She'd take this path with a fresh step, with a clear mind, an uncluttered perspective. Wherever she went and whatever happened, she would follow her path. Make her way. And find what she sought. Just like Gleaming Head and Jilly would do. Just like her dad would do.

She took a step forward.

Just like her mother would do.

Soarsha crossed the threshold past the rolling door and into the warehouse. Sure, it stank. But if she didn't go forward, if she didn't follow this path to the end, that would leave her with something far worse: the stench of a soul rotting in cowardice, alone forever in an abandoned world.

She thought of all her father had been through. Dying. Losing her mother. Fighting the scathtor.

There is no power and love but what you grow in yourself. That's what made someone a gleam in the dark. Not being a hero.

Just doing what needed doing, for the sake of those you cared about. That was what mattered. And that's what would drive her onward. No matter what.

Soarsha's eyes narrowed as she took another step into the labyrinth, pushing back the wall of stink, all the while wanting to run away and retch. But she didn't. If her father could endure all he had suffered, then she could keep finding her way for the sake of finding him.

She would face the labyrinth. Go to the center. She reached a tender hand inside the neck of her shirt and touched the purple stone around her neck. She would face down the scathtor and rescue everyone left. She would be Soarsha the Kid. Last of the Mrazas. Living, striving, and enduring in joy and love, no matter what else.

Tired and hungry and homesick as she was, nonetheless she plodded down the straights and around the turns of the dimly lit labyrinth. At every moment she expected to hear the thunk of the rolling door slamming shut, but the only sound was her footsteps. She wondered if the lights would go out, leaving nothing to see by except, she hoped, the bright light of her heart. Yet throughout the labyrinth, only silence went with her. Horrible as it was, even the stench lessened, or at least she got used to it. Now and again, Soarsha stopped and stared at the walls around her and the roof above her. All corrugated, wavy green metal. It wasn't the rolling hills of her dreams, for sure, yet in the midst of the labyrinth, Soarsha realized she had never felt as close to her dream as she did right now.

Perhaps, she realized, just maybe, the scathtor wasn't here after all. Maybe it was out looking for her. Maybe she could find everyone, discover what secret must lie at the center of the labyrinth, and they could all be on their way before the scathtor was any the wiser. Maybe. It was nice to think so, anyway, and even if it didn't happen that way, well, a girl could dream.

As she walked, Soarsha pondered the words on the mirror. She understood being the gleam in the dark. That made sense. If you couldn't find a light, then you had to become a light.

But the center is not the heart?

She shook her head. That still didn't make sense.

The path of the labyrinth sometimes ran in straight lines, sometimes long and sometimes short, depending on how close to the outside edge or the inner center the path was taking her. Sometimes the curves were tight, and sometimes they ran on long arcs, lazy as a Saturday afternoon on her bed reading *Wandering Heroes* comics. Now, though, as she rounded one more turn—so short and tight she'd almost careened into the wall—the dim light of the labyrinth blazed up with gold and silver light, bright as sunrise, bright as the hope, even now, that one day Soarsha's dream would be more than just a dream.

There it was.

The end of the labyrinth. The center of it all.

Soarsha's heart beat faster and faster, and she rested her hand on her chest, right above her heart. Her eyes widened, and she glanced down.

That was it.

Her heart wasn't resting on the dead center of her chest, but was off to the left, just slightly. Not quite in the center. But at the heart.

The Spire was at the center of the city, but the Spire wasn't the heart. The warehouse with this labyrinth, culminating in this chamber in front of her—this was it. You didn't find answers by getting to the middle of the matter or the center of the matter. You found answers by getting to the heart.

Whatever was causing the glow, she couldn't see it yet. As she stepped closer, in fact, the light became brighter, and she had to cover her eyes. She smiled, though. She was almost to the chamber, and she had that sense that beyond the tight, narrow passageway of the labyrinth, the final chamber at the heart widened, and was deep, and tall, and held the answer she had sought and sought and sought, throughout loss and heartbreak and despair. A place where she could breathe easier, before the final plunge, into whatever would come next.

Then the light went out.

Soarsha lowered her arm.

A massive shape blocked the entire entrance of the passage, and by reflex Soarsha took a few steps backward.

Raising its arms of shadowy blades, the scathtor seemed to grunt, or perhaps it was some sort of muffled cry of rage and pain. The shadows that formed its head swirled, fast as tornadoes, and Soarsha couldn't see past the darkness there. But she didn't have to see it to know. The good thing about being a girl who dreamed was that even when she couldn't see the truth, she knew the truth was still there.

The scathtor took another step toward her. Little light remained in the passage now, just enough to see the monster approaching.

Lunging its head forward, the scathtor roared at Soarsha.

She wanted to run. Give in. Go hide under her bed. Under her dad's bed. Go beat against the gate until she broke it down. Anything to get away from the scathtor. Instead she narrowed her eyes. Set her feet. Stared straight into the stormy shadows of the scathtor's face. For just a moment, Soarsha saw a glimpse of brown eyes—and she smiled.

Loud as the Spire crashing, the monster roared again. Dust and flecks of metal rained down from the roof of the warehouse. Yet she heard it now. Not just the roar, but the stagger in it, the hesitation, the stutter. Not just a cry—but crying.

Soarsha gave the scathtor a nod. "Hello," she said. "You must be terribly frightened. But it's going to be okay. I promise. All you've done, I don't think you've hurt anyone, and what's more, I don't think you want to hurt anyone. You were doing what you thought you had to do. The others are free, off to whatever is next for them. It's just us now. You and me. Together, we can understand. Together, we can make it right."

The scathtor shook its head. Stepped toward her—and she stepped toward it. Strong and steady, the hero of her heart came to life as her true self.

The next roar sent Soarsha's hat sliding up her head slightly, but Soarsha tugged it back down and kept going. Unarmed. Unprotected. Around her, the lights of the warehouse went out, and she could see nothing except the smoldering reddish-brown darkness of the scathtor's eyes.

"Must protect you," said the scathtor, raising its shadow arms, curved like scythes. With a snarl, it lunged forward. But its looming shadows stayed still, as if it could not bring itself to do something that might harm her.

"I know," said Soarsha. "I don't know why, but I understand."

She set her left hand on the scathtor's face. "It's going to be okay. I forgive you." She smiled. "Mr. Adbad."

The shadows of the monster's face stopped swirling. Behind them she could see the brown eyes now, scared and full of sorrow. Not for itself, though.

For her.

"You must not go in there," said the scathtor. For a moment she could hear the warmth of her teacher's voice, a voice that sounded kind and ancient and despairing and full of hope. "Had to stop the others. In case... In case..."

"In case what, Mr. Adbad?" said Soarsha. "You can tell me. We can figure this out."

Then the scathtor shook its head and tipped backward. The monster's roar tore holes in the walls and the roof, and Soarsha staggered.

"You must stay!" The scathtor came toward her, raising its arms again. "It's the only way!"

The shadows were swirling again, and she could no longer see the scathtor's eyes. Mr. Adbad's eyes.

The scathtor lowered its arms toward her. Soarsha reached into her shirt and found the purple stone. The stone that had been her mother's, and her father's, and now hers. Lavender moved through the air. The scathtor recoiled, but Soarsha leaped forward. Holding the stone tight, she plunged it into the scathtor's chest. Not toward the middle, but just to the left. Not for the center.

For the heart.

35

DEAD MAN'S TALE

Without a trace of smoke or ash, the smoldering fire of the scathtor's eyes snuffed out. The eyes of Soarsha's teacher stared back at her, confused and hurt and scared, but Mr. Adbad's eyes nonetheless.

The shadows went still, then drew backward, toward Mr. Adbad, like needles of water flowing backward into a showerhead. Soon the darkness was gone, and the teacher remained. His tweed suit was scuffed and torn. Bruises and scratches covered the rich brown skin of his face and bald head. Sinking to his knees, Mr. Adbad stared up at his student with dry eyes that wanted to cry.

He went rigid. His eyes swirled, black and shadowy. Then the darkness drained out of his eyes, dripping out of his fingertips like water, until the dribbling shadows had formed puddles on the floor—and vanished.

Tucking the purple stone in her pocket, Soarsha sat down on her knees before her teacher, and she took his hands.

"I'm sorry for everything," said Mr. Adbad.

"Why don't you want me to get to the end of this?" said Soarsha. "You taught me. You brought me to the city in the first place. Don't you want me to find answers?"

"I want you to run through those green hills you dream about," replied Mr. Adbad. "I want you to stand squished and smiling between the hugs of your mother and father. I want so much for you, but they are all things you can't have. Not here. Not anywhere."

"Is that why you took everyone?" said Soarsha.

"People were starting to help you," replied Mr. Adbad. "They wanted to see you on your way. I couldn't let that happen."

"Like Carl," said Soarsha. "Like Finley. Carl told me what he thought had happened to you. You're... You're Gleaming Head. And the shadow monster that you fought outside the city. Is that true?"

"All of it," said Mr. Adbad. "Had you had a chance to read that last *Wandering Heroes* comic, you would have learned all about it." Her told her, quickly, about the ride across the Barrenburn, the gates of Dedalo opening, and the battle between the shadow and the Mrazas—and how Jilly defeated the monster.

"Then a bus came," said Mr. Adbad. "And she got on, and sat down near a man with green eyes that were bright but full of sorrow."

"My dad," said Soarsha. "So Jilly is me, and Gleaming Head is you."

Mr. Adbad ran a hand over his bald head. "I'm more than that, though, and so is your father, but we'll get to that. Soon. Very soon." He sniffed, and together they stood. "The scathtor and I, fallen in battle, somehow we... merged. When the bus came, I snuck up behind it and leaped onto the back, but no one saw."

"So you came to the city with me and Dad," said Soarsha. "But you... you already knew about Dedalo? About the people here? Did you... Did you die in the battle with the shadow?"

"Yes... and no," said Mr. Adbad. "Though I didn't come to this world alive. I was dead too. Gleaming Head... Mr. Adbad... Scathtor... I'd had so many names here. Not one is my real one, but soon you'll learn the truth." He stared at her, and he shook his head. "I figured I'd be a wandering sage, Soarsha. Then I found you."

"Was that a bad thing?" said Soarsha.

He chuckled. "Anything but," he replied. "The surprise of finding you was the best thing there is to know of anything in this place, or in the world I left, or, I would wager, in any world that lives or has lived or may someday come to exist."

"Why was finding me such a surprise?"

Bewilderment flashed in Mr. Adbad's dark eyes. "You didn't come here with me," he said. "You... appeared."

"That's why I'm alive," said Soarsha. "Because I... I hadn't died yet."

"That's exactly why I needed to keep you in this world, though," said Mr. Adbad. "That's what I need you to understand."

Soarsha shook her head. "The world beyond the wall is nothing to see at all?"

"You never would accept it." He sighed. "There is no power and love but what you grow in yourself, Soarsha, and yours has always been vaster than what I could hope to contain."

Mr. Adbad turned, and Soarsha could see down the passage again. The light beyond had dimmed, though it still shone silver-gold. Four figures lay on the floor, head to toe with one another, as if forming the edge of a circle.

Soarsha rushed past Mr. Adbad, through the end of the passage and into the chamber beyond. The corrugated metal walls ended. The chamber she stood in was lined with green stone, deep green like rain-kissed hills, and lined with curving, jagged white lines, as if lightning had painted itself across every surface.

At the back of the room, carved into the stone wall, a golden-brown door covered most of the width of the wall, and ran from the floor to the ceiling, which was engraved with a silver-gray material that made the ceiling look like low, rain-swollen clouds. The door was closed, but gold and silver light glowed from behind its cracks, obscuring the trim.

Mr. Adbad stood next to her. His eyes were red. "I wish I could cry, Soarsha. I never wanted you to come here. I had hoped that if I hid the others here, you wouldn't find this place. Then we could wait just a little longer, and it would never happen."

"What wouldn't happen?" said Soarsha. "Please tell me. I deserve to know."

"The rest of the story," he continued, "is one I need to share with the others."

Running to her dad, Soarsha kneeled down next to him and kissed his forehead.

His eyes opened, green and sorrowful, but brightening like the light behind the golden door as soon as he saw his daughter.

"Rainbow," said Das. "You're okay." He smiled as he raised himself off the floor and hugged Soarsha. "I knew you'd find me."

Around them, the others stirred too. One by one, Iandel, Garen, and Nabraig also sat up.

Then the four of them saw Mr. Adbad.

Das leaped to his feet. "Soarsha! He's not what we thought. He's—"

"The scathtor," said Soarsha. "I know. I... I brought him back. Though I don't fully know how."

"Yes you do," said Mr. Adbad. He stepped into the room, beyond the circle of the four people, and he stood next to Soarsha. "That's what you've always done," he continued. "Whether sorrow or fear, it's never mattered. You've always brought back your father."

"I don't understand," said Soarsha, leaning away from her teacher, toward her father.

"Me neither," said Iandel. "What are we doing here?"

"Amazing," said Nabraig. "All this time I've been negotiating for this plot of land with an annoying bald man. Incredible how just a pair of glasses kept me from recognizing you, you hard-sell, hard-nosed, son of a—"

"That's why you all need to be here," said Mr. Adbad.

Garen shook his head. "Why would we believe you?"

Mr. Adbad's gaze kindly yet firmly settled on the happiness coach. "Because what I'm about to say, you already know in your hearts to be true. It's just a matter of whether you can come to terms with it, as I've done."

Soarsha leaned forward, afraid to know yet yearning to understand. "Then tell us, please," she said.

"It's not a nice tale," said Mr. Adbad. "But it's a true one." He sighed. "Then... well, then I guess we'll need to see what you decide, Soarsha. Everything I'm about to say, it's all about you. And really... you're the only one who can say should happen next."

"What?" said Nabraig. "You think we don't deserve a say?"

"Of course I do," replied Mr. Adbad. "Once you hear me out, though, I think you'll see why we'll be in agreement."

"I'm listening," said Nabraig.

"Me too," said Garen.

Iandel snorted. "Not like we have anywhere else to be right now."

Mr. Adbad tried to smile. "We are here for a simple reason," he said.

"We know that," said Das. "We died."

Mr. Adbad bobbed his side to side, as if he were trying to touch his ears to his shoulders. "Not in the way you think." He looked at each of the adults in turn. "What do you remember about how you died?"

As if as one, each of the four adults put a hand over their heart.

"Something happened to my heart," said Garen. "I don't really remember." He winced. "Nothing like dying to make you forget that ole end-of-life trauma, I suppose."

"That sounds about right," said Das. "Something happened to my heart too. But it's not like we have to remember the gory details."

Soarsha looked back at Mr. Adbad—and saw he was holding a hand over his heart too.

"I remember," said Mr. Adbad. "Every moment. Every pain. Every detail. It's not pleasant, I assure you."

"How did you die, then?" said Nabraig.

Mr. Adbad chuckled. "Helping save the world," he replied, shaking his head. "It feels like forever ago, down a road now covered in shadows. That's how I died." He paused, and looked at the four adults again. "That's how we all died."

"I don't understand," said Garen. "What? Were we all fighting in a war?"

"Let's say it was a small one," replied Mr. Adbad. "A great evil was about to obtain an unstoppable power. We gave our life to save someone else's, and that person, in turn, saved the world."

Soarsha's brow scrunched. Something about what he said was hard to follow. She couldn't figure out what it was but knew that it was there, like a tiny splinter in your foot that you couldn't see, but poked into you like a needle with every step.

Then he turned to Das. "You are not Soarsha's father," he said.

Das's hands clenched into fists. "I've raised her," he replied. "Been here, day after day, so she always had at least one parent in her life."

"Please let me finish," said Mr. Adbad. "You are not Soarsha's father. Yet you are. And yet you are not the only one."

"Now just a damn minute," said Das. He leaned forward, and his red face reminded Soarsha of Garen. Though as the four of them sat there, near Mr. Adbad, Soarsha realized she hadn't noticed it before. A similar yearning in their eyes, like what one person had was the hole in another person's gaze—on in their heart.

Soarsha's eyes widened.

"Our life," she said.

Mr. Adbad turned to her. "Yes."

"Don't you mean our *lives*?"

Mr. Adbad smiled. "Head of the class," he replied. "I do, in fact, mean 'our life.' We are not five different people. We are one person, split into pieces."

Soarsha reached into her pocket, and took out the four pieces of pendant. "Like this," she said.

"Just like that."

Iandel shook her head. "How does a soul break into pieces, like, what, a dropped glass?"

"We are one person," said Mr. Adbad. "Named Jay. He is Soarsha's father... and we are Jay." He looked from one to another. "Tell me," he said, "have you ever felt complete? Or have you always felt like part of you is missing?"

No one had a reply.

"When Jay died," continued Mr. Adbad, "he went... on."

"To the city of gates," said Soarsha.

Sadness and pain crackled in Mr. Adbad's voice. "Where he made a choice. Difficult and agonizing, yet done out of love and hope."

"You know?" said Soarsha.

"Everything they have forgotten lives in me," said Mr. Adbad. "I remember dying. And I remember what happened afterward."

"What is this city of gates?" said Nabraig.

Soarsha explained what Carl had told her in the Spire.

"Jay," said Mr. Adbad, "was about to go through the Summer Gate. He was about to return not only to the world of the living, but to the life he had left. Imagine that? Picking up where you left off. Like leaping off a bus and then hopping right back on. Whole and renewed."

"It sounds like a one in a trillion chance," said Das. "Why would he... Why would we... pass that up? Wouldn't he... Wouldn't we... have wanted to get back to Soarsha?"

"That's the thing," said Mr. Adbad. "When Jay died, he didn't have a daughter."

"I don't understand," said Soarsha. "I was told that my mother is alive. And that's in a world where I'm alive."

"That's true," replied Mr. Adbad. "Your mother is alive. But you had not been born yet. You... You are like a visitor from Jay's future. From our future." Mr. Adbad raised his hand, palm up, and pointed his fingers toward Soarsha. "When Jay neared the Summer Gate, he met a friend from our old life. That friend told us something. A truth about the future."

"He told you that I was in the future," said Soarsha.

"Sort of," replied Mr. Adbad. "He revealed that you would be in the future... if Jay didn't go through the Summer Gate yet. Timing was everything. If Jay went through the Summer Gate, he would have an amazing life. A life of travel and power and riches and glory beyond compare."

Soarsha let that sink in. "But he wouldn't have me."

"So he chose to wait." For such a momentous choice, her father's voice was so small, so choked. "Because any world with your child is better than one where your child doesn't exist."

"Spoken like a true father," said Mr. Adbad.

"It makes sense," said Nabraig. "What you're saying is we are... all Jay. And that means we're all Soarsha's father."

"All of us feel protective of her," said Garen.

"We want the best for her," said Iandel.

"Exactly," said Mr. Adbad. "That's why, instead of returning to his life, Jay turned away from the Summer Gate and went through the Winter Gate. To Dedalo. He was—we were—supposed to be here long enough to ensure that Soarsha would exist, in the real, living world."

"Mr. Adbad?" said Iandel. "When were we supposed to leave?"

Mr. Adbad glanced at the golden door, shining behind them. "Soon," he said. "That's why the door is shining. It's been dark the entire time we've been here. Until recently, as the time got close."

Das stared at the door. "As we got close to the anniversary of when we came here."

"Trouble is," said Mr. Adbad, "something came with Jay. Something he did not expect."

"Me," said Soarsha, tears stinging her eyes. Never had she realized that being alive could be such trouble.

"You," said Mr. Adbad. "That pendant in your pocket, that was a symbol of Jay's soul, a key to the Summer Gate that only he could use." He pointed at the golden door. On the left side of the frame was a circular depression—exactly the size of the complete pendant. "When the pendant broke, Jay broke into us. A soul in five pieces. Except once we came to Dedalo, I realized a horrible truth."

Mr. Adbad turned to Soarsha, and his eyes were full of a sorrow that wished it could cry.

"You weren't supposed to be here, Soarsha," said Mr. Adbad. "You were a dream to come true, not be true yet. Despite that, even in potential, even in the imagination, you are so alive that the mere understanding of you existing was enough to make you real."

He sighed and shook his head. "And that brings us to the problem. Why I wanted that door to stay closed. Why we can't go through. Can't go back. We can never leave Dedalo, Soarsha. I know it's not what you want, but it's the best we can do for you. It's a half life... but it's better than no life."

She shook her head. "But why? I don't understand. I could live. You could live again, and we could find Mom and be together. Why can't we leave?"

"You did not come from the land of the living," said Mr. Adbad. "You came to life in the land of the dead. You were not alive, but now you are. If we go through the Summer Gate, aye, Jay will live." Agony crossed his face. "But you, my dear, our daughter, you will die."

36

THE FINAL PIECE

Das held his daughter's gaze. "I understand what he means now," said Das. "I can't risk losing you, Soarsha."

Then he looked away. So did all the others, staring at the wall instead of at the girl who could either have a partial life, or no life at all.

Soarsha stood and grabbed her father's sleeve, and made him turn around. "What sort of life do you think I can possibly have here?" said Soarsha. One by one she went to them, turning them around. They would look her in the eye, their dry eyes to hers that were ringed with tears. They would see.

"This place is empty," said Soarsha. "Dedalo has collapsed. The only thing left is the ringwall."

"But you'll live," said Garen.

"I'll exist," replied Soarsha. "I won't really live. There's no one here. Am I supposed to stay a child forever too?"

Iandel took a step toward her. "Is that really so bad?"

"Some people want to be children their whole lives." Soarsha stared at the embalmer. "I want to grow up. I want to become the woman I want to be. I don't want to wander through an empty world where there's no one to play with, no one to grow up with, no one to be friends with, no one to fall in love with. Living here is no life."

Garen shook his head. "Life isn't always about getting what you want, kid," he said. "Sometimes all you can get is what you need."

"We'll be your everyone," said Nabraig. She touched Soarsha's hand, but Soarsha pulled away. Pain flashed across the business-woman's face. "That's all we'll have to do from now on," continued Nabraig. "Just be with you."

Soarsha stared at her. Focused her gaze. "You don't get it, do you?"

"Your life or no life." Kindness and resignation flickered in Nabraig's eyes. "No contest. I'll gladly sign on that dotted line."

"I won't," said Soarsha. "You could live again. Not broken up into five bits of soul, but the whole person you were. And even more... you'll be in the world again. In the world where, one day, I can exist." She turned around and stared at Mr. Adbad. "That's the whole point, right? We leave at the right time, then this Jay, my dad, will be with my mom, and one day they will have me."

"That's the risk, though, Soarsha," said Mr. Adbad. "You didn't exist. Now that you do... you may not only stop existing, but now never exist at all."

She looked at them. One to the other. "You've lost so much," she said. "You died. And here, you've tried to be complete. But you can't. You have helped me, but you can't go on helping me. I will die of longing in a world of the dead. Is that what you want?"

Das touched her shoulder. "But if we did what you want, and go through..."

Soarsha knocked his hand away. "Then you take a chance. A risk. You saved the world. Do you think that was without risk?"

Das's hand went to his heart, and pain struck across his face. "This is different," he said. "You're... You're my child."

"Every parent wants their child to have a better life than what they had," said Soarsha. "That's what you've always told me. Tell me, Dad: How is this life going to be better than what I can have in the real world?"

Das said nothing and looked away.

Soarsha shook her head. Then she remembered one crucial detail. The hot fury, the pulsing drive to live, faded.

"Not that it matters anymore," she said. "Everywhere I've looked for the fifth piece of the pendant, I haven't found it. So I guess that door will go dark soon... and we'll be trapped here regardless of what we want or don't want."

Everyone looked away from Soarsha. Soft sighs and dry sobs filled the chamber. Soarsha stared at the golden door. The light glowed strong, pulsing slightly, as if waiting for something, as if beckoning her to come to the door—and through the door, to what lay beyond.

A tear streaked down her face, and she kneeled down to the ground.

"I want my dad to live," she said. "I want to live. And I want to meet my mom." She shook her head. "But maybe you're right. Maybe what we want isn't always what we can have."

Someone touched her shoulder. She turned. And stood up. Mr. Adbad was behind her, an apologetic look in his eyes.

"What?" said Soarsha. "I don't think you have anything left to teach me."

"Just one thing," said Mr. Adbad, his voice sad and weary. "To listen carefully to someone's words."

Soarsha shook her head. "I don't understand."

"You do understand, Soarsha, that if you and your dad go through that gate, anything could happen."

"That's why I want to go," said Soarsha. "That's why I want to live. Anything can happen. And I accept that. We have to keep going. Move onward, see what happens, and make the best we can with what we've got. That's living. I'm alive. And I want to live, not live a little bit, but live fully with all the time and being I have."

"Then... as part of the soul of your father," said Mr. Adbad, "one of the things any parent learns is to listen with their heart to the desire of their child's heart."

The teacher unbuttoned his scuffed and ripped tweed jacket, and reached his right hand inside.

"Please hold out your hand," he said.

From his jacket's inside pocket, he pulled his hand back out, and opened his fist, and set the fifth piece of the pendant in her hand.

"I never lied," said Mr. Adbad. "I stole it from you, that day on the bus when we came to Dedalo. I just didn't wear it around my neck."

Tears trembled in Soarsha's eyes, leaping with the joy beating from her pounding heart. Four jagged tapering prongs, like compass points, jutted out from the rim of a perfect circle. Soarsha gasped. She remembered the comic page, with the hole in the center so she couldn't see what was there. Now she knew. In the center of the fifth piece, a pale stone gleamed, like a blue summer sky.

"I don't know, though," said Mr. Adbad, "what happened to the other pieces, in the labyrinth. But for my part..."

Soarsha grinned. Then she reached into her own pocket, and took out the other four pieces of the pendant.

Das came over to his daughter. "This is what you really want," he said.

She looked from the pieces to her father. "Can you be okay with it?"

"Whatever you want, Rainbow." The fragments of a smile began on her father's face, small but growing. Hoping. "Just... Just let me catch up with you after you've had some time with your mom, okay?"

She laughed, and kissed her dad on the cheek. "Always, Dad. Always. We'll be waiting for you. Just get on down the path to us as soon as you can, okay?"

Pride like summer sunlight shone as Das looked at his daughter.

The five adults stood in a circle. Soarsha stood in the center, setting the pieces on the floor and aligning each one with the fifth piece.

Nothing happened.

All the pieces were there. Except.

Soarsha's eyes widened.

She traced her finger along the blue stone in the center. In all the excitement, no one had noticed that there was still a hole. Not quite in the center. Just off to the side, slightly. A sliver in the shape of a crescent.

Fingers trembling, Soarsha reached into her pocket and dug.

"Where is it?" she said.

"Where's what?" said Das.

Soarsha pulled the purple stone out of her pocket. "The final piece," she said. "From Mom."

She pressed the purple stone into the crescent hole. The pieces of the pendant began to glow with a soft, silver-gray light. As if drawn by magnets, the pieces snapped together. Soarsha held her breath.

The door changed first. The silver-gold light shuddered—then turned to a brilliant, pure gold that smelled like hot sun on earthen paths. From the pendant, a golden light filled the room so that Soarsha couldn't see anything but the green hope beyond her dreams. When the light in the room faded, where five people had stood around her, now one stood next to her.

He looked like Das, only shinier, but she could see the others in his body, his face, and above all, his eyes. The eyes of her father, green as bright grasses under golden sunlight. Iandel's skepticism and Nabraig's vision and determination flowed through her father's gaze. Woven through like a red thread, Garen's intense fire gleamed too, the spark of discontent that made all change possible in a reluctant world. Yet underneath all that, Mr. Adbad gleamed there, a wandering hero of the ages, ready to do all he could for those he loved.

Jay was a little taller than Das, a touch wiry, and his clothes had changed too. Cargo pants had replaced jeans—but what really caught Soarsha's eye was his brown T-shirt. A little orange rowboat flowed down a river as bright blue as a goddess's eyes. Soarsha was certain, though, that when she looked away, the shirt changed, and for a moment, the barest moment, she saw long red curly hair, blowing in a breeze, on a green background.

"So," said Jay, "what do you think?"

Soarsha hugged him tight. "Hi, Dad."

"It's okay?"

She breathed in his scent. That hadn't changed. Spices and hot dust. High sun, a whiff of beer, and the first hint of garlic hitting hot oil in a pan.

"It's you," she said.

Jay touched her under her chin, and lifted up her face so they could look each other in the eye.

"I'm a little surprised," said Soarsha.

"Why do you say that?"

"Dunno," said Soarsha, grinning. "Figured you'd be shorter. Do you feel okay?"

"I do," said Jay. "I remember... Everything. Being here... as everyone. I remember my life too, and what happened afterward. Death has been a strange ride, my daughter, but even that's nothing compared to my life." He laughed. "I can't wait to tell you about it. Someday." He winked. "When we're both alive."

Soarsha picked the pendant up off the floor. "We're not done yet."

Jay stared from the pendant to Soarsha. Uncertainty crackled in his bright eyes. "You're still sure?"

"I am," said Soarsha. "Because I see what you didn't. Do you see it now?"

"I was so afraid," said Jay. "Being a parent is about being

afraid... but only in part. Being a parent is also about being hopeful. And, as you learn over time, being a parent means trusting not only your child, but yourself."

"It's one of the silly things people do," said Soarsha. "They get so afraid of what they might lose, they lose sight of what they can gain. You're not going to lose me, Dad."

"You're right," said Jay. "I'm going to find you. When the time is right."

Soarsha smiled, and set her hand on her father's cheek. "I think you've got some good potential for this dad gig."

"I'll be sure to remind you of that when you feel like you're ready to sack me."

"You still don't get it, though," said Soarsha.

"What do you mean?"

"I mean... My being alive here. I'm not an anomaly." Soarsha sighed, and looked into her father's eyes. "You've been through so much. Death and grief. Suffering and fear. Yet there was one thing you needed. One thing you deserved."

Jay's eyes were trembling—though, Soarsha noticed, he still had no tears to cry.

Her father's voice shook. "What's that?"

"Something to live for," said Soarsha. "A purpose." She looked around the room. "However all this happens, or if there's anything beyond what we do, I think I came to life here, with you, because it was like the world was making you a promise."

Jay smiled back at her. "You are wise beyond your years, my daughter."

"Maybe I got it from my dad."

Jay chuckled. "I don't know about that," he said, "but I also know something you don't know."

Soarsha cocked her head. "What's that?"

"Your mother." Jay held out his hand. "How about you go meet her?"

Hand in hand, together they walked to the doorway. Soarsha

held the pendant up toward the depression there. Daughter and dad nodded at each other. The light held steady, and she set the pendant in place.

They waited. Barely breathing.

Then looked from the pendant to the door to each other.

Nothing was happening.

Soarsha pressed on the pendant. Jimmied it from side to side. Tried to turn it.

Nothing.

The golden light dimmed, ebbed, and began to grow pale and feeble. Flickers and embers now, but soon darkness. The door wasn't opening. Soon, it would never open at all. Soarsha wondered what rain would have smelled like. What warm sun would feel like on her skin. How it would sound when her mother laughed. She wished, just once, to see where the hills ended and the sea began.

Pulling the key away, Jay and Soarsha stared at it closely.

"Is it broken?" said Jay, his voice a gasp.

Soarsha's eyes widened. She shook her head—and handed him the pendant. "Your soul," she said. "Your life. Not mine. This key is for you to use."

Jay set the pendant into the keyhole again.

The feeble light shuddered. Barely gold, paling against a growing darkness.

Then the light went out.

Soarsha grabbed the doorframe. "No!" she yelled.

Her father's mouth fell open, but he had no words, only the despair in his eyes, and that was screaming. Their heads bowed.

Then raised.

From behind the door, a scent like a breeze blowing through green grass wafted through the cracks in the doorway. It was soon followed by roses and barley, tea and coffee, the scent of dew just before the sun gets high enough to turn it into the ghosts of the world's tears. Rain and salt. The tang of old earth. And something else.

Lavender in summer sun.

The door faded, replaced by a gleaming golden light, the light of sun on thick meadows—or on the green grasses of endless rolling hills.

"I don't know what will happen," said Jay.

"No one does," said Soarsha. "But isn't that life?"

They smiled at one another. Held hands. Golden light surrounded them, filled them, and went with them through the Summer Gate.

PART VI

JUST LIKE A DREAM

37

THE PROMISE OF US

Somewhere in the light, he kissed her forehead, leaving not only the reminder of his kind touch, but also the salty wetness of fresh tears. He squeezed her hand, then was gone. She was certain of it. As certain as she was that the air now smelled of salt and earth, of recent rain and the promise of sun.

After the hard black streets of Dedalo, the soft springy green stuff under her boots would take some getting used to. So would the low gray sky, whether it had hints of blue or not.

Soarsha smiled. She figured she'd manage.

The hills around her rolled as far as she could see—and not once, in any direction she turned, did she see any sign of a wall.

Through the green grass, a worn, bare ribbon of brown path meandered along the rises and dips of the rolling earth. Coming down the path toward her, a scent like sunlight on lavender filled and enwrapped Soarsha. Her gaze followed the path, up a hill, to the crest—where a flash of red came into view.

Long red curls caught the wind and swung around in it, like children playing at a park.

Over the hill the woman came walking, and her brown skirt

and creamy shirt fluttered in the breeze. Thick brown boots stepped through the world with strength and confidence. Her tan freckled skin seemed lit from within by a gentle, gold and silver glow. As blue as the sky beyond the clouds, the woman's wide eyes shone with fear, hope, destiny, decision, light, answers, and questions. So many questions.

Soarsha hoped she'd be able to answer them. The world she'd left was still there, at the edge of her mind and on the tip of her tongue, but it seemed to be slipping, or smudging at the boundaries, like a vivid dream that becomes fragments upon waking.

Turning to look more squarely at the woman, Soarsha felt a tug and realized something was around her neck. She ran her fingers along her collarbone, at the edge of her purple shirt and overalls, and tugged at a brown leather cord. The pendant, whole and complete, as if it had never been broken, hung over her heart.

The woman crested the hill and paused. She stood still, as if deciding that what she saw before her was real, not some hopeful dream making her see things. Above the two of them, the clouds broke up. Golden summer sunlight shone down, mingling with the scent of lavender. The woman breathed deeply, deliberately, holding off so much as the hint of a tremble in her body, and her voice rolled like the hills yet was kind, steady, and certain.

"Soarsha." A tear slid slowly down her cheek.

Soarsha felt her own body tremble, her own eyes fill with tears.

"Mom."

As they ran to each other, Soarsha pulled the hat off her head and threw it into the breeze. Her own shorter red hair fluttered—and she wondered how long it'd be before it matched her mother's.

Mother and daughter held each other in the sunshine, swaying in the breeze but standing steady.

"I missed you," said her mother.

"I missed you too," said Soarsha.

Side by side they stood, arms around each other, and they stared at the crest of the hill.

"This is just like my dream," said Soarsha.

"Aye. Only better." Her mother smiled, and kissed her daughter's forehead, leaving the lightness of her touch—and a hint of fresh tears. "This is real, and this is living." Her mother touched Soarsha's cheek, then gently touched her forehead to her daughter's. "And it is limitless."

Her mother leaned away slightly and stood tall. "When the time is right, your father will arrive. There's things he's got to do in the meantime. A path he has to follow, so that once he gets here, gets to the promise of us, he's ready."

Soarsha looked from her mother to the path. There wasn't exactly much to do around here. "So... we wait for him?"

As her mother laughed, her shoulders shook. "Oh, last thing we need to do is stand around here all day," she replied. Her eyes gleamed. "In the meantime, we've got plenty to catch up on."

She gave Soarsha another squeeze, then laid a gentle hand on her daughter's cheek. "He'll be along," she said.

They turned and walked over more hills, toward, Soarsha saw at last, in front of a stand of tall leafy trees, a little white cottage with a brown thatched roof. Smoke, earthy and invigorating, puffed out of a chimney, and it wove with the scent of sunlight on lavender. In front of the cottage, purple rows of lavender waved welcome in the breeze.

Soarsha squeezed her mother's hand and smiled. Looking over her shoulder, she glanced one more time at the path in the distance. Then she turned back to her mother, and the cottage before them, and all the days and nights and stories and moments to come.

"Aye," said Soarsha as they went inside. "He'll be along."

THE...
End? Nope!
More adventures await in the acclaimed Rucksack Universe.
Start your next journey at...
rucksackuniverse.com

THANK YOU FOR READING

Please **tell people** about this story and **review it at your favorite online bookstore or social network**.

Reviews are the best way readers discover great new books, and I would truly appreciate it. Even a couple of sentences is a big help.

BECOME A WANDERER

Early access to new stories... and much more
Support the Rucksack Universe on Patreon

This story is made possible in part by my Wanderers, my patrons on Patreon. In return for backing my work each month, Wanderers get special rewards, exclusive access to me, e-books, signed books, early access to new stories, and more. Learn more and become a patron today:

patreon.com/anthonystclair

Free story!

When you join Anthony's free Reader Club via email, you'll get a free ebook, and be the first to hear about new stories, events, news, and more!

rucksackuniverse.com/freestory

PRAISE FOR ANTHONY ST. CLAIR

"Left me completely gobsmacked. Great concept, fun characters, and beautiful writing... High-stakes story, told with wit and compassion."

— Nth Degree

"Brings the reader into the story and holds them there with every sight, smell, sound, and feeling.... St. Clair is now one of my favorite authors and I truly cannot wait to read more."

— Online Book Club

"Fans of travel, fantasy, and beer will circle around this story. Matching Indian lore with universe building reminiscent of Terry Pratchett, St. Clair's tale will make readers reconsider fate."

— Kristi Chadwick, *Library Journal's* Self-Published Ebook Awards

What Readers Say

"Cheeky and sophisticated."

"Pulls you in fast and keeps you on the edge of your seat."

"The characters and story swept me into their grasp and whisked me into their world."

"A page turner for sure."

"Fascinating new universe."

"Modern fantasy writing with very real characters and situations."

"Easy to read, wildly entertaining, and full of imagination."

"St. Clair is a fine storyteller who will keep you reading to the end and still wanting more."

"Anthony seamlessly combines quirk, wit, travel, and magic."

"Grabs your attention and doesn't let go."

"Entertaining fantasy full of twists and turns."

"Challenges and trials that will keep you fully engaged as you read St. Clair's beautiful prose."

"Delightful and artful adventure into an intriguing world."

"A wonderful read for all levels, St. Clair uses humor, his love for travel, and his love of beer to create a fascinating universe that draws you in and doesn't let go."

"Sharp writing and dialogue."

"A variety of amazing characters that have been masterfully brought to literary life."

"Beautiful prose, smart humor and a slanted take on reality."

"If you love strong characters, witty repartee, beer, and occasional sword-play, this book and series is for you."

"Anticipation of what's to happen next kept me turning the pages."

"A great familiar setting for those of us living on earth, with a nice twist of fantasy splashed throughout. Perfect for fans of Terry Pratchett and Neil Gaiman."

"I am curious as to what happens next."

"A delightful read, especially for those who love to travel— even if only in their armchairs."

"Intriguing, magical underbelly!"

"Lots of exciting scenarios, with several twists/turns & a great set of unique characters."

"Easy to slip into the myths of the situations and places."

"Anthony's got an amazing sense of the epic, and each of the stories in the Rucksack Universe keeps building on the groundwork that came before. There's a lot of long play being worked out through the stories and I just can't wait to see how it all weaves together and falls into place."

"Goes down smooth and leaves the reader poised for another round."

"Armchair Travel! I love going to new places in the literature I read.... Food and conversation are just as telling as the scenery he paints on the page. Read it."

"Just when you think you have it all figured out there is a twist that keeps you guessing."

"I love books with lots of dialog and character interactions. I am more interested in how a person perceives their environment and how they react internally and externally to it than what the scenery is. This book delivers. Just enough detail of the surroundings and full of wonderful character interactions."

"Buoyant with a unique humor, twist and focus on international travel."

"The story telling is exquisite and makes it hard to put the book down."

"A stand-out writer and author to watch (and read) for the future! This is not Douglas or Pratchett, this is St. Clair!"

"An abundance of love, light, and wonder."

"Left me wanting more!"

ALSO BY ANTHONY ST. CLAIR

Rucksack Universe titles are available worldwide in popular formats. Visit rucksackuniverse.com to learn more and buy from your favorite bookstore:

Novels

Novellas

Short Stories

Box Sets & Collections

Libraries & Bookstores

News, special features, and more

rucksackuniverse.com

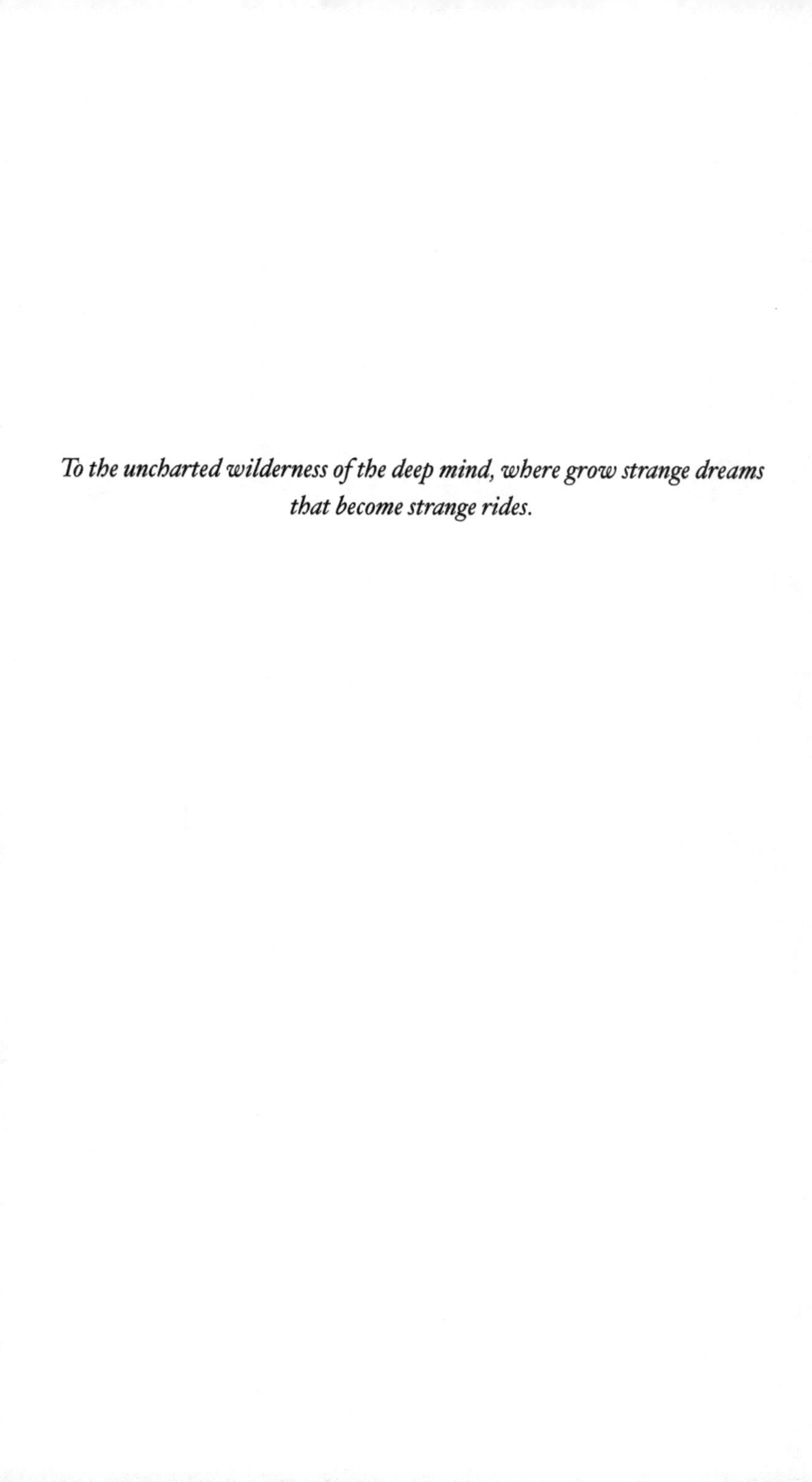

To the uncharted wilderness of the deep mind, where grow strange dreams that become strange rides.

ACKNOWLEDGMENTS

This book began as a dream about a young girl searching for her missing father. She rode a bus through a dusty city, and found herself at a strange warehouse full of golden light.

STRANGE RIDE came to fruition, thanks to the support of my friends, family, and patrons. I also want to give a special shout-out to Dean Wesley Smith: By completing his year-long, write-a-short-story-a-week Great Challenge, I was able to lay much of the groundwork that became this book. More about Dean's books and writing courses are at his website: DeanWesleySmith.com.

Rucksack Universe stories are made possible in part by the ongoing support of my Wanderers, my patrons on Patreon. Special thanks to patron Sean Keener. Patrons can get special rewards, exclusive access to me, early access to new stories, free books, and more. You can be a patron too. Learn more and become a patron today:

patreon.com/anthonystclair

Thank you to Bonnie Donaghy for cover design, and to Scott Alexander Jones for the spot-on copy editing, story advice, and proofreading. Any mistakes—especially when it comes to languages and cultures—are mine.

Above all, my thanks to my family. Connor and Aster, you inspire every story I write. Jodie, with you I am the man I'd always hoped to be.

ISBN, Trade Paperback Edition: 978-1-940119-51-9

ISBN, ePub Edition: 978-1-940119-52-6

ISBN, Kindle Edition: 978-1-940119-53-3

Library of Congress Control Number: 2020916497

Ordering & Queries: info@rucksackpress.com

Cover design by Bonnie Donaghy. All other trademarks and copyrights are property of their respective owners.

This is a work of fiction. All of the characters, organizations, events, and references portrayed in this story are either used fictitiously or are products of the author's imagination. Any resemblance to real persons, entities, or organizations is purely coincidental.

Find a mistake? Corrections are welcome and often rewarded. Email the publisher at editor@rucksackpress.com.

anthonystclair.com | rucksackuniverse.com

SPECIAL FEATURES

Go behind the scenes of the Rucksack Universe:

Become a patron for behind-the-scenes special access
patreon.com/anthonystclair

Reading Order
The Rucksack Universe is an ongoing, non-sequential series. Read
it in any order you like. If you want to know the order of release
or the order of the storylines, here are suggested reading orders:

Choose your reading itinerary
rucksackuniverse.com/reading

SNEAK PEEK

THE QUIRK, WIT, TRAVEL, AND MAGIC OF THE RUCKSACK
UNIVERSE CONTINUES!

The myths, intrigue, and adventures never end! Enjoy this FREE sneak peek of the novel Forever the Road, and find out why *Library Journal* says the Rucksack Universe has "universe building reminiscent of Terry Pratchett."

Get the full book now:
rucksackuniverse.com/forever

Chapter 1

"It could be a mirror eclipse," Rucksack said to Jade. Her hand jerked. The pint glass banged against the tap, sending the black Galway Pradesh Stout foaming and sloshing. She set it down so the beer could settle before resuming the seven-minute pour that made for a perfect pint of GPS.

"But there hasn't been a mirror eclipse since The Blast," she replied. "And that was nearly two hundred years ago."

Rucksack looked up from the newspaper and ran his gloved left hand over his bald brown head. A dark sadness flickered over his eyes, as brown and black as earth and trees. "Well, in two month's time, there may be." His accent, an ambiguous combination of Irish and everywhere, refused as usual to acknowledge the sound "th," so "there" sounded more like "t'ere." His gaze flicked from Jade's face to the bottles at the back of the bar, then slowly came back to her.

"Mirror's not for certain, though," he said. "They won't know till closer to the time. Just says the atmospheric conditions may be right." He harrumphed. "Bloody irresponsible, saying that. All it'll do is scare people. And mentioning the damn Blast on top o' it..."

Jade poured, then set down the brimming pint so it could finish settling, black beer under snow-white foam. "Let me guess," she said. "There's no cause for alarm."

"O' course," Rucksack said. "It's all coincidence." His thin, tight smile said the rest.

Even the steaming-hot India day outside couldn't alleviate the chill in Jade's gut. She remembered talking of The Blast as a schoolgirl, scared hushed whispers after history lessons about the strange double-sided eclipse that had burned before Night's Day, then a world changed and scarred. As an adult and a Jade, many times she had tried to ask The Management what role The Blast was supposed to play, but they never spoke of it. Then again, there were many things they never spoke of.

Jade handed Rucksack his pint. The heat didn't matter. At her touch, the glass and beer became the perfect temperature for the stout, as if the Irish pub were in Ireland itself, instead of the middle of one of India's hottest cities.

"I'll be outside," Rucksack said. "Suddenly I feel a chill."

You're not the only one, Jade thought as her first customer of the day opened the double mahogany doors. Flat yellow sunshine spilled heat into the pub, but she still felt cold.

Once the doors closed, Jade eyed the liquor, where not so much as a speck of dust dulled the bottles or the glass shelves. The bar's lights glinted off the bottles, which sat on shelves against the mirror that ran from the ceiling to Jade's waist, as wide as the length of the bar. It was well stocked for now, though later she knew there'd be a run on the cheaper stuff: Ram Rum, Liquid Courage, Manager's Reserve, Jimmy Runner, Potato Juice, Blue Label Special, Nirvanic, Captain's Special Box.

The knock-off Indian booze might all taste like sugary antifreeze, but it had the best names. Jade chuckled and wondered who had thought of them all. In the mirror, the light caught her smile and her blue-and-gold eyes, framed by her almond face, olive skin, and the kinky brown-and-black hair that hung just past her shoulders.

Then she reached down, just there on the paneling, just below the bottom shelf of the mirrored bar, just below the phone that never rang. Jade tapped the spot and the cabinet opened. Unseen and unseeable by anyone but her—though lately she wondered about Rucksack—the cabinet held her true duty.

A soft, silvery light shimmered from no distinct source. The cabinet could have opened to the sky; the small space inside seemed to have no back, no bottom, no sides, no top. *All these years,* Jade thought, *and sometimes I still don't know.* She reached inside, wondering if she would just keep reaching and reaching, but as always her knuckles rapped on the wood at the back of the cabinet, the same deep mahogany of the bar and the doors.

The bottles seemed to float on the light: Green #2, Red #4, Brown #5, Yellow #6, Blue #7, Orange #9, Silver #10. Almost an ordinary day, except that there was extra Blue #7 and Red #4. No Gold #1, Gray #3, Purple #8, or Black #11, but those came only with special circumstances. Two or even three could be combined. All eleven were never supposed to be mixed together, except under personal guidance from The Management. For a moment Jade wondered why The Management had never been able to figure out a twelfth elixir. It was said that they nearly had, just before The Blast, but after the catastrophe they had stopped trying. The twelfth elixir remained a myth that could not be made real.

Jade glanced at the clock. Early the hour and empty the pub, but hot was the day, and people would be thirsty. The news spoke of The Blast and another mirror eclipse. People would be scared, indecisive, unsure. The people would need those extra elixirs, and Jade would be ready to steer them.

She closed the cabinet, rose, and turned to face the doors. Her eyes blazed, but her insides still felt cold. For a moment, her mind faded back to long ago, to another life that seemed further away than The Blast.

"Why are you posting me here?" she had asked The Management.

"Because of who you are," the three hooded, floating figures had replied. The voices of The Management always seemed at once like three voices in perfect unison and like one voice that they passed to each other like a ball.

"But I'm just me," she had said.

If they knew her thoughts, they gave no indication. Jade couldn't figure out if they read minds or not. All you could ever see were the hoods—never a face or limb or any indication of what The Management were behind their cloaks. In a way that still haunted her every move and decision, they had replied, "You are here because you are the best of us, Jade Agamuskara Bluegold."

She hoped she still was. Lately, she didn't feel so certain. No matter how perfect the drink, no matter how she steered the drinker down the path that life needed him or her to take, she no longer fully trusted her decisions or her own path. Whoever she helped, her own choices rang in her mind all the time. *Who am I now?* she thought. *Why did I choose this, instead of saying yes in Hong Kong when he asked?*

But that was another life ago.

When the pub door opened again, her thoughts returned to where she was: behind the bar of the best pub and hostel in Agamuskara, India. A man entered and sat at a table. His straight black hair hung ragged, as if he'd given himself a haircut after drinking a few beers—a common look with many of the budget backpackers she'd seen pass through the hostel. His clothes suggested a young American, and in his brown eyes hung doubts of his place in the world, how he was trying to find it but had a hard time knowing where to look. He stuck his nose in his guidebooks, a dry thirst in his throat and a yearning in his heart.

Jade ignored him.

A few minutes later, a woman came in, sat at a different table, and quickly buried her nose in her guidebooks. The pub lights gleamed off her short blonde hair. A ferocity burned in her, one that Jade knew well: a brittle wall, hard voice, and driving velocity that concealed intense fear and doubt.

Jade ignored her too. *The less you do,* she thought, *the more they do what they were supposed to do anyway.* So Jade stood behind the bar, her back to the tables. After a few more minutes, first the man and then the woman approached the bar. Jade kept her back to them, waiting.

"Excuse me," the man said.

"Oy!" the woman said.

Jade turned around. "Oh, hello! What can I do for you both?"

"I've been here for—" they both began in unison.

"Oh, oh, so sorry!" Jade replied. "What can I get the two of you?"

"We're not together," the woman said, looking at the man for the first time.

"No, um," the man said, looking back at the woman, "I'm, um, over there."

"I'm surprised," Jade said. "I would've thought you were traveling together."

The woman's eyes widened. "Why do you say that?"

Jade pointed at the book each was carrying. "You each have *Deep's Enlightened Guide to Spiritual Travel* and *India Through the Third Eye*. Seemed like a for-sure." Jade shrugged. "Even a bartender can't be right all the time."

"Oh," the woman said, not just looking at the man but also paying attention to him for the first time. He looked at her, then at the worn, identical book in her hand. "Are you heading to Godhpur?"

"Um, yeah," said the man. "Yeah, I was, I mean, it's—"

"It's amazing!" the woman said. "I've been wanting to find myself there for years!"

"Me too!" the man said. "Well, I mean, find myself, not yourself. I, um, you know..."

Gotta be Californian, Jade thought as she smiled at him. "You want a Deep's Special Lager," she said, then nodded to the woman. *Australian, no doubt*. "And you want a chardonnay."

Both nodded.

"I'll bring your drinks right over. Why don't you sit and swap travel plans."

They both wandered over to the woman's table and resumed talking.

Now for the hard part.

While they pointed to the same highlighted sections in their guidebooks, Jade looked at the paths of their lives—how they connected, intertwined, ran together for so long.

How they broke apart.

Falling in love, Jade thought. *It's easier than falling down the stairs.*

But he would never show his confidence, and she would never let down her guard. In time, their bright eyes would turn cold, their words sharp. Eventually, there would come a day when they would turn away from each other, preferring the coldness of the world to the frigidity of each other's company.

That's the future, Jade thought. It was all there in the paths that only Jakes and Jades could watch—and influence. She grinned as the tapped the cabinet.

Unless I do my job.

Neither the man nor the woman saw Jade pour the beer and the wine. Nor did they see her smile as she pulled out Red #4 and Blue #7. "Best to you both," Jade whispered, tipping drops into each glass. The drinks brightened for a moment, as if revealing some inner divinity, then faded back to their usual merely golden selves.

They should be lifelong, Jade thought. *But they will let themselves get in the way, instead of trusting each other enough to be their true selves with each other.* Jade set the drinks on the table.

The challenge isn't falling in love, she thought. *The challenge is landing safely and staying in love.*

An hour later and well past their first round, the man no longer stammered, and the hard edge of the woman's voice was gone. The woman looked deep into his eyes, one hand near his, almost but not quite touching. Not yet. Though too far away to hear, Jade needed only to watch to know what was happening. They sat closer now, knees touching, hands occasionally tapping a shoulder, arm, or thigh. From serendipitous wonder had come laughter. Now the talk was serious with "you do? me too!" moments.

Then it happened.

Mid-sentence, the talk ended. The man and the woman looked deeply into each other's eyes. He leaned toward her, his hand on her hand. She leaned toward him. They connected in the smallest, most passionate, tender, relieved-to-have-found-you-in-such-a-random-heartless-world first kiss.

The couple left soon thereafter, toward their shared lifetime ahead. Jade smiled, but only for a moment. *I can help anyone fall in love*, she thought, *but myself.* Like the smile, this thought lasted only a moment. *I am a Jade,* she thought, *and I am the best. Love has no place in decision and destiny.*

She went back to work.

Chapter 2

The no-shocks, no-worries truck clunked in and out of another pothole. For the millionth time since hopping in the back of the truck at Mt. Everest Base Camp in Tibet, Jay bounced up and slammed back down into the truck bed. His bruised body seared under the blazing Indian day. He hardly winced anymore. The effort wasn't worth it.

When Jay was crammed into the corner where the truck bed met the cab, the jarring and jostling affected him less. He tried sitting on his backpack again. Instead of merely pounding his arse, each bump nearly tossed him onto the cracked road.

Jay sat back down on the hot metal of the truck bed and

patted his backpack. Faded, black, waterproofed by dust, nearly as wide as Jay, and as tall as his tenderized torso, the backpack dozed next to him like a dog beside its master. A round lump stretched the fabric at the top of the pack.

It had come back.

Again.

A triple shot of fear, awe, and revulsion washed through him. Jay had lost track of the number of times he'd dropped the *thing* off cliffs, flushed it down toilet holes, and lobbed it into rivers. Each time, he'd hardly zipped up his pack when the lump would appear again. Jay looked away. Instead of thinking about the... thing, Jay tried to think about Agamuskara. Guru Deep's *India Through the Third Eye* called it "India's holiest and unholiest city," though the guidebook never explained why.

Jay couldn't explain to himself why he felt so compelled to go there. It was said that people went to Varanasi to die holy, but they went to Agamuskara to live fully. Jay figured he really must want to live, even if his manner of getting to the city suggested otherwise.

After three days of the truck's tires barely not going over the edges of cliffside roads in Tibet, nearly crashing to a halt from axle-bending potholes in Nepal, and using endless horn blasts to navigate the oncoming trucks and standstill cows of northern India's river plains, Agamuskara couldn't be much farther now. Before setting out this morning, the driver had told Jay they would not be going to the city center, but that was fine. He'd make his own way to the middle of town, even if he had to walk. With his skin clogged with grit and his throat caked in dust, all Jay wanted right now was a hot shower and a cold beer. India was India, though. He suspected he would get the opposite. But he would rest and clean up. Then he'd find his way through the city and figure out what he had to see, what drew him so.

The rattling truck moved so fast that the world passed in a

blur, but Jay marveled at all he saw. Countless people wore brilliant colors and smiled from weathered, driven faces. They defied the washed-out landscape and the humid mat of the air. Every village had been here before time was time, it seemed. Each village also brought a glimpse of temples and shrines, elephant-headed gods, bulls, monkeys, multi-limbed deities rendered in brick, stone, concrete, and reverence.

Approaching Agamuskara, Jay now understood that India was four things: heat, humans, history, and gods. They shaped India not so much into a country or a culture but a world. India was all of the world, all of time in every passing moment, and every emotion, every depravity and transcendence, every hope realized and every futility suffered, of all the human race.

And, gods, was India heat. Humid, blazing, sopping heat. India felt as if wet blankets had been baked for an hour in a pot of water, then, steaming and boiling, wrapped around the country. Even Jay's sweat glands felt sluggish. The humidity jellied the will. It softened the wood of the few meager trees. Even the concrete blocks of houses and shacks seemed to sag, drip, and simmer in the midday, clear-sky blaze of sunlight.

The truck turned onto a highway, renown throughout north-eastern India for being maintained. The road reminded Jay of the interstate highways of his left-long-ago home, except that as far as the traffic was concerned, the four lanes were simultaneously one lane, three lanes, twenty lanes, and no lanes. Still, the truck's consistent speed and motion brought a soothing breeze to Jay's skin, and the smooth road took him from a blazing sear to a nearly gentle simmer.

For once, Jay's tenderized rump stayed in one merciful, bounceless spot. After a few kilometers, he relaxed like a roast chicken resting after coming out of the oven.

The view from the highway wasn't as interesting. The heat haze dulled the flatlands, and it seemed as if a wink and some rupees had made the scenery vanish. Jay almost pined for the cliffs that, just a couple days ago, had dropped off from the side of the truck. Every rock bouncing down into nothing had terrified him, but the trees, cows, and occasional village had been fascinating.

"Namaste la vista, baby," Jay said, mimicking the formerly white t-shirt he was wearing. He lifted the shirt to gain access to the treasures below. Wrapped around his waist and tucked into the front of his tan, dusty cargo pants, the thin fabric of his money belt was already soaked through. But no matter. The treasures would be dry and safe. Jay took out a wad of plastic, then unrolled, unfolded, flipped, and eventually unwrapped his most prized possession: the small, dark-blue booklet of his US passport.

The formalese of government speak greeted him: "...requests all whom it may concern to permit the citizen/national named herein to pass without delay or hindrance and in case of need to give all lawful aid and protection..."

Jay wondered how much he still looked like the photo. The green-and-gold eyes were the same, as was the light-brown hair. But the skin of that face? Dust, heat, sun, cold, ice, rain, beer, hot breakfasts, cold breakfasts, no breakfasts had all leathered his face, hardened his eyes, softened his smile. But it was still Jay. Jay, once from Idaho, now of the world.

He flipped through the pages—past the backgrounds of cacti and mountains, past the important information that addressed everything from about your passport to loss of citizenship. Then he opened the last five years. Visas, stamps, signatures—most of them official and some, to put it mildly, questionable. Jay thought about the so-called visas that had been added not at an official immigration checkpoint, but by hands unsteadied after a bit of backroom blather, boozing, and baksheesh. He flipped through the countries: South Africa, Tanzania, Kenya, Gambia, Morocco, Ireland, England, Scotland, Belgium, France, Spain, Italy, Austria,

Croatia, Germany, Sweden, Russia, Kazakhstan, Mongolia, China, Tibet.

There should have been a visa for Nepal, but instead there was only a blank page. Before arriving at the border checkpoint between Tibet and Nepal, the men in the truck had hidden Jay under a blanket. Jay didn't ask why. They'd hardly slowed down since.

And now—officially—Jay was in India.

Adventures taken, people met, sights seen—all condensed to stamps on pages. Jay re-wrapped his passport in the plastic and stuck it back in his money belt, behind the photo where the man and woman always smiled at him.

"I hope you're still having a good time," Jay said to the couple in the photo. For a moment, his anywhere voice lost all the twangs and lilts of his globetrotting, and he was just a regular guy from Idaho again. He started to take out the picture, but the truck's grinding, slowing gears stopped him. The driver stopped blaring on the horn just long enough to slap the door twice. Jay rustled his money belt and clothes back into place.

End of one road, he thought. *Now for another.*

The truck stopped. Jay grinned. He grabbed the pack, ready to lose himself in all the adventures that came from putting one foot in front of the other on an unknown road—a road that could be the one that would finally go on and on forever, as long as he just kept traveling.

At the edge of the city, Jay jumped out, thanked the two men, and handed them some worn notes. The drivers nodded and laughed at the crazy traveler who thought he'd just stroll into the center of the city. As the truck rumbled off, the indistinct faces of the two men slipped out of Jay's memory. He couldn't understand why it was so hard to remember what these men looked like, especially after spending so many days traveling together. *Must be fatigue,* he thought.

Jay swung on his backpack, set its buckles, and adjusted its straps. Despite the ringing in his head, the tiredness, the bruises, and the extra weight, the touch of the pack to his back brightened his eyes and straightened up his stooping body. It'd be a good walk. A long walk. A tough, hellish walk, sure, but then again, travel wasn't supposed to be easy. The pack did feel heavier, though, now that the little... thing spun in there again.

If anything weighed him down, it wasn't the road-weary fatigue, the not-quite-remembered moonlit night at Mt. Everest, or the Chinese police and all those Dalai Lama portraits. It was the quiet, slow, incessant *shr-shr-shr* as the thing turned, rubbing the fabric of his faithful backpack.

"One foot in front of the other will put it out of your head," Jay said, the Idaho gone from his voice and replaced by the patchwork of places stamped in his passport.

The city center couldn't be that far. *Once there,* he thought, *I'll beeline to a pint, a shower, and a bed—in whatever order works best. For once, I even know where I want to go.*

Backpack-laden, his skin and clothes were so soaked he wondered if sweat glands could get sore. With every step, Jay tried to understand how the Indians did it. Children ran, laughed, smiled, circled him, joked, and asked for a pen or a piece of candy. Women, wrapped head to toe in yards and yards of sari fabric, walked everywhere carrying baskets. Men in pants and long-sleeve shirts held hands with each other and talked like they were all brothers. Their animated voices and gestures defied the dulling, steaming humidity.

Jay had no idea what the men said. The women didn't look in his direction. The kids tired of him and returned to their games.

With every step, the age of the country seemed to whisper alongside the *shr-shr-shr.* All around him, in every pebble and blade of grass, in every buffalo-dung patty drying as fuel on the sides of shacks, Jay saw and felt the gods whose presence and personality had shaped all people, all moments, all things.

The acrid scent of burning tires stung the air. A cow rooted through plastic and garbage. Jay wondered why the gods couldn't have made things smell better.

As he pressed on, the heat melted his resolve. He was now wearing a boulder, not a backpack. Sweat poured and feet dragged, but Jay kept going. Some old saying about single steps and thousand-mile journeys flitted through his mind. It had to be close, though, had to be. The miles pounded the bottoms of his worn boots, and the scene around Jay changed. At least the ground was flat. Other than a tall hill off to the west, the land here was even, with hardly a rise at all.

Covered in drying dung-fuel patties, the shacks gradually gave way to one- and two-story buildings. Shops. Homes. Offices. Sometimes distinct, often all jumbled.

The humid floating dust changed character too. The scent of fields, cow dung, and fires still clung to his pores and his soul, but a new layer of sound and soot settled on him: car and rickshaw exhaust, cooking food, open sewers. Jay had always heard of India as a land of diversity. Walking it now, he understood they meant the smell.

Stopping a moment to rest, Jay had hardly stood still when an open-sided, three-wheeled black-and-yellow rickshaw taxi pulled up next to him like a buzzing, rattling bumblebee.

"You need a ride?" the driver said. "Get in. I will take you to my friend's hotel."

"No, I'm fine," Jay replied, but the driver was already running over to him.

"So tired," the driver said, reaching for Jay's backpack. "Let me put that in for you."

Jay's eyes widened and he stepped back.

"I'm fine," he repeated, his voice flat and final. "No taxi."

"Cheap ride."

"No taxi."

"Special price, my friend," the driver said.

Jay flung out his hands, shook his head, and started walking away.

The driver shrugged. "You tourists."

"I'm not a tourist," Jay replied. "I'm a traveler."

The driver smiled. "You tourists. Always walking around with houses strapped to your backs! But it is okay, my friend. Sooner or later, you always need a ride, and when you need a ride, I will take you."

Jay left the taxi behind, but the taxi didn't leave him. As he trudged onward, the taxi would flit beside him or buzz behind him or singe Jay's nose with a whiff of putrid blue-black exhaust.

A few kilometers later, Jay stepped wrong and tripped.

Banging his knee on the rough asphalt, he winced and his eyes watered.

When he looked up, the rickshaw had stopped in front of him.

"My friend," the driver said. Something about the man's indistinct face seemed familiar.

Jay sighed. He looked past the driver to the skyline of the city proper.

"The heat makes things seem closer," the driver said, "but it is still far."

"How far?" Jay asked.

"Farther than your feet."

The rickshaw's back seat looked soft. There weren't any springs poking out, and the roof would keep the sun off him. Jay's knee throbbed. His feet threatened mutiny and blisters. Jay sighed and surrendered.

"Everest Base Camp," he said, limping into the rickshaw and setting his pack between his grateful feet.

Chapter 3

"Oy! Jade!"

The laughter-laced shout blasted through the pub door and nearly made her drop the glass she was polishing.

Ah, Jade thought. *Rucksack must be ready for his next pint.* She brought a fresh glass to the tap. As she did, The Management's strange warning rang in her head, the way it did every time Rucksack was around: "This man is dangerous."

She thought back over the last few months to when the three hooded figures had appeared in the pub. It was just minutes after the letter had arrived and she'd read it. Later that day Rucksack had come in for the first time—but The Management had visited first.

The surprise had made her drop the letter. The Management hardly ever came to the Jakes and Jades in person. Or in being. Or whatever they were. "Why is he dangerous?" she had asked, picking up the sheet of paper. "Who is he?"

"Some say he's a broken hero," said the figure in blue and green.

"Some say he's the world's only Himalayan-Irish sage," said the figure in brown and black.

"Some say he's just a freeloading drunk," said the figure in silver and gold.

"None of these things has ever been proven," they all said together. "All we know is that he is an unknown quantity."

"An unknown quantity?" Jade had said. "What does that even mean?"

"It means he has no destiny. He is as a ghost to us. He is outside of us all."

"How is that even possible?" Jade had looked at each of the three figures. If they could look sheepish, this was the closest they had ever seemed to it. "What do you want me to do?"

"Your duty has many guises, Jade Agamuskara Bluegold, and some are more dangerous than others. We know little about Faddah Rucksack and far less about his path. Be wary of him but watch him. Learn from him but keep your distance. Stay close but do not get involved. A man without a destiny is a man who might do anything."

The Management faded away into nothing, as they always did. Jade stood alone, still holding the letter.

She came back to the finished pour. *Who are you, indeed?* Jade thought. Blinking at the glaring midday sun, she carried the brimming glass out into the bright world.

The white walls of Agamuskara collected light, stored it, packed it tightly, and shot it back into the world like munitions. People, bicycles, vehicles, and animals trudged and flowed—a river of thousands moving past one-story, two-story, and three-story buildings.

The brown-and-black sari was a shadow amongst the white glare and the thousands of colors. The woman caught Jade's eye for a moment. Then the woman was gone, downstream in the river of flesh and steel.

Scooters, rickshaws, taxis, trucks, cows, dogs, children, men, and women teemed through the streets. Many things tried to occupy the same place at the same time. Not even a square of dirt or pavement showed beneath the slow incessant press of tires, feet, and paws. From the people rushing and meandering to the buildings that seemed to shimmer and wobble in the light, all the world moved.

Except for him.

Faddah Rucksack sat at the black iron table, the pub's single table outside, to the right of the door and near the corner of the building, where two wide streets met at an acute angle. His back to the pub and dressed all in black, he sat like the city's shadow—the only shadow amidst the white walls and brilliant colors of the people and trucks. Clad in a black leather glove, his left hand rested on the table next to an empty pint glass. His bare right hand seemed simultaneously earth-brown and cloud-pale.

He read a sheet of paper covered in a scrawl whose language

Jade couldn't determine. As she approached, he turned it over and set it down. Rucksack looked toward the roving people. Jade couldn't see his eyes, but everything in how he stared said that the man sitting right here was also hundreds of years and thousands of miles away. He set his left hand on top of his right.

Jade blinked. Coming from the low lights of the pub, it was hard adjusting to the sunlight. She looked at his hands again. Maybe it was the glove, but his left hand seemed smaller than the right.

"Rucksack?" she said. "Are you okay?"

He turned his head and noticed her for the first time. It took but a moment for the faraway man to return. Rucksack's face was everyone and no one, everywhere and nowhere; he could've been from Ireland, Tibet, Kenya. For all Jade could tell, he could've dropped out of the clouds. His tight face let loose a wide smile, bright as the city walls. "There's never a fear, as long as there's beer, there's only smiles and glee," Rucksack sang. "Now that you're here, let's drink in good cheer. Hey, barkeep! How about a couple for free?"

Jade laughed. "Have you ever paid for a beer?"

"It's like a dog, only more loyal and useful," Rucksack said. "I cannot help the extensive credit that insists on following me wherever I go."

And that comes ahead of you too, Jade thought. The letter had arrived an hour before he had first walked into the pub all those months ago. The Deep, Inc. stationery was familiar enough, having appeared on many an invoice and letter accompanying kegs of Deep's Special Lager ("Thank you for making *Every Night Special!*") and Galway Pradesh Stout ("The World's #1 Beer!"):

One Faddah Rucksack, a traveler of worlds and doer of deeds, does come to Agamuskara for an indeterminate length of time. Mr. Rucksack's purchases are free of charge and will be reimbursed to you. Thanking you in advance for your understanding.

The scrawled signature had been as indecipherable as the strange language on the paper Rucksack had been reading, but the money had come every week. *Good thing too,* she thought. *It's so bloody hot here, I hardly ever carried GPS until he arrived. I swear the man could put a straw in a keg and drain it.*

Jade set the pint on the table. The beer's white head wobbled just above the rim. "I'll never understand how you drink stout in this heat."

"A pint at a time, my lass," Rucksack replied. With a tilt of his head, he raised his glass to her. "Besides, o' all the barkeeps from Ireland to India, not a one pours a GPS as fine as you do, Jade. And believe you me, I would know."

Jade couldn't help but grin. All these months and they had hardly spoken, except to exchange pint orders, natter about the weather, or discuss the day's headlines. "Such a compliment," Jade replied. "You're not... drunk... are you?"

Rucksack dimmed his smile, a seeming seriousness in his eyes. Then he winked. "There are two things I never do," he said. "I never stop drinking. And I never get drunk."

"It's just that when I came out here, something about you seemed off."

Rucksack looked at her in a new way. His gaze moved from Jade to the paper, then back to her. "Have you ever lost someone, Jade?" he said. "Someone close to you? Someone who mattered more than all the world?"

For a moment, she was there again: painted concrete, his outstretched hand, the shape of his mouth, the glint of the ring in his fingers—and then all the world had gone still. "Yes," she said. "Long ago. In a different life."

"In a different life." He nodded, clenching and unclenching his left hand. "Yes, that's a good way to put it. I have too," he said. "Lost someone. Long ago."

"I'm sorry."

"And I thank you, as I am for you too." Rucksack traced a bare finger over the sheet of paper. "I got a letter recently, saying that the someone I lost, I only thought I lost. And that if I came to Agamuskara, I'd find her."

A lover? A wife? she thought. *A sister?* Jade took a step toward the table. "Who was she?"

Rucksack opened his mouth to reply, but the words froze. All the world seemed to hold its breath.

Both Jade and Rucksack doubled over, as if they'd each been punched in the stomach. On the two streets, everyone and everything stopped moving. No one spoke. Thousands of eyes only looked around, wondering what was so suddenly different about the world.

The glaring walls of the city grew brighter yet softer. From the Agamuskara River, a breeze blew whispers and wet earth, caresses and cool summer nights. A million dawns rose from every soul in the city. Every dream shimmered like gardens in the first morning light, dewy green leaves scintillating. Though it was midday, the world seemed like the slimmest golden glimmer of sunrise, like the birth of a child, like the first time you see the person you fall in love with.

Jade fell onto one knee, her right hand grabbing the other chair at the table. All that had happened, all the doubts, all the wonderings and questions, all washed away. She was only Jade, no longer a Jade or the Jade. Just Jade. Just herself. Not her decisions and her destiny, only her possibilities. *I can do anything,* she thought. *I can be anyone. I can choose anything and nothing and everything.*

The world shimmered. Double helixes of silver-and-gold light rained down.

Shaking, Jade staggered back to her feet. Helixes. Ever since her training, The Management had said to think of decision and destiny as a double helix, the DNA of existence that flowed forever, intertwining without touching, influencing the other without crossing paths.

Of course, no one else noticed that part. She glanced.

Except Rucksack.

As quickly as the world had held its breath, it exhaled. Life began moving again.

Jade looked at Rucksack and caught him staring at her. The world teemed by again. Rivers of endless people, animals, and objects flowed and flowed as if nothing else had happened but moving forward.

"No one else saw it," he said. "But you did, didn't you?"

She said nothing.

Rucksack smiled. "I figured you were one o' them. You're not the first I've ever seen or known, Jade Agamuskara Bluegold. I've seen as many o' you as pubs I've lightened kegs in over the years—dozens o' you the world over. I still don't know quite what you do with that special wee cabinet that no one else is supposed to see, but near as I can tell you don't do anyone evil by it, and I'm okay with that. So, let's not lie to each other here."

Confusion flooded her. *How did he know my full name?* she thought, looking away from Rucksack to the people. *How could he have seen the helixes? Only Jakes and Jades can see them, and I'm the only one in Agamuskara.*

The Management's cryptic warning whispered through her: "Learn from him but keep your distance."

But Rucksack wasn't shying away from what they'd seen. *If I were to get close,* she thought, *if I wanted to understand him, then he would have to understand some of me too.*

The Management hovered in her mind, and their warning coursed through her again: "A man without a destiny is a man who might do anything."

Okay, she thought, *so what is he going to do?*

Jade smiled. "Seeing destinies," she said. "We've got that in common. Usually it's obscured, tucked just beneath the skin of all things. What we just saw, it's like suddenly seeing the air we breathe."

Rucksack sighed and drained his pint. "There was a time I would've been able to read every one o' those lives wandering by, helixes to heads. I would have known them all." His fingers touched the paper in front of him. All the bluster, the bombast, the big smile, and the bigger words all vanished. He looked away from her. "I can't do that anymore."

The rest of him seemed as withered as his hand. Jade's confusion turned to pity. She pulled out the chair and sat down. "Maybe. Maybe not," she said, getting her mind out of the way and letting her instincts, her training, take over. "But I know what you can do."

"What?"

"You can help me figure out what that was."

Rucksack shrugged. "Things happen that don't necessarily mean anything."

"Tell that to anyone in western Ireland just before The Blast," Jade replied. "That meant a lot."

"What does The Blast have to do with any o' this?" The letter crumpled beneath his fingers.

It happened so long ago, Jade thought. *Why does it bother him so much?* Instead she leaned forward, locked her gaze onto him, and said, "From every person and animal and object, the helixes trailed away like paths. They should flow like bright water."

Rucksack stared at the wrinkled sheet of paper and nodded.

"Then tell me, Faddah Rucksack, why did so many of them wither into black and ash and nothing?"

He turned to look at her, his left hand closed tight. "We don't know," he said.

"We don't," Jade said kindly. "But I think we owe it to these people to find out. It just might save their lives."

For a while, Rucksack said nothing. The city wandered. The sun blazed. A meandering cow walked by and left behind a steaming pile of dung.

Forget it, Jade thought. She started to go back into the pub, when at last he spoke.

"Whatever changed just now," he said, "we'll figure it out."

Jade turned around. "Where should we start?"

Something in Rucksack relaxed, as if he were relieved. When his gaze held hers, earth turned to stone and a fire blazed up inside his brown-and-black eyes. "I'm going to start right here, have a think and a pint. There's tales o' this city I need to remember. That... and I need to wait for something."

Jade nodded. "Okay," she said. "It's a start. What should I do?"

"Make sure you have a bed available," Rucksack said. "And bring me another pint o' GPS. I need to see clearly."

"I thought you were staying a few blocks away?"

"I am," he replied. "It's not for me. We'll find out who it's for soon enough."

"Then I'm going to get back inside and see what else the day brings."

She walked to the door, thinking of helixes. Then it hit her—the last thing she'd seen before the helixes had faded from sight. They had trailed from every person, every object, every animal. So many of them flashed like bright chains, only to blacken, char, and disappear.

Except him.

Rucksack had sat there, staring out at the still crowd, at the shimmering helixes. But no helix had come from Rucksack. No chain of destiny, no flowing paths of decisions and possibilities. The Management was right. Rucksack was like a ghost yet alive. Wandering but without a path.

His voice stopped her at the door. "Who were you before?"

Jade looked down at the cracked, somewhat-white pavement.

Years and lifetimes coursed through her like blood. She opened the door and said, "Who were you?"

Neither answered.

Chapter 4

A pothole sent Jay lurching to the right, and he nearly tumbled from the rickshaw. A chunk of asphalt bounced the three-wheeled putt-putting bumblebee into the air and flung Jay back into his seat. Through the open sides of the rickshaw, the blazing blue sky for a moment took on a silvery glow. The world seemed to pause, as if holding its breath, but Jay realized that it was just him not exhaling yet.

The wheel smacked back down onto the pavement. Like a punch in the stomach, Jay doubled over as the impact knocked the air out of him.

He gasped and coughed, seeking air amidst bumblebee exhaust and the scent of cow manure. The driver smiled over his shoulder. "Welcome to Agamuskara, my good friend!" he said. "We are now in the city proper!"

"How can you tell?" Jay asked, coughing again.

"You are not truly in Agamuskara," the driver said, "until you see the river." He pointed west, to their right.

For a moment Jay thought back to his time traveling through England, the only place in the world where people drove on the left. Madness, he'd figured at the time. It was absurd, but you couldn't give the Brits too much flack. *Given how the entire island was nearly wiped out by The Blast,* Jay thought, *the Brits can drive on whatever side of the road they want.* But here in India, Jay was glad the traffic went on the right. Otherwise, he wouldn't have been able to see the river.

After the truck had passed through the Nepal-India border and resumed its bouncing, jostling ride toward Agamuskara, Jay had passed some kilometers looking through his guidebook, Guru Deep's *India Through the Third Eye*:

Agamuskara shares its name with the river that runs through India's holiest city, which is also its unholiest. While no records survive to tell us when Agamuskara was founded, local lore maintains the area was settled by the first people to come to the Indian subcontinent. History also does not explain why the city and the river should be named what, in the Hindi, translates as "smiling fire."

As Jay stared at the wide river, he understood how it could be mistaken for a smiling fire. The ruddy water glowed harsh and golden in the sun, and it burned Jay's eyes to look at it too long. Even the ancient river flowed sluggishly in the heat, but the driver was right. The Agamuskara's bends and straightaways, every curve and line, held a majesty that belied the brown water. As they drove, the river coursed along with them.

The map in the guidebook had shown that the river flowed from the north, out of the Himalayas. At Agamuskara the river's course turned sharply west, then curved south and east, creating a nestle of land where, it was thought, the original riverside village had been founded. As the city had grown, it had built up on the north side of the river. Then the city crossed south and continued growing. Today, the Agamuskara bisected the city then emptied into the Ganges farther east.

"It is beautiful," the driver said, looking more at the river than the road in front of them.

Jay turned to agree. Then he saw the cow standing still in front of them and instead he screamed.

The driver hardly turned his head, but he pounded on the horn. The cow blinked but did not move. Not bothering to look, the driver swerved right. Jay looked over. Beside them, chains flapped from the yellow bed of a large truck. Red wheel wells blurred as they turned. Jay grabbed the supports of the rickshaw.

I'm going to die, he thought. *And I only just got here.*

As the horn blared, a hole opened between the truck and another vehicle. The rickshaw swung into place with inches to spare on either end.

As they passed the cow, Jay was certain it winked at him.

The driver spat at it. "Bloody cows."

"Aren't they holy?" Jay replied.

"Cows give us many gifts," the driver said. "Milk and butter to nourish us, dung for our fires. We do not eat them and we do not hurt them, but it doesn't mean we like them."

"Since they think they own the road?"

The driver laughed. "Yes, my good friend. I like how you say that." One foot on the gas and one hand on the bleating horn, the driver swerved, zipped, and putted. The rickshaw swerved in and slipped out of every scant space not possibly big enough for it, yet somehow there was always just enough room.

Jay stared at the river as they traveled farther into the city. Had this water come down from the Himalayas at the same time that he had? As the rickshaw zipped in and out of meandering livestock, bell-ringing bicycles, grumbling trucks, and horn-tooting taxis, a breeze passed over Jay. It wasn't particularly cool, but it felt good on his skin. If his clothes couldn't dry out in the soggy hot air, at least they didn't feel as sticky. And the drive was certainly not boring. Jay let go of the rickshaw supports and sat back in his seat.

The river disappeared behind some buildings. Jay's backpack sat quietly on the floorboards between his knees, and he rested his hand on top of it. As they passed the white walls of the city center, the close buildings reflected the light and trapped the heat. The weight of gods and ages pressed on Jay, compressing humanity and humidity in a slow boil.

Out of the corner of Jay's eye, in front of a copy-machine-and-long-distance-calls shop, a blue humanlike figure sat proud and smiling on a cow. Dressed in gold, the figure was maybe male, maybe female, but it definitely had four arms and held some sort of staff. It winked.

Jay's head snapped to the right to look more closely, but only the cow remained.

He'd barely seen it, but since of course there was no way it could have been there to begin with, he hadn't seen it anyway.

I'm so tired and dehydrated, Jay thought. *I'm starting to hallucinate. That's all.* Jay swallowed dust. *I need a beer. Even a Deep's Special Lager would be good enough for right now, though I wouldn't really call that beer. I've drunk more flavorful water and passed tastier piss.*

The rickshaw squealed to a stop. Jay folded forward. Five years of traveling clamped his hand to the top of the pack so it didn't tumble out of the rickshaw. The driver stomped the brakes and cut the engine. Jay tried to ignore the *shr-shr-shr,* but the outline of the thing pressed into his hand.

Hundreds of people banged instruments, sang songs, and paraded down the cross street in front of them. Jay couldn't understand the words, but he understood the feeling—a hope for tomorrow, a wish for the next life, a joy in spite of today. The singing cooled him like water, like a spring night back home. He sighed. For a moment, his addled weariness faded. The *shr-shr-shr* seemed louder.

Another flash of blue turned his head. So did flashes of gold, brown, white, and red.

Cows flanked the rickshaw. Taxis, bicycles, and large trucks all stopped at the edge of the procession. When Jay looked directly at any of the motionless cattle, he saw only cows. When looking from the far edge of his peripheral vision, though, Jay thought he saw more figures, multi-armed and gold-adorned, aiming inscrutable smiles at the parade. But whenever he turned to look directly, he saw only cows.

Jay tapped the driver's shoulder. "What is the parade for?"

"For the gods, my good friend."

"Which one?"

The driver shrugged. "All sing to all, and all listen, and all praise."

Jay wished he didn't suck so badly at languages. Other than a rough French *bonjour*, the only other language Jay knew was the "I'm not dangerous" smile, the "where's the nearest toilet?" anguished leg scrunch with side-to-side wiggle, and the cupped fingers raised to the mouth that could serve for "hungry" or "oh great keg in the sky do I need a beer." But this? This was all Hindi to Jay.

Hundreds upon hundreds of paraders passed. All of their disparate songs should have been disjointed caterwauling, but they weren't. The upbeat danced around the slow. Low, mournful notes fell low in Jay's ear, but songs of celebration leaped over them. Jay picked out harmonies and tunes; they blended, played side by side, built on each other's pitch and cadence. His hand pressed harder on top of his backpack as he leaned out of the rickshaw to better see the procession.

Out of the corners of Jay's eyes, all the multi-armed, multi-colored blurs turned to look at him. Before he could cry out, the tune and the lyrics skipped his ears, stunning him silent as the paraders' songs sang directly into his mind.

"Let the love of ages be the love of my heart..."

"A hot meal and a warm thigh, a hard kiss and a soft sigh..."

"May my sons be as the sun and my daughters as the earth..."

"Return the life to the flame and to the Smiling Fire, be the cinders and the burn of the life of the world..."

Jay sat up, banging his head on the rickshaw's roof. His hand flung from the pack to the top of his aching head. The song vanished. Out of the corners of his tearing-up eyes, he saw nothing but stalled traffic and shuffling cows.

The driver turned around at the noise. "Are you okay?"

"I think so."

The driver smiled, looking at Jay's head and the slightly dented roof. "Not the way one usually sings, my friend, but then, you tourists have strange ways."

"I'm not a tourist," Jay said. "I'm a traveler."

The driver bobbed his head side to side. Jay didn't need to speak Hindi to know that this meant, "Maybe yes, maybe no, maybe maybe. All the same to me."

The parade ended, its fading songs mere whispers to the words sung and singed into Jay's mind. The pain faded only once the street had cleared and they could continue again.

The driver soon stopped at a nondescript hotel. "Here we are," he said, getting out and reaching for Jay's backpack.

Jay batted away his hand. "This isn't Everest Base Camp."

"No, no, much better, you will like it, my good friend. Much better."

Head still throbbing, feet still hurting, and throat a cup of desert sand, Jay felt how tempting it was. He was here. He was so tired. It was so hot.

But there were no signs of a pub. He recalled what he'd been told: when in Agamuskara, the only place for a traveler to stay was at the Everest Base Camp. Some said it was the best pub and hostel in town. Some said it was the best in India. Everything else was for tourists and tossers—which was he?

Jay pulled up all the will he had left, along with some money in his pocket. He set the bills on the seat, grabbed his pack, and got out.

The driver cried out, but Jay ignored him. Then, from behind, an impact made him stagger. Jay couldn't ignore that he was almost falling.

One hand on the pavement to keep from smacking the road, Jay looked up. His backpack grew smaller as it bounced down the street, seeming to struggle in the arms of a teenage boy but already far away.

Jay's feet protested with pain and fatigue, but his backpack was everything. He began to run.

What happens next?
Get the full book now

rucksackuniverse.com/forever

ABOUT THE AUTHOR

Anthony St. Clair, a freelance writer and entrepreneur, is the author of over 500 fiction and non-fiction works, including novels, short stories, articles, and more. *Library Journal* calls Anthony's storytelling "reminiscent of Terry Pratchett," and his fiction has been celebrated for its "quirk, wit, travel, and magic." In addition to his global travels, Anthony spent fifteen years in media and business before turning full time to writing in 2011. Together with his wife, son, and daughter, Anthony lives a life of everyday adventure at home in Oregon and on the road anywhere.

For more information:

rucksackuniverse.com | anthonystclair.com

patreon.com/anthonystclair

instagram.com/rucksackuniverse

twitter.com/anthonystclair

facebook.com/anthony.stclair.author

pinterest.com/anthonystclair

amazon.com/author/anthonystclair

goodreads.com/anthonystclair

linkedin.com/in/anthonystclair

youtube.com/anthonystclairauthor

bookbub.com/authors/anthony-st-clair